University of
Chester

CHESTER CAMPUS
LIBRARY
01244 513301

This book is to be returned on or before the last date stamped below. Overdue charges will be incurred by the late return of books.

PARTISAN POLITICS, NARRATIVE REALISM, AND THE RISE OF THE BRITISH NOVEL

PREVIOUS PUBLICATIONS

Rachel Carnell is co-editor (with Ruth Herman) of *The Selected Works of Delarivier Manley*, 5 vols. (Pickering & Chatto, 2005). She has published articles in *Eighteenth-Century Studies, Eighteenth-Century Fiction, Nineteenth-Century Literature,* and *Studies in the Novel.*

Partisan Politics, Narrative Realism, and the Rise of the British Novel

Rachel Carnell

palgrave
macmillan

First published in 2006 by
PALGRAVE MACMILLAN™
175 Fifth Avenue, New York, N.Y. 10010 and
Houndmills, Basingstoke, Hampshire, England RG21 6XS
Companies and representatives throughout the world.

PALGRAVE MACMILLAN is the global academic imprint of the Palgrave Macmillan division of St. Martin's Press, LLC and of Palgrave Macmillan Ltd. Macmillan® is a registered trademark in the United States, United Kingdom and other countries. Palgrave is a registered trademark in the European Union and other countries.

ISBN-13: 978–1–4039–7013–8
ISBN-10: 1–4039–7013–0

Library of Congress Cataloging-in Publication Data
Carnell, Rachel.
    Partisan politics, narrative realism, and the rise of the British novel / Rachel Carnell.
        p. cm.
    Includes bibliographical references and index.
    ISBN 1–4039–7013–0 (alk. paper)
        1. Political fiction, English—History and criticism. 2. English fiction—18th century—History and criticism. 3. English fiction—17th century—History and criticism. 4. Politics and literature—Great Britain—History—18th century. 5. Politics in literature. 6. Literature and society—Great Britain—History—18th century. I. Title.

PR858.P6C37 2006
823'.509358—dc22   2005058613

A catalogue record for this book is available from the British Library.

Design by Newgen Imaging Systems (P) Ltd., Chennai, India.

First edition: August 2006

10 9 8 7 6 5 4 3 2 1

Printed in the United States of America.

For my parents
and in memory of my grandmother
Alice Klingelhofer Powel (1909–2004)

CONTENTS

ACKNOWLEDGMENTS

After having spent so many years studying the partisan shrill of late seventeenth- and early eighteenth-century Britain, I am struck by similarities between it and political rhetoric today: voices on both sides of the contemporary partisan divide in the United States routinely humanize their adherents and dehumanize their opponents, rendering the former "real" or "human" and the latter an "extremist" faction. Within this world of dehumanizing partisan soundbites, it is a pleasure to be able to thank the truly humanizing community of friends and scholars that has contributed to this project over the many years it has taken me to complete it.

In its initial stages as a dissertation (before it was a study of either partisan politics or narrative realism), this project was overseen by Michael Prince, Jon Klancher, and Susan Jackson; their early advice and mentoring (especially that of Susan Jackson) were invaluable. In subsequent years, my colleague Gary Dyer has generously read the manuscript several times through, offering incisive insights and suggestions at every turn. Glending Olson and Jane McIntyre have also offered helpful feedback on individual chapters. Comments on the manuscript by Catherine Ingrassia, Christopher Flint, and Chris Mounsey were essential to bringing the project into publishable form. More recently, my colleague David Larson read the whole thing through, under a tight deadline, with a careful ear for logic and clarity. My graduate assistants Al Cliffe and Lee Zickel have also both greatly improved the manuscript through their assiduous attention to detail and their mastery of Microsoft Word's indexing features. Helen Liggett, Dan Melnick, Paula Bloch, Adam Thurschwell, Cathy Robertson, and Tayyab Mahmud—my interdisciplinary intellectual family in Cleveland—have kept me alive to the life-affirming resonance of contemporary critical theory.

The community of scholars at Cleveland State University is supported by superb staff members and an administration sympathetic to the needs of research. I must thank the three department chairs whose mentoring and encouragement helped this project at every point in its development: Earl Anderson, John Gerlach, and Louis Barbato. Jane Dugan, Anne Barnett, and Rita Hammond so capably assist the department in so many ways that faculty are able to stay focused on their work as scholars—particular thanks are due to Jane Dugan for all of her extra assistance in helping me manage my recently increased administrative responsibilities. Research for this project was generously supported by two faculty travel grants from Cleveland State: an Established Full-Time Faculty Research Grant from the Graduate College in 1997 and a College of Arts and Sciences travel grant in 2000. Preliminary research for an early stage of this project was supported in 1993 by a grant from the Angela J. and James J. Rallis Scholarship Fund, through the Humanities Foundation at Boston University.

Librarians and staff members at Cleveland State University Library, Case Western Reserve University's Kelvin Smith Library, the British Library (both old and new locations), Harvard University's Houghton Library, Oxford University's Bodleian Library, Cambridge University Library, the National Library of Scotland, the Cleveland Public Library, and the Boston Public Library have been unfailingly helpful and courteous. I must also thank the University of North Texas for granting me permission to include in my second chapter material that was originally published, in a slightly different form, as "Revising Tragic Conventions: Aphra Behn's Turn to the Novel," in *Studies in the Novel*, 31:2 (Summer 1999), 133–51. I likewise thank the editors of *Eighteenth-Century Fiction* for permission to use in my fourth chapter material originally published in an earlier version by that journal as "Clarissa's Treasonable Correspondence: Gender, Epistolary Politics, and the Public Sphere," *Eighteenth-Century Fiction* 10:3 (April 1998), 269–86.

My greatest debt is to my parents, John Evans Carnell and Sue Powel Carnell, whose enthusiastic interest in my intellectual activities has sustained me throughout my life. My mother, editor par excellence, has read the manuscript almost as many times as I have read it myself, offering each time incisive queries and superb suggestions. My mother's mother, Alice Klingelhofer Powel, who unfortunately did not live long enough to see this book in print, has been an inspiration to us all.

My daughter, Alison Carnell Lupton, who is now counting the days until "Mommy finishes her book," has infused my life with joy during the last stages of the work. Gregory Lupton, best possible partner in life, has made everything possible.

Introduction: Realism and the Rise of the Novel

To scholars of the eighteenth-century novel, it may seem "a truth universally acknowledged" that "narrative realism" and "the rise of the novel" are outmoded categories. We are now cautious about focusing on formalist conventions that have been used to distinguish "great" from "lesser" works of literature. We are likewise skeptical about the teleological implications of the term "rise," even when our students innocently remind us that the novels of Jane Austen are more structurally sophisticated than those of Aphra Behn. Perhaps not surprisingly, one prominent critic has reasserted the "intellectual/aesthetic power . . . of the line that begins with Defoe and flourishes in Richardson, Fielding, Smollett, Sterne, and Burney and that is not fully achieved by other eighteenth-century novelists."[1] By returning to the formalist trajectory of the traditional canon, this critic implicitly protests against two decades of scholarship more focused on political and cultural history than on aesthetic or formalist analysis. In doing so, he challenges us to reconsider the political history of the novel in light of the formal quality by which the genre has traditionally been judged: its narrative realism.

Partisan Politics, Narrative Realism, and the Rise of the British Novel reintroduces a consideration of formal realism to the political history of the British novel by focusing on an aspect of that history which has not yet been fully recovered: its connection to the partisan political discourses of its time. Late seventeenth- and early eighteenth-century British novelists—both female and male—had a common grounding in the partisan political discourses of their day. This partisan grounding, I show, helped determine the formal structures we have come to call narrative realism. Furthermore, the impulse for novelists and political writers to articulate their own partisan vision as a universally human "reality" ultimately helped to shape the conventions of novelistic realism, which would appear to future readers as less political than they were originally. In other words, the very partisan nature of the novel's early history may in part explain the impulse of subsequent generations—an impulse that certainly lingers to this day—to understand that history in aesthetic rather than political terms.

By linking the rise of the novel to the rise of individualism in *The Rise of the Novel* (1957), Ian Watt connected the emergence of narrative realism to certain developments in British social history. Emergent Protestant, capitalist, and empiricist ideologies, which Watt describes as "the rising tide of individualism," led eighteenth-century Britons to become interested in the stories of "particular individuals having particular experiences at particular times and at particular places" and in novels that give the impression of "a full and authentic report of human experience."[2] Watt's analysis of the formal features of eighteenth-century narrative realism within the larger frame of ostensibly "universal" human experience was easily reconciled with mainstream New Critical approaches to literature during the 1960s and 1970s, especially in American universities,[3] even though his argument was at least as indebted to materialist social theory as to formalist New Criticism.[4] In more recent decades, social and cultural theory has been a central feature of scholarship on the novel's origins: materialist critics have corrected Watt's linear version of history while feminist critics have expanded the literary canon for which he had written a history.[5] The topic that has been of less interest to scholars over the last several decades is the category of narrative realism itself.

Realism, of course, was not necessarily an ideal for all early eighteenth-century novelists, and it should not necessarily be understood as the single defining feature of the early British novel.[6] Nevertheless, the techniques now associated with formal realism had become important conventions of prose fiction by the middle of the eighteenth century. Moreover, if we tiptoe too carefully around the category of realism in our analysis of the early British novel, we only end up returning to Watt's 1957 characterization. As one critic observed in an article published four decades after Watt's book: "no one, to my knowledge, has ever convincingly displaced Watt's notion of formal realism as a dominant characteristic of narrative during the early eighteenth century, particularly in England."[7] This comment suggests that traditional perceptions of narrative realism will continue to inform the way teachers and students discuss the early eighteenth-century novel, whether or not we continue to explore the topic as scholars.[8] Although it is tempting to circumvent the category, as much recent scholarship has done, by doing so we may end up leaving in place the exclusionary tendencies of previous definitions.

In analyzing the history of novelistic realism, William Warner concludes that the category of realism has always been contingent upon the "social network of readers who produce, consume, and criticize" at a given time and place.[9] Warner ultimately argues that no single vision of realism has ever been uniformly accepted by "novel readers and writers" (36). In so doing, he clears a critical space in which to rewrite the history of the novel as a "subset of the cultural history of print entertainments" (xi), a cultural history in which three traditionally noncanonical novelists, Aphra Behn, Delarivier Manley, and Eliza Haywood, become the central figures. However, by separating the works of these three important early novelists from scholarly histories of the novel and by detaching the genre of the novel from Watt's original definition of formal realism, Warner permits a rearguard attack on the significance of the very novelists to whom he has just granted a central place.

The plea for us to acknowledge the "intellectual/aesthetic power" of the "line" of novelists from Defoe to Burney is a plea for us to take seriously the formal and literary achievements of the early British novels that we study. However, in John Richetti's "line" of development, Burney is the only female novelist accorded a place.[10] To be fair, Richetti wrote one of the first modern studies of early eighteenth-century women writers.[11] Nevertheless, by reasserting a traditional canonical trajectory, Richetti relegates to second-class status female novelists such as Aphra Behn, Delarivier Manley, and Eliza Haywood whose contributions to the development of formal realism have not yet been fully understood. One reason for the continued marginality of these women writers in the eighteenth-century canon, I argue, is that their work has been analyzed most frequently in terms of political or cultural history, rather than in terms of the development of the novel's formal structure.

A recent study of eighteenth-century women's contributions to narrative realism unfortunately may have the effect of reasserting the second-class status of women's formal contributions to the novel by attaching to them a separate definition of realism, focusing on "their self-consciously different, perhaps even perverse, 'feminine' angle on reality."[12] As Paula Backscheider has observed, "Students of the eighteenth-century novel *must* now ask if the early women writers should be treated as a rival or counter tradition or, apparently most difficult of all, as an integral part of the history of the 'rise' of the English novel."[13] One reason why this integration may seem "difficult," I argue, is that in the process of asserting women writers' significance to cultural and political history, scholars have neglected to revisit the category of formal realism, within which women novelists have always been viewed as second-class citizens.[14]

Backscheider seeks to redress the tendency to see women writers as part of a rival or secondary canon by locating "the formative decade for the English novel" in the 1720s, rather than the 1740s, and in articulating the similarities between the works of Daniel Defoe and those of the influential women writers of the 1720s.[15] I propose that we locate the novel's origins even earlier: during the last two decades of the seventeenth century, starting with the Exclusion crises of the early 1680s, when debates about the social contract prompted political philosophers, partisan pamphleteers, playwrights, and early novelists to articulate their own versions of the political subject as more "human" (and so more "real") than other versions of this political individual. These debates about the nature of "the individual" continued throughout the first half of the eighteenth century as Britons negotiated several peaceful monarchical successions and entered a period of Whig hegemony; it was during this period that the novel developed into a genre recognizable to modern readers.

Despite the recent scholarly tendency to avoid the terms "rise" or "origin" because of their teleological implications, in this study I retain the term "rise," a term that acknowledges that British prose fiction did evolve between 1680 and 1760 as certain features of novelistic structure became accepted as conventions among readers, writers, and booksellers. I also retain the word "novel" in broad terms, without distinguishing it from "romance" in early eighteenth-century Britain, since the terms were frequently used in tandem—"novels and romances"—and distinctions made between them were not uniform.[16] Moreover, the category of "romance" has been used in twentieth-century criticism with the effect of marginalizing the works of women writers;[17] I argue that the category of "romance" has similarly been used to marginalize prose fiction promoting a pro-Stuart or Jacobite position.

During the last two decades of the seventeenth century and the first half of the eighteenth century, early novelists, both male and female, offered strikingly different partisan versions of human experience and of the normative political individual. Thus, the development of novelistic realism corresponds not with the rise of one particular type of Enlightenment Whig individual, as Ian Watt suggested, but with the competition among different versions of political selfhood, each of which sought to be perceived as universal human selfhood. In other words, when we move beyond traditional Whig histories of the novel and uncover the early British novel's multifaceted partisan history, we discover that male and female writers were equally significant in shaping the features of novelistic realism and in determining which partisan version of reality would be allowed to be counted as "real."

Partisan Caricature and
Realistic Character

Formal realism is usually understood as a set of narrative qualities that make characters appear to be particular individual people living particular individual lives. According to Ian Watt, these narrative conventions include a choice of "new" over traditional story-lines, a development of "individual" over idealized characters, and a stylistic "air of" veracity or authenticity,[18] in contrast to the idealized depictions of courage and virtue in seventeenth-century French heroic romance. Wayne Booth long ago pointed out that Watt may have overstated the importance of this detailed "realism of presentation."[19] For Booth, detail in and of itself is never enough; he approvingly acknowledges Watt's recognition that "the accurate transcription of actuality does not necessarily produce a work of any real truth or enduring literary value."[20] In Booth's analysis, the art of writing is "the art of choosing what to dramatize fully and what to curtail" (64). Although Booth is concerned with the techniques of "good writing" across the centuries whereas Watt is concerned with understanding the political history of eighteenth-century narrative realism, in tandem their approaches to literary analysis helped to articulate the basic features of novelistic realism that have been taken for granted by scholars and students over the last fifty years. In the traditional New Critical account, incorporating both Booth's and Watt's work, narrative realism is associated sometimes with a profusion of quotidian detail and sometimes with a deft omission of such detail.

In understanding how detail, in its abundance or its scarcity, determines how we gauge whether or not something feels "real," it is helpful to consider Deidre Lynch's research into eighteenth-century conceptions of character. Drawing on Hogarth's analysis of portraiture and Fielding's distinction between the comic and the burlesque, Lynch explains that "Caricature becomes a contingent stage into which character passes, and vice versa. Caricature, far from being the antithesis of character, may be read as its extension."[21] Lynch draws our attention to Hogarth's concern with overdrawing, which is as great a risk as underdrawing: "Here, the finishing touch, the increase in detail that enables the image to realize its claim to truth value, is reconceived as, past a certain limit, something else that disrupts rather than extends" (69–70). Hogarth often associates the universal, abstract, or "realistic" character with less detail, rather than more.

This contrast between character and caricature in drawing, which Lynch relates to the history of materialism and commercialism, also helps us to understand the partisan history of novelistic realism. For example, whereas Richardson's Pamela and Defoe's Robinson Crusoe seem real because of the detail with which their inner thoughts are described, other eighteenth-century characters seem real because they are sketched with less detail than certain comically overdrawn caricatures with which they are contrasted. Sophia Western, the heroine of Fielding's *Tom Jones*, is not the most developed of novelistic characters, but she functions as a plausible heroine in part because her apolitical femininity is juxtaposed to the "unnatural" Amazonian caricature of Jenny Cameron for whom she is comically mistaken. In Austen's *Pride and Prejudice*, the properly Tory hero, Fitzwilliam Darcy, is drawn with relatively little detail, but is ultimately rendered more "human" than his aunt, Lady Catherine de Bourgh, a caricature of Tory impropriety. Darcy also emerges as more human than the anti-hero, Wickham, who, although plausibly developed early in the novel, eventually reveals enough features of the villains of anti-Jacobin fiction that he comes to seem less human as the novel progresses and more like a partisan caricature.[22]

Early eighteenth-century philosophy was, as Watt observes, "still governed by the strong classical preference for the general and the universal."[23] In an essay first published in 1709, Anthony Ashley Cooper, the third earl of Shaftesbury, asserts that the "mere Face-Painter indeed has little in common with the poet, but, like the mere historian, copies what he sees and minutely traces every feature and odd mark."[24] In Shaftesbury's estimation, real poets and geniuses achieve their ideas from "*many* objects of nature, and not from a *particular* one" (66). In other words, truth is better exemplified by a universal ideal than by a particular example: "the best artists are said to have been indefatigable in studying the best statues, as esteeming them a better rule than the perfectest human bodies could afford" (67). For Watt, early "realist" novelists such as Defoe and Richardson broke with the aesthetic tradition of idealized universals by creating characters that seemed as if they were particular and ordinary, rather than ideal, individuals. On the other hand, what makes *Crusoe* "great," for Watt, is its portrayal of the "universal image of individualist experience" (89). In other words, *Robinson Crusoe* is "great" for Watt in part because of its depiction of the "universal" human experience of being "isolated" (88). Watt's account, however, does not specify what determines a character's "universality."

Drawing on Renaissance developments in mathematics and natural and aesthetic philosophy, Elizabeth Ermarth suggests that narrative realism derives from the way in which multiple narrative perspectives coalesce into a "consensus" that defines individual characters in relation to the universals of human experience.[25] However, novels that limit their perspective to the point of view of the narrating protagonist may not fit this model. Robinson Crusoe's isolation, described from the character's limited first-person perspective, is the particular isolation of one stranded merchant sailor and not the isolation experienced by his servant Friday (who never learns enough of Crusoe's native tongue to establish a full human connection with him), the slave Xury (whom Crusoe sells for sixty pieces of silver shortly after swearing lifelong loyalty to him), the wife Crusoe takes upon his return, or the children he fathers (whom he abandons in order to take up the voyages chronicled in his *Farther Adventures*). Such limitations on Crusoe's potential "universalism" also define for us the limitations of most formalist accounts of eighteenth-century realism: their reliance on a transhistorical assumption of a "universal" human nature, drawn largely from a Protestant, Whig, male, property-owning head of household.

Watt identifies the impulse to provide a "full report" of particular human lives with an emergent ideal of individualism that coincided with political events such as the Revolution of 1688–89 and philosophical breakthroughs such as the publication of Locke's *Essay on Human Understanding* (1689). Curiously, however, although Watt recognizes the importance of the political and philosophical upheavals of the 1680s, he identifies as the first true novel *Robinson Crusoe* (1719), which appeared thirty years after these upheavals. However, as J. A. Downie has observed, there does not seem to have been a linear increase in the number of novels published between 1719 and 1740 although there was a small surge of such publications in the 1680s and 1690s, a second surge in the 1720s, and a more significant increase in the 1740s.[26] It is also important to remember that Locke's *Two Treatises of Government* (1689) did not achieve widespread popularity until the middle of the eighteenth century, by which time his work's most radical implications seem to have been forgotten.[27] As Linda Colley and J. C. D. Clark have shown, even though Whigs dominated Parliament for decades, they did not necessarily have the support of the majority of the population.[28] While a Lockean idea of selfhood gradually gained favor, eighteenth-century Britons also encountered a range of competing versions of political selfhood in the partisan productions of political journalists and pamphleteers.

Partisan disagreement marked the decades of the late seventeenth and early eighteenth centuries, during the time when the formal features we now associate with formal realism first began to develop as novelistic conventions. As Britain negotiated the effects of the transition from divine-right to parliamentary monarchy, "party strife" became a key feature of daily life for many Britons. Geoffrey Holmes writes of Anne's reign: "In spheres far removed from the confines of the Court and 'the Parliament-House', or for that matter of the parliamentary boroughs, a man's party allegiance became a fact of considerable, and often of supreme, importance."[29] Tories, Whigs, and Jacobites often socialized in separate clubs and separate coffee houses, and during Anne's reign, "it became increasingly rare for leading partisans of the Whigs and the Tories to meet each other socially, unless they happened to be relatives or to have strong local interests in common" (21).

Although such intense partisan resentments abated somewhat during the Hanoverian years, strong responses to Walpole's power and control marked both political and novelistic discourse during the 1730s and 1740s,[30] and the possibility of Jacobite risings continued to inflect the way in which Whig "reality" distinguished itself from other political visions until the mid-1750s. This particular version of reality corresponds to what Margaret Anne Doody has described as Whig "Prescriptive Realism": an "all-or-nothing Realism," that "cuts out fantasy and experiment, and severely limits certain forms of psychic and social questioning."[31] In this account, Charlotte Lennox's *The Female Quixote* (1752) functions as an example of a novel that thematizes the increasing ideological preference, by the mid-eighteenth century, for Whig reality over earlier forms of romance. The moderate rational individualism embodied by that novel's hero ultimately triumphs over the exaggerated heroics of aristocratic French romance and Jacobite mythology.[32] The developing taste for Whig realism by the 1750s and the Whigs' continued political dominance provide the background for the Whig versions of the political individual and Whig versions of the novel's history so familiar to twentieth-century students and scholars. However, from the 1680s into the 1750s, this Whig version of reality had not yet emerged as normative, and the novels written during those decades reveal the spectrum of different partisan versions of realism that were still competing for cultural dominance.[33]

NARRATIVE REALISM AND POLITICAL HISTORY

The qualities that make a narration "feel real," of course, have varied from century to century and from culture to culture. Even within a given period and a given selection of novels, readers have not necessarily agreed about what creates a feeling of reality, nor have subsequent critics agreed upon what seems "realistic" in works produced in earlier eras. Across the centuries, some reviewers and scholars have found

Pamela's first-person narrative compelling and believably voiced, while others have found implausible Richardson's attempts at "writing to the moment." More generally, a feeling of "reality" or "plausibility" has been ascribed by critics sometimes to a third-person and sometimes to a first-person narrator, and sometimes to a free-indirect style that marries the two. In traditional scholarship, realism is sometimes identified with an apparently objective or ironic narrative detachment, sometimes with a "stream of consciousness" monologue, and sometimes with a narration perceived as too subjective to be "reliable." Similarly, the depiction of "realistic" character has been ascribed sometimes to an abundance and sometimes to a scarcity of detail. However, in mid-twentieth-century accounts of narrative realism, realistic character was typically conceived of as both concrete and universal, hence implicitly apolitical, or at least nonpartisan.

When considering the connection between "literary" and "political" history, it is useful to remember that the impulse to draw a sharp division between the literary and the political is a twentieth-century phenomenon, one that has affected the way we study both literature and social history.[34] Scholarship on the connection between the literary and the political public spheres, for example, has sometimes drawn on the popular twentieth-century assumption that there once was a "literary" sphere inculcating "affective humanism" which was separate from, although necessary to, a "public" sphere of commercial and political concerns.[35] This association of affective humanism with the literary rather than the political public sphere frequently led twentieth-century scholars of literature to be more interested in the aesthetic rather than the political development of the novel; it also may have prevented critics from noticing that eighteenth-century political discourse was just as active in helping shape our ideas of what sort of person feels "human" or "real" as were the emergent discourses of narrative realism.

Although novelistic "realism" has traditionally been understood in relationship to "life itself," this study demonstrates that early British novelists were frequently depicting "reality" and "human nature" in relationship to other textual depictions of them. In many instances, these other depictions of "life" and "human nature" were partisan in nature. Not surprisingly, given the outcome of the events of 1688 and the subsequent emergence of Whig political dominance in eighteenth-century Britain, those writers handed down to us as serious, "realistic" novelists have frequently been either Whig or anti-Jacobite Tory. Defoe has been admired since the early nineteenth century for his "natural painting."[36] Fielding and Austen have been touted for their use of irony in depicting the social realities of their eras. By contrast, the narrative irony in Eliza Haywood's late pro-Jacobite novels has rarely been mentioned by critics, and the pro-Stuart Behn is seldom considered a realistic novelist, even though she employs many of the techniques associated with narrative realism in traditional scholarship.

This study offers not a comprehensive formalist treatment of eighteenth-century novelistic realism, but an analysis of the political discourses that shaped the context in which early British novelists were narrating their versions of "reality." In offering this analysis, I do not mean to suggest that novels in early eighteenth-century England had no connection to other key developments in economic, religious, and social history so frequently associated with the rise of narrative realism.[37] Rather, in addition to its role in mediating these broader social and economic concerns, the early British novel also responded to the competing Whig, Tory, and Jacobite versions of political self-hood, evident in both formal political treatises and partisan occasional tracts, that emerged in response to the upheavals of the 1680s and persisted through the final challenges to the Hanover line of succession in the mid-1750s. Thus, rather than viewing the early British novel as a product of Protestant Whig capitalist selfhood, as Watt proposed, or of Tory virtue, as has been more recently suggested,[38] we should acknowledge that many narrative techniques now associated with narrative realism were part of the cultural discourses competing to determine which political version of selfhood would be perceived as normative.

HIGH POLITICAL THEORY AND PARTISAN PAMPHLETS

Paula McDowell describes the years from 1678 to 1730 as a period when "the English press was undergoing some of the most important transformations in its history."[39] She argues that the continued political unrest that began with the first Exclusion crisis and ended with the consolidation of Whig hegemony in 1730 helped to forge a "professional literary subculture" that "created new opportunities for diverse oppositional communities" (5–6). As J. A. Downie has shown, the passing of the Triennial Act in December 1694 and expiration of the Licensing Act in 1695 signaled the "rise of a virulent political press," which the government eventually learned to harness to its advantage through a variety of propaganda writing teams.[40] Lennard Davis notes that the repeal of the Licensing Act in 1695 was later undercut by the 1724 revision of the Stamp Act.[41] I argue that both the 1695 repeal and the 1724 revision were crucial to the novel's development: the first because it encouraged the spread of certain types of political discourse with which I associate the novel, and the second because it made the extended novelistic political tract, and by extension the novel itself, a likely choice of genre for propaganda. I would also extend the period of virulent partisan activity that helped shape the novel's development into the early 1750s, since the brutal response to the Jacobite rising of 1745 must be recognized as part of the Whigs' ultimate consolidation of political power.

Jill Campbell's study of political allegory in Fielding's fiction suggests a way of linking the formal quality of character development to various types of political discourse. She demonstrates, for example, that *Tom Jones* (1749) "actively shows us the interconnections between historically specific political purposes and [the] experiences of private pursuits."[42] When Campbell points out that Fielding "fails to locate Sophia [Western] clearly on either side of the opposition" between Whig or Jacobite ideals of femininity (170), she suggests how Sophia is drawn in direct contrast to a familiar partisan stereotype. Campbell's analysis, however, slights the crucial generic distinction between occasional tracts and political treatises that purport to construct a more general theory of the civic individual's relationship to the state. For example, Campbell juxtaposes polemical anti-Jacobite tracts from the 1740s with abstract political philosophy, such as Locke's, from the last decades of the seventeenth century; in doing so she overlooks the discursive continuity between anti-Jacobite pamphlets from the 1680s and the 1750s and therefore misconstrues genre difference as an ideological shift.[43]

When uncovering the early novel's political history, we must be careful to differentiate between the characteristics of different modes and genres of political discourse.[44] Formal political treatises in late seventeenth- and early eighteenth-century Britain frequently constructed a political self in general terms, making such an individual seem "human" and "universal" by omitting particularizing detail. Meanwhile, during the same era, polemical occasional pamphlets routinely defined their partisans as ordinary or "normal," hence "real" or "universally human," in contrast to the caricatures of their excessively "zealous" partisan opponents. Early British novelists were clearly responding to the general and particularizing discourses of both of these genres.

As is now well known, formal political treatises from the late seventeenth and early eighteenth centuries cast their arguments about state structure not in terms of an abstract universal individual existing in a philosophical vacuum, but in terms of the relations between particular individuals within the domestic household. Proponents of both divine-right and social-contract theory deployed analogies between the household and the state, with the former group promoting a patriarchal family structure and the latter promoting a type of power-sharing or joint dominion between husbands and wives. The difficulty for these early liberal political theorists was that in their attempt to define an abstract political self in the person of the male head of household, they were confounded by the presence in their analogies of the wives, children, and servants, who were not yet conceived of as full citizens.[45] For example, social-contract theorists such as John Locke and James Tyrrell refuted the patriarchalism of Robert Filmer's traditional family model by elevating Eve from helpmate to joint ruler over the household. However, this elevation was never intended to improve a wife's status in the home, as Mary Astell made clear when she demanded of social-contract theorists, "if Absolute Sovereignty be not necessary in a State, how comes it to be so in a Family?"[46] As Joan Wallach Scott has observed, "The abstract rights-bearing individual who came into being as the focus of liberal political debate in the seventeenth and eighteenth centuries somehow became embodied in male form and it is his-story that historians have largely told."[47] At the same time, the analogy of the domestic household on which these treatises rely staged the question that is at the heart of both the political theory and the prose fiction of late seventeenth- and early eighteenth-century Britain: who has the right to exert power over whom within or outside of the household?

As Nancy Armstrong has argued, the early British novel "concealed the power exercised by discourse itself" by translating political relations into sexual ones, a translation that would eventually lead British domestic fiction to be perceived as a domain of "apolitical subjectivity."[48] However, we must remember that in the early to mid-eighteenth century, arguments about domestic relations, gender, and power were frequently used and understood to convey specific partisan political messages. The theme of the subjugated female, a commonplace in early British fiction, for example, has obvious partisan resonances. Richardson's Pamela protests against tyranny in ways that echo Whig protests against tyranny and call attention to the paradox that the Tory proto-feminist Mary Astell articulated so eloquently: if propertied men use the analogy of domestic tyranny to justify overthrowing a tyrant, how should we respond to their tyranny in their own households? Richardson's Clarissa draws on a traditional Tory discourse of liberty, while her friend Anna Howe talks like a Whig. These characters also frequently use language that is universal and humanizing, as do the authors of seventeenth- and eighteenth-century political philosophy who claim to describe the situation of a universally human political subject.

In depicting human experience, British novels engaged the abstract gestures of high political theory as well as the particulars of partisan political rhetoric, the goal of which was to depict the opposing political party as less than human, that is, less than "real." Whig readers, for example, would be familiar with images of Tory and Jacobite selfhood from pamphlets such as *Simeon and Levi* (1696), *The True Picture of a Modern Tory* (1702), and *A Seasonable Warning Against Jacobites and Papists* (1712), which describe Jacobites as hot-blooded "papists" or cannibals (because of the Catholic belief that the host is literally the body of Christ).[49] Elaborating further on the dangers of Jacobitism (and hence, Catholicism), *The History of the Jacobite Clubs* (1712), *The Jacobite Curse* (1714), and *The Counsel to the True English* (1746) describe priests who commit adultery and depict monasteries or nunneries as places that would sexually corrupt young girls or boys.[50] In anti-Jacobite publications such as these, masculine versions of selfhood range from the reasonable Whig to the hot-blooded Jacobite or the treasonous "Papist." Pro-Jacobite pamphlets usually reverse these partisan stereotypes, making the Whig unreasonable and the Jacobite a model of measured calm. Nor was political selfhood necessarily coded as male: partisan pamphlets also feature the overly political Tory woman, the apolitical Whig lady, and the monstrous Amazonian Jacobite. In his misogynistic, anti-Catholic dramatic tragedy *The Female Prelate: Being The History of the Life and Death of Pope Joan* (1680), a production obviously designed to incite fear of Charles II's Catholic brother and the then heir-apparent James, duke of York, Elkanah Settle deploys partisan images of corrupt Catholic priests alongside the figure of Pope Joan, a monstrous depiction of female sexuality and ambition.

The competing versions of political selfhood familiar from both abstract political philosophy and from partisan tracts are recognizable in the pages of many early British novels, although novelists often borrowed such character types only to modify and adapt them. Defoe's Robinson Crusoe exhibits various characteristics of Whig individualism, including an interest in the contractual aspects of human relationships, although he by no means represents an ideal Whig individual. Aphra Behn's Oroonoko provides a significant variation on the theme of martyred Tory innocence. Fielding offers contrasting images of the pro-Hanoverian Squire Allworthy and the Jacobite Squire Western, whereas Richardson tries to create male heroes who transcend partisan caricature. Haywood's Jenny Jessamy provides a new model for a pro-Stuart lady in contrast to the frequently misogynistic Whig depictions of Jacobite "Amazons." As the rest of this study will show, early British novelists, rather than forging a consensus about the "universal" nature of human experience, often focused on the sharp differences among individuals that stem from their contingent domestic, social, economic, and partisan positions. Moreover, the subtle narrative maneuvers that novelists cultivated in order to convey or, if necessary, to be able to deny their political allegiances helped to effect some of the complex narrative techniques that have come to be associated with formal realism.[51] This is the case, even though traditional histories of realism have typically only acknowledged as realistic the formal techniques of Whig and anti-Jacobite Tory writers.

In the chapters that follow, I develop this argument first by analyzing the rhetorical structures of a range of late seventeenth- and early eighteenth-century political texts. I then examine the relationship between these different genres of political discourse and the formal structure of novels by Aphra Behn, Daniel Defoe, Samuel Richardson, and Eliza Haywood, four novelists whose work was central to the development of the British novel during the first half of the eighteenth century, and whose political biases represent the range of partisan positions that seem to have influenced the novel's development. This selection of novelists also juxtaposes two canonical novelists, Defoe and Richardson, whose formal realism has become a truism, with Behn and Haywood, two novelists whose work has not yet been fully integrated into the traditional "line" of realistic novels.[52]

OVERVIEW OF CHAPTERS

Chapter 1 focuses on a range of material from formal political treatises to highly charged partisan tracts. Although political philosophical treatises from 1680 to 1760 usually assumed an abstract political subject (tacitly a male head of household), there are often narrative tensions evident in the domestic analogies used to establish such an abstract universal. Meanwhile, partisan writings from the same period relied on more specific stereotypes of different partisan "selves," which novelists of the period both deployed and revised in developing "realistic" characters. A rhetorical analysis of both formal political treatises and partisan occasional tracts helps us understand how different genres of political writing broached the problem of the universal and the particular so crucial to the development of novelistic character. The chapter concludes with an analysis of an anti-Jacobite "memoir" of the Jacobite folk heroine Jenny Cameron, a liminal text that exemplifies the interconnections between novelistic and political discourse in early to mid-eighteenth-century Britain.

Chapter 2 demonstrates how Aphra Behn, a comic dramatist loyal to the Stuarts, challenged the boundaries between comedy and tragedy in the still-nascent form of the novel. In doing so, she offered a Tory version of narrative realism that revised the standard partisan discourses of Tory propaganda. If we accept traditional formal definitions of the novel, Behn's work seems to have little place within the history of the form. However, once we cast her protagonists within the context of political polemics from the 1680s, we see how she was reworking the rhetorical figures of pro-Stuart propaganda while simultaneously refusing the individualism of social-contract theory. By scripting tragedy outside the conventions of Restoration drama, Behn was able to maintain her critique of Whig ideology without relying on the misogynistic paradigms standard in Tory Restoration tragedy. In her novella *The Dumb Virgin* (probably written in 1684), an adaptation of the classical tragedy of Oedipus, Behn offers an alternative Tory version of political selfhood and of novelistic character development through her revision of traditional dramatic models of tragic heroism. In *The Fair Jilt* (1688), a potentially tragic tale that ends happily, Behn further revises the dramatic conventions of character, as she offers her own model of "realistic" femininity in her Tory variant of the story of Lucretia.

Whereas Behn approaches narrative realism by revising stereotypes of Tory virtue, Defoe offers a parallel critique of Whig ideology by creating characters who test the domestic analogies through which the Whig social contract was originally articulated. In chapter 3, I juxtapose the protagonists of *Robinson Crusoe* (1719), *Moll Flanders* (1722), and *Roxana* (1724) with stock characters from Defoe's own political writings and conduct books. I then demonstrate how Defoe complicates the familial analogies of social-contract theory—the disobedient son, the wife who insists on full equality within marriage—and thereby differentiates between the experiences of different household members under the social contract. Although Defoe's political views have often been reduced to a simplified version of social-contract theory or dismissed as inconsistent because of his work as a paid propagandist, the depth of his political thought becomes apparent when we understand the critique of the social contract offered by his version of formal realism.

Chapter 4 focuses on the works of Samuel Richardson. Through the example of his protagonists' verbal and epistolary debates, Richardson offers a model for polite exchange that contrasts sharply with the slander and misogyny of pro- and anti-Jacobite pamphlets from the 1740s. Pamela and Mr. B. articulate their disagreements by means of the political discourses of tyranny and treason; Clarissa Harlowe and Anna Howe recapitulate debates from the 1680s between social-contract and divine-right theorists that in many ways were anachronistic by the 1740s. Sir Charles Grandison offers a paradigm for moderation politics while challenging standard partisan images of virtuous masculinity. By reanimating earlier political debates through the discourses and life experiences of his idealized protagonists, Richardson achieves a new version of narrative realism, complicating the abstractions of mid-century political treatises even as he protests against the rhetorical tropes of partisan political slander.

In chapter 5, I contend that the usual binary division scholars find in Eliza Haywood's oeuvre, contrasting her early scandalous work with her later reformed fiction, fails to accommodate either the consistency of her political viewpoint or her significant contributions to formal realism. Haywood acknowledges her opposition to Walpole in her overtly political novel *The Adventures of Eovaai* (1736) and hints at her Jacobite sympathies in her political periodical *The Parrot* (1746) and her *A Letter . . . to a Particular Friend* (1749), for which she was arrested for seditious libel. Her political texts and her novels apply a similarly partisan approach to character development. Although the didacticism of her later novels has led nineteenth- and twentieth-century critics to read them solely in moral terms, these works actually represent Haywood's challenge to the new hegemony of Whig realism. In *The Fortunate Foundlings* (1744) and *The History of Jemmy and Jenny Jessamy* (1753), Haywood offers pro-Jacobite paradigms for both masculine and feminine virtue, thereby undermining the Whig prescriptive realism whose triumph Charlotte Lennox stages in *The Female Quixote* (1752). Haywood's late-career response to this increasingly dominant mode of realism illustrates how fully the conventions of realism were grounded in the discourses of party conflict.

By the mid-1750s, when the Hanoverian succession and Whig control of Parliament had become accepted facts of life in Britain, openly partisan debates about the nature of the self were less usual in novels. At the same time, novelists who promoted anything other than a conventional Whig position frequently veiled their partisan preferences within a coded discourse of domestic harmony. However, until the mid-1750s, competing partisan versions of selfhood and reality continued to influence the conventions through which reality itself would be written and understood in the pages of British novels.

CHAPTER 1

Political Selfhood and Novelistic Character

When William and Mary replaced James II in 1688–89, the abstract subject of liberal political theory was still in the process of being articulated. Opposing versions of the domestic household—the divine-right patriarchal household and the less authoritarian household of social-contract theory—were deployed as analogies by the political philosophers Robert Filmer, James Tyrrell, John Locke, and Algernon Sydney in treatises published with an eye toward influencing the Exclusion crises of 1679–81 and justifying the Revolution of 1688–89. The domestic situations deployed as both ideal and cautionary analogies in these treatises—including families with patriarchal fathers, oppressed wives, rebellious children, and servants—are of course familiar scenarios in eighteenth-century British novels. However, after the Revolution of 1688–89, formal political treatises began to excise potentially disruptive domestic analogies and to construct an abstracted political individual who appeared universal but was in fact a Whig (or a least an anti-Jacobite Tory), Protestant, propertied male head of household.

As the Revolution (or Whig) principles of 1688–89 became more universally accepted, the abstract subject of liberal political theory gradually emerged rhetorically: there was less reason to spell out the domestic analogies on which the arguments of social-contract theory originally relied. Liberty and tyranny could be discussed without reference to the contingent position in the domestic household of those seeking freedom from tyranny. Moreover, writers from different political stripes incorporated many of the resonant terms of Whig ideology into their own discourse. Writing in the mid-eighteenth century, the Tory philosopher David Hume would refer to an abstract concept of "liberty," although he would not use the analogy of the domestic household. At this juncture, the analogy might have been disruptive even to the Whigs in power, since it could call attention to the potential rights of wives, for example, whose oppression had been of interest not for its own sake but as an analogy for the oppression of those who opposed James II in 1688. References to the domestic family would become important again in political treatises written during the crises of the French Revolution,[1] but by the middle of the eighteenth century, these analogies were relatively infrequent in high political theory. The significance of a person's gender, household position, religion, and partisan sympathies, however, continued to be relevant to the conflicts and characters described by early British novelists long after Britain's Protestant succession had been determined.

We might conclude that by depicting the particular situations of wives, servants, children, and foundlings, early British novelists kept alive the domestic analogies on which late seventeenth-century liberal political theory had originally relied. Of course, not all novelists would necessarily have read the treatises articulating liberal political theory, and so they would not have directly engaged these now-canonical texts of political philosophy. However, an abstract but tacitly Whig male political self is also evident in popular abridgments of Locke's theory, in particular the best-selling *The Judgement of Whole Kingdom and Nations* (1710), and it is through works such as this that the ideas of high political theory were probably most familiar to eighteenth-century novelists and their readers. The formal conventions of novelistic realism—which convey an aura of reality and universal humanity to stories depicting particular people at particular times—thus may have arisen at least in part as a response to the increasing abstraction of high political discourse. At the same time, novelists were certainly conversant with the clichés of contemporaneous partisan propaganda; they were also apparently familiar with the narrative technique of humanizing certain characters by juxtaposing them to partisan caricatures.

The tendency of late seventeenth- and early eighteenth-century political writing to construct an abstract but ostensibly universal individual in contrast to the excised domestic analogies of high political theory or the dehumanizing particulars of partisan caricature is thus crucial to understanding the development of novelistic realism, which has long been understood to depict universal humanity through the particular details of particular individuals. The first three sections of this chapter trace the narrative techniques by which political philosophers and pamphleteers constructed the difference between abstract and contingent selfhood in three different genres of political writing: formal political treatises and their derivative abridgements, partisan occasional pamphlets, and pamphlets about women that probably were influenced by partisan debates of the day. The final section considers a highly novelistic work of partisan propaganda from the 1740s in which the features of "realistic" narration and character development seem to derive directly from the author's engagement with contemporaneous political discourse.

THE ABSTRACT POLITICAL INDIVIDUAL AND THE FAMILY

Formal political treatises written during the Exclusion crises of the early 1680s and the Revolution of 1688–89 relied on the pivotal analogy of the domestic household, whereby two different versions of Genesis were at stake: a patriarchal divine-right version in which God granted dominion of the Earth to Adam and to all kings directly descended from him, and a Whig social-contract version in which God granted dominion of the Earth to Adam and Eve jointly, in a power-sharing arrangement that justified the accession of William and Mary as joint sovereigns and, more generally, the interruption of the Catholic line of Stuarts. The analogy of the household, of course, did not originate in seventeenth-century England, but had been established by Aristotle when he articulated a parallel between the role of wife and the role of citizen: both are free in some respects, yet their virtue lies in their subordination to their ruler. Aristotle's analogy is, in fact, more complex than this simple parallel suggests, since he identifies specific differences among the positions of wives, children, and slaves.[2] This complex paradigm would probably have interested eighteenth-century novelists, who frequently depicted a variety of domestic power-struggles—between husband, wives, parents, children, and servants. However, Aristotle's complex web of analogies did not travel to Elizabethan England intact.

Aristotle's *Politics* was not readily available and certainly not available in an accurate translation; moreover, his complex system of power dynamics did not necessarily suit the needs of British monarchs, who were consolidating their absolute power at the beginning of the seventeenth century. In the *Trew Lawe of Free Monarchies* (1598), by characterizing all of the monarch's subjects as children, James I devised a purer patriarchy than that articulated in Aristotle's Politics. James does not mention the mother's or wife's function per se, except to align the "mother" with the commonwealth and then to assert that the subjects or children "are better off if their 'mother', the commonwealth, is ruled by a tyrant than not ruled at all."[3] In other words,

James borrowed a parallel from the classical period only to erase the differences between the contingent positions of any subordinate member of the household. In so doing, he helped construct the father or monarch as an abstracted universal individual by contrast to the other members of the household, who are all equally subordinate to the father.

Robert Filmer's *Patriarcha: A Defence of the Natural Power of Kings Against the Unnatural Liberty of the People* (1680) articulates a similar patriarchalism.[4] The foundation of Filmer's argument lies, like Aristotle's, in the assertion of an analogy between family hierarchy (which he holds to be natural) and state structure. Unlike Aristotle, who makes only an imprecise analogy between household and state, Filmer insists on a closer connection, in fact an identification, between the two: "it follows not that a family and a commonwealth are distinct, because, as well in the commonweal as in the family, both these communities are found" (76). In insisting on the similarity rather than the difference between family and state, Filmer attempts to transform Aristotle's complex domestic analogy into a precise *identity* between family and state; moreover, in contrast to James I's version of patriarchalism, Filmer's depiction of the family emphasizes the relationship between husband and wife, rather than the relationship between the mother and her children (or infantile subjects). This decision elides the differences between the contingent positions of the subordinate individuals in the household, as also occurs in James I's *Trew Lawe*; those who are not the head of the household are all equally subordinate and particular, rather than abstract and universal.

While Filmer carried to an extreme the exact identification of the state with the household, his political opponents disassociated the two spheres. James Tyrrell published his *Patriarcha non Monarcha* (1681) in direct response to the publication of Filmer's *Patriarcha*. Tyrrell counters Filmer with examples from Classical, Saxon, and European history in order to prove, by precedent, that ruling families have often overthrown and replaced other ruling families. Tyrrell's account may be seen as a model for most subsequent justifications of contract government, including Locke's *Two Treatises of Government* (1689).[5]

By contrast with Filmer, Tyrrell generally finds similarity rather than exact identification between household and state. However, he reasserts the family-state analogy by speculating about what would happen if "the Father of a Family, in the state of Nature, should in a mad or drunken fit go about to kill or maim the wife."[6] The wife, like the individual subject in the social contract, must retain her capacity for judgment, in order to know when it is appropriate to ignore her husband's right to rule her. In other words, Tyrrell refuses to use Genesis as a justification for divinely ordained sovereignty; instead, he uses a different analogy of the household to justify replacing a monarch who has abused the liberties of his citizens.

In *Bibliotheca Politica* (1694), a series of political dialogues designed to promote social-contract theory, Mr. Freeman argues with a Gentleman and Mr. Meanwell, who adopts Filmer's view that Adam was endowed by God as "the great Father and Monarch of Mankind." Mr. Freeman, whose arguments triumph thirteen dialogues later, responds with an argument typical of social-contract theorists: "I deny this Power of Superiority of Adam over his Wife and Children, was at all a Despotical or Civil Power, but merely Oeconomical, for the Good and Convenience of Adam and the well ordering and preserva-tion of his Family."[7] Tyrrell concludes that the power of fathers over wives and children is perhaps similar to but clearly distinct from the power of monarchs over their subjects. By acknowledging the different contingent situations of various family members, Tyrrell objects to the construction of an overly abstracted political individual. In so doing, he acknowledges the significance of the precise details of household position to political power; not surprisingly, early British novelists, both the Whigs who agreed with social-contract theory and the Tories who opposed it, would frequently take up the theme of what wives and children should do when a father or guardian acts tyrannically.

When the threat of "popery and arbitrary government" loomed in the early 1680s because the succession of the king's Catholic brother seemed unavoidable, the "liberty" of wives, children, and servants was deemed instantly relevant to anti-Catholic political theorists.[8] However, the right of actual women and children to resist oppression was regarded with caution. In *Patriarcha non Monarcha*, Tyrrell ulti-mately qualifies his position by stating, "Not that I give Children any Right . . . to disobey their Parents or resist them upon every slight occasion . . . but in the case of extreme Necessity" (42). In his *First Treatise of Government*, John Locke likewise expresses ambivalence about the simultaneously similar and yet distinct circumstances of husband and wife. In one sense, Adam and Eve share the same dilemma of having been expelled from Eden; at the same time, Eve has the further burden of being subservient to Adam. Locke, moreover, seems unable to decide whether he wants to emphasize the sameness or the difference of their situation. As he refutes Filmer's rather absurd assertion that the divine right of kings dates from Adam and Eve's expulsion, Locke also expresses his confusion about the precise differ-ence in their situations: "For tho as a Helper in the Temptation, *Eve* was laid below him, and so he had accidentally a Superiority over her, for her great punishment; yet he too had his share in the fall as well as the Sin."[9] Locke's struggle over whether or not Adam and Eve are equally guilty is emblematic of the struggle that faced most social-contract theorists when they dealt with the relative positions of power among different household members. This dilemma would be addressed repeatedly by early British novelists, especially during the decades when domestic analogies were gradually disappearing from high political theory.

Although social-contract theorists rewrote the Filmerian interpretation of Genesis, they often obscured the details of the domestic analogies they implicitly invoked by suggesting that government may not have had a single knowable origin. Instead, they often alluded to an unspecified earlier era when an incipient form of social contract already existed. William Atwood, in his *The Fundamental Constitution of English Government* (1690), explains that "our Constitution . . . depends not upon a single Contract between the People and a Prince and his Heirs."[10] He adds, however, that "there plainly was a farther Contract among themselves, to prevent Anarchy and Confusion, at any time when the Throne might be vacant" (102). This reference to a "farther Contract" serves to shift the focus away from the image of the jointly governed family. The political journalist and novelist Daniel Defoe relied on a similarly ambiguous source for the origin of monarchy in *The Original Power of the Collective Body of the People of England, Examined and Asserted* (1702). He explains that although the members of the House of Commons represent their constituents, the citizenry does not give up all its power upon electing parliamentary representatives: "Now it cannot be suppos'd this Original Foundation should give up all its Waters, but that it reserves a Power of supplying the Streams." He continues, "There must always remain a Supream Power in the Original to supply, in case of Dissolution of Delegated Power."[11] Having revised the Filmerian version of the family, Defoe then obscures the relevance of family structure to social-contract theorists' version of the state by referring elliptically to an already extant contract from an always infinitely earlier period.

Social-contract theorists helped to construct an abstracted political subject by first invoking and then obscuring the contingent differences between individuals but, because of the problem of female succession, they could not deny these entirely. The right to the throne that contract theorists needed to grant to Mary and Anne made it difficult to subjugate women entirely to men, but gender roles were often distinguished so that, in some pamphlets, Mary was responsible for the morals of the nation, William for its military protection. In *A Brief Justification of the Prince of Orange's Descent into England*, Robert Ferguson describes Mary's ability to "reform" England "by her Manners."[12] Algernon Sidney similarly struggles with his desire both to uphold England's distinctive tradition of allowing female monarchs and to reaffirm woman's "natural" sweetness and submission in the home. He finally concludes that "as the Apostle says, *The Woman is not the head of the Man, but the Man is the head of the Woman.*"[13] The merging of the metaphor of the family and the metaphor of the body vividly demonstrates the problem raised by gender for social-contract theorists at the end of the seventeenth century—a problem that formal political treatises tended to obscure but that early British novelists would not ignore.

Like Tyrrell, Sidney can recover the husband's right to dominion over the wife only by reverting to Hobbes's declaration that a state, like a body, can support only one head. Sidney elsewhere deploys the apparently "natural" category of class difference in order to construct a household paradigm compatible with his version of social-contract theory: "a hard Father may use his Children as servants . . . and a gentle and good Master may shew that kindness to faithful and well-deserving Servants, which resembles the sweetness of a fatherly rule: but neither of 'em can change their nature; a son can never grow to be a Servant, nor a Servant to be a Son" (59).

By contrast, in Locke's *Two Treatises*, the difference between the category of child and the category of servant is not quite so explicit. In his *First Treatise*, Locke obscures the distinction between children and servants by suggesting that the father's power over both was once unlimited. The text suggests that both are better off now than in earlier times, although Locke does not examine the advances made by either group:

> God also hath given to the Father a Right or Liberty, to alien his Power over his Children to any other; whence we find the Sale and Gift of Children to have been much in use in the Beginning of the World, when Men had their Servants for a Possession and Inheritance, as well as other Goods, whereupon we find the Power of Castrating and making Eunuchs much in use in Old Times. (par. 8)

Linking abuse of children or servants to an ill-defined but barbarous past, when castration was presumably more common, Locke distances the contemporary domestic power structure from an earlier and presumably more tyrannical one. However, although the position of children in some aristocratic and bourgeois households may have improved since "Old Times," the legal and financial positions of the peasant or the servant classes had not necessarily advanced significantly by the time Locke was writing. Passages such as this in the major works of social-contract theory help to blur the differences between men of different ranks. Interestingly, however, social-contract theorists generally left the subordinate position of women unchallenged, maintaining a distinction to which various early eighteenth-century novels would allude. The eponymous heroine of Defoe's *Roxana* (1724), for example, analyzes the marriage contract by comparing a wife's position to that of a servant. The heroine of Richardson's *Clarissa* (1747) specifically defines the tension between the abstracted self of high political theory and her own constrained circumstances when she cries out to Lovelace, "permit me the freedom which is my birthright as an English subject."[14]

Locke's popularity grew and his ideas reached an ever wider audience as he became known as a philosopher concerned with the systematic functioning of the human mind and as he came to be perceived as less radical than the potentially universalizing claims of his *Treatises* might otherwise suggest.[15] Although treatises by James Tyrrell, Algernon Sidney, and William Atwood, which were explicit about their exclusion of women and other subordinate household members, were more popular than Locke's during the 1680s and 1690s, Locke's *Treatises* gained in popularity as his fame as an abstract philosopher spread during the eighteenth century.[16] However, his ideas were disseminated not only through his own writings: equally influential were several popular abridgments of Locke's *Treatises* that helped render an abstracted Whig individual even more central to the dominant discourses of eighteenth-century British politics.

Vox Populi, Vox Dei (1709), which was reissued the following year as *The Judgement of Whole Kingdoms and Nations* (1710) and became one of the best-selling pamphlets in eighteenth-century Britain, was crucial to popularizing the tenets of Lockean liberal political theory. As Richard Ashcraft and M. M. Goldsmith explain, "it was through the means of its influence that not only Lockean principles, but also the actual phrases taken from the *Two Treatises*, entered into the political consciousness of many Englishmen."[17] This text, which consists of concise, abstract statements about the right to resist a monarch and the mutual obligations of subject and ruler, avoids the level of detail about the household that even Locke's *Treatises* hazard. Little emphasis is placed on refuting Filmer, and there are only a few passages about the family. Organized as a series of aphorisms, this popular pamphlet includes observations such as "The Preaching or Promoting of Passive-Obedience without Reserve is a much greater crime than the encouraging of Rebellion," "The Doctrine of Absolute Passive Obedience is a treasonable, pernicious Doctrine," and "*Vox Populi, est Vox Dei*" (the voice of the people is the voice of God).[18] Since it does not explore the complicating differences between household members, this influential work clearly helped construct an abstracted "universal" Whig subject whose position as household head is obscured.

Although revisionist historians such as Clark, Speck, and Colley are right to remind us of the persistent conservatism of eighteenth-century British culture, Britons gradually came to accept the idea that a citizen's liberty should be understood as the right to resist a tyrant. However, once the crown had passed from William and Mary to Anne and from Anne to George I, the priority for Whigs was no longer refuting divine-right theory but supporting the monarch without appearing to contradict the revolutionary precedent set in 1688–89. The aphoristic structure of *The Judgment of Whole Kingdoms and Nations* thus conveniently familiarized readers with Revolution principles, and led them to support the Revolution settlement without asking them to give any thought to the particular circumstances or domestic situation of the abstract civic individual under liberal political theory. In other words, as the eighteenth century progressed and the Whigs continued to dominate Parliament, the language of the best-selling pamphlet that helped to disseminate the principles of social-contract theory to the general populace also increasingly helped to reify an apparently abstracted but nominally Whig, male, Protestant political individual.

Three decades later, *A Dissertation on the Liberty of the Subject in Great Britain* (1737), another pamphlet helpful in disseminating Locke's ideas to the mid-eighteenth-century reading public, imitated the still popular *Judgement of Whole Kingdoms* by emphasizing an abstract universal citizen's right to liberty. The anonymous *Dissertation*, usually ascribed to William Keith, relies on the idea that it is the law, not the monarch, that reigns supreme. However, rather than diminishing the monarch's power by dividing it metaphorically between husband and wife, this treatise deploys instead a mechanical image of "that most beautiful Machine, which, the Coalition of three different Estates and Conditions of Men, composes one united, arbitrary, and legislative power."[19] In choosing the image of a machine, Keith, clearly a supporter of the Whig majority although not of the powerful minister Robert Walpole, then describes the "Publick

Good" as "the only Principle which can effectually unite the three great and independent Parts of the Legislature in *Great Britain*"(16–17). Only rarely does this treatise refer to monarchical power in terms of the household analogy, and when it refers to the king's "Tenderness of a Parent" (44), it carefully avoids distinguishing between father and mother, but seems to evoke both in a single phrase. William Keith also celebrates a parliament that operates through the "Application and Judgment of above 700 Persons of different Ranks and in different Capacities" (17), and thus effectively ignores all those whose household position, gender, lack of property, or religious conviction excluded them from this ostensibly heterogeneous group of seven hundred.

The abstract language of liberty that informed mid-eighteenth-century Whig discourse can also be found by the 1730s and 1740s in the writings of political theorists from the opposition. As an opponent of Walpole but a supporter of George II (after having renounced his earlier allegiance to the exiled Stuarts), Henry St. John, Viscount Bolingbroke, devised a compromise between social-contract theory's reliance on the rule of law and divine-right theory's reliance on God's authority: in Bolingbroke's view, God simply wants us to obey the law. In his *Idea of a Patriot King*, written in 1738 but not published until 1749, Bolingbroke explains that God "exacts our obedience to the laws of those communities, to which each of us is attached by birth, or to which we may be attached by a subsequent and lawful engagement."[20] Moreover, Bolingbroke describes God himself as a "monarch, yet not an arbitrary but a limited monarch, limited by the rule which infinite wisdom prescribes to infinite power" (18). In staking out this compromise position between divine right and divine precedent, Bolingbroke relies on abstracted ideal of "liberty," rather than on the potentially troubling analogy of the domestic family. The logic of his essay hinges on axiomatic explanations such as the following: "because popular liberty without government will degenerate into licence, as government without sufficient liberty will degenerate into tyranny, they are mutually necessary to each other" (30). When reiterating such elegant generalities about "liberty," Bolingbroke never specifies exactly which part of the population he believes should share in this ideal.

Although insisting that "Mr. Locke condescended to examine [the works] of Filmer, more out of regard to the prejudices of the time, than to the importance of the work" (30), Bolingbroke himself borrows a Filmerian turn of logic when he proposes that "The true image of a free people, governed by a Patriot King, is that of a patriarchal family" (46). We may see here how, by the mid-eighteenth century, support for a limited monarchy and a Protestant line of succession no longer required the notion of equal sovereignty between husband and wife. Moreover, Bolingbroke, in one of his few references to the domestic household, denies any difference between the contingent positions of its members by emphasizing their shared interest in the good of the whole: "the head and all the members are united by one common interest, and animated by one common spirit" (46). Bolingbroke never acknowledges the inequities that might make any member of a family articulate an interest other than that of his or her "superior." Rather, he takes to task those who would dare to hold any opinion other than that of the "common spirit" expressed by those of the superior view: "if any are perverse enough to have another, they will be soon borne down by the superiority of those who have the same; and, far from making a division, they will but confirm the union of the little state" (46–47).

David Hume, like Bolingbroke both a Tory opponent of Walpole and a supporter of the Hanoverian line of succession, demonstrates a predilection for abstract political concepts.[21] He generally avoids the analogy of the family and thus the particulars that would undermine the abstraction of his political subject, although his historian's eye for detail sometimes complicates his theoretical assertions. In his essay "Of the Original Contract," Hume attempts to mediate traditional disagreements between rights-based and obedience-based models of government by suggesting that "*both these* systems *of speculative principles are just.*"[22] One of his few references to the familial basis of authority describes the absurdity of believing "the consent of the fathers to bind the children, even to the most remote generations" (447). In other words, in dismissing Filmer's outdated logic of paternal law, Hume overlooks the fact that many of the arguments against passive obedience during the 1680s were grounded not in the rights of sons but in the rights of wives to disobey tyrannical or abusive husbands. In a passage in the chapter "The Origin of Justice and Property" from his *Treatise of Human Nature* (1739–40), Hume conflates the very different economic situations of men and women entering into marriage: " 'Tis easy to remark that a cordial affection renders all things common among friends, and that married people in particular mutually lose their property, and are unacquainted with the *mine* and *thine* which are so necessary and yet cause so much disturbance in human society."[23]

Throughout the rest of the essay, Hume relies on the "universal concepts" of liberty and sympathy: "The *general rule* reaches beyond those instances, from which it arose . . . *Thus self-interest is the original motive to the* establishment *of justice: but a* sympathy *with public interest is the source of the* moral approbation, *which attends that virtue*" (499–500). When he relies on the "general rule" of sympathy, which was crucial for the construction of the moral ground for his political philosophy, Hume obscures the different ways in which men and women are expected to demonstrate it. The elision between men's and women's legal situation in the rare passages in which Hume mentions women confirms the sense that only persons who were propertied and male could fit the universal concept of the "individual."[24] In this regard, Hume's work may be seen as representing, by the mid-eighteenth century, a culminating moment in high political theory, which since the start of the eighteenth century had increasingly obfuscated the contingent differences among individual citizens and so helped to reify a certain abstracted and ostensibly universal political individual.[25]

PARTISAN CONSTRUCTIONS OF THE INDIVIDUAL

Traditional Whig narratives of British history point to the Revolution of 1688–89 as a turning point in the development of civic individualism and hence in the construction of a Whig version of political individualism. The restrictions on their power to which William and Mary agreed when they were brought to the throne and the subsequent passage of the 1701 Act of Settlement greatly increased Parliament's control over the monarchy. As parliamentary power was strengthened, so by extension, at least theoretically, were the rights of men. Moreover, the successful assertion of rights in 1688 arguably led the way to similar assertions in America in 1776 and in France in 1789.[26] Yet, although it is tempting to identify a linear progression from 1688 to 1789, such a narrative belies the many serious threats to the Protestant line of succession and to the Whig control of history. Early in his reign, William was obliged to fight the Stuart-led risings in Ireland and to elude various French-led assassination attempts. Although James II died in exile in 1701, his son James Edward Stuart (the "Old Pretender") was recognized as king of England both by France and the Vatican. In 1708 Jacobite supporters invaded Scotland; after Anne's death, Scottish Jacobites led significant though unsuccessful risings against the Hanoverians in 1715 and again in 1718. The Jacobite rebellion of 1745, led by James II's grandson Charles Edward Stuart (the "Young Pretender"), was put down only after rebel forces had descended into England as far as the Midlands.

These repeated challenges to the post-1689 Protestant succession kept alive for over six decades a political debate that helped shape the way in which competing partisan versions of the individual were portrayed in the early British novel.

Following the Exclusion crises and the Revolution of 1688–89, Whig pamphleteers attempted to associate the extremes of Jacobite caricature with all Tories, while anti-Whig propaganda painted Whigs as hypocritical, unfaithful to the principle of liberty they had invoked in 1688, and guilty of the same tyranny they ascribed to Tories and Jacobites. A sequence of pamphlets in the early years of the eighteenth century distinguishes the "modern Whig," as a hypocritical Tom Double, from a more principled Whig predecessor.[27] In the early- to mid-eighteenth century, anti-Whig discourse also increasingly took the form of personal attack against powerful individual Whigs. Sarah Churchill, duchess of Marlborough, was demonized in strongly misogynistic terms in the first decade of the eighteenth century, because of her perceived political influence over Queen Anne. From about 1727 to 1742, Robert Walpole became an easy target for Tory and anti-Walpolian satirists, who painted him as monstrous tyrant, borrowing descriptions once used against James II.

The pamphlets mentioned in the introduction articulate the features of typical anti- and pro-Jacobite discourse. *Simeon and Levi* (1696), *The True Picture of a Modern Tory* (1702), and *A Seasonable Warning Against Jacobites and Papists* (1712) attempt to characterize Jacobites as less-than-human "papists" or cannibals.[28] In *The History of the Jacobite Clubs* (1712), *The Jacobite Curse* (1714), and *The Counsel to the True English* (1746), reasonable Whig masculinity is contrasted to hot-blooded and unnatural Jacobite masculinity, which is again aligned with Catholicism, lust, and outlawed sexuality. Meanwhile, in a parallel manner, "reasonable" (i.e., apolitical) Whig femininity is contrasted to Amazonian Jacobite femininity.[29] Pro-Jacobite pamphlets reverse these stereotypes, depicting Jacobite men as stronger and less cowardly (less prone to cuckoldry) than Whig men and Jacobite women as models of strength, beauty, and loyalty. These partisan stereotypes, unlike other features of political discourse, did not evolve substantially between the late seventeenth and the middle of the eighteenth century. At moments of perceived Jacobite threats—1690, 1715, 1719, and 1745—familiar anti-Jacobite imagery simply reappeared.

Whereas formal political treatises from the late seventeenth to the mid-eighteenth century deployed increasingly abstract descriptions of the political subject, across the same period there was little change in the style of discourse of partisan occasional tracts: the authors of such tracts consistently depicted members of their own political parties as normal, ordinary, or "realistic," while partisans of any other parties were depicted as caricatures, prone to divisive and factional behavior. As factionalism between the parties became part of the fabric of everyday life in early eighteenth-century Britain, each party increasingly insisted that it was not a "faction." The word *faction* itself became personified in tracts such as "Faction Displayed" (1704) and in the portrait of "Miss Faction" in *The Examiner*.[30] Whigs, Tories, and Jacobites all declared their own universal humanism in contrast to their opponents' zealous partisanship. Political pamphlets from the first Exclusion crisis until the middle of the eighteenth century continued to rely on predictable stereotypes of aggressive women, cuckolded men, and lascivious priests and nuns, even though more philosophical treatises gradually stripped themselves of familial analogies as they adopted the abstract discourses of "high politics."[31] At the same time, partisan pamphlets also exploited and reinforced tension between the universal and the particular by describing their own adherents as abstract universal character types—ordinary, moral, and objective—and contrasting them with the zealous, "interested," amoral members of the opposing factions.

Whereas some anti-Jacobite tracts, such as *A Treatise on Government* (1746), simply demonstrated in laborious detail the obvious fact that the chronology of monarchs in Britain during the previous millennium did not include any direct descendants of the biblical Adam,[32] most partisan pamphlets from the late seventeenth to the mid-eighteenth century deployed much more divisive language. During and following periods of Jacobite unrest, anti-Jacobite pamphleteers frequently went so far as to declare that the Whigs were not even a "party" in the sense of having private, partisan interests, whereas supporters of the Jacobite cause were partisan in the worst sense of the word. For example, the anonymous author of *A Comparison of the Spirit of the Whigs and Jacobites* (1745) attempts to cast most Whig conduct as normal, ordinary human behavior in contrast to the excessive zeal of Jacobite sympathizers:

[A] *Whig*, in Consequence of personal Connections and private Interests, he may hope to serve . . . *may* be a *Party-man*, yet he is under *no Necessity* of being one, if he truely be in earnest about the Principles of *Whiggism*, and strictly adheres to them in his Conduct. Whereas a *Jacobite*, be he ever so much in earnest about the Principles that distinguish his side; *must* be a Party-man.[33]

Given as a public lecture and subsequently published in Edinburgh, *A Comparison* was clearly designed to counteract complaints, presumably made by certain supporters of the Jacobite cause, that the local Whigs were themselves overly zealous party men. Thus George II is described as "the Servant of the People" (10) while Charles Edward Stuart is portrayed as interested in "the Prerogative of *only one Man*, and the Interest of *only one Family*" (13).

Since the Whig definition of the public good helped to marginalize the supporters of the Stuart cause, it is not surprising that Jacobite pamphleteers attempted to turn the rhetorical tables by declaring those in power to be similarly motivated by selfish, particular interests. A pro-Stuart writer explains in a 1692 pamphlet that "we [the British people] have been blindly following the Dictates of our own personal Prejudices and intoxicated Judgments, rather than tracing the Footsteps of our Predecessors, or of the most zealous Assertors of publick Liberties in other Nations."[34] For this writer, the change in power must be attributed to the "Ambition of the Prince of *Orange*" (2) for his own self-aggrandizement rather than for the good of the English people. A half-century later, just before the last Jacobite rising, another Jacobite supporter deemed it prudent to disguise his critique of the Whig administration as *An Attempt Toward A Natural History of the Hanover Rat* (1744). He suggests not only that the current administration is fueled by particular, selfish interests, but that these interests are so far removed from the universal that they are not even human. The writer further emphasizes the commercial and monetary interests served by the Hanoverian monarchy and the Whig establishment when he describes the rat's eating habits: "it doth not only digest Iron, but Steel, Brass, Pewter, Tin, Copper, Silver, and Gold."[35]

The occasional pamphlets described here demonstrate how political propagandists characterized their opponents as factional and self-interested and so implicitly constructed their own partisans in terms of a humanized universal selfhood familiar from the more abstract discourses of high political theory. As the next section demonstrates, gender difference was often a key means of rhetorically distinguishing the abstract from the particular in both political and novelistic discourse.

GENDER AND PARTISAN SELFHOOD

In the six or seven decades following the Revolution of 1688–89, there are examples of both strongly proto-feminist and strongly reactionary misogynist rhetoric. On the one hand, the upheavals of 1688–89 were sometimes aligned with a history of courageous women from earlier times. On the other hand, because women were politically marginal and because their experiences were often represented as "particular" and "subjective" rather than examples of universal human experience, political writers from every partisan position often rhetorically "feminized" their opponents in order to denigrate them. Thus, representation of gender difference was key to the depiction of "humanity" associated with narrative realism, and early British novelists frequently depicted tensions between men and women in ways that suggest an engagement with contemporaneous political discourse.[36]

Published during the year in which James II was ousted from power, *Female Excellency, or the Ladies Glory* (1688) is an example of a text in which courageous women are shown as politically empowered and capable of overthrowing a tyrant. This text rehearses the histories of Deborah, Judith, Esther, Susanna, Lucretia, and Marianne, exemplary women from classical and Old Testament sources; it also includes accounts of Queen Boadicea of Britain, Queen Clotilda of France, and Princess Andegona of Spain. Apparently written in response to an essay in which Montaigne asserts a dearth of "Good Women," these lives are set down to refute the "commonly reckoned" belief that women are "uncapable of noble Undertakings."[37] The themes of the chosen tales, however, highlight not only women's courage generally, but also women's particular courage in response to political oppression. Deborah, Judith, and Esther are described as having risked their lives for the sake of the Israelites; Boadicea risks hers for the sake of the British under Nero's rule; Clotilda helps convert her husband Clovis to Christianity. In Exclusionist social-contract theory, the right of wives to protest against oppressive husbands was crucial as analogy to the right of men to protest a tyrant; in *Female Excellency*, strong women from history function as exemplars of courageous humanity in general as well as of courageous females in particular.

In contrast to High-Church Tory conduct books such as *The Whole Duty of Man* (1658) and *The Whole Duty of Woman* (1695), which define women's role in terms of their subordinate household duties, *Female Excellency* provides a counter-narrative of strong, loyal women willing to fight tyranny, whether tyranny is represented by the Tarquins or the current line of Stuarts. When describing Lucretia's death, Brutus's language seems remarkably consistent with the language used to justify excluding James II and his progeny from the throne: "Who can imagine the Sons will be better than the Father; Their tempers are composed of the bloud of two wicked ones; They are educated by a Tyrant, born into the proud commanding family of the *Tarquins*, and therefore like to be altogether as insupportable as their parents" (80). Other examples of illustrious women appear in Madame de Scudéry's *The Female Orators*, which was published in English translation in 1714, the year Queen Anne died. This work includes ostensibly verbatim accounts of the speeches given by such historical figures as Zenobia, Artemisa, and Lucretia. Whereas in *Female Excellency* Brutus narrates most of Lucretia's story, here Lucretia eloquently articulates her own tragedy, as she does in Shakespeare's *Rape of Lucrece* (1594), reinserting her version of domestic tragedy into what sounds like a typical Whig objection to Jacobite "tyranny."

In contrast to these strongly proto-feminist treatises, which seem inspired by the Revolution of 1688–89, many of the overtly partisan pamphlets of the first half of the eighteenth century make their rhetorical points through the language of sexual difference and a misogynist feminizing of the opposing faction. While we might expect Tory propaganda to rely on a Filmerian preference for passive obedience in the household and Whig propaganda to rely on a more egalitarian treatment of women, neither partisan propaganda nor partisan-inflected prose fiction from the first half of the eighteenth century followed neatly such a formula.[38] Whig and anti-Jacobite propaganda, in particular, relied on misogynistic, anti-Catholic diatribes contrasting ordinary lawful behavior to a Jacobite factional zeal that ostensibly triggered physical violence, oftentimes between women. Although during Anne's reign anti-Tory propaganda was less overtly misogynistic, anti-Jacobite writers from 1680 to 1760 continued to cast their opponents as particular or feminized caricatures in contrast to the emerging normative Whig political individual. The debate inscribed in *The Anatomy of a Jacobite-Tory in a Dialogue between Whig and Tory* (1690), for example, ends with the Tory growing impatient with dialogue and drawing his sword. *The Female Duel* (1700), an anti-Jacobite song, involves a Jacobite woman challenging a Whig woman to a duel: the Jacobite is clearly too hot-blooded to win; the Whig woman, although disinclined to fight, ends up being a better mistress of her weapon because she is less hot-blooded.[39] *Reflections on a Jacobite Plot* (1701) sums up the Whig attempt to associate its cause with abstract rational masculine selfhood by asserting: "There never yet were Measures concerted towards the Destruction of a Kingdom, but a Woman (and she generally a Whore) or a Priest, was embarqued in the Design" (9).

Tory propagandists were not necessarily able to refute the misogyny of anti-Jacobite propaganda because they themselves relied on the patriarchal theory of passive obedience. The Tory proto-feminist Mary Astell, of course, incisively critiqued the inconsistencies in Whig political theory, but Astell's work was not typical of most Tory propaganda, which, like the sermon promoting passive obedience for which Henry Sacheverell was impeached, tended to support a parallel form of patriarchy in both the household and the state.[40] Whigs during Anne's reign sometimes refuted the misogyny of standard Tory and Jacobite discourse by challenging those who resist a woman's rule. For example, a 1710 pamphlet ascribed to John Toland castigates High-Church nonjuring clergy by insinuating that their refusal to swear an oath to Queen Anne implied that they would rather swear allegiance to the pope than to a woman: "nothing can be more inconsistent then the Supremacy they claim by Divine Right over the Queen . . . And can we think that such Men as these wou'd ever scruple, when they found their interests to prefer to the Supremacy of a Woman, that of the Pope, as Patriarch of the West."[41]

In Whig political writing from the period between 1702 and 1714, when Whig political rhetoric was less overtly misogynistic than in other eras, we still see tendencies to subordinate women to men. In the final years of Anne's reign, anti-Jacobite rhetoric focused on the threat of a Jacobite rising to the innocent women and children of the nation. The anonymous author of *A Dissuasive from Jacobitism* (1713) evokes supposed images from the Irish rising, which was instigated by the ousted James II in 1689. He describes Jacobite supporters as "[r]avishing Women in the presence of their Husbands, hanging them up by their heels, ripping up the Big-belly'd, with delight beholding the unborn Children struggling for Life."[42] This reliance on images of the vulnerable women and children of England connects anti-Jacobite rhetoric during 1714, the year that Anne died, to a traditional divine-right image of the family—that of a country needing a father figure to rule it. In an invitation to George III to become monarch, an anonymous broadsheet in 1714 appeals to the "Affectionate Concern of a Prince who is Father to his Country."[43] Thus, even though social-contract theorists might describe joint dominion between husband and wife in formal political treatises, pro-Hanoverian tracts nevertheless frequently depicted women as vulnerable and naturally dependent.

Another anti-Jacobite pamphlet, published in Glasgow in the same year, denigrated the Jacobite cause by publicizing a curse ostensibly circulated by Jacobite supporters against the enemies of "King James VIII" (i.e., James Edward Stuart). This curse reads: "Let their Children be Fatherless and their Wives widows, let them beg their Bread in a strange

Land, and let there be none to pity their Fatherless Children."[44] By associating the Jacobite cause with the destruction of family structure, this writer casts the Jacobites as less than fully human, indifferent to the ties of family or homeland, motivated only by their own allegiance to their lawless party. When the author asks "Is this Party by Law to be tolerated?" (3), he implicitly defines his own party as composed of ordinary individuals, inclined to lawful, moral behavior and a naturally hierarchical family structure.

In other words, while Whig writers of formal political treatises between 1680 and 1760 struggled with the position of women because of their reliance on the analogy of the power-sharing household, Whig propaganda writers consistently deployed misogynistic imagery throughout the entire period, except for a hiatus during Anne's reign. During the decades after Anne's death in 1714, anti-Jacobite pamphleteers were perhaps even more misogynistic than they had been before her accession in 1702. Henry Fielding's anti-Jacobite rhetoric in *The Jacobite's Journal*, published during the aftermath of the 1745 rising, when anti-Jacobite sentiment was running high, is typical of anti-Jacobite discourse after 1714. He denigrates Jacobite women because "the very Scandal at their Tea-Tables is political" while he compliments Whig women for their "Silence on that Head."[45] This passage is typical of anti-Jacobite writings from the 1740s, which promoted not only a subordinate but an apolitical role for women. It also reinforces the traditional Whig conventions of gender difference that defined women as "too virtuous" to enter the political fray. The narrator's attempts to define and defend Jacobitism through an absurd proliferation of pseudo-scholarly details are also clearly intended to associate the Jacobite fascination with the minutiae of lineage and, more generally, with the particular, the factional, and the feminine.[46] By contrast, Fielding implicitly defines the anti-Jacobite "realist" character of his partisan *Journal* as abstractly human, politically normative, and tacitly male.

The Counsel to the True English (1746) and *The Female Rebels* (1747) are typical of mid-century anti-Jacobite propaganda that defined women as too passionate for proper political activity. *The Counsel* reiterates the threats of promiscuity and outlawed sexuality familiar from earlier anti-Jacobite tracts. In *The Female Rebels*, various strong female supporters of the Stuarts (the duchess of Perth, Lady Ogilvie, and Florence MacDonald) are castigated for their devotion to the Jacobite cause. The author ultimately observes: "It is remarkable of the Fair Sex, that whatever Opinions they embrace, they assert them with greater Constancy and Violence, than the Generality of Mankind: They seldom observe any Medium in their Passions, or set any reasonable Bounds to those Actions which result from them."[47] For mid-eighteenth-century Whig propaganda the worst fault of Jacobitism was its extreme partisanship, or its inability to support a Whig understanding of the public good; once again, it is implicitly defined against an abstract ideal of more moderate political selfhood.

Although Tory and pro-Jacobite propaganda was usually as misogynistic as anti-Jacobite propaganda, some pro-Jacobite tracts nevertheless contested the misogyny of the Whig propaganda, and so also contested the construal of "natural" femininity as subordinate and apolitical. *The Highlanders Salivated* (1746) takes the form of a declaration made by "We the *Ladies of Pleasure, Women of the Town, Nightwalkers, Strollers, Bunters,* and other loyal Members of the *Amazon* Society at *King's* Coffee-House, *Covent-Garden.*"[48] The anonymous pamphleteer clearly attempts to associate the infamy of public prostitution with the Whig cause. Yet, at the same time, the discourse aligns the anti-Jacobite cause with patriotic women who are "moved with the justest Indignation against the bold Invaders of the precious Liberty we enjoy, and which we are sensible . . . can only be preserved to us inviolate by the Protestant Succession in these Kingdoms" (18). By putting the Whig principles of liberty into the mouths of these saucy "Nightwalkers," the pamphleteer clearly intends to mock both Whig principles and women who are bold enough to express political ideas in public.

These witty "Nightwalker" ultimately disrupt the standard tropes of political propaganda by calling attention to its hyperbole. Moll King intones ironically, "what Influence, the daring insolent attempts of this *Pretender*, may have upon the thoughtless giddy part of our Society, I know not; but the bare Apprehension of *Popery*, almost frightens me into Fits" (7). She then adds slyly, emphasizing the hypocrisy of anti-Jacobite rhetoric, "How I tremble at the dismal Thoughts of being caress'd in a Corner, by a dirty *Capuchin*, with a long sweeping Bear . . . instead of one of our fine smug-faced Parsons" (7). Through such witty and ironic comments, the narrator of this tract herself resists being reduced to the standard misogynistic stereotypes of partisan propaganda—to a vulnerable victim or unfeminine Amazon. Like Defoe's Moll Flanders, this Moll is rendered engagingly sympathetic to readers. Although only the disembodied narrator of a pamphlet, not a fully drawn character, Moll King nevertheless demonstrates how a character may begin to come alive (or seem "real") through her difference from standard partisan caricatures. Comparing this pamphlet to the earlier *Moll Flanders* (1722) also reminds us that not only would political discourse have influenced novels during this period, but with the increasing number of novels by the mid-eighteenth century, novelistic discourse would have begun to influence political discourse as well.

On the one hand, partisan occasional tracts helped to reinforce the tendency of formal political treatises to construe an abstracted and ostensibly universal political subject. On the other hand, the very openness with which partisan tracts asserted gender difference as part of their arguments helped provoke continued debate about women's position within emergent liberal political theory. We should not assume that the dominant Whig political individual was necessarily becoming an abstracted and universalized entity by the middle of the eighteenth century merely because the language of formal political treatises was becoming increasingly abstract. Rather, this abstracted individual of high political theory was continually being challenged and redefined in specific and gendered detail by a broad spectrum of partisan pamphlets, novels, and proto-novelistic writings. Certain eighteenth-century narratives, like the one analyzed in the next section, are difficult to categorize as either partisan propaganda or proto-novels; the very difficulty of categorizing these works underscores the discursive interplay between political and novelistic discourse during this period.

Proto-Novelistic Partisan Propaganda

Certain genres of seventeenth-century political propaganda have long been connected to the emergence of the novel. For example, the secret history, a genre often acknowledged as a precursor of the novel, was an important tool in opposition politics in mid- to late seventeenth-century Europe. Anecdotal counter-histories of the court of Louis XIV appeared in underground French presses in the aftermath of the Fronde (1648–53). In England, counter-histories such as Sir William Temple's *Memoirs of What Past in Christendom from the War Begun 1672 to the Peace Concluded 1679* (1692), detailing the deceits of Charles II, became central to Whig historiography in the aftermath of the Revolution of 1688–89.[49] In the preface to his *Anecdotes de Florence*, published in France in 1685 and translated into English in 1686, Sieur de Varillas distinguishes the "Anecdoto-grapher" from the official historian in a description that gestures toward the writing style of later novelists:

> The Historian considers almost ever Men in Publick, whereas the Anecdoto-grapher only examines 'em in private. Th'one thinks he has Perform'd his duty, when he draws them such as they were in the Army, or in the tumult of Cities, and th'other endeavours by all means to get

open their Closet-door; th'one sees them in Ceremony, and th'other in Conversation; th'one fixes principally upon their Actions, and th'other wou'd be a Witness of their inward Life, and assist at the most private hours of their leisure.[50]

In these works, the emphasis is on the revealing anecdote, a detail from the personal life of a political figure that casts suspicion on his ability to rule, making these works similar to later eighteenth-century novels in which political concerns are couched in the rhetoric of domestic relations. For example, *Hattigé: ou Les Amours du Roy de Tamaran* (1676, English translation 1680), casts suspicion on the reign of Charles II by reminding readers of a disturbing aspect of Charles's domestic situation: the perception that he was overly governed by his powerful mistress, Barbara Palmer, duchess of Cleveland.[51]

This genre of anecdotal political satire was developed in Britain most notably by Delarivier Manley, whose anecdotal anti-Whig histories *The Secret History of Queen Zarah and the Zarazians* (1705) and *Secret Memoirs and Manners of Several Persons of Quality, of Both Sexes; From the New Atalantis* (1709) define a liminal genre between political satire and proto-novel.[52] In these romans à clef, certain powerful political figures—such as the Whig Sarah Churchill, duchess of Marlborough, and the Whig journalist Richard Steele—are demonized in scathing detail. By contrast, Tories, such as George Granville, Baron Lansdowne, and Henry Somerset, second duke of Beaufort, are depicted as eminently humanized characters, although they appear in very few scenes and are presented with little specific detail. In other words, like many early eighteenth-century political writers and novelists, Manley caricatures her political enemies with unflattering detail and renders her political favorites more "real" or "human" by giving them only a cursory but complimentary description.[53]

By the 1730s and 1740s, certain extended works of partisan propaganda appeared that were almost indistinguishable from the domestic and picaresque fiction of the same period, demonstrating the overlap between "literary" and "political" discourse in mid-eighteenth-century Britain. Archibald Arbuthnot's *Memoirs of the Remarkable Life and Surprizing Adventures of Miss Jenny Cameron* (1746), a novel-length text that straddles the border between political propaganda and novel, offers insights into the discursive connections between the two genres in the 1740s. This text, written from a moderate anti-Jacobite Whig position, also demonstrates a feature that is crucial to the "realisms" of the more canonical novelists of this period: manipulation of the stereotypes of the author's own partisan bias.

A colorful figure from Jacobite folklore, Jenny Cameron, sometimes said to have been a mistress to Charles Edward Stuart (the "Young Pretender"), apparently dressed as a man in order to fight for James Edward Stuart in the 1715 rising and advised Charles Edward Stuart in 1745. She became the subject of numerous accounts in the aftermath of the 1745 rising; her military courage and personal loyalty to the exiled Stuarts made her an easy target for anti-Jacobite propagandists, who typically portrayed Jacobite women as overly promiscuous and unnaturally masculine. *A Brief Account of the Life and Family of Miss Jenny Cameron, the Reputed Mistress of the Pretender's Eldest Son* (1746), for example, gives a short version of her life and adventures, focusing on the standard stereotype of Jacobite supporters as undisciplined, promiscuous, and overzealous. In its account of Jenny's life, this pamphlet emphasizes the importance of proper education to curb a child's—but especially a daughter's—passion: Jenny's parents are blamed for making the mistake of letting her run wild during her youth, as if that decision accounted for her subsequent political commitments.

Arbuthnot's *Memoirs of Jenny Cameron* shares with shorter accounts of Jenny Cameron's life the tendency toward moralizing commentary about the proper education for daughters: Arbuthnot's narrator clearly blames Jenny's father for spoiling her by not thwarting "any of her Childish Humours and Passions."[54] Unlike shorter accounts of Cameron's life, however, which focus on her youthful promiscuity, Arbuthnot's longer text transforms Jenny into a sympathetic character, one who matures and learns life's lessons, like the heroines of so many works of prose fiction from the 1740s. In Arbuthnot's longer narrative, Jenny becomes a respected Highland queen, and after her Highland husband dies, she grows old gracefully. She eventually loses interest in sexual adventures; she relocates her long-lost family members and helps her brothers financially. The narrator describes her, at age forty-six, as no longer beautiful, but improved "in the Excellencies of her Mind" (259). Middle age, moreover, has humanized her: "Her Wit was no longer a Flash, and then extinct, but a Fire continually burning, whenever she was pleas'd to light it up; her natural good Sense was matur'd into a solid Judgment; and the various Vicissitudes of Life, and the different Scenes of Action in which she had bore a Part, had given her a very comprehensive Knowledge of Mankind" (259). Like Defoe's Moll Flanders, Jenny becomes a sympathetic heroine whose thoughtful middle-aged reflections on her promiscuous past mark her development as a character.

Arbuthnot, who is identified on the title page as "Minister of *Kiltarylaty,* in the Presbytery of *Inverness*" and as "One of the Society for propagating the Christian Knowledge," concludes his description of the middle-aged Jenny in such a way as to underscore his credentials as a loyal Hanoverian: "And had she not been so violently prejudic'd in Favour of a bad Cause, she wou'd have appear'd in the first Class of the Female Worthies of the present Age" (259–60). Although Arbuthnot borrows from standard anti-Jacobite clichés of promiscuous Amazons, this *Memoir* pushes the boundaries of predictable partisan discourse. While Arbuthnot clearly blames Jenny for choosing the wrong side on which to fight, he uses the format of the "realistic" fictional autobiography to inculcate sympathy for the heroine of the *Bildungsroman* that Jenny's life's story has become. A verse below the atypically feminine portrait of Cameron on the frontispiece concludes, "*Thy Spirit Jenny had deserv'd applause / Hadst thou engag'd in George's nobler Cause.*"[55]

Following John Richetti's conception of the novel as a text that creates "those verbal energies and accents that signify novelistic character at its fullest and most complicated,"[56] Arbuthnot's *Memoir* certainly qualifies as a novel. The "realism" here, significantly, derives not from the "real-life" details of Jenny's story, since these are the same as in the less novelistic *Brief Account* and since in both cases the "facts" are merely based on well-known myths about Cameron. Rather, Arbuthnot's history of Jenny Cameron conveys an appearance of "reality" because of the way in which its characterization of Jenny deviates from typical partisan cliché: the narrative provides a more critical view of Jenny than would a Jacobite hagiography but a much more sympathetic account than a standard Whig political tract. Despite his stated loyalty to the Hanoverian regime, Arbuthnot not only delivers his heroine from the flattening clichés of partisan tracts, but he also simultaneously critiques a central assumption of high political discourse—that the voices of women and marginalized political groups are too particular to be considered part of the essence of the abstracted political subject.

When analyzing how Fielding, an anti-Jacobite supporter of the House of Hanover, borrows and subverts standard tropes from the political rhetoric of his time, Jill Campbell contrasts his novels with representations of masculinity and femininity in the anonymous *Brief Account* of Cameron's life.[57] Fielding's passively feminine Sophia Western seems to be defined by the absence of partisan bias, in contrast to the zealously pro-Jacobite Cameron. Such apparently apolitical femininity, however, should be understood in contrast to anti-Jacobite representations of powerful Jacobite women, rather than a representation of a priori or "natural" womanhood per se. Fielding's novels, of course, were written in the context of partisan polemics; it would be misleading, however, to assume that his novels should be judged as "literary" against a backdrop of other more purely "political" works. The comparison between Fielding and Arbuthnot demonstrates the overlap between partisan and novelistic discourse during this period; both authors craft the literary through the political. Whereas Fielding sketched Whig models of femininity in contrast to extreme Jacobitism, Arbuthnot modified the very stereotypes against which Fielding was defining his "realistic" women.

In a scene in Arbuthnot's account in which Jenny is advising the Highland leaders, her male auditors listen intently and approvingly to her military counsel: "The Gentlemen were all supriz'd to hear a Proposal so rational and judicious, and so full of good Policy, from a Woman . . . They unanimously applauded the Prudence and Solidity of her Advice" (249). We might object that these men are all on the wrong political side, in Arbuthnot's opinion, and so their respect for her participation just proves the standard Whig innuendo that Jacobite men are impotent. However, the text then turns around and complicates the very gender roles usually assumed by mid-eighteenth-century Whig patriarchy. Dressed as a man, Jenny attracts the attentions of Lady Mackintosh because of his (Jenny's) refusal to take physical advantage of her. In realizing the mistake, Jenny reflects that Lady Mackintosh "has shewn me, from her own Example, what are the most valuable Accomplishments of a Woman; and by her Instructions has taught me what are the most commendable Qualities in a Man" (128). Arbuthnot thus refutes the traditional assumption that rakish behavior in men is justified if it corrects forward behavior in women. This scene might be construed as a means merely to reinforce a Whig heterosexual norm, intended to keep women in an apolitical position of passive virtue, as at the Whig tea-tables to which Fielding alludes in *The Jacobite's Journal*, where politics is apparently never mentioned.[58] However, because Jenny is cross-dressed, she becomes the exception to the rule: moreover, had she not been playing the role of a chivalrous man and thereby deviating from the mid-eighteenth-century Whig paradigm of femininity, readers would not have learned the cautionary lesson about rakish behavior in men.

By contrast with the shorter *Brief Account*, which introduces an entirely gratuitous account of incest between Jenny and her brother, Arbuthnot's novelistic *Memoir* accords Jenny a certain amount of respect—suggesting that she was never mistress to Charles Edward Stuart but rather a loyal adviser who had done her best to achieve harmony between squabbling rebel factions. Arbuthnot's text never deviates from its anti-Jacobite principles, but insists that Jenny was mistaken in preferring *"Popish* Bigotry and *French* Tyranny" over *"English* Liberty, and the Constitution" (273). However, Arbuthnot modifies and supplements masculine Whig narratives of individual liberty by suggesting that some women might be courageous and intelligent enough to be considered full political individuals.

The narrative frame established by Arbuthnot's preface further demonstrates the interrelation between political and novelistic depictions of gender difference during this period. The author begins with a misogynist tirade on "the Humours, the Fancies, the Whimsies, the Schemes and Pursuits of the Fair Sex" (iii) only to have his own text interrupted by some scribbling of his sister Bel, whom he describes as "a pert Hussy . . . who passes for a Wit" (viii). Arbuthnot claims to have left his sister's interruption in his preface "in order to shew the World how weakly she [his sister] has managed her Defence" (ix). However, because of the narrative frame that includes her voice, his sister is able to make her case against men "who pretend to an unlimited Sovereignty" (ix–x) over women. Moreover, she enforces his demands for a better education for women by reminding him that "were there Academies and Universities erected . . . for the Instruction of the Ladies in all Parts of Literature," they might produce works that would greatly exceed "any Thing that ever yet dribled from any of their hum-drum Noddles" (xi). This playful exchange suggests to us a Bakhtinian "system of languages" or a Foucauldian "enunciative field" of different discourses.[59] This preface also permits Arbuthnot, who allows his sister's voice to be heard even as his narrative persona belittles her, to challenge the basic assumption of high political discourse—that legitimate political voices are to be male, Protestant, and anti-Jacobite—even as the text repeatedly reiterates a typically anti-Jacobite position. Arbuthnot's juxtaposition of the domestic tension within his own household (between himself and his sister) with the story of an obviously political heroine underscores the novel's ability to reassert the relevance of domestic analogies to the mid-eighteenth-century abstractions of Lockean and Humean political theory. We may thus appreciate the genre's engagement with both the particular details of partisan propaganda and with the more generalizing abstractions of high political theory.

In describing how Arbuthnot's liminal narrative develops novelistic complexity, I do not mean to suggest that in order to seem "realistic" a novel must necessarily exceed the boundaries of its author's probable partisan purpose. Certainly when Haywood, Fielding, or Austen sketch characters in response to particular partisan caricatures, their political purposes are not necessarily undercut by the excess verbal energy of the text. However, insofar as Arbuthnot's *Memoir* has the feel of a "realistic" novel, it demonstrates how mid-eighteenth-century techniques of narrative realism might derive as much from a critique or manipulation of dominant Whig ideology as from a simple reiteration of it. As the rest of this study demonstrates, between the last decades of the seventeenth and the middle of the eighteenth century, writers with a range of different partisan commitments contributed to the narrative conventions we have come to associate with the novel by engaging with both the philosophical abstractions of high political discourse and the static stereotypes of partisan argument. My argument relies upon and vindicates the premise that no single political position was more responsible than others for the novel's evolution. What Doody terms Whig "Prescriptive Realism"[60] is certainly more familiar to modern readers than Tory or Jacobite realism, probably because certain pro-Stuart and Jacobite novelists (including Behn and Haywood) were eventually dropped from traditional Whig versions of history.[61] Once we return these traditionally noncanonical novelists to the history of the novel, we are able to recognize the polyvalent threads of partisan discourse that helped to determine the structure of early British novels.

CHAPTER 2

Tory Ideology and Aphra Behn's Turn to the Novel

In her "Essay on Translated Prose" (1688), which appears as a preface to her translation of Fontenelle's *Entretiens sur la Pluralité des Mondes* (1686), Aphra Behn (1640–89) reflects at length on the genre of translation and on a translation's relationship to the original work. Similarly, in several of her prologues, epilogues, and published prefaces to her dramatic works, she comments on the difference between comedy and tragedy, and on the reception of her own works vis-à-vis the reception of works by male writers in the same genre. In order to defend her forays into dramatic comedy, Behn redefines the genre even as she mocks the male critics who insist on faulting her for flaunting some of its conventions. Mocking "their musty rules of Unity, and God knows what besides" in her preface to *The Dutch Lover* (1673), Behn insists that if the rules "meant any thing, they are enough intelligible, and as practible by a woman."[1] However, despite this suggestion that she is indifferent to the formal rules of a genre, Behn obviously thought deeply about the differences between comedy, tragedy, poetry, and prose translation and about the significance of a woman daring to author any of these genres.[2] Such an awareness of the formal and ideological conventions of these different genres also appears to have shaped her forays into writing novels.

Following a decade of success as a playwright and poet, Aphra Behn turned her hand to prose fiction in the early 1680s, when the political turmoil of the Exclusion crises and the amalgamation of the Duke's and King's Companies reduced the demand for new plays. Her *Love Letters Between a Nobleman and His Sister* (1684–87), a three-part epistolary scandal chronicle, and her *Oroonoko: or, the Royal Slave, a True History* (1688) were both immediate successes and stayed in print until the middle of the eighteenth century. Behn also wrote a dozen other shorter novels, five of which were published just before she died; the other seven appeared during the decade after her death. Although her prose fiction comprises less than one third of her total literary production,[3] her experiments with fiction are crucial to understanding the formative stages of the British novel, especially its connection to partisan political discourses of its day.[4] Behn was a loyal Tory who understood "Plays and publick Diversions [as]. . . one of the most essential parts of good government."[5] When she turned to writing novels and freed herself from the conventions of the Restoration stage, she revoked the traditional patriarchalism of pro-Stuart Restoration drama, especially that of dramatic tragedy. Instead she offered new paradigms for Tory ideology, which she articulated through a variety of narrative techniques that have come to be associated with formal realism.

During the 1680s, pro-Stuart ideology typically relied on a patriarchal model of the household, as is evident in political treatises such as Robert Filmer's *Patriarcha* and in the stage tragedies of the Tory dramatist John Dryden. Behn frequently refutes domestic hierarchy in her prose fiction, especially in her prose tragedies, and challenges the partisan stereotypes of Tory virtue. In so doing, she reconfigures the domestic analogies of high political theory, both Tory and Whig; she also frequently refutes the partisan caricatures of Tory selfhood. In order for her to assert the "reality" of her new Tory versions of self-hood and household structure, she experiments with different narrative techniques subsequently understood as central to formal realism—sometimes interjecting a first-person "eye-witness" narrator, sometimes opting for a quasi-journalistic attempt at objectivity. Behn also develops complex characters that break conventional paradigms of both Restoration drama and political discourse. Insofar as they broke conventions that shaped readers' perception of "reality," these characters might not always have seemed "real" to readers (in Behn's own time or subsequently); nevertheless, they represent Behn's narrative attempts to naturalize a different Tory version of reality through formal innovation. What is striking is how frequently Behn's innovations in formal structure appear to have a political motivation or foundation.

THE POLITICS OF TRAGEDY

During the 1680s, when it became difficult to make a living writing for the stage, Behn, like other playwrights, tried her hand at many different types of writing in hopes of finding another lucrative medium. Her 1685 translation of La Rochefoucauld's *Réflexions ou Sentences et*

Maximes morales (1675) was well received, and she continued to publish prose translations for the last four years of her life. Her epistolary scandal chronicle *Love Letters Between a Nobleman and His Sister* also sold well. Despite this success, however, Behn did not try to follow the paradigm in her other prose works: most of the dozen or so novels or novellas she wrote during the last decade of her life were short parodic anecdotes, quite unlike *Love Letters*. Moreover, although only about half of her short novels were published during her lifetime, she continued to write several of these short works each year until she died in 1689. Although financial considerations certainly played a part, Behn also appears to have been experimenting with different genres and styles of prose.

More often than not, Behn crafted stories with tragic endings in the form of prose fiction rather than drama. With the exception of *Abdelazer: or, The Moor's Revenge* (1676), her only dramatic tragedy, and *The Forced Marriage: or, The Jealous Bridegroom* (1671), *The Amorous Prince* (1671), *The Young King, or The Mistake* (1679), and *The Widdow Ranter* (1689), which may be classed as tragicomedies, Behn's fifteen other known stage productions are all comic.[6] In adopting or adapting tragic story-lines, Behn most frequently turned to the novel, for which there were fewer established conventions. In fact, seven of her fourteen novels (five of the seven published during her lifetime) end tragically—that is, in a death or multiple deaths.[7] In other words, her preference in telling a tragic story was to craft it as fiction, a move that allowed her to circumvent the conventions of Restoration tragedy.

In order to understand why Behn chose to write tragic novels or novellas more frequently than tragic plays, we should consider the formal and political conventions of Restoration dramatic tragedy as delineated by John Dryden in his preface to *Troilus and Cressida* (1679). He explains that unlike comedy, a lesser genre that involves lower-class characters, tragedy should concern men who occupy positions of public responsibility and possess a superior social rank. Following Aristotle's *Poetics* and the example set by Shakespeare, Dryden insists that a tragedy should describe in a unified, dramatic action the fall of a virtuous hero. This hero should be someone "of the highest Quality . . . so that when we see that the most virtuous, as well as the greatest, are not exempt from such misfortunes, that consideration moves pity in us."[8] For a Tory writer of Restoration dramatic tragedy, however, it was not enough merely to create a virtuous hero, a unified action, and an effect of catharsis: beyond that, he or she also needed to communicate a vision of passive obedience that underscored the newly reinstated monarchical order.

By the 1670s and 1680s, when Behn was writing for the stage, and during the Exclusion crises of 1679–81, Stuart ideology was still represented in hierarchical and patriarchal terms.[9] The schema for tragedy that Dryden outlines in his openly Tory adaptation of Shakespeare's *Troilus and Cressida* parallels Robert Filmer's conflation of household hierarchy with passive obedience in the state and so obliges a parallel between female submissiveness in the household and male obedience to the crown. In Dryden's *Troilus and Cressida* (1679), Troilus's loyalty, underscored by a final couplet exalting obedience to the king, and Cressida's suicide help define this gender-specific loyalty. In *All For Love* (1678), Dryden's Antony suffers tragedy, as in Shakespeare's *Antony and Cleopatra*, because his loyalty to love interferes with his loyalty to the state. But Dryden also uses the final speech of his play to reinforce an ideal type of female devotion not emphasized in Shakespeare's version. Whereas Shakespeare's final references to Cleopatra are devoted to Caesar's speculation about the method by which she took her life, the final speech by Serapion in Dryden's version describes the all-consuming power of Cleopatra's devotion to Antony: "Th' impression of a smile left in her face, / Shows she dy'd pleas'd with him for whom she liv'd."[10] Although not every Restoration playwright followed Dryden's example, the way in which he mapped political loyalty onto domestic relations nevertheless helped to define particular types of heroic virtue—both male and female—for the Restoration stage.

Aphra Behn shared Dryden's Tory political sympathies, but did not follow his lead by writing Tory dramatic tragedy. In her comedies—both dramatic and novelistic—she supported Tory ideology, even as she followed the increasingly prevalent trend in Restoration comedy of undermining household patriarchy by depicting rebellious children and unhappy marriages.[11] In 1681, after Charles II had defeated the Exclusion movement, drama became, according to Derek Hughes, "overwhelmingly Tory."[12] Comedies in particular tended to demonstrate "Tory triumphalism combined with gestures of reconciliation and comprehension" (133). Behn's major comedies from the 1681–82 season, *The Roundheads* and *The City-Heiress: or, Sir Timothy Treat-all*, are not exceptions. In these plays, as in her earlier comedies, *The Dutch Lover* (1673) and *The Rover* (1677), she portrays Puritans and Whig leaders as adulterous or otherwise unjust in their domestic relationships, thus reinforcing standard Tory caricatures of Whigs.[13] However, as Hughes has observed, Behn does not automatically depict her Tory heroes as flawless: her plays reveal "the way in which male orders that were opposed in relation to each other could be identical in their oppression of women."[14] In these comedies, Behn "combines clear support for the establishment with gloomy recognition that women are excluded from its workings" (155–56). Thus, even in her early dramatic comedies, Behn demonstrates a willingness to adapt narrative conventions to her own personal version of pro-Stuart loyalty.

Behn was one of the most popular writers of dramatic comedy of her era; even during the troubled political years of the Exclusion Crises, when there was less demand for comedy, Behn was, according to Hughes, "the only writer to remain productive . . . without writing a tragedy" (70). While her *Abdelazer* (1676) was, in Hughes's words, "a modest success" and "one of the best new tragedies since the Restoration" (70), Behn chose not to return to the mode of dramatic tragedy. We can only speculate as to why she did not choose to write more tragic drama, especially given that so many of her novels and novellas have tragic plot lines. However, it is certainly significant that conventional dramatic tragedy, like classical tragedy, usually has as its protagonist a great man, specifically a significant public figure. By contrast, only one of Behn's fourteen novels, *Oroonoko*, has a male protagonist: most of her novels concern the plight of little-known women. Furthermore, although half of her works of prose end tragically, these stories do not follow the standard outlines of classical or Restoration tragedy.

In her first published novel, the three-part epistolary *Love Letters Between a Nobleman and His Sister* (1684–87), Behn concludes the action with a description of Cesario's (Monmouth's) final attempt for the crown and his ultimate military defeat, a dénouement befitting a heroic tragedy. However, rather than focusing on the details of the battles, she insists that "it is not the Business of this little History to treat of War, but altogether Love; leaving those rougher Relations to the Chronicles and Historiographers of those Times, I will only hint on such things in this Enterprize as are most proper for my purpose" (2:426). Had Behn made war, not love, her main focus, her novel—which ends with Cesario's death and the completion of the moral ruin of Silvia (who represents the real-life Lady Henrietta Berkeley, who eloped with her brother-in-law, Lord Grey, once an ally of Monmouth)—might have been written as heroic tragedy.[15] Her decision not to make Cesario into a tragic hero is overtly political: her disapproval of Monmouth's attempts to unseat his uncle was well known, especially after her 1682 arrest for criticizing the illegitimate royal claimant.[16]

Behn's depiction of Philander (the real-life Lord Grey) is also shaped by political concerns. *Love Letters* begins with Silvia voicing

Tory caution to Philander, warning him not to oppose the king, while Philander supports Monmouth not out of true principles but because he is ambitiously self-serving—a characteristic that Tory propaganda generally ascribed to Whigs.[17] Over the course of the three-part novel, Silvia devolves from a model of Tory prudence into a fallen, degenerate aristocrat, while the Whig Philander is partially rehabilitated by the end of the final section. As Janet Todd suggests, the earl of Sunderland may have commissioned part III, and his own shifting loyalty, transferred from William to Monmouth, coupled with his possible intervention in Lord Grey's escape, may have dictated the evolution in Philander's character.[18] In other words, it may have been an explicit partisan commission that was responsible for Philander's development from a mere Whig caricature to a complex character, neither entirely treacherous nor entirely cowardly, whose precise partisan allegiance is difficult to pinpoint by the novel's end.[19]

In her subsequent novels and novellas, none of which approached the length of *Love Letters*, Behn continued to develop narrative innovations by rupturing conventions of Restoration tragedy and traditional Tory discourse. While Dryden accepts classical conventions by insisting on unified action, the action of Behn's tragic novels proceeds rather haphazardly, sometimes over the space of days, sometimes over the space of years. Dryden articulates a theory of catharsis, but Behn's protagonists often evoke more puzzlement than pity. Rather than scripting heroes who struggle with political loyalty, in her short novels *The Unfortunate Bride: or, The Blind Lady a Beauty* (1698), *The Nun: or, The Perjured Beauty* (1698), and *Agnes de Castro: or, The Force of Generous Love* (1688) Behn describes heroines who struggle with the real but not usually narrated dilemma of falling in love with more than one man. The texts that will be analyzed in the rest of this chapter likewise refute conventions central to Restoration drama as they rescript the central domestic analogies of formal political theory, both Tory and Whig, and refute the misogynistic caricatures of divine-right propaganda.

As this chapter demonstrates, Behn develops narrative structures now associated with formal realism, including both subjective "eye-witness" narration and ostensibly objective and detached narration, in order to naturalize her particular pro-Stuart vision of reality. In the sections that follow, I first examine Behn's tragic yet parodic novella *The Dumb Virgin: or, the Force of Imagination* (1698) in which she retells the traditional story of Oedipus as a proto-feminist Tory "tragedy in reality" rather than a conventionally "moving scene" on stage.[20] I then examine two novellas written during the last year of her life, *Oroonoko* (1688) and *The History of the Nun: or, the Fair Vow-Breaker* (1689), both of which were later revised by Thomas Southerne into more conventional sentimental tragedies, in which Behn continues to define the features of Tory tragic novelistic realism in contrast to the conventions of the Restoration stage and the political discourses of her time. The last section of this chapter demonstrates how Behn articulates a vision of political pragmatism and compromise in *The Fair Jilt* (1688), a novella that resists categorization as either comic or tragic. It offers instead a quasi-objective style of narration that encourages readers to suspend conventional moral judgments and acknowledge as "human" characters with whose political motivations they might otherwise disagree.

The Oedipus Saga Revisited

Just as she engaged the caricatures of partisan propaganda in *Love Letters*, Behn also reworked partisan depictions of virtue and heroism in her shorter works of prose fiction from the same era. In *The Dumb-Virgin: or, the Force of Imagination* (probably written in 1684, published posthumously in 1698), Behn rewrites the classical tragedy of Oedipus, rupturing patriarchal conventions of both classical tragedy and political propaganda and achieving, in this effort, her own style of novelistic Tory realism. Although seen by post-Freudian society in terms of individual psychological development,[21] the tragedy of Oedipus is in fact concerned with the decline of a nation state, a decline linked to incest within the ruling family. Sophocles' original tragedy emphasizes an implicit, if somewhat blurred, connection between order in the family and order in the state. It should come as no surprise, then, that this story reappeared in England and France during the second half of the seventeenth century, when, after the British civil wars and Louis XIV's ascension to the throne, questions of tyranny and monarchical succession were actively being debated, often in terms of metaphorical parallels to family structure. It is also predictable that, in the face of the first Exclusion Crisis (1679), Dryden and Lee's jointly authored *Oedipus: A Tragedy* should further reinforce the patriarchal domestic analogy so central to pro-Stuart ideology.

Dryden and Lee, as well as Behn, would almost certainly have been familiar with Pierre Corneille's *Œdipe* (1659), in which Oedipus is a tyrant who has usurped the throne from Dircé, his own sister, and is attempting to prevent her marriage with Thésée (Theseus). In contrast to the ways in which Corneille complicates his audience's view of the tragic hero, Dryden and Lee, in their version of Oedipus, simplify the story's domestic relations by having every member of the family line (including Oedipus and his children) die, by murder or suicide, at the end of the play. They thus avoid the question of who has the greater claim to the throne—Creon or Oedipus's children—in a play produced during the year of the first Exclusion Crisis when the right of the Catholic James to ascend to the throne was being hotly disputed. Dryden and Lee circumscribe the quagmire of a contested succession by killing off an entire branch of the ruling family. Whereas Sophocles, by focusing on Antigone's position after the death of her mother and brother, and Corneille, by introducing Oedipus's sister and her potential claim to the throne, complicate a merely patriarchal vision of the domestic family, Dryden and Lee simplify both the classical and the French models by reasserting for the English Restoration stage an uncomplicated parallel between household and nation, in which the household is not itself a subject for debate but only a static analogy. Aphra Behn offers a pointed response to Dryden's patriarchalism and contributes to the development of formal realism by reintroducing the importance of the domestic household to the Oedipus story. At the same time, her emphasis on the centrality of household structure also refuted Exclusionist (Whig) political theory from the 1680s, which frequently deployed a liberating analogy of the household but was cautious about extending its relevance beyond the realm of political imagery to the actual sphere of domestic reality.

In contrast to both Corneille's 1659 and Dryden and Lee's 1679 dramatic tragedies, Behn's short novel *The Dumb Virgin: or, the Force of Imagination* provides an odd parody of the Oedipus myth. Cosmos, lost at sea as an infant and raised to manhood in England, appears in Venice as the dashing naval hero, Dangerfield. Within twenty-four hours of his arrival, he forcibly seduces a young beauty, who turns out to be his sister, and mistakenly stabs their father during a mix-up in a duel. The story concludes with Dangerfield's outburst "O! *horrour, horrour, I have enjoyed my Sister, and murdered my Father*" (3:359). Although brother-sister incest was not uncommon on the Restoration stage, the repetition of the words "*horrour, horrour*" suggest the horror evoked in Sophocles' *Oedipus Rex*, especially to a playwright herself familiar with Dryden's version of *Oedipus* (on which she comments in her preface to *The Luckey Chance*). Aside from the obvious echo in the final passage, other references to an unavoidable "fate," so central to classical tragedy, are also evident. The narrator emphasizes the protagonist's predetermined destiny as she describes him leaving the arms of the beautiful young woman he has seduced: he surely would have pursued a speedy marriage, "had not the unhappy *Crisis* of his fate been so near" (3:357). Earlier in the tale Cosmos's mother is described as reflecting on an enigma that echoes the predictions of Oedipus's own destiny: "the strange riddle of her Sons fortune, who by shunning one fate, had (in all probability) fallen into a worse" (3:343).

By parodying the references to tragic destiny typical of classical and Restoration drama, Behn undermines the pathos of such models. When Dangerfield cries "*horrour, horrour,*" his words reflect anguish, but his moral mistakes—the too-swift seduction of a pretty girl and his over-readiness to draw his sword in an argument—are those of a hot-blooded rake or perhaps the villain of a revenge tragedy, not of a classical hero. Had he waited until after dinner to seduce Maria (whose vulnerability is scripted by her congenital inability to speak), he might have found out that they were siblings; had he asked questions before drawing his sword, he might not have stabbed his own father. Dangerfield is a naval hero and so presumably concerned with the good of the nation's honor at war, but his insistence on applying methods of combat to the vulnerable inhabitants of the household undercuts his legitimacy as a potential public leader. Here he differs from Corneille's Thésée (Theseus) who, when he is briefly led to believe that his fiancée may be his sister (and he the long-lost infant son), virtuously recasts his amorous feelings for Dircé into those of a loving brother.[22] Thésée's heroism stems largely from his willingness to subordinate his personal feelings to the good of the state; Behn mocks the naval hero Dangerfield because he lacks Thésée's understanding of the connection between private morality and public good.[23]

The final skirmish that kills Dangerfield, Rinaldo, and two other gallants starts during an argument among the three young men over which will have a chance to seduce one of Rinaldo's daughters. This bloody ending is so abruptly tacked on to what otherwise reads like a comic tale, however, that it is difficult for the reader to feel pity for any of the men involved. When Rinaldo is inadvertently stabbed by the naval hero he does not yet know is his son, he responds simply, "*you have ill rewarded me for my care in your concerns in the Senate to day*" (3:358), a matter-of-fact reply that hardly effects either pity or fear. When moments later, as both men lie dying, they recognize their kinship, Dangerfield muses to "*ye impartial Powers . . . how happy had been the discovery some few hours ago, and how tragical is it now*" (3:358). This one-line echo of high tragedy sounds awkward, even parodic, in an otherwise farcical account of gallant impetuosity.

Although Dangerfield initially appeared to be a traditionally courageous hero, the events of the story prove him to be little more than a
shallow stereotype of an ambitious, self-interested Whig.

Complicating these depictions of standard political caricatures,
Behn's decision to name the dashing naval-hero figure "Dangerfield"
also had distinct party implications. A pro-Catholic, pro-Stuart pamphleteer, who was active in staging the faked Protestant "Meal-Tub"
plot intended to divert attention from other popish plots against the
monarch, the real-life Thomas Dangerfield was someone with whom
Behn might have sympathized, as is suggested by the narrator's hope
that she has "done him the justice . . . to make him be pity'd for his
misfortunes, not hated for his crimes."[24] However, Behn's reference
to Dangerfield may be more complicated than her narrator's final
comments suggest, since Dangerfield was not merely an active player
in the Meal-Tub plot; he was also a turn-coat and double-dealer, who
gave evidence against fellow plotters and fellow Catholic sympathizers
Mrs. Cellier and Henry Nevil Payne, the latter of whom was the ded-
icatee of Behn's *The Fair Jilt*. Although the narrator claims to want to
portray Dangerfield sympathetically, Behn's distinctly un-heroic representation of this Oedipal figure hardly qualifies as a flattering portrait. Behn in fact may have cast Dangerfield as a typical Tory
caricature of Whig ambition and recklessness, whose double-dealing
undermines the valor of his partisan cause. If we are to locate a lin-
gering sympathy for the real-life Dangerfield it would lie in the fact
that, on his deathbed, this character points out that his name is "*not*
Dangerfield, but *Cla*—" (3:359). This unflattering portrait of Whig
ambition thus represents either a fictional or some other real-life Whig
scoundrel, whose mercenary ambition is revealed in the ease with
which he hides under a false name. In either case, clearly it is Behn's
own Tory position that fuels her depiction of the Whig scoundrel as
mere partisan caricature. In contrast to this rakish stereotype, the loyal
but lightly sketched Rinaldo, a diligent senator who attempts to
accomplish his professional duty by assisting the career of a war hero,
is shown as more "human."

Recrafting the pathetic conventions of both classical and
Restoration tragedy in order to mock the impulsiveness of rakes, Behn
faults politicians who take their governmental responsibilities more
seriously than their duty to protect the subordinate members of their
own households. Locating her version of Oedipus in Venice, a republic governed by a parliament, rather than in Britain, a parliamentary
monarchy, Behn is able, during the year that James II was being
ousted from power, to satirize the Whig social-contract theorists,

whose vision of a parliamentary monarchy seemed to her just as oppressive as patriarchal tyranny. Changing the tragedy's focus from a crisis in monarchical succession (in which Creon replaces Oedipus as ruler) to a crisis among ordinary members of the political sphere, Behn casts the figure of Oedipus's father, Laius (her Rinaldo), not as a monarch but as a senator in the republican city-state of Venice. Rinaldo's position in the senate is not an inherited post, and so the mistakes his son makes do not suggest a pollution to the whole nation, as they do in Sophocles' original tale; the crisis is not a succession crisis, like that prompted by the evil "usurper" Creon in Dryden's adaptation or by the "tyrant" Oedipus in Corneille's adaptation of the classical story. In Behn's novel, the deaths of father and son do not make up the most significant part of the tragedy. All we know of Rinaldo is that he is an important person in the Venetian Parliament and generously inclined toward this mysterious British stranger. In contrast to the Whig caricature of Dangerfield, the underdrawn Tory Rinaldo feels more "human" and hence more "real." The focus of Behn's story, however, is not the father or the son, but the fate of Rinaldo's two daughters, Dangerfield's sisters.

In making central the plights of the adolescent girls, Behn draws our attention to what is ignored by the "serious" political debates of "great men" in a public sphere that conflates the role of the head of the family with that of the abstract citizen.[25] Significantly, it is at the precise moment when Rinaldo and his fellow senators were in the Senate busily debating Dangerfield's own promotion to naval captain that Dangerfield "at last gained the Fort" (3:357) of Maria's chastity. Behn clearly questions the heroism of a naval leader who in his spare hours uses his military prowess to seduce innocent women. In connecting Rinaldo's absence from the household with the forced seduction, or rape, of his daughter, Behn further suggests that the benevolent household head—the tacitly "universal" subject of formal political treatises, both Tory and Whig—who moves freely from home to the outside world of politics and economic affairs, may inadvertently cause tragedy in the lives of the individual women who have power in no other realm but the household. Behn has shifted the focus of the traditional classical tragedy away from the hero altogether, so that none of the male characters are as developed as the female characters, with whose struggles the story is primarily concerned.

Behn narrates the rape itself from the perspective of Maria, who "held out against his assaults above two hours, and often endeavoured to struggle from him, but durst make no great disturbance, thro fear of alarming the Company below" (3:357). Depicting the sharp contrast between the situations of rapist and victim through an omniscient narrator, Behn deftly shifts from the feelings of the rapist "who fatally enjoy'd the greatest extasy of bliss" to those of the "ruined Lady" who "now too late deplored the loss of her Honour" (3:357). This deft switching of perspectives permits Behn to depict the different contingent realities dictated by household position and gender. Behn also narrates the scene as the ruin of a young woman, rather than as a crime against her family or father, as rape was legally defined during this period. This narration, which is consistent with the particularizing detail associated with formal realism, here stems from Behn's taking the analogy of the domestic household in Whig social-contract theory more seriously than the political theorists who deployed it.

The sisters themselves, in fact, are not fully developed novelistic characters: Maria functions as an emblem of beauty without wit, Belvideera wit without beauty. Behn seems to be making an ironic commentary on a culture that appreciates female beauty but cannot quite acknowledge the value of female wit, but this commentary does not of itself render them "real." What makes these sisters feel somewhat "real" is probably less the single defining quality of their personalities than the attention the narrator draws to their plight, as well as the rivalry described between them.[26] More emphasis is given to jealous rivalry between the sisters, and their attempts to out-maneuver each other in seeking Dangerfield's attentions, than to the duel fought between the rival gallants, of which the reader receives only a second-hand account. Behn also introduces a female narrator in *The Dumb Virgin* who steers the reader away from the ostensible tragic hero. Positioning herself as a neighbor of Senator Rinaldo and a confidant of the two daughters, this nameless first-person narrator (presumably Behn herself) claims to be an eyewitness to the novel's final scene of bloodshed:

> I lodged within three doors of *Rinaldo's* House, and running presently thither, saw a more bloody tragedy in reality, than what the most moving scene ever presented; the Father and Daughter were both dead, the unfortunate Son was gasping out his last, and the surviving Sister most miserable, because she must survive such misfortunes . . . (3:359)

Consciously removing this "tragedy in reality" from the "moving scene[s]" that mark the stage tradition of heroic drama, Behn uses this first-person interjection to loosen the patriarchal underpinnings of

Tory Restoration tragedy. In so doing, she also introduces a narrative device typical of later "realist" fiction.

After this brief description of the abrupt deaths of father, son, and sister, Behn ends the novel by mentioning the financial situation of the second sister, who signs her estate over to her uncle, "reserving only a competency to maintain her a Recluse all the rest of her Life" (3:360).[27] By concluding the story with this brief explanation of what happens to the forgotten daughter, Behn challenges the focus of political debate in which the model for the civic individual is a husband or father whose virtuous actions in the political sphere lead to the all-too-real tragedy of violation in the household. By having one daughter survive the death of her father, brother, and sister, rather than following Dryden's example of eliminating all the offspring, Behn insists on the family's difference from the state and reclaims the complexity of Sophocles' original drama. In focusing on the contingent details of domestic life, however, Behn offers a version of "reality" that refutes any model of political selfhood that is overly abstracted from the analogy of the domestic household.[28]

Tory Heroism and Domestic Reality

In the second half of 1688, after James II's wife had borne a son and when William of Orange was being encouraged by Whig leaders to invade Britain, Behn published two short tragic novels both treating the question of loyalty and vows: *Oroonoko; or the Royal Slave*, probably begun after the announcement of Mary's pregnancy and published shortly after the birth of James Edward Stuart in June of 1688, and *The History of the Nun: or, the Fair Vow-Breaker*, which was licensed on October 22, 1688, just two weeks before William's landing at Brixham. Anyone who had taken an oath of allegiance to Charles II after the Restoration or pledged loyalty to James after his accession to the throne in 1685 would clearly be breaking a vow or bond of loyalty in declaring or recognizing William of Orange as king of England. Thus the dilemma of whether or not to acknowledge any sovereign other than James would cut across party and class lines, although it would particularly affect men who were members of Parliament or office holders of any sort. In *Oroonoko*, the sovereign rendered slave is African, not English; in *The History of the Nun*, Behn recasts the issue of political loyalty into a matter of religious vows and locates the dilemma of divided loyalty in the story of a once virtuous woman who, Behn's narrator suggests, took her convent vows at too young an age. By translating the problem of loyalty across lines of gender and race in *Oroonoko*, Behn manages, as in *The Dumb Virgin*, to recast traditional Tory models of loyalty away from the standard model of the patriarchal household and toward a new pro-Stuart paradigm for domestic "reality."

Unlike Behn's other novels, in which the leading characters are women or adolescent girls, *Oroonoko: or, the Royal Slave* (1688) has as its protagonist a man of royal blood who suffers the most significant tragic reversal possible: from royalty to slavery. The hero, Oroonoko, an enslaved African prince, is described in terms that echo the physical characteristics of heroes from classical or European tragedy. Had Behn merely intended to create a Tory heroic tragedy from the lives of one of the martyred Stuarts, she might have followed Dryden's lead in creating a noble hero, such as his Troilus or his Oedipus, whose virtue is highlighted by the unscrupulousness of his opponents. Behn could have chosen to pit Oroonoko against the governor of Surinam—as does Thomas Southerne eight years later when he recasts her novel as dramatic heroic tragedy—and have them vie for the love of Imoinda. However, Behn's novelistic tragedy is formally less conventional and morally more ambiguous than Southerne's later revision. As in *The Dumb Virgin*, the complexities of character and narrative voicing that we now associate with the development of formal realism stem once again from the tension between Behn's Tory position and her refusal to countenance the usual divine-right patriarchalism associated with a Tory stance.

In Southerne's 1696 stage production *Oroonoko: A Tragedy*, the protagonist resolves the tragedy of star-crossed love and revenge in a swift triple murder: he requests his wife's suicide, which she quickly performs; he stabs the governor, then himself, in quick succession. In Behn's original novel, the tragic dénouement is not so simple. Oroonoko cuts the throat and severs the head of his "heroick Wife" (an action she approved), then is himself captured and disemboweled. He is sewn back together and allowed to heal for a few weeks, with the approval of one faction of the local plantation owners. Finally he is dismembered and quartered by another faction of colonial landowners. Although depiction of the horrors of vengeful landowners taking justice into their own hands in the absence of monarchical control would be consistent with pro-Stuart propaganda during the 1680s, there is nevertheless a problem in Behn's description of Oroonoko's otherwise noble decision to save his unborn child from the horrors of slavery. A murder that might have been narrated as tragic heroism is complicated by Behn's description of the public reaction to Imoinda's corpse; a group of persons seeking Oroonoko

> ask'd him, what he had done with his Wife? For they smelt a Stink that almost struck them dead. He, pointing to the dead Body, sighing, cry'd, *Behold her there.* They put off the Flowers that cover'd her with their Sticks, and found she was kill'd, and cry'd out, *Oh, Monster! that hast murther'd thy Wife.* (3:116)

The physical detail of this passage provides a troubling revision of the cleaner heroism of Restoration tragedy, which occasionally incorporated violence against women, but did not usually depict the mutilation of heroines or mention the decay of their rotting corpses.[29]

Readers are left uncertain how to view the eponymous hero of *Oroonoko*: they may feel sympathy for his plight as an exiled and enslaved monarch but horror at what he has done. The classical language of honor and virtue, with which Oroonoko explains his decision to murder his wife, would be central to a dramatic tragedy, but is undercut by the realistically detailed description of Imoinda's corpse; readers are here likely to feel ambivalent toward Behn's protagonist. This ambiguous depiction of a Tory hero challenges the patriarchalism of standard depictions of Tory virtue. At the same time, it contributes directly to the development of a complex and not wholly admirable protagonist, a development that we have come to associate with narrative realism. Southerne's revision of Behn's novel into affective dramatic tragedy, marked by the swift double suicide of the lovers, reminds us of the threat that Behn's novelistic tragedies must have posed to the tacit assumptions of male Restoration dramatists, Tory and Whig alike.[30]

The challenge that Behn's tragic novels offered to the traditional patriarchal assumptions of the Restoration stage is emphasized most dramatically by Southerne's addition of a comic sub-plot to his 1696 stage version of *Oroonoko.* Two sisters, fleeing England for lack of marriage opportunities, are forced to resort to tricks and disguises to land men with fortunes. Against the high tragedy of the wronged monarch, Southerne's sub-plot instills in women the fear that men are hard to get and reiterates that a woman's powerlessness without one makes a man desirable at any emotional or moral cost. As Paula Backscheider has pointed out, Southerne's adaptation of *Oroonoko* "naturalized or even eradicated Behn's transgressive woman."[31] I would argue that Southerne's drama also reinscribed the assumption central to late seventeenth-century political theory of every ideological stripe: the hierarchical family is a natural structure, irrelevant, except as analogy, to the functioning of the state.

The traditional patriarchalism of Restoration tragedy that Dryden articulates and Southerne reinvokes requires that women be subordinate to men, as men are to God and to their king. It is against this backdrop that Behn turns to the novel to write a different version of Restoration tragedy, offering her own pro-Stuart version of reality. In previous political decodings of Behn's novel, Oroonoko has been plausibly linked to Charles I or James II.[32] Consistent with this partisan stance, Behn employs the bloody mutilation of Imoinda and the drawn-out death of Oroonoko to represent the messiness of factional disputes and the potential chaos of interrupted monarchical succession, images typical of Tory drama from this period. However, Behn does not depict her Tory hero as flawless; her depiction of Imoinda's decaying corpse, for example, undermines her readers' ability to sympathize with her hero, even if the murder he committed was theoretically consistent with a pro-Stuart ideology.

In a further mark of her refusal to deploy standard Tory representations of reality, Behn articulates her distrust of decentralized power without a direct display of support for patriarchy in the family. Behn expresses her distrust of parliamentary government and social-contract theory, under which any sort of "Villains" might gain power, when she describes the Governor's council with scarcely veiled contempt:

> his Council, who (not to disgrace them, or burlesque the Government there) consisted of such notorious Villains as *Newgate* never transported; and, possibly, originally were such who understood neither the Laws of God or Man, and had no sort of Principles to make them worthy of the Name of Men: but at the very Council-Table would contradict and fight with one another, and swear so bloodily, that 'twas terrible to hear and see 'em. (3:112)

Even though Behn's narrator is at times herself fearful of Oroonoko and seems to cooperate in spying on him, she ultimately blames this council of scoundrels—a fraternal rather than patriarchal governing body—for preventing her, in the Governor's absence, from delivering Oroonoko the protection she claims should be in her power.[33] In passages like this, she critiques the tyranny she locates in fraternal parliamentary power without directly reinforcing the divine-right assumptions of hierarchy and subordination of women in the household.

Although there are several moderate plantation owners in *Oroonoko*, these men are overruled by the others' strong impulse for revenge against the escaped royal slave; there is thus no effective voice of protest against Oroonoko's brutal dismemberment. The only opposi-tional voice is the posthumous offering of Behn's own narrative, which she sardonically refers to as the work of "only a Female Pen" (3:88). Nevertheless, it is clear that despite her self-deprecating pose, Behn recognizes the importance of her political critique. She concludes her novel with the hope that the "Reputation of [her] Pen is considerable enough" to make Oroonoko's "glorious name" survive (3:119). Moreover, she dares to assert in her preface that this chronicle will provide significant but overlooked knowledge to those, like Lord Maitland, who seek to serve the public good. She once again claims a voice in public debate but only by writing, "a Short Chronicle of those Lives that possibly wou'd be forgotten by other Historians" (3:54)—that is, by writing a type of tragic chronicle that has not been written before.

By reconfiguring Tory Restoration tragedy as tragic novel, Behn reveals that true tragedies often occur in the private space of the house-hold, a zone that she insists is artificially disconnected from and ignored by the politically powerful, articulate men who controlled both government and the public sphere. She thus insists that the domestic household, so central to political theory as analogy, should be taken seriously for its own sake. Although none of the characters in this novella is fully developed according to subsequent novelistic conven-tions, Behn undermines the standard partisan depictions of Tory tragic heroes and insists on the real-life tragedies effected by political figures on subordinate members of the household. In her preface to *The Luckey Chance*, Behn recounts that in viewing Dryden's *Oedipus*, she has seen "the Gown open'd wide, and the Man shown in his Drawers and Wastecoat."[34] In her novelistic recrafting of heroic drama, Behn uses the building blocks of formal realism to strip the emperor of tragedy of his fine clothes and show the public that the good of the nation depends on more than the tragic plight of its heroes.

Not Quite Virtuous Protagonists

A few months after the appearance of *Oroonoko*, Behn returned to a mode of tragic novella more typical of her prose fiction, in which the heroine is more central than the hero. Her *The History of the Nun: or, The Fair Vow-Breaker* begins with a pious and beloved daughter, who willingly takes convent vows at age thirteen. At that young age she is "resolv'd and inflexible to all contrary persuasions" (3:216) in her desire to take holy orders. Early in the tale Behn introduces a first-per-son narrator who cautiously observes that she wishes for the prevention of abundance of Mischiefs and Miseries, that Nunneries and Marriages were not to be enter'd into, 'till the Maid, so destin'd, were of a mature Age to make her own Choices; and that Parents would not make use of their justly assum'd Authority to compel their Children, neither to the one or the other. (3: 213)

Behn makes clear that the heroine was not coerced against her will into taking vows; however, she describes how Isabella was subtly influenced from a very young age to prefer the convent life. As we see from the heroine's subsequent passion for Henault, the brother of another nun, Isabella at thirteen was not fully mature enough to know her own desires. Here, as in *The Dumb Virgin*, Behn's focus on the complex situations and decisions facing adolescent girls helps to render her heroines subtly realistic in comparison with standard depictions of virtuous Tory innocence. The above passage also disputes the central analogy of divine-right political theory: if father does not always know best in deciding his children's fate, should the patriarchal household be the analogy or model for the Tory state?

After trying in vain to suppress her passion, Isabella breaks her convent vow and elopes with Henault. If loyalty to the church here represents loyalty to the Stuart monarchy,[35] then Behn makes a strong case for this loyalty by having the newly married Henault and Isabella face a host of difficulties. Henault's father cuts Henault out from his inheritance, settling the estate on his younger son; when Henault tries to live by farming, "he found nothing of his Industry thrive, his Cattel still dy'd in the midst of those that were in full Vigour and Health of other Peoples; his Crops of Wheat and Barly, and other Grain, tho' manag'd by able and knowing Husbandmen, were all, either Mildew'd, or Blasted, or some Misfortune still arriv'd to him" (3:239–240). It seems that Isabella's initial act of disloyalty to the church has instigated a blast of retribution from an angry heaven. By analogy Behn seems to be suggesting that, in 1688, disloyalty against James II could result in a similar act of divine retribution against the people of England. However, the story does not end with Henault's failure as a farmer. Isabella achieves a partial reconciliation with the abbess of the convent, and receives some financial maintenance in recognition from the large dowry she had brought to the institution. Meanwhile, Henault goes into the army in order to win back his father's respect; only when he is left for dead by his commander, a previous suitor of the young Isabella, do the problems begin. Isabella waits an appropriate period of mourning and eventually marries Villenoys, who respectfully renews his suit after waiting a decent interval; they are happy together for five years. When Henault, who had in fact not died but been taken prisoner, finally returns home, Isabella smothers him in a moment of panic; then, in a fit of shame, she sews the sack with the dead man on to the back of Villenoys's coat, so the latter drowns when trying to dispose of the body.

We might conclude from this bizarre sequence of events that, as Janet Todd puts it, "inclinations change."[36] Certainly this is one of Behn's points in portraying a heroine whose inclinations evolve naturally as she matures from naïve convent girl, to impoverished wife, to brave widow, to pious wife of her second husband, and finally to murderer of both first and second husbands. More significantly, in describing the tragic evolution of her heroine, Behn does not make Isabella into a cliché of feminine monstrosity. Isabella is not Lady Macbeth, urging her husband into treacherous deeds; nor is she the lustful, ambitious Pope Joan from Settle's Exclusionist anti-Catholic tragedy *The Female Prelate* (1680). Behn's heroine is neither a monster nor a wronged innocent who commits suicide, Lucretia-like, as testimony to her virtue. By contrast, in Thomas Southerne's subsequent adaptation of the novel, staged as *The Fatal Marriage: or, The Innocent Adultery* (1694), Isabella is so anguished at the reappearance of her first husband that she goes completely mad and, rather than injuring either husband, stabs herself, thus maintaining the tradition of tragic heroines who posthumously restore their lapsed virtue through repentant suicide.

While Southerne's Isabella utters a mad Ophelia-like soliloquy as she perceives the horror of her unintended bigamy, Behn's less conventional heroine is mercilessly rational as she calculates not so much the horror of her deed, but the "Infamy, that, she saw, must inevitably fall upon her," no matter how innocent she believed she was in remarrying. Thus she "resolv'd upon the Murder of Henault, as the only means of removing all Obstacles to her future Happiness" (3:251). Southerne rescripts Behn's Isabella into a conventionally virtuous heroine, who is persuaded into a second marriage only out of desperate financial need and expresses genuine love for her first husband upon his reappearance. However, Behn offers a much more ambiguous commentary on first love; her narrator observes upon Henault's return: "One may a while suffer the Flame to languish, but there may be a reviving Spark in the Ashes, rak'd up, that may burn anew; but when 'tis quite extinguish'd, it never returns or rekindles" (3:249).[37] Not yet the dryly ironic narrator of Austen's fictions, offering sardonic insights about the true nature of love, money, and constancy, Behn's narrator nevertheless offers a foretaste of such a voice in her critique of the myth of first love. Describing Isabella's situation, this narrator explains, "had she believ'd, *Henault* had been living, she had lov'd to the last moment of their Lives; but, alas! the Dead are soon forgotten, and she now lov'd only *Villenoys*" (3:249).

Despite the narrator's glib acknowledgement of how soon the dead are forgotten, Behn's heroine, having murdered the sleeping Henault, nevertheless "fell into a Swound with the Horror of the Deed . . . and, she finds, he conquers anew, being Dead, who could not gain her Pity, while Living" (3:252). In response to her panic, readers are likely to feel pity for this panicked heroine, even as they are horrified at what she has done. Rather than playing the role of tragic heroine, she seems to have taken on the role of tragic hero. Like Oedipus, Isabella has transgressed fundamental social codes, but has done so unwittingly. In committing a murder herself that she, following the example of Lady Macbeth, might have persuaded her second husband to carry out, Isabella is further masculinized. Again like Oedipus, Isabella suffers in the knowledge of her mistakes, yet rather than blind herself as if hoping to black out the horror of her deeds, Isabella kills her second husband so as to avoid his reproaching her. Although Isabella told Villenoys that Henault died naturally in his sleep from the shock of learning she had remarried, she realizes that in his heart he could not believe this lie: "Villenoys would be eternal reproaching her, if not with his Tongue, at least with his Heart" (3:253), and so she stitches Villenoys' cloak to the sack of the dead Henault, as the former prepares to carry the latter's corpse to the river.

The guilty heroine atones for her crime by facing the scaffold "Chearful as a Bride" then making "a Speech of half an Hour long, so Eloquent, so admirable a Warning to the *Vow-Breakers*, that it was as amazing to hear her, as it was to behold her" (3:257). In concluding with this speech against vow-breaking (resonant for those contemplating oaths of loyalty to a new sovereign), Behn offers a loyal Tory conclusion to this tragic pro-Stuart novella, which was licensed shortly before William of Orange's invasion (an invasion predicted by many followers of court politics).[38]

Behn follows the conventions of classical and neo-classical stage tragedy in having a heroine who sinned die to demonstrate her repentance of her vow-breaking; however, Behn never fully demonizes her vow-breaker. Rather, Behn helps the reader sympathize with her protagonist by allowing readers access into the latter's inner thoughts. Behn provides, for example, an extended description of Isabella's emotional turmoil at the moment of her first husband's sudden reappearance in a passage that concludes in language approaching free indirect discourse:

> [S]he was not able to lift her Eyes up, to consider the Face of him, whose Voice she knew so perfectly well. In one moment, she run over a thousand Thoughts. She finds, by his Return, she is not only expos'd to all the Shame imaginable; to all the Upbraiding, on his part, when he shall know she is marry'd to another; but all the Fury and Rage of *Villenoys*, and all the Scorn of the Town, who will look on her as an Adulteress: She sees *Henault* poor, and knew, she must fall from all the Glory and Tranquilllity . . . she dyes, to think that he [*Henault*] should know she had been so lightly in Love with him, to marry again; and she dyes, to think that *Villenoys* must see her again in the Arms of *Henault* . . .(3:249)

Although the novel ends with a speech against vow-breaking, the narrator herself suggests that Isabella's predicament was not simple. In comparing Isabella's decision to send Villenoys to his death to her decision to kill Henault, the narrator describes the second action as having: "in my Opinion, far less Excuse" than the first (3:253), suggesting that perhaps the first murder was in some sense excusable, given Isabella's predicament. Ultimately, Behn allows Isabella to repent and to die "generally Lamented" (3:258).

The narrator seems to situate this second murder within the classical idea of fate compelling a certain horrifying but inevitable sequence of events: "when Fate begins to afflict, she goes through-stitch with her Black Work" (3:253). On the other hand, by offering her own measured comparison of the relative horror of the two deeds, Behn's narrator suggests a moral economy in which crimes must be weighed against each other, through an appreciation of their relative contexts. Isabella may have been wrong to have broken her original vow to the church and eloped with Henault; on the other hand, the abbess forgave her, and Henault's father would have eventually forgiven him. Isabella was not personally to blame for having married Villenoys, since, like the tragic hero Oedipus, she transgressed a cultural taboo unknowingly. In other words, rather than creating an ambitious anti-heroine, such as Lady Macbeth (whose role in urging the murder of the Scottish Banquo might have had particular resonance as the fate of another Stuart King hung in the balance in 1688), Behn borrows traits from classical male heroes to create a more realistically ambiguous novelistic heroine, who is neither an ambitious lustful Whig caricature (in a Tory reversal of anti-Stuart misogyny) nor a conventionally subordinate wife from Filmerian political theory.

Isabella's breach of her convent vows might represent, if we understand the church here standing for the monarchy rather than disloyalty to James II, the first instance of disloyalty to the Stuart line: the execution of Charles I in 1649. From a Tory viewpoint, this original act of disloyalty provides the logic for a second act of disloyalty—in an overthrow of James II, that might well result in his death or the death of his infant son. By asking for pardons from aunt and father respectively, Isabella and Henault might represent the many political officeholders under the Protectorate who deftly negotiated for Charles II's pardon when they saw Richard Cromwell's hold on power fading. In allowing Isabella and Henault to gradually return to favor, Behn seems to acknowledge the political necessity of changing loyalty, even though her heroine ends the novel with a final speech against vow-breaking as she approaches the scaffold.

Although Behn's novel was published before history showed that James and his son would be allowed to escape alive, Isabella's murder of her two husbands represents at some level the bloody possibilities that might result from William's anticipated invasion of England. At the same time, even this act of murder does not render the heroine wholly repugnant to readers. Isabella's confession of her guilt, her final discourse against vow-breaking, and the "Majestick and Charming" mien with which she faces her execution, demonstrating "no Languishment or Fear" (3:257), helps create a heroine for whom, despite her sins, readers would probably feel some sympathy.[39] To the extent that she becomes sympathetic despite her crimes, Isabella refutes the partisan caricatures of both anti-Whig political propaganda and pro-Stuart dramatic tragedy and becomes an increasingly developed novelistic character. The sympathy that she inspires, more-over, pushes the novel beyond the realm of simple Tory propaganda against vow-breaking. Behn complicates both the clichés of political propaganda and the domestic analogies of Tory political theory in her refusal to subordinate her heroine to the traditional moral and domestic strictures. As in Archibald Arbuthnot's *Memoirs . . . of Miss Jenny Cameron*, discussed in the previous chapter, the techniques associated with complex and realistic narratives are here again connected not to an apolitical humanism but to a nuanced partisan position that complicates rigid political categories.

TRAGEDY, COMEDY, AND THE NOVEL

Although many eighteenth- and nineteenth-century novels resolve like comic drama, in happily-ever-after marriages, or tragically, in pathos and death, the conventions of novelistic realism as developed in subsequent periods frequently demonstrate a reality neither wholly comic nor wholly tragic. In reworking the conventions of Restoration drama, Behn creates certain liminal works of prose fiction that explore the boundary between comedy and tragedy in a way that prefigures the ambiguities of later fiction, rather than looking backward to the conventions of dramatic tragicomedy.[40] Behn's *The Fair Jilt: or, The History of Prince Tarquin and Miranda* (1688) makes many allusions to heroic tragedy, but it does not end tragically; of course, neither does it have the harmonizing conclusion of a romantic comedy. If we follow classical and Restoration conventions in assuming that both comedy and tragedy are properly intended to encourage virtue and denigrate vice, *The Fair Jilt* fails as comedy because the characters who survive are not models of virtue. On the other hand, it is not straightforward tragedy: Janet Todd refers to its "joltingly strange morality," in which the brutal and manipulative Prince Tarquin and his wife never quite get their "comeuppance."[41] It may be seen as a liminal work, neither comic nor tragic, whose nascent realism stems in part from its revocation of the dramatic conventions of both comedy and tragedy.[42] Refusing the pathos of heroic tragic drama and the resolution of romantic comedy, Behn instead offers a seemingly objective narration that neither encourages readers to admire nor to wholly demonize her ambitious and manipulative protagonist. In so doing, she also conveys, as in *The History of the Nun*, a Toryism more nuanced than rigid.

Miranda, the wealthy heroine of *The Fair Jilt*, orphaned as a girl and passing her adolescence in a convent, enjoys making conquests, as would a stereotypical male rake, without herself falling in love or agreeing to be married. Christopher Flint sees Miranda as helping to "define the social contract, even as presented in the more liberal articulations of Lockean doctrine."[43] However, this novella, which appeared before Locke's *Two Treatises* had been published, seems to have less to do with Lockean versions of selfhood and subjectivity than with refuting simple Whig (Exclusionist) caricatures of aggressive pro-Stuart women. Because of her nonchalant attitude towards the men she jilts and her sexually aggressive tendencies, Miranda provides a certain echo of Pope Joan, the lustful, ambitious, masculinized heroine of Settle's misogynist anti-Stuart dramatic tragedy *The Female Prelate* (1680). By contrast to the unselfconscious ambition displayed by Pope Joan, however, Miranda moves beyond mere partisan caricature in that she demonstrates at least some awareness of her own nature:

> She knew the strength of her own Heart, and that it cou'd not suffer it
> self to be confin'd to one Man, and wisely avoided those Inquietudes,
> and that Uneasiness of Life she was sure to find in that married Life,

which wou'd against her Nature, oblige her to the Embraces of one, whose Humour was, to love all the Young and the Gay. (3:12)

This passage, in which the narrator takes us inside the mind of a confident and egotistical hypocrite, anticipates passages in Jane Austen's *Emma*, in which Austen fully acknowledges Emma's failings, but manages to make the reader admire her anyway. This way of depicting Miranda also sets up the potential for the traditional comic plot of independent woman humbled, as in Shakespeare's *Taming of the Shrew*. As if following Shakespeare's or anticipating Austen's heroine, Miranda falls passionately in love almost as soon as she has articulated her disinclination for marriage; however, her first passion is for a priest who respects his vows too much to threaten her autonomy.

After being rejected by the priest, Miranda takes revenge by falsely accusing him of attempted rape; she then immediately falls in love with Prince Tarquin, who is celebrated and admired enough to break any number of women's hearts. Significantly, however, rather than humbling this proud, dangerous woman, Tarquin ends up being so devoted to Miranda that he continues to adore her even after her greed and ambition cause him to risk his fortune, his honor, and his very life. Once married to the prince, Miranda shows the extent of her avarice by convincing first her page and then her husband to attempt to murder her sister so that she can retain full possession of the legacy from their uncle, which was to be shared between the two sisters upon the younger's coming of age. Tarquin, whose love for Miranda never lessens even during his imprisonment for this attempted crime, is, like the page, sent to the scaffold for his attempt. He escapes death only because his neck is not fully severed; severely wounded but not dead, he is taken to a Jesuit refuge and ultimately released and pardoned upon a promise never again to see his wife (a promise he finally evades by returning to Flanders and reuniting with Miranda there). Through all these plot twists, we fully expect Miranda's ultimate downfall when she finally apprehends the horror of her own actions and, like Lady Macbeth, becomes overwhelmed by her own guilt. However, in an unexpected inversion of a more conventional tragic plot, Miranda, whom the general population has come to hate, is finally pardoned by her sister, released from prison, and welcomed by her husband and his family in Flanders.

Despite the protagonist's cunningly evil propensities, the narrator does not wholly demonize her or reduce her to caricature. Miranda is not Settle's Pope Joan, a Whig representation of overly ambitious authoritarian (Stuart, hence Catholic) governance. Nor is Miranda simply an anti-Whig inversion of Settle's anti-Stuart creation. She does not come to be hated and condemned by those around her or by those closest to her. Prince Tarquin, most notably, never stops loving her. As soon as Tarquin "was permitted to speak," after recovering from his wounds, "the first News he ask'd was after the Princess [Miranda]" (3:46). We are given fewer narrative glimpses into Tarquin's apparently noble and loyal thoughts than into Miranda's cunning and manipulative ones. However, despite its unlikely continuance, readers, along with Tarquin's associates, may accept Tarquin's love for Miranda as real, in part because he simply never deviates from it and in part because it defies even his own reason. We are told that Tarquin's "Friends were very much afflicted to find, that all his Loss of Blood had not quench'd that Flame, nor let out that which made him still love that bad Woman" (3:46). Tarquin's companions in fact do everything they can to malign his wife and to extol his own virtues. Nevertheless, the narrator informs us simply that "in his Heart he resolv'd never to abandon her; nor was he able to live, and think of doing it: However, his Reason assur'd him, he cou'd not do a Deed more justifiable, and one that wou'd re-gain his Fame sooner" (3:46). This depiction of "love beyond reason" is certainly resonant with standard myths of love, and so in that sense would have been plausible to readers. The matter-of-fact tone with which this stubborn devotion is narrated also serves to humanize both its bearer and its recipient.

The narrator simply informs the readers that Tarquin's companions and family accept and acknowledge his loyalty to Miranda; Behn also informs us that Miranda's sister is so impressed by "this great Man" (3:47) that she pardons him for the crime of attempting to murder her. Just as Tarquin's friends and relations come to take as real his devotion to his wife, so might readers here begin to accept the unconventional possibility of an ending in which Miranda is not obliged to die to prove her virtue, like Isabella in *The Fair Vow-Breaker*, but can be "penitent for her Life past" and reach "as perfect a State of Happiness as this troublesome World can afford" (3:48). Behn insists in her dedication that the narrative is "Truth," and at least some of the story's less plausible aspects were drawn from the life of Prince Francisco de Tarquini, who attempted to murder his sister-in-law and yet escaped death, pardoned after the executioner's stroke failed to kill him.[44] Although readers may never fully forgive Miranda's bloody schemes or understand Tarquin's remarkable loyalty, the matter-of-fact narrative nevertheless comes to feel like a journalistic account of a true, if implausible, sequence of events. In continuing to assert the "facts" of a narrative that refutes the reader's expectations of tragedy, Behn uses the form of the novel to blur the formal and ideological differences between dramatic tragedy and comedy. In so doing, she refutes the anti-Stuart clichés of powerful, sexually forward women without re-imposing traditional pro-Stuart patriarchalism.

When Miranda first demonstrates the "masculine" characteristics of proud rake and even attempts to lure the priest into ravishing her, readers would expect, following conventional plots, that these "unnatural" tendencies will be comically corrected when she is finally "conquered by" a man—or at least that she will die tragically. However, as is the case in her novelistic tragedies, Behn here again refuses to make her political point through a reactionary paradigm for household hierarchy. Instead, Behn raises the specter of political upheaval by having the young Miranda, before she has even met the prince, somewhat perversely resolve "to be the *Lucretia*, that this young *Tarquin* shoul'd ravish" (3:28). Ignoring the true history of the rape that resulted in the overthrow of the Tarquin monarchy and the foundation of the Roman republic, Miranda dreams only of the ambition of marrying "A young King of *Rome*" (3:28). As Janet Todd suggests in her biography of Behn, Behn "may have indulged in a little fantasy of how a woman might do what she pleased if she could only handle men."[45] There may also, however, be a partisan political message in Miranda's comment.

As a pro-Stuart Tory, Behn pointedly revises the tale of Lucretia: her Tarquin has no intention of raping Miranda, only of marrying her honorably and returning with her to his native Holland. As Todd observes, Behn's fictional Prince Tarquin is a somewhat more appealing character than the real-life Tarquini, who "seems to have been the harshest and most violent of the trio" of family members (112). Thus, in Behn's fictional adaptation of the stories of both the real-life Tarquini and the tragedy of Lucretia, the occasion for overthrowing a monarchy never arises because Behn's Prince Tarquin—at this juncture, a figure for James II—becomes a figure for her new vision of masculine Tory selfhood. Behn's Tarquin is not morally perfect, as Behn acknowledges in the preface: his devotion to Miranda provokes him to engage in criminal acts. He offers a new model of Tory heroism, one that allows a hero to give a sinning woman a second chance; his devotion may not seem plausible to all readers, but Behn's insistence on the truth of her narrative and on the appeal of her hero helps to naturalize this version of heroism and to challenge classical models of masculinity as well as rigidly patriarchal divine-right representations of the household.

In rescripting the story of Lucretia, Behn is not just working against a timeless version of a classical myth and divine-right political theory but is also specifically refuting depictions of Lucretia from contemporary Whig (or Exclusionist) propaganda. *Female Excellency, or the Ladies Glory*, published in the same year as *The Fair Jilt*, show-cases heroines of antiquity and the Old Testament who demonstrate the courage to challenge political tyrants. The chapter about Lucretia in *Female Excellency* includes a specific diatribe against tyranny that leaves no doubts as to the author's view of the House of Stuart. Carefully casting his political propaganda in the mouth of the classical hero Brutus, the author—probably the printer Nathaniel Crouch[46]—observes when denouncing Tarquin that "A Tyrant is a Monster who is by nature intended only for a scourge to men and therefore none can be safe under him, he equally fears and hates both good and wicked men, and despiseth lukewarmness and indifference."[47] Further insisting on the need to depose a whole royal line (rather than, for example, deposing James II but allowing his sons to return to the throne), the author continues: "What is it you expect? perhaps the old kings death; Who can imagine the Sons will be better than the Father; Their tempers are composed of the bloud of two wicked ones; and therefore like to be altogether as insupportable as their parents" (80). No doubt alluding to the Catholicism of both James II and his wife, Crouch reintroduces both parents as potential tyrants, recon-figuring the positive Whig image of joint dominion, such as that described in Tyrrell's *Patriarcha Non Monarcha*, into a darker, more ominous family portrait. Crouch, a printer of nonconformist religious books whose progressive social views are suggested by his having once having bound a female as an apprentice,[48] warns readers of the importance of distinguishing the true abstract principle of liberty from the false "inchantment" of "the name of Liberty, which carries an universal influence with it though very few truly understand what it is" (80).

One of the reasons why Behn may have drawn Miranda as such an odd mixture of lust, deceit, and narcissism is that she was working against the image of the virtuous, coup-inciting Lucretia. Rather than risk Miranda becoming a virtuous martyr against tyranny, Behn scripts her as politically naïve and morally immature, heedlessly wishing to be "ravished." Although this unflattering portrait of a lascivious woman might initially seem consistent with the anti-Stuart stereotypes of ambitious women, such as Settle's demonic Pope Joan, who meets a tragic end befitting the awfulness of her character, Behn once again ruptures the conventions of dramatic tragedy, allowing her heroine to break the conventional binary choice for women between immoral tyranny or chaste resistance.

The classical tragedy of the rape of Lucretia, which resulted in the overthrow of the Tarquin monarchy, becomes domestic romance characterized by political calm: the pardoned couple live out their days in private tranquillity, "retir'd to a Country-House" (3:28), their financial needs subsidized by Tarquin's forgiving father and Tarquin's own subsequent success in the French army. Miranda's original fears of losing her autonomy in marriage are put behind her; the "Joy unspeakable" with which Tarquin welcomes her home is matched by her gratitude to "Heaven . . . for having given her these Afflictions, that have relcaim'd her" (3:48). This symmetrical domestic bliss might seem to resemble the metaphorical joint sovereignty articulated by social-contract theorists, but it is in fact pro-Stuart: partly financed by the French, it is achieved without overthrowing a royal line. Behn further indicates her novel's political resonance by dedicating it Henry Pain, a known Stuart sympathizer, whose unswerving loyalty to James II she likens to the loyalty of her hero, although she distinguishes between them in moral terms. Just as her Tarquin remains relentlessly faithful to fickle and selfish Miranda, so does she suggest that she knows of no "more faithful Subject" than Pain, whose "Imprisonment and Sufferings, through all the Course of our late National Distractions, have sufficiently manifested" (3:5), demonstrate his loyalty to the beleaguered James II.

In crafting a heroine who is not killed or obliged to commit suicide, despite her transgressions against the rules of virtuous female behavior, Behn refigures standard distinctions in Restoration tragedy between comedy and tragedy. Miranda should, by the rules of tragedy, commit suicide in recognition of the horrors of what she has done, or else, by the rules of comedy, be swiftly shamed or punished so that true virtue might be rewarded, but Behn instead crafts a version of novelistic realism through the possibility of repentance that refutes the conventional closure of either dramatic comedy or tragedy. In other words, by recrafting the classical political tragedy of the Tarquin monarchy into a "true history" of loyalty and forgiveness, Behn creates a novel whose matter-of-fact refutation of literary and political conventions defines her own version of pro-Stuart political "reality" against the conventions of both misogynistic Whig political propaganda and patriarchal Tory political theory.[49]

Behn's text also seems to promote a calm, moderate acceptance of the reality at hand that hearkens towards Richardson's subsequent novelistic humanizing of political moderation. Tarquin and Miranda's unexpectedly happy ending probably figures, for the pro-Stuart Behn, a promise to England that, however disloyal, malicious, or bloody the country's intentions to the Stuart dynasty, the Stuart monarchs will remain ineffably loyal. On the other hand, the matter-of-fact narrating of a story that defies the expectations of both characters and readers might offer yet another political message in 1688 (when James II's political future was so uncertain): accept what comes, however unexpected, for it will be the reality we will inhabit together. As in the other novellas written during the last few years of her life, *The Fair Jilt* naturalizes a pro-Stuart political reality more flexible than rigidly partisan.

By refuting the conventions of Tory Restoration drama, including its fundamental distinction between comedy and tragedy, Behn articulates a Tory version of novelistic realism that reworks depictions of virtue and villainy, both male and female. In so doing, she also challenges the caricatures of contemporaneous partisan propaganda, both Whig and Tory, and insists on the centrality of an accurate depiction of the domestic household to political debates, rather than the idealized versions deployed as analogies in high political theory. Like the subsequent versions of Whig, anti-Jacobite, and Jacobite realisms that are discussed in the following chapters, Behn's late seventeenth-century Tory realism sought to naturalize a version of political reality that previous genres—either literary or political—had not yet articulated.

CHAPTER 3

Daniel Defoe and the Whig
Ideal of Selfhood

Considered mainly a political writer or a partisan "scribbler" in his own time, Daniel Defoe (1660–1731) was not included in histories of the novel until the early nineteenth century and not considered a significant contributor to the novel's evolution until the middle of the twentieth.[1] Since Watt's *Rise of the Novel*, scholars have usually acknowledged Defoe's contributions to "formal realism," but remain uncertain as to whether the "realistic" formulae of his narratives are what make them truly "great."[2] As Homer Obed Brown observes, over the past two centuries scholars have rarely agreed on exactly what formal innovation Defoe contributed to the novel: there is little consensus as to whether or not his characters are drawn with emotional depth or whether the "plotlessness" of his novels makes his texts more or less "novelistic."[3] Interestingly, the problem of defining Defoe's precise contribution to the formal evolution of the novel mirrors the difficulties critics have had in pinning down his political position.

Since Defoe's best-known political writings demonstrate Lockean or "Whig" political principles, scholars have traditionally had difficulty explaining his decision to work for the moderate Whig-turned-Tory M. P. Robert Harley for reasons other than financial necessity and gratitude for helping him get out of jail.[4] Thus Defoe becomes a pragmatic chameleon, a master of disguises; his precise political position is as difficult to pin down as the structural qualities that make us describe his works of prose fiction as "novels." Defoe, of course, would have been influenced throughout his life by financial concerns, but he was a thoughtful and complex writer, whose political and novelistic writings all indicate a serious engagement with the political ideas, discourses, and analogies of his day. I propose that we can shed light both on his political position and his contribution to the novel's formal structure by examining these two conundrums simultaneously.

Perhaps because Defoe scholarship did not begin in earnest until the twentieth century, when the nuances of early eighteenth-century political debates had been smoothed over by dominant Whig versions of history, it has been commonplace to reduce Defoe's political thought to simplified Lockean contractarianism and reflexive anti-Jacobitism, with occasional pragmatic lapses into Toryism. In an incisive correction to the standard version of Defoe's political beliefs, Manuel Schonhorn has painstakingly delineated the points of Lockean political theory with which Defoe disagrees. Acknowledging Defoe's hatred of tyranny, Schonhorn nevertheless disputes the notion that Defoe was either distrustful of sovereignty as an institution or at all in favor of republicanism.[5] By tracing in Defoe's political verse epic *Jure Divino* (1706), a subtle but pointed parody of Clarendon's *History of the Rebellion* (1704), D. N. Deluna likewise sets the stage for viewing Defoe not as a mere scribbler or paid propagandist but as a highly conscious stylist, perfectly capable of mocking Clarendon's neo-classical prose style even as he refutes Clarendon's Tory version of seventeenth-century political history.[6] Recognizing Defoe's skill in manipulating genre, style, and tone helps us to understand that just as he deployed the form of blank-verse epic as part of his political critique, so might he have deployed the other genres he attempts—political pamphlets and periodicals, conduct books, and prose fiction—in a similarly self-conscious fashion.

Once we recognize that Defoe was neither an unconscious mouth-piece of some abstract ideal of Whig individualism nor an unconscious artist who inadvertently developed the formal category of narrative realism,[7] we may see that Defoe's contribution to the formal structure of the novel derived from his exploration of the contradictions inherent in the Whig ideal of political individualism. Ian Watt locates Defoe's "individualist" ideology both in the real-life detail of his individualized characters and in their position as supposedly universal representatives of the human predicament.[8] Maximillian Novak extends this theory a step further by claiming that Defoe's greatness lies in his development of the individual of "mythic significance."[9] And yet, Defoe's characters are particular individuals within a particular social and political context, juxtaposed against other individuals occupying different positions within the same context. While Watt and others have been reluctant to ascribe the moral inconsistencies of Defoe's heroine narrators to a conscious attempt at irony, Defoe's political writings and conduct books suggest a keen awareness of the way in which characters demonstrate moral and political hypocrisy. Therefore, in addition to locating incipient formal realism in the first-person narration that brings us "close to the consciousness"[10] of his characters or in the empiricist detail that Doody would describe as Whig "Prescriptive Realism,"[11] we may also identify it in the ironic critique of Whig political hypocrisy that Defoe's novels offer when read in dialogue with the partisan political writings of his day, including his own.

Christopher Flint suggests that "Defoe reimagines domestic relations in such a way as to transform them into novel forms of power without endangering the self-sufficient masculinity of conventional models of government (even those problematically related to the Stuart monarchy's legacy)."[12] I would argue that without entirely rejecting conventional forms of patriarchal government, Defoe is nevertheless concerned with thoroughly examining and exploring the Whig model of the social contract. Like the Tory Aphra Behn, who narrates the "reality" of her protagonists in contrast to standard partisan depictions of Tory heroes and heroines, the Whig Defoe asserts "realistic" characterization through his depiction of the difficulties different individuals face in their attempts to live out the ideal of the Whig social contract and develop beyond mere partisan stereotypes of the Whig individual. As this chapter demonstrates, Defoe develops certain techniques now recognized as important to formal realism through his increasingly subtle engagement with the contradictions and complexities of Whig social-contract theory, a theory he apparently believed was solid enough to withstand the rigorous critique to which he subjected it. In the sections that follow, I first establish the narrative techniques Defoe uses in his political writings and conduct books and then show how he achieves a more complex political critique of Whig ideology through a further development of these techniques in his prose fiction.

POLITICAL APHORISMS AND PARTISAN CARICATURE

Born in the first year of the Restoration and educated at a Dissenting academy during a period of High-Church supremacy, Defoe lived out his early manhood during the tumult of the Exclusion crises and the removal of the Stuart monarchy. Defoe was so familiar with the writings of John Locke that Richard Ashcraft and M. M. Goldsmith suggest that he may have been the author of the three anonymous distillations of Locke's *Two Treatises of Government*, specifically *Political Aphorisms* (1690), *Vox Populi, Vox Dei* (1709), and *The Judgement of Whole Kingdoms and Nations* (1710),[13] the latter of which became one of the most popular pamphlets of the eighteenth century and helped to shape the way that Lockean political theory became known to the British populace. Furbank and Owens do not acknowledge this attribution, and Manuel Schonhorn has complicated the direct link that Ashcraft asserts between Defoe and Locke.[14] Furbank and Owens's de-attribution is supported by the fact that the Whig analogy of the domestic household, in which women and children have a right to resist a tyrant father, is not prominent in *The Judgement of Whole Kingdoms*, whereas in the political writings definitely ascribed to him, Defoe does not avoid the analogy of the domestic household in making his political point. In fact, his most successful or popular political pamphlets rely on developing characters in relation to other characters, if not always within a household, at least in emotional bonds similar to those found in a family. This type of character development, in which the contingent details of human relationships challenge and correct the abstracted ideal of the Whig individual, also anticipates Defoe's development of "realistic" character in his prose fiction.

Defoe's *The True-Born Englishman* (1700), a verse satire written in response to John Tutchin's *The Foreigners*, reiterates citizens' fundamental rights to resist a tyrant monarch even as it establishes the inherent "foreignness" of all Englishmen:

> When Kings the Sword of Justice first lay down,
> There are no Kings, though they possess the Crown.
> Titles are Shadows, Crowns are empty things,
> The Good of Subjects is the End of Kings;
> To guide in War, and to protect in Peace:
> Where Tyrants once commence the Kings do cease:
> For Arbitrary Power's so strange a thing
> It makes the *Tyrant*, and unmakes the King.[15]

In these lines, which were catchy enough to be memorized and chanted about town by subjects loyal to William III, Defoe limits his analysis of political principles to an idea that may be conveyed within a single rhymed couplet—that by practicing tyranny a monarch repudiates his right to govern. Without getting bogged down in theoretical details such as a precise definition of tyranny, Defoe casts William of Orange as an unambiguous hero. William may not have been born an Englishman, but Defoe reminds his readers that all English people are descended from immigrants from other continents. Here, Defoe defines the essence of Englishness as varied or heterogeneous: "Thus from a Mixture of all Kinds began, / That Het'rogeneous *Thing*, An Englishman" (13:42).

In this immensely popular verse pamphlet, which would see more than fifty editions by the mid-eighteenth century, Defoe takes a complex idea about the nature of Englishness and identity and particularizes it through his characterization of the tract's hero, William III. Although this tract was in part a response to the Jacobite threat to Protestant succession that was perceived after the death of heir apparent Anne's only surviving child in July 1700,[16] Defoe does not rely on the standard misogynist clichés of anti-Stuart rhetoric, which describe, for example, the "Whoredomes of your mother Jezebel, and her Witchcrafts."[17] Nor does he turn to a purified image of a "True and Loving" Whig wife, as did many anti-Jacobite propagandists of the period.[18] Rather, Defoe locates heterogeneous Englishness itself as the progeny of a violated woman. Envisioning a pre-history of Europe in which the "Torrid Zone of *Italy*" (13:34) was governed by "Lust" and France by "Ungovern'd Passion" (13:35), Defoe at times reiterates standard anti-Jacobite slander of England's Catholic rivals even as he casts "yet unpeopled" England as a prey to "ev'ry Barbarous Nation . . . Who Conquer her as oft as they Invade her" (13:36). England is an innocent romance heroine, raped by all and sundry other nations: "*So Beauty guarded but by Innocence, / That ruins her which should be her Defence*" (13:36). Innocence violated produces "Barb'rous Off-spring left behind" who "Blended with *Britains* who before were here." Thus "From this Amphibious Ill-born Mob began / *That vain ill natur'd thing, an* Englishman" (13:37). In offering a new image of Whig virtue in female form, Defoe thus avoids the misogynist, xenophobic partisan rhetoric familiar from anti-Jacobite tracts.

The second half of the poem continues to circumvent standard tropes of anti-Jacobite rhetoric by depicting William as a new type of male hero. By contrast with the rakish cavalier hero of pro-Stuart Restoration drama, Defoe's William is apparently not immediately attractive to women, but Defoe insists that "He needs no Character, but his own Fame, / Nor any flattering Titles, but his Name" (13:62). Creating a modest male Whig hero, so different from the arrogant cavaliers of Restoration comedy, Defoe pleads the cause for his protagonist: "*Listen ye Virgins to the Charming Sound . . . Your early Offerings to this Altar bring; / Make him at once a Lover and a King*" (13:62). Anticipating the virtuous but unappreciated Dutch merchant in his own *Roxana* (1724), Defoe could be said to begin a tradition of male characters whose virtue lies as much in their respectful behavior off the battlefield as their valor thereon. William III, whom Schonhorn describes as Defoe's ideal "warrior-king,"[19] is seen here as needing a propagandist to make him attractive to women. This renders him all the more appealing as an under-appreciated hero.

The success of Defoe's early satirical tracts probably derived from the way in which he reduced complex political thought to pithy aphorism and rendered the characters into heroic individuals, rather than mere partisan stereotypes. By contrast, the commercial failure of *Jure Divino* (1706), the verse epic with which Defoe hoped to improve his financial situation, may well have stemmed from his focus on political theory rather than character development. He begins his analysis of sovereign right with a catchy couplet, in the aphoristic style of his earlier verse tracts: "First Government was Nat'ral all and Free, / And Fix't in Patriarchal Majesty."[20] However, rather than moving from easy aphorism to the appealing character of his hero (here again William III), Defoe instead introduces a rather complex alignment of civil right with property right:

> From thence convey'd by Right to Property
> Where he bestows the Soil, and gives the Law
> The Right of that's the Right of the Command,
> There can be no Pretence of Government,
> Till they that have the Property consent.
>   (2:16–17)

As he moves away from the rhymed couplets to blank verse, and as he moves from ideas that may be expressed in a single couplet to ideas that require six or more lines to explicate, Defoe no doubt loses his appeal to the general reading public, as the poor sales of his epic suggest.

Moreover, while Defoe had rendered William a charmingly modest hero in his shorter pamphlets, in *Jure Divino* William becomes more heroic but less developed as an individual character. Maximillian Novak explains that William is being cast as one of the new heroes in the "Whig myth of history," as one of the monarchs "who respected the laws and rights of their subjects."[21] Established as a mythic force against tyranny, Defoe's William is no longer a character in his own right as potential lover, husband, or father. Justifying his hero to his readers and invoking his muse, Defoe pleads:

> If any ask thee what High Place Remains,
> And what bright Orb thy WILLIAM's Star contains;
> Tell 'em that he who pull'd down Tyrants here,
> Proclaims Eternal Wars against them there.
>   (1:26)

Making William an epic hero on a mythic scale, rather than a more humanized male character engaged in romantic or familial relations, deflects the emphasis away from William's actual domestic situation, a monarch who died a widower with no children. Avoiding the hero's relationship to his domestic household also would have deflected attention away from the domestic situation of Queen Anne, the actual monarch in 1706, who was head of the nation but not head of the family, and who had been pregnant many times but had no surviving children.

As I have already explained, social-contract theorists who revised the domestic analogy from patriarchal to household to joint dominion between husband and wife, in a refutation of patriarchal sovereign right and in defense of Anne's rule, struggled with the awkward specter of real-life women who might actually want more power in the home. Defoe skips over this problem in the passage below, one of the few in the epic in which he even mentions the domestic analogy:

> If family is united by consent,
> There we come back to Laws of Government;
> Compact and mutual Treatises of Accord,
> Between a willing People and their Lord.
>   (2:3)

The family "united by consent" here stems from an almost automatic "Compact" between "a willing People and their Lord," but Defoe does not allude here to the difficulties he explores in his conduct books and his prose fiction, that is, what happens when the wives or children are less than obedient to "their Lord." In *Jure Divino*, Defoe may have created, as Novak suggests, a new mythic hero for the Whig cause. However, unlike his earlier tracts and his later prose fiction, *Jure Divino* makes its hero a static caricature of Whig patriotism rather than a more developed character. By contrast, the characters developed in his conduct books and novels would increasingly be represented as particular individuals living particular lives, rather than as reified images of the Whig individual familiar from both formal political treatises and the static tropes of partisan slander.

VIRTUOUSLY DISOBEDIENT CHILDREN

In 1715, after almost two decades as a writer of political tracts and periodicals, Defoe began writing conduct books. Had he followed standard models for the genre, he would have found no place for the character development that marked his most successful political writings. However, even in his conduct books Defoe puts the development of believable characters and plausible domestic scenarios above the rules of this traditional genre.

First published during the last year of the Protectorate, Richard Allestree's *The Whole Duty of Man* (1658), a High-Church conduct book that reappeared in almost yearly editions for more than 150 years, had clearly established for eighteenth-century Britain the formal conventions for conduct literature: provide dogmatic rules for the moral behavior of every category of the household member, including children, servants, unmarried daughters, wives, widows, and the household heads themselves. Allestree's rules emphasize the principle of passive obedience and the obligation and respect due to all superiors in a clearly defined household hierarchy that parallels a strict social and religious hierarchy. In brief, wife, children, and servants obey fathers and husbands as the latter obey priests and monarchs and as these latter obey God. At first glance Daniel Defoe seems to follow Allestree's model in his conduct books *The Family Instructor* (1715) and *Religious Courtship* (1722). His conclusions sound remarkably similar to the rules set down by Allestree, with whose High-Church doctrines Defoe would not have agreed: teach your children the catechism; make certain your daughters marry men who share their religious beliefs. However, there is a significant difference in the formal structure of Defoe's and Allestree's moral guidebooks: while Allestree structures his guide as a series of dogmatic maxims or rules, Defoe structures his first two conduct manuals as a series of dialogues in which the contradictions and complexities of individual characters can be developed.

Each of these works is written as a sequence of conversations between family members; in *The Family Instructor* "notes" are provided at the end of each dialogue, summing up the moral lesson already made evident by the exchange itself. In *Religious Courtship*, Defoe does not add notes at the end of each dialogue but has the central characters voice the moral lessons he intends to convey. For example, a pursuing swain, hitherto indifferent to his spiritual state, finally reaches "this General and happy Conclusion . . . That he should never be a complete Gentleman, till he became a religious man."[22] Thus, as with some of his early political tracts, Defoe's moral guidebooks at first glance seem to assert their truths in aphoristic, even dogmatic, terms. The notion that authority figures have all the answers, however, is undermined by a dialogic structure through which the rational morality of his protagonists, often children, becomes evident as they challenge and resist the advice of their parents. The precocious and self-chastising child of the first dialogue in *The Family Instructor* realizes that he has been on Earth six years already and has not yet adequately thanked God or loved him. He questions his father in detail about the nature of God and realizes that, while he has said his prayers every day, he "never thought a word what they meant," but "only said them by rote."[23] The father eventually realizes that he and his wife are guilty of religious hypocrisy, of teaching their children only the outward appearance of religious faith. Defoe here contradicts Allestree's High-Church conduct manual which sanctions no authority but the father's, although the "moral conclusion" still stands.

The tension between the dogmatic authority of Defoe's moralizing narrator and the impertinent resistance of his child heroes becomes more evident as the dialogues treat family situations of increasing complexity. Later dialogues consider what happens, for example, to adolescent children in a family when the parents suddenly perceive the hypocrisy of their daily lives. Defoe acknowledges that it may be more difficult for a parent to persuade a teenager than a young child that the conduct that has hitherto been deemed acceptable—such as going to the theater on Sundays—is suddenly forbidden. In part II of *The Family Instructor*, an adolescent son and daughter object to the newly stringent moral rules that their parents have announced. The son runs away to join the army; the daughter marries a religious man, achieves a superficial reformation of manners, and then finally, after a brush with death, achieves full spiritual reform. The narrator's moral conclusion about these complex clashes between older children and parents is predictably authoritarian and monolithic: "a Contempt of paternal Instruction is nothing else, but laying in a great Stock for Repentance" (294). The stubborn resistance of the teenage children in this later dialogue seems reasonable, however, in light of the young boy's demonstration of parental error in the first dialogue. It is also significant that no resolution is reached within the confines of the immediate family: the full moral conversion of the daughter is achieved not by her dogmatic, newly converted father, but by her more tolerant, more forgiving husband. Although the narrator insists on the primacy of heeding paternal instruction, the behavior of the savvy son-in-law undermines such a general conclusion. Perceiving his own inadequacy in fulfilling his "natural" role as household leader, the father in the dialogue bursts out to his son-in-law: "You are fitter to be the Father than I am!" (391). This concluding line, which ironically inverts a prior, though apparently only provisional, lesson about paternalistic control, demonstrates how Defoe subjects his characters to ironic narrative inversions, thereby challenging political caricatures, both Tory and Whig.

The advice Defoe offers in *The Family Instructor* and *Religious Courtship* may seem limited to relations within the family. However,

Defoe was well aware that any advice suggesting a child's right to disagree with his parents would have political resonance. It is significant, therefore, that Defoe emphasizes his reversal of household hierarchy in the subtitle to part I of *The Family Instructor*: "Being the Family Inverted: or the Child Chastising the Father With the Happy Consequences of it in an Eminent Family in London" (1). Defoe's subtle analysis of family hierarchy and his choice of the formal structure of dialogue underscore his obvious political differences with the High-Church Tory position. Perhaps not surprisingly, given the difficulties that contract theorists had in negotiating the wife's position in the household after their metaphorical elevation of Eve to joint sovereign, Defoe's domestic scenes focus more frequently on the right of children to resist morally deficient parents than on the right of the wife to resist a morally deficient husband.[24] However, Defoe does stage scenes that depict a household governed jointly by mother and father: for example, in the third dialogue of book I, an equally repentant wife and husband vie to take blame for neglecting the Christian upbringing of their children. As the dialogues treat domestic scenarios of increasing complexity and move away from traditional partisan versions of identity, the characters become comparatively more "real." Although Defoe's first novelistic hero is perhaps best known as an individual in isolation, Defoe's contribution to formal realism, as we see in *The Family Instructor*, derives from his ability to develop characters in relation to other characters, both within and outside the family circle. Moreover, it is through this complex series of relations and through his increasing reliance on ironic narrative inversions that Defoe develops his ideal of the Whig individual beyond the static confines of partisan caricature.

Defining the Individual

When Ian Watt situates Defoe's novels within an intellectual history of individualism, he describes the state of political ideas at the end of the seventeenth century by quoting F. W. Maitlin: "for the first time, the Absolute State faced the Absolute Individual."[25] Watt thus set the stage for several decades of scholarship in which Defoe's fiction would be mapped against the complex relation of self to society in eighteenth-century Britain.[26] His presumed relationship to Lockean individualism remained largely unchallenged, however, until Manuel Schonhorn described certain key differences between Locke's and Defoe's positions. Relying on readings of *Jure Divino* and *Robinson Crusoe*, Schonhorn suggests that Defoe's notion of individualism insists on strong monarchical power in a way that might seem inconsistent with his support of Revolution principles. Schonhorn appropriately casts Defoe in the position of many eighteenth-century Britons, who, in the words of W. A. Speck, "albeit illogically, acquiesced in the Revolution but still hankered after some kind of divine sanction for government."[27] However, rather than simply reading the allusions to family and sovereignty in *Robinson Crusoe* in light of contemporary debates about sovereignty and paternity, as does Schonhorn, we must also map Crusoe's image of the family against the analogies of the domestic household in early social-contract theory.[28] As explained in chapter 1, Whig political theory from the 1680s protested against a tyrannical patriarchal household, but this liberating revision of the patriarchal model was in fact deployed with caution by Whig political theorists not necessarily intending to change the actual political situation of women. The complex descriptions of marriages, families, and households in Defoe's novels fully acknowledge how potent the analogy of the domestic household was in contemporaneous political debate.

Christopher Flint interprets the fraught representations of domestic life in *Robinson Crusoe* as "the unsuccessful attempt to incorporate individualism within traditional patterns of social behavior."[29] Once we understand Defoe's subtle critique of Whig individualism, we should also recognize that Defoe uses Crusoe as an intentionally flawed model of Whig behavior in order to warn citizens not to lose sight of the proper functioning of the social contract. Crusoe is the model we both ought and ought not to follow if we truly believe in the ideals of the social contract and want to bring them to fruition. *Crusoe* may well be intended, as Defoe says in the preface to *Moll Flanders*, for "those who know how to read it."[30] Moreover, it may be most appropriate to read it like *Jure Divino*, as a satiric commentary on other well-known texts, including some of Defoe's own political works. Thus, in addition to noticing (as in traditional formalist accounts) Defoe's development of narrative realism through the powerful first-person accounts of his persuasive protagonist-narrators, we should also notice that his novels frequently establish an ironic distance between the limits of a character's particular viewpoint and the larger political view alluded to through the analogy of the domestic household.

The aphorism that sums up so many of Defoe's early political pamphlets, " *Vox Populi est Vox Dei* " incorporates the conundrum that "the people" rarely speak in a single voice. As Defoe clearly demonstrated through the domestic squabbles that illustrate his best-selling *Family Instructor*, the ideal of a people governed by their own consent is attractive as abstract theory, but might never exist in real life. In *The Life and Strange Surprizing Adventures of Robinson Crusoe of York, Mariner* (1719), Defoe first reduces contract theory to its simplest formulation, a community of one person on an island, and then gradually introduces other characters whose circumstances call our attention to the difficulties inherent in the social contract when there is a community of more than one. Schonhorn insists that because the state of nature on Crusoe's island incorporates an essential hierarchy between Crusoe as sovereign master and Friday as servant, Defoe differs from other eighteenth-century social-contract theorists, who conceive of the state of nature as a community of equals.[31] However, Schonhorn's reading of Crusoe assumes what few critics have ever assumed of Defoe's *female* protagonists, that the reader is expected to admire and respect every decision made by the protagonist-narrator. I would argue, rather, that given the imperfections in paternal author-ity that Defoe demonstrates in *The Family Instructor*, he would have expected his readers to treat ironically the political and moral hypocrisy of Crusoe's logic.

When the voice of "the people" is literally one and the same as the voice of the sovereign, social-contract theory achieves its ideal repre-sentation. Robinson Crusoe, both subject and king, embodies not just a parallel between household and state, but an exact identity between the two realms:

> It would have made a Stoick smile to have seen, me and my little Family sit down to Dinner; there was my Majesty the Prince and Lord of the whole Island; I had the Lives of all my Subjects at my absolute Command. I could hang, draw, give Liberty, and take it away, and no Rebels among all my Subjects.[32]

Here, Crusoe apparently recognizes no difference between being head of a household and head of a state: he holds dominion over all of the "Subjects" in his "little Family," none of which at that moment are other human beings. Schonhorn insists that Defoe demonstrates his difference from Filmer by making Crusoe's "Family" not really a family and thus showing his power as merely political not familial (7:160). However, we might argue instead that Defoe is consciously exploring the standard political analogy between family and state. Rather than representing some pre-social innocent state of nature, Crusoe's island seems to embody the fundamental dilemma of the social contract. As Defoe makes clear in *Jure Divino*, the consent of the governed is forthcoming most easily when the sovereign and citizens are truly equal parties under law; the easiest scenario in which to imagine this consent between sovereign and citizen would naturally be when they are one and the same person.

Although Crusoe may in some sense represent William III, or Defoe's ideal warrior-king, as Schonhorn suggests, in fact Crusoe alternates between viewing himself as slave or monarch, as head of the state or as subordinate retainer in the household. Crusoe describes himself as "like a King" when he dines at his table, with the company only of his servants and domestic animals: "Poll, as if he had been my Favorite, was the only Person permitted to talk to me" (7:171). In referring to the length of time he has been on the island, however, Crusoe refers to "the sixth Year of my Reign, or my Captivity, which you please" (7:159). Crusoe's uncertainty as to whether he is slave or monarch is significant: by referring to himself as both captive and monarch he tends to gloss over the plight of a real captive, his first servant, Xury. Out of gratitude for having helped him escape from the Moors, Crusoe had promised Xury that he would make him a "Great Man." Shortly thereafter, however, Crusoe sells Xury for "60 pieces of eight," an act rendered tragically ironic by the allusion to Judas's betraying of Jesus.[33] Crusoe's inability to recognize the obvious biblical lesson about betrayal simply underscores the limitations of his own subjective moral and political perspective. Moreover, Crusoe's naïve and pompous political self-representation seems to offer, more generally, a satiric critique of overly abstract political theory.

Just as social-contract theorists from Locke to Sidney frequently stumbled over the differences between child and servant, so Crusoe's situation embodies the awkward question raised by the social contract when applied to real people in real situations: does it oblige us to treat servants as full citizens, with the chance to become "Great" men, or may they be dismissed as mere property, to be disposed of as chattel, by other men? If we view Crusoe as a sovereign rather than as a prisoner, his treatment of Xury is even more troubling, for his actions represent the cruel and arbitrary whims of a tyrant monarch. Given that the novel begins with the narrative frame of Crusoe himself disobeying a father depicted not as a tyrant but as "a wise and grave Man" who provided "excellent Counsel" (7:2) against Crusoe's plan of going to sea, the main narrative must be viewed against the ironic relief of its opening scene, with Crusoe having become the tyrant his own father was not.

The limitations of Crusoe's subjective viewpoint, depicted in formal terms through the self-absorbed perspective of the controlling first-person narrator, are further demonstrated when Crusoe spies Friday attempting to escape from cannibals: his first impulse is not a purely humanitarian instinct to save him, but rather a desire to acquire a servant. As with Xury, the language Crusoe uses to refer to his fellow human being blurs the question of whether Friday will develop a friendly, feudal, or filial relationship with his rescuer: "It came now very warmly upon my Thoughts, and indeed irresistibly, that now was my Time to get me a Servant, and perhaps a Companion, or Assistant; and that I was call'd plainly by Providence to save this poor Creature's Life" (7:235). Although his rescue of Friday is in some sense a humanitarian act, Crusoe's initial motive is purely selfish. The epithets "Companion" and "Assistant" suggest a relationship between equals, as would exist in the ideal fraternity of peers implied by the social contract. These labels obscure, however, the actual relationship, which we may recognize in Crusoe's materialist impulse "to get me a Servant." Crusoe's relationship to Friday, like his relationship to Xury, requires a verbal displacement to meet the utopian vision of the social contract. When Crusoe has successfully rescued Friday, the latter's mute response is to lay his head upon the ground at Crusoe's feet and to make "all the Signs to me of Subjection, Servitude, and Submission imaginable, to let me know, how he would serve me as long as he liv'd" (7:239). In teaching his new companion to speak English, Crusoe names this assistant and himself according to his vision of their relationship. The names that Crusoe assigns to himself and to his servant describe the nature of the contract between them: Friday must always remember to be grateful for the day when his life was saved; he must call "master" the person to whom he owes perpetual obedience for having saved his life (7:239).

In describing his servant's loyalty to him as the devotion of loving child to a benevolent parent, Crusoe introduces a traditional, hierarchical version of family structure: "never Man had a more faithful, loving, sincere Servant, than Friday was to me; without Passions, Sullenness or Designs, perfectly oblig'd and engag'd; his very Affections were ty'd to me, like those of a Child to a Father" (7:242). Crusoe casts Friday's loyalty in terms that echo his earlier description of himself as patriarch of both home and nation. He casts himself as a benevolent father, whose very position in the family engenders loyalty naturally. By narrating the only human relationship on the island in patriarchal terms, however, Defoe does not necessarily articulate an "illogical" urge for "divine sanction," as Schonhorn suggests.[34] We could assume equally well that Crusoe's reference to absolute power should be read as satirical commentary on a par with that in *The Shortest Way with Dissenters*. Through this reference to Crusoe's selfish materialism, Defoe may well be calling our attention to the difficulty of maintaining equality and mutual respect between persons of different rank, as a thorough application of the social contract would require.

Just as Defoe gestures to the fraught position of the servant in political discourse, so by his brief references to the wife whom Crusoe takes upon his return to England does he introduce the problem the social contract raises about the wife's role in the domestic family. Crusoe's return to Britain underscores the difference between the image of Adam and Eve's harmonious joint dominion, so crucial to social-contract theory, and the depiction of an actual eighteenth-century family, in which the wife was not a full person under law, but a *feme covert* (a woman under the cover or protection [of her husband]), whose political selfhood was subordinated to her husband's. The woman Crusoe marries, whom he describes after her death as "the Stay of all my Affairs, the Center of all my Enterprizes,"[35] seems, like their children, incidental to his life, even an obstacle to his pursuing any more adventures. He first mentions his wife obliquely by noting that he married "not either to [his] Disadvantage or Dissatisfaction" (8:104). Even while married, Crusoe confesses that he "could not keep the Country out of [his] Head, and had a great mind to be upon the Wing again" (8:104). Married and with "all that the World could give" him (8:115), Crusoe recounts his wife telling him that she imagines *him* thinking "if *she* was dead, [leaving on another voyage] would be the first thing *I* would do" (8:114, emphasis added). Even when he might quote his wife directly, the protagonist-narrator instead paraphrases his wife's response to his desire to travel; the formal structure of this passage thus emphasizes the limitations of the narrator's perspective.

The unopposed head of an imaginary household—whose sole inhabitants are goats, a parrot, a dog, and himself—may liken himself to a monarch of a country in which the inhabitants are so happy that the concept of rebellion is unknown to them. Apparently, a real household with a real wife and children can function this smoothly only if the wife is completely subservient, or if she is dead and the children are the responsibility of someone else. Crusoe calls our attention to the harmonious possibilities of the social contract when he describes, in two short paragraphs, his life on a farm as a "Country Gentleman," a situation that prompts him to remind the reader of the novel's narrative frame when he describes himself as enjoying "the middle State of Life, that my Father so earnestly recommended to me" (8:116). At the same time, the brevity of this description, relative to the prolixity of the rest of the narrative, draws our attention to the obvious fact that Crusoe still sees the need to travel, or to rebel once more against the advice of a nontyrannical father. As soon as his wife dies, Crusoe parcels off his children to a sympathetic widow and so disbands his only real domestic household in order to return to the sea.

The structure of the text itself, in which the protagonist-narrator tells his own story, has long been assumed as one of the qualities that give the text its air of verisimilitude. Of course, *Robinson Crusoe* often draws less directly from life itself than from its relationship to other texts. Defoe may have discovered the idea for a story of a shipwrecked survivor from an incident in a real travel text, such as, for example, Woodes Rogers's *A Cruising Voyage Round the World* (1712).[36] Assuming that Defoe was familiar either with this text, or some similar travel narrative, it is worth noting that this type of account was not necessarily narrated from the point of view of an individual who imagines himself as a ruler of island kingdoms. Woodes Rogers's *A Cruising Voyage*, for example, is a model of deference, in which he apparently feels obliged to justify every single decision, in his lengthy description of a lengthy voyage, to his financial backers. Rogers insists in the preface and reiterates in various ways throughout the narrative, "that I used my utmost Endeavours to promote your Interest, which was always prefer'd to my own."[37] This deferential tone strikes a sharp contrast to that of Crusoe, who seems unable to perceive the world from any point of view but his own. Crusoe, in fact, seems less a paradigm for the ideal individual under the Whig social contract than an example of someone who does not quite fully grasp its ideals. The narrative perspective of his text, in marked contrast to the deferential viewpoint of an actual voyaging narrative, calls attention to the difference between the ideal Whig individual and an actual person who does not quite live up to such a model. Although *Robinson Crusoe* has long been taken as embodying what Doody has described as Whig "Prescriptive realism,"[38] the ironic possibilities of its intertextual allusions in fact articulate a version of Whig realism that is not merely prescriptive, but also interrogative.

Defining the Individual Woman

If Robinson Crusoe represents the ostensibly self-reliant individual who has difficulty recognizing others around him as equal partners under the social contract, then the heroine of *The Fortunes and Misfortunes of the Famous Moll Flanders* (1722) represents a woman whose final domestic alliances may ultimately satisfy Defoe's Whig ideal model for the social contract but who seems neither to understand nor appreciate its significance. Like *Robinson Crusoe*, *Moll*

Flanders creates an impression of "reality" as much through its adherence to a single individual perspective as through its ironic acknowledgment of the limitations of this vision. In other words, the novel achieves its formal realism both through the first-person narration that helps the reader identify closely with Moll's consciousness, and through the allusions to external political events or situations that rupture Moll's perspective and allow us to recognize its limitations.

The difference between Moll's and Crusoe's situations is, of course, that Moll is female and born into poverty. Her rhetoric suggests the ways in which the language of romance obscures the inequality between parties in the social contract. Moll's explanation of how she was first seduced points to the over-determined word "happy," an adjective that only sometimes implies a formal, contractual agreement:

> [H]e did as it were put Words into my Mouth, telling me how passion-ately he lov'd me, and that tho' he could not till he came into his Estate, yet he was resolv'd to make me happy then, and himself too; *that is to say, to marry me*, and abundance of such fine things, which I, poor Fool, did not understand the drift of, but acted as if there was no kind of Love but that which tended to Matrimony. (1:20)

What would make Moll "happy" in the long run is far different from what will make the mayor's eldest son happy in the heat of the moment; however, his conversation suggests a symmetry between their situations, as if they were two equally free parties entering into a legal contract. Moll herself later refers to their ultimate arrangement as if it were contractual; once her eyes are opened to the different uses of the term "love," she chides herself for not having managed the negotiations better: "If I had known his Thoughts . . . I might have made my own Terms, and if I had not capitulated for an immediate Marriage, I might . . . have had what I would" (1:21). When Moll is finally offered a genuine proposal of marriage by the mayor's younger son, she and the older brother continue to dispute the nature of the contract they have entered into by their liaison and his implicit promise to marry her. She insists that they are, in essence, already married, and so her marrying the younger brother would be adultery. She challenges the older brother to define her as he might define the other party through a legal contract—to say whether she is his "whore" or his "wife"—and demands to know if he considers her an alienable piece of property: "[W]ill you Transfer me to your Brother? Can you transfer my Affection?" (1:37).

The pseudo symmetry of the original contract through which Moll loses her virginity interrogates the possibility of a truly symmetrical contract either in the domestic sphere or in the civil sphere. Moll's insistence on knowing whether or not the older brother views her as a piece of property links this passage to Locke's definition of individual rights. In his *Second Treatise of Government*, Locke defines a man's right to own property through the property of his own labor:

> Though the Earth, and all inferior Creatures be to all Men, yet every Man has a *Property* in his own *Person*, This no Body has any Right to but himself. The *Labour* of his Body, and the *Work* of his Hands, we may say, are properly his. Whatsoever then he removes out of the State that Nature hath provided, and left it in, he hath mixed his Labour with, and joyned to it something that is his own, and thereby makes it his *Property*. It being by him removed from the common state Nature placed it in, it hath by this *labour* something annexed to it, that excludes the common right of other Men. (par. 27)

In wondering whether the older brother would translate a theoretically sacred marriage vow into a contract, with herself as the alienable piece of property, Moll implicitly demands to know what he has done to "own" her affection in the first place, thus implying that her affection, like her labor, is implicitly her own property. Although Schonhorn insists that for Defoe, property, not labor, determines power and political dominion,[39] Moll is an eloquent spokesperson for the social contract at the moment when she protests the older brother's attempt to alienate her affections. However, after subsequently having married the younger brother and been widowed by him, Moll in essence is allowed to begin life anew, a respectable widow with an inheritance of £1200. Moll then makes a poor choice in marrying a smooth-talking draper: because of the laws governing a wife's property, this husband is able to squander her valuable savings. This second marriage demonstrates the problems in a social contract in which one party has more legal power (or control over joint resources) than the other. However, Moll herself admits that she enjoyed her husband lavishing her money on her and thus shares the blame in the mismanagement of their household; her acceptance of blame here confirms the wife's obligation to help govern the household, as set down in the Edenic analogy for the state originally preferred by social-contract theorists.

The univocal perspective of Moll's self-rationalizing narrative makes it difficult to imagine other options that she might have pursued. When early in her narrative Moll complains about the lack of government provision made for orphans in England, we easily accept it as an explanation for her having fallen "into a Course of Life, scandalous in itself, and which in its ordinary Course, tended to the swift Destruction both of Soul and Body" (1:2). Moll's early complaint about England's lack of orphanages, however valid, also suggests a fundamental inconsistency in her narrative, since the actual trajectory of her life does not prove that being orphaned necessarily caused her turn to crime. It is from logical inconsistencies such as this that we question the reliability of the text's main narrator. Moll also indicates that at certain junctures she realized that she should have broken off her life of crime, but neither her mature narrator nor her younger self ever seriously pursues an alternative course of life, such as living frugally in Manchester, an option that she once acknowledges as possible. While in some cases formal realism may result from a simultaneous convergence of multiple perspectives,[40] in the case of *Moll Flanders*, realism seems to derive from the lack of convergence between its different narrative perspectives. Confronted by this disjunction, readers are asked to interrogate their own assumptions and complacency about the Whig social contract.

In the novel's romantic conclusion, Defoe outlines a marriage bond in which the ideals of the social contract are maintained—in which two individuals who are equal in rationality, affection, and material goods achieve a harmonious life together. Moll's happy and penitent final union provides a sharp contrast to the indeterminate domestic situation of Crusoe at the end of the third volume of his *Adventures*. Unlike Crusoe, who has been unable to conceive of his position as responsible citizen or joint partner in a household, Moll and her "Lancashire husband" help us visualize a symmetrical bond of shared dominion and property. When Moll's grateful husband finally catalogues their riches, he concludes: "Who says I was deceiv'd when I married a Wife in *Lancashire*? I think I have married a Fortune and a very good Fortune too" (2:174). This exchange, in which the happy functioning of a marriage seems to depend on both parties bringing financial independence, reminds us of C. B. MacPherson's observation that, in Locke's writings, men without property are "rightfully both in and not in civil society."[41] The financial balance of Moll's final harmonious reunion seems emblematic of a broader symmetry in marriage that represents an idealized analogy for the Whig social contract. Despite the political import of this analogy, however, neither Moll nor her Lancashire husband seem at all cognizant of the political implications of their happiness. The husband focuses solely on his own material comfort, both when he leaves Moll to become a highwayman and when, after they are reunited, they relocate to the colony of Maryland. Moll meanwhile remains throughout her text obsessively concerned with which details of her past or present life she needs to hide—and she is usually entering into contracts with at least some deception on her part.

In a telling rhetorical aside, when her Lancashire husband abandons her to pursue a lucrative life of crime, Moll cries out, "*Oh Jemy!*. . . *come back, come back*" (1:163), echoing the familiar "lost-lover" motif of popular Jacobite ballads after 1714, in which Jemmy represents James Edward Stuart (the "Old Pretender"), the true king, whose lover mourns his absence. Because of the efforts of a few energetic Jacobite printers and their ballad-hawkers, such ballads would have been familiar to a large portion of the British populace during the early decades of the eighteenth century, despite the fact that loyal Jacobites comprised a relatively small percentage of the population.[42]

Moll Flanders, published in 1722 during the reign of George I, after the failure of the 1715 and 1719 Jacobite risings, was ostensibly "written in the Year 1683" (2:175), that is, before James II had abdicated. Thus the young Moll's plea for Jemy's return would probably have occurred (within the chronology of her fictional life-story) some time in the 1660s. Nonetheless, the echo is striking enough to suggest a double time-scheme (representing simultaneously the 1660s and the 1720s), a narrative technique already established in *Crusoe* and one that would be developed more fully in *Roxana*.[43] The time scheme might even be triple here, if we consider that in 1683, the ostensible year in which the narrator was recounting this story, another "*Jemy*"—that is, James Scott, duke of Monmouth, illegitimate but Protestant son of Charles II—was in exile for his association with the Rye-House plot against Charles II. A ballad written in 1683 mourning Monmouth's exile describes "*Jemy*" as "a Foe to no Man, / Till wheedl'd in by *Shaftesbury*" and so "forc'd to fly, / . . . For disturbing *Monarchy*."[44] The illegitimate Monmouth is rendered innocent here, manipulated by ambitious Whigs such as Shaftesbury; according to this pro-Stuart ballad, Monmouth's own wife was aware that interfering with the natural succession of monarchy was no less than "Treason." Whether Defoe is suggesting an echo to the exiled Scott in 1683 or to a subsequently exiled James II or mission James Edward Stuart (The "Old Pretender"), Moll and her Jemy are certainly exiled, however comfortably during their term of "transportation," in colonial Maryland (a haven for Catholics). Moll, who takes the role of breadwinner and manager of the estates, in a gender reversal typical of anti-Jacobite propaganda, humors her Jemy by presenting him with elegant wigs, pistols, and swords. The alert reader, rendered suspicious by Moll's earlier echo of a Jacobite ballad, notices the lack of congruence between the usual Edenic image of the social contract—Adam and Eve jointly tilling the soil—and Moll's marriage to this somewhat dandified highwayman, whom she perhaps naïvely arms for combat. The reunion of Moll and Jemy might instead also correspond to the Jacobite image of "The Happy Pair," representing Britain's reunion with the exiled "Pretender."[45]

How we should interpret Defoe's over-determined echo to "*Jemy*" is not clear. If in a work published in 1722, the reference is to the exiled James II or to James Edward Stuart, then Moll may represent a naïve English populace, unappreciative of the efforts of William III, as Defoe suggested in *The True-Born Englishman*, and less interested in the social contract than in amassing material possessions. If, in a variant reading, Moll's Jemy, who insists that they return to England at the end of the novel, represents the Protestant James Scott in 1683, preparing for his final attempt in 1685 to "save England" from the Catholic James II, then Jemy and Moll become more admirable as potential protectors of English liberty. Defoe's novel, however, does not allow us to define a precise extratextual referent for "*Jemy*." Rather than the one-to-one correspondence between exaggerated Whig caricatures and real-life political figures that Delarivier Manley effects in her political romans à clef, Defoe gives us characters whose relationship either to real political figures or to simple partisan carica- tures is over-determined. For example, Moll Flanders shares some of the characteristics of the courageous, ostensibly promiscuous Jenny Cameron, but Moll differs from most anti-Jacobite accounts of the female military leader in her desire for a quiet, monogamous domes- tic existence. Following the echoes of Jacobite ballads, Moll might represent the Jacobite heroine Jenny Cameron safely guiding and arming the James Edward Stuart for a potential invasion of England. But Moll, in contrast to the mythic heroine, is rendered femininely "human" (and thus seen as "realistic" for generations of readers) by her apparent lack of interest in political affairs.

The "realism" of *Moll Flanders* stems not only from the way that the protagonist is humanized, in contrast to partisan discourse, but also from the sustained critique the text offers of the domestic analogies familiar from high political theory. Like Robinson Crusoe, Moll cor- responds at some level to the abstract Whig individual, competing to survive or succeed. On the other hand, by focusing on Moll's initially subordinate position within the domestic household, Defoe draws our attention to the differences between her situation, as orphaned female, and that of the usual abstract (non-Dissenting Protestant male) subject of Whig political theory. Although critics have traditionally connected the concrete details of Moll's life to the empiricism usually associated with realistic narratives, in fact, the same detail—the improbable number of husbands, coincidences, and adventures—is here too excessive to feel "real": Moll has too many adventures, too many husbands; her good fortune results from too many improbable coincidences. The "realism" of her character depends not merely on Defoe's description of her life, as pre-textual reality, or on her difference from partisan caricature, but also on the tension between this representation of an individual woman and other familiar representations of political individuals, male and female. Just as *Robinson Crusoe* demonstrates the risks of mistaking an unequal contract for a contract between equal parties, so *Moll Flanders* teaches us how easy it is to focus on the benefits of peace, liberty, and political contract without fully understanding the labor, sacrifice, and rational analysis necessary to maintain this political model. The "reality" that Defoe depicts in *Moll Flanders* is thus reducible neither to some abstract mercantilist Whig demand for empiricist detail nor to an easy reaffirmation of Whig social-contract theory.

Misunderstanding the Social Contract

Like *Robinson Crusoe* and *Moll Flanders*, *Roxana; or, The Fortunate Mistress* (1724) achieves its formal realism not merely by reinforcing an ideal of individualism, but by demonstrating the complexity of the household analogies frequently used to represent the social contract. Like *Moll Flanders*, *Roxana* calls our attention to the weakness of a contract that is entered into by two persons who are not equal in circumstance. The eponymous heroine's life of crime begins because she marries an attractive man who has no business sense. In a few years he squanders her fortune and his own, then deserts her, leaving her devoid of financial resources and with five children to support. Roxana's advice, "Never, Ladies, marry a Fool,"[46] echoes Defoe's advice in all his conduct manuals against marrying in haste or because of a purely physical attraction. Once she has made the mistake against which she warns other women, Roxana descends into sin because, still married but deserted by her husband, she has no method of remarrying legally. When her landlord, known only as the "Jeweller," offers her a pseudo-nuptial agreement and maintenance contract, he emulates the mutual affection and responsibility Defoe describes as necessary to a marriage in his moral writings. In this case, the legal contract binding

Roxana to the husband who ruined and deserted her appears in stark contrast to the symmetrical, if illegal, contract offered by the generous and devoted jeweler.

When Roxana anticipates that the jeweler is about to suggest an extramarital liaison, she interrupts him to observe:

> There was a vast Difference between our Circumstances, and that in the most essential Part; namely, That he was Rich, and I was Poor; that he was above the World, and I infinitely below it; that his Circumstances were very easie, mine miserable, and this was an Inequality the most essential that can be imagined. (11:45)

Roxana's concern seems justified when we recall what happened to Moll Flanders and to many other novelistic protagonists from the 1720s who allowed themselves to be seduced by the lure of the symmetrical language of love when their financial position and their seducer's were not symmetrical. Yet the jeweler tenders a legal agreement that provides, as he suggests, "such Measures as shall make an Equality still" (11:45). Just as the social contract between citizens and monarchs potentially renders all citizens equally empowered to repudiate a tyrant, so the jeweler makes provisions through a "Contract in Writing" in which he promises sexual fidelity, financial support, and a substantial sum of money should he abandon her. The contrast between this contract, which provides Roxana firm guarantee of security, and her own marriage contract, which allowed her husband to ruin her financially, is striking. Moreover, this bigamous union, of genuine love and mutual respect, seems to approximate the ideal conjugal agreement Defoe describes in his subsequent conduct book *Conjugal Lewdness; or, Matrimonial Whoredom* (1727): "The Matrimonial Duty is reciprocal; 'tis founded in Love, 'tis performed in the height of Affection, its most perfect Accomplishment consists not in the Union of the Sexes, but in the Union of the Souls."[47] Although Roxana's union with the jeweler clearly exceeds the traditional moral strictures promoted in *Conjugal Lewdness*, readers are asked to interrogate the very meaning of the social contract when its logic seems to uphold actions that may exceed a traditional moral order. The jeweler dies relatively early in the novel. One reason why Defoe writes him out early may be to eliminate the irreconcilable conflict between the moral order and the legal order posed by his pseudo-marriage contract with Roxana.

Given the political and moral orders that Defoe upheld in most of his writings, it is difficult to understand why, after the death of the jeweler, Roxana refuses the marriage proposal of an honest Dutch merchant. Following the pattern of Moll's Lancashire husband, who respects Moll for her ability to manage money, this Dutchman is sensitive to Roxana's fears that her fortune may be squandered by an irresponsible spouse. He proposes to let her retain control of her money after marriage and even offers her control of his. Defoe scholars have traditionally assumed that the Dutch merchant's offer of financial equality exceeded Defoe's sense of a "natural" moral order.[48] While such an order does seem fundamental to Defoe's thought, his works also demonstrate his predilection for subjecting even his most fundamental beliefs to rigorous interrogation. Appreciating the fact that the social contract depends on two parties joining together as free and autonomous individuals, Defoe already demonstrated the dangers of unequal unions through his depiction of Moll's and Roxana's first conjugal agreements. However, in refusing the Dutch merchant, Roxana is not refusing an asymmetrical union but an exceptionally egalitarian and generous marriage contract.

The reason that Roxana gives for rejecting the Dutch merchant is the inequality of the marriage bond. She explains, "That the very Nature of the Marriage-Contract was, in short, nothing but giving up Liberty, Estate, Authority, and every-thing, to the Man, and the Woman, was indeed, a meer Woman ever after, that is to say, a Slave" (11:172). Although this description is potentially true of the traditional marriage contract and certainly true of Roxana's first marriage, it does not characterize the offer that the honest Dutch merchant tenders. What is striking about Roxana's narrative, unlike other fictional accounts of conjugal liaisons written during the 1720s (for example, those in Eliza Haywood's early novels) is that, with the exception of her first husband, the men Roxana becomes involved with are exceptionally reliable and treat her with scrupulous attention and generosity. Roxana, in fact, proves herself hypocritical by claiming to want full equality in a marriage and then rejecting the merchant's offer of real equality in order to debase herself by becoming paid mistress to an English nobleman with whom she will never be an equal partner.

The Dutch merchant plausibly represents William of Orange, the heroic Dutch-born guarantor of English liberty in Defoe's political tracts. Roxana then embodies the English citizenry which inadequately appreciated him and never fully understood the nature of the liberty he protected. French-born and "promiscuous," Roxana echoes standard anti-Jacobite depictions of loose women. The protagonist of a novel written during a decade when Jacobitism was not considered an urgent threat, Roxana may also echo the discourses of those citizens who mouth the vocabulary of equality but are diverted by political favors and short-term gain. Like the members of the court of George I, whom Defoe mocks for their preoccupation with luxury and finery, Roxana forgets, in her fascination with wealth and titles, the meaning of the liberty she claims to be seeking. Were she to accept the Dutch merchant's offer she would become, like the figure of England in Defoe's *True-Born Englishman*, the "ruined" but noble mother of the nation's heterogeneous populace. However, this would require her to acknowledge and accept her own children, both legitimate and illegitimate, and, although in the later sections of her story she seems inclined to offer financial assistance to some of her legitimate children, Roxana never seems concerned about her illegitimate offspring. Roxana's fall is thus both the descent of a woman who fails to recognize the value of an equitable union when she is offered one and the fall of a nation that fails to understand the value of the liberty it gained under William of Orange and so may be threatening to revert, under George I, into the luxury and immorality of the reign of Charles II. The novel's "double time-scheme," in which the action takes place during the dissolute era of Charles II but also refers to the reign of George I (during which it was written), obliges us to read with a kind of double vision that allows us to appreciate Roxana's perspective but simultaneously to cast judgment on it.[49]

In *The Great Law of Subordination considered; or, the Insolence and Unsufferable Behaviour of Servants in England* (1724), published in the same year as *Roxana*, Defoe explains that for the average British citizen, the concept of "Liberty" functions much as a "Mistress" or a "Whore":

> In like manner *Liberty* is a word of Endearment, 'tis the Hereditary Favourite of the People; 'tis the Nation's Mistress, I was a going to say it was the Nation's Whore; in a Word, 'tis talk'd of by every-body, valu'd by every-body, and understood almost by no-body; this *English* Liberty is as blindly espous'd, as I said Popery was blindly hated by those who mistake it in the grossest manner.[50]

A perfunctory interpretation of this analogy might suggest that Roxana, in choosing to become a "Whore," which is how she describes herself as soon as she consents to the jeweler's contract, misunderstands the true meaning of liberty. However, Defoe also clearly distinguishes between a reflexive response to a word such as "Liberty" or "Popery" and a deeper understanding of its meaning. In the previous paragraph, he mocks those whose only understanding of "Popery" is something against which "100,000 stout Fellows . . . would spend the last Drop of the Blood" without really knowing "whether it be a Man or a Horse" (20). In looking back over her life as she narrates her story, Roxana explains that it was not the "sin" of technically "being a Whore" that weakened her union with the jeweler, but rather her "Conviction that was from the beginning, upon me, that I was a Whore, not a Wife" (11:49). It is this conviction that persuades her to force her maid Amy to sleep with her new pseudo-husband and so potentially strain the pseudo-marriage.

Roxana's disturbing treatment of Amy might have been used to further align Roxana (a French-born adulteress after all) with the "French promiscuity" with which Whig tracts usually associate the Jacobite cause. However, in developing Roxana's character through this fictional autobiography, Defoe seems more interested in exploring the foundational principles of liberal political theory than in gratuitously denigrating French or Jacobite women. Ultimately, Roxana's union with the jeweler comes to represent a successful combination of liberty and love, even if it is not ultimately compatible with Defoe's traditional version of the moral order. However, by becoming a mistress, after the jeweler's death, to various members of the nobility and royalty, Roxana mistakes the liberty that comes through a union of equals for the pseudo-liberty of sleeping with aristocratic men she does not love in exchange for money she does not need. In other words, she misunderstands the boundary between liberty and license so important to eighteenth-century political thought. Although she eventually marries the honest merchant after her other liaisons end, Roxana continues to misunderstand the value of liberty by seeking titles of nobility rather than embracing an honest union of equals. The formal realism of the text thus derives from the extratextual irony— through references to the politically charged terms of "Whore," and the politically potent analogy of an equitable domestic household—that obliges us to pass judgment on Roxana even as we are drawn into sympathy for her through the controlling power of her narrative voice.[51]

The "realism" of this text derives in part from Roxana's difference from familiar political caricatures: she is more humanized than the anti-Jacobite caricatures of courageous women, yet she is more independent and more outspoken than Eve in the Edenic model of the domestic household deployed by social-contract theorists. She also moves beyond the standard virtuous heroines typical of Restoration dramatic tragedy, although her story resolves more darkly than was typical of dramatic comedy. Roxana achieves, finally, all the trappings of outward success—wealth, a marriage to the Dutch merchant who purchases for her titles of nobility in England and Holland—but her story ends in a tragic loss of all these gains through a sudden "Blast of Heaven." This switch from comedy to tragedy takes place abruptly within the final paragraph of the narrative:

> Here, after some few Years of Flourishing, and outwardly happy Circumstances, I fell into a dreadful Course of Calamities, and *Amy* also; the very Reverse of our former Good Days; the Blast of Heaven seem'd to follow the Injury done . . . and I was brought so low again, that my Repentance seem'd to be only the Consequence of my Misery, and my Misery was of my Crime. (12:160)

Roxana's story, which at first parallels the financial progress and material gain of Moll's, diverts abruptly from the redemption and happiness of Moll's final experiences. The fine line between the paths that Moll and Roxana follow—one to repentance and redemption, the other to divine retribution and punishment—seems to represent two women's differing relationships to the ideal domestic representation of the Whig social contract: Moll accepts it as soon as it is offered; Roxana defers too long. For Defoe, the formal or structural difference between comedy and tragedy resides not in classical conventions of tragic or pre-ordained fate but in the conscious political choices made by individual characters. Defoe's novels, like Behn's, challenge rigid partisan stereotypes that might be reinforced by the conventional distinctions between comedy and tragedy.[52] The abruptness of tragic closure that Defoe imposes on *Roxana* in the last few pages helps provoke the reader to renounce Roxana's mistaken understanding of the social contract. This sudden shift from comedy to tragedy thus moves this novel beyond simple prescriptive Whig realism into a more interrogative Whig realism.

The theoretical contract between monarch and individual citizen is not a contract that can be described by a single, universally applicable paradigm. Defoe's novels, from *Robinson Crusoe* to *Roxana*, describe the connection between the state and the household not as a binary analogy, in which one is a static or mythological emblem of the other, but as a continuum of obligation and carefully wrought negotiation. As someone who understood through personal experience the ease with which a respected businessman or writer could become persona non grata—through debt, imprisonment, or Dissenting religious beliefs—Defoe certainly understood how an individual's opportunity for participating in the social, political, or commercial contracts depended on contingent circumstances that were frequently out of his or her control. Hypothesizing the most complicated possible variants of the preferred Whig analogy for the social contract, Defoe's novels push the boundaries of the Whig empiricism that they have traditionally been thought to embody. They achieve their dissonant narrative perspectives and their realistic characterization by acknowledging the complexity of Whig political theory that, by the mid-eighteenth century, abstract political treatises increasingly obscured. As the next two chapters demonstrate, Samuel Richardson and Eliza Haywood further develop the structures of formal realism by acknowledging and interrogating the discourses of mid-eighteenth-century political debate from their own different partisan perspectives.

CHAPTER 4

Partisan Debate and
Moderation Politics in
Samuel Richardson's Fiction

For several decades, scholars took for granted the connection between Samuel Richardson's "bourgeois" or "progressive" politics and his contributions to formal realism, although the bulk of twentieth-century criticism did not focus on Richardson's political stance.[1] According to the biographers Duncan Eaves and Ben Kimpel, Richardson (1689–1761) was opposed to any abuse of power that verged on tyranny, whether in the hands of Tories or Whigs. They point out that while Richardson is known to have bragged that his father sided with Monmouth during the 1685 rebellion, in the 1720s he probably printed several issues of the pro-Jacobite *True Briton*.[2] For Margaret Anne Doody, Richardson's novels are more Tory than Whig, although they are not reducible to either. Doody describes Mr. B. as a "Country Gentleman," neither quite Tory nor Whig, who names his first son Charles; Lovelace could be either a tyrannical Robert Walpole or a sinister, plotting "Pretender"; Grandison is simultaneously a "Whig patriot" and a new image of "what the true Tory Prince should look like."[3] Doody argues that, especially in *Sir Charles Grandison*, Richardson articulates "a dream of restoration, reconciliation, and wholeness [for] an England badly divided and given to division" (126). Richardson's interest in conciliatory politics is certainly a defining feature of his work, but it is important to emphasize that Richardson was not interested in a reconciliation that involved simplifying the complexity of the political debates of his day.

Just as Defoe re-examines the fundamental principles of the social contract through his depiction of domestic conflict and harmony, Richardson likewise restores the analogy of the domestic household to the increasingly abstract language of mid-eighteenth-century political theory. In doing so, he challenges and redefines the paradigm for both moderate political selfhood and for rational political debate. Richardson also draws our attention to the limitations of overly rigid partisanship by insisting that his virtuous characters develop beyond the limits of mere partisan caricature. This does not mean that he recommends "forgetting traditional political categories and understanding all social relationships in domestic terms,"[4] as Nancy Armstrong argues. Rather, Richardson re-deploys the analogy of the domestic household, previously central to political debate, for his own moderate political purposes. Adopting the viewpoints of individuals in different contingent circumstances, Richardson examines in detail power relations in the domestic household. He thereby helps formulate the conventions of mid-eighteenth-century narrative realism, refusing both the caricatures of partisan discourse and the abstractions of high political theory.

The examples of the tyrannical Mr. B. and Lovelace demonstrate the dangers of using the abstract mid-eighteenth-century discourses of the "public good" without fully understanding the complexities of the domestic analogies on which the social contract was originally articulated. In Richardson's first two novels, the female characters provide the real models for political selfhood through their careful negotiation of power relations within and outside the household. Moreover, in *Clarissa*, Richardson provides a model of political debate through the epistolary exchange between Clarissa Harlowe and Anna Howe, two women who respectively represent paradigms for Tory and Whig selfhood. *The History of Sir Charles Grandison* offers a male model of political virtue in the figure of the eponymous hero. Unlike Richardson's earlier tyrannical male protagonists, Grandison is never content to base his actions or judgments on the clichés of abstract political philosophy; instead, he always takes into account the contingent particulars of the domestic and interpersonal relationships, and so offers a paradigm for patient, tolerant governance.

As shown in previous chapters, early British novelists often engaged in the political debates in language that tended to humanize the discourses of the genre within which they were working. By the middle of the eighteenth century, conflict over how the emergent novel should be viewed—whether as political intervention or humanizing entertainment—was already apparent. Richardson's works mark a turning point in the novel's formal development. Although their "realistic" attention to the detail of quotidian domestic life and individual psychology represented a response to the abstract discourses of contemporary partisan debates, it was by no means an apolitical response. However, this stylistic development tended to reinforce a moral humanism that would encourage later generations of readers to conflate realism with a representation of apolitical universal selfhood.

The Abstract Subject and the Particular Self in *Pamela*

Pamela's spectacular "rise" from lady's maid to the wife of a country squire has traditionally been understood within a rubric of Whig or bourgeois individualism.[5] More recently, it has come to be viewed in Tory terms.[6] Part of the difficulty in categorizing *Pamela: or, Virtue Rewarded* (1740) and its sequel *Pamela*, Part II (1741) as definitively Whig or Tory is that by the middle of the eighteenth century both parties voiced abstract ideas about liberty, while the analogy of the domestic household was gradually disappearing from formal political philosophy. When Mr. B. announces shortly after marrying Pamela that he believes "the Distinctions of *Whig* and *Tory* odious,"[7] he seems to be offering a model of moderate political behavior that eschews the extremes of partisan positioning. He insists that he has never "given a Vote but according to what I thought was for the publick Good, whether *Whig* or *Tory* proposed it" (2:229). The integrity of this comment, so closely following Mr. B.'s own capricious impatience with Pamela for not having arrived at the Darnford's at the time he had requested (in fact she was being held "prisoner" by his own sister), is ironically undercut by Mr. B.'s own tyrannical comments a few moments earlier. In other words, Mr. B.'s reliance on the easy abstractions of "the publick Good" permits him to continue to act tyrannically in the household while assuming that such behavior is irrelevant to his role as good citizen. The detailed descriptions of Pamela's daily life and thoughts, made available through the first-person epistolary structure, of course, provide a picture of "virtuous femininity" and moderate civic individualism that would help shape the emergent perceptions of normative (hence "realistic") selfhood. However, Richardson's depictions of domestic life also derive from a direct engagement with the competing partisan versions of selfhood of his day.

Pamela's "treasonous papers" (1:312), as Mr. B. describes her letters home, at first seem to represent a potential rebellion of certain oppressed groups, such as women, children, dependent servants, Jacobites, or other marginalized political or religious interests. Mr. B.'s assertion that Pamela is a "great Plotter" (1:312) might associate her either with the "plotters" of the Jacobite cause during the 1740s or the Whig orchestrators of the events of 1688–89.

Mr. B.'s descriptions of Pamela, however, tell us less about Pamela's actual political stance, which is a complex combination of resistance and deference, than about Mr. B.'s own political naïveté, in which anyone who attempts to thwart his single-minded pursuit of his own pleasure must be described as a rebel. The ease with which Pamela is able to assure Mr. B. that, once they are married, she will have "no Will but" that of her husband (2:41) might suggest that her postnuptial politics will be more Tory than Whig, following the domestic analogies of formal political treatises from the 1680s. However, such analogies to the domestic household had largely disappeared from high political theory by the 1740s. Pamela's assertion seems instead to represent her subtle ability to manipulate political discourses in order to maintain her (Whig) right to resist through a careful coding of (Tory) deference. Pamela thus helps to naturalize and humanize a model for moderate political selfhood that combines a Whig discourse of contract with Tory discourse of virtue. In other words, her discourse helps to associate humanized or "realistic" character with political moderation.

In contrast to Defoe's Roxana, who is several times offered financial settlements (both for illegitimate cohabitation and for legitimate marriage) that parallel the equitable domestic analogies of Locke's and Tyrrell's versions of the Whig social contract, Pamela is offered a less literal allegiance to the Revolution principles of 1688–89. Rejecting the sort of extramarital contracts from which Defoe's Moll and Roxana benefited, Pamela demonstrates little interest in the material details of the "Articles" Mr. B. offers in exchange for her becoming his mistress. Her refusal of Mr. B's articles is not based on the monetary value of his offer, although we might note that the landed Mr. B., unlike Roxana's generous jeweler and Dutch merchant, does not offer to share the full measure of his wealth. Defoe's merchant heroes may be identified by their willingness to split their assets equitably with Moll and Roxana, respectively; of course, their wealth consists mostly in tangible, rather than real, property, and there is less of it to divide than there would be in Mr. B.'s estates. In any case, had Mr. B. offered Pamela an actual "shared dominion" through a literally equitable division of property (rather than 500 guineas and a farm in Kent), she would probably still have refused to become his mistress, given her implacable protection of her "virtue." In other words, Richardson's conception of the social contract, unlike Defoe's, is not articulated through the details of shared wealth, but through a vision of reciprocal virtue within the domestic household.

Pamela's political sensibilities, even before marriage, indicate a conservative reluctance to divide estates. By refusing to become his mistress, she in effect keeps Mr. B.'s property intact for his legitimate heirs and guarantees their offspring's legitimacy. In this sense, her behavior fits into a standard Tory model. Yet we should also note that Pamela remains aware of the language of liberty and contract, and insists that she is possessed of a free will, at least insofar as it allows her to turn down Mr. B.'s inappropriate offers. Protesting that she will "make no Free-will Offering of my virtue" (1:260), she insists that she will offer her virtue only in exchange for joining Mr. B. in a legal union that defines his will and her will as one. Although in one sense Richardson renders Pamela "an independent party with whom the male has to negotiate,"[8] as Nancy Armstrong suggests, Pamela's actions also depict a typical 1740s version of the social contract, in which a Whig discourse of free will has merged with more conservative language of obligation. She insists on her right to assert her "free will" although she is quite prepared, upon marriage, to subsume her will to her husband's. In this sense, Pamela enacts Hume's Tory account of the social contract. However, in Richardson's 1741 sequel to *Pamela*, Pamela's actions after marriage bring back into play allusions to "realistic" domestic scenarios that respond to and complicate Hume's abstracted articulation of Tory selfhood.

Despite her self-effacing demeanor after her marriage and her apparently conservative political inclinations, Pamela asserts her right to resist her husband's authority when she believes that he is about to commit adultery. At this point Richardson alludes to the Old Testament, casting Pamela as the biblical Esther, valiantly saving the Jews from destruction through her courageous but always deferential demands. Faced with the possibility of her husband's imminent descent into "polygamy," as she describes it, Pamela manages to preserve her vision of the social contract—reciprocal virtue within marriage—by daring first to disobey her husband and then to give him an ultimatum: either he remains faithful, or she will live separately with their son. Yet, following Esther's example, and thereby invoking a crucial biblical anecdote to counter her husband's oppression, her actions suggest that tyranny is most effectively thwarted when the oppressed retain a respectful attitude toward their tyrants. Like the wife facing the tyranny of a drunken husband in James Tyrrell's *Patriarcha Non Monarcha*, Pamela retains her right to judge for herself when she should obey or disobey a tyrant.

Having angered her husband by bursting into tears after meeting the countess, whom she suspects of pursuing a romantic intrigue with him, Pamela sends Mr. B. a note requesting to meet with him and explain why she was crying. Refusing to see her that evening,

Mr. B. writes in response, "I will give your cause a fair hearing, when I am more fit to hear all your pleas, and your excuses" (4:171). By changing her request to speak with him into a request for a "hearing," Mr. B. renders Pamela a criminal who needs to plead her case rather than a joint partner in the social contract. Pamela seems at first to concede Mr. B.'s label of her criminality and the loss of power it suggests. Ultimately, however, she ignores his warning to stay away from him and provocatively knocks on his door, excusing herself by translating her situation into that of the biblical Esther (or "Hester"), who "ventur'd her Life" to "break in upon" her husband "unbidden" (4:172). Following the example of Esther, Pamela accepts her husband's characterization of her position as suppliant and so renders him "that *Eastern* Monarch" (4:172), that is, King Ahasuerus, the Old Testament tyrant whom Esther persuades to save the Jews from massacre.

Rather than recognizing Pamela's reference to "poor Hester" for what it is, an allusion to a successful political plaintiff, Mr. B. seems to assume Pamela has made another reference to Lucretia, or some other heroine from classical tragedy. He responds with an echo of his earlier plea that they resolve their story as "a pretty story in romance" (1:31) by saying, "I hope, my Dear, by this Tragedy Speech, we are not to expect any sad Catastrophe to our present Misunderstanding" (4:172). In his earlier reference to their pretty "romance," Mr. B. refused to acknowledge the dramatic political effects of Lucretia's rape. Again attempting to diminish the tragic conclusion of the most famous classical rape narrative, he now asks, "Who ever blamed *Lucretia!*" (1:31). If his first allusion to tragedy demonstrated an unwillingness to acknowledge either the tragedy of a woman raped or the threat of such a rape to a tyrant monarch, Mr. B.'s second reference indicates how little he has learned by reading either classical literature or the Bible. Mr. B.'s reluctance to acknowledge the possibility of tragedy demonstrates his desire to ignore the risk that his tyrannical behavior poses to those within his dominion. His more general inability to hear the political overtones of literature also means that he will conflate nontragic biblical history with classical dramatic tragedy, and then ignore the political implications of both, as eager as he is to cast every story as domestic romance. Mr. B's tone-deafness to political interpretation confirms that he can easily mouth political abstractions—including the glib observation that the difference between Whig and Tory is "odious"—without recognizing the political resonance of his own actions. This tone-deafness helps make Mr. B. seem, at this juncture, more a caricature of tyranny than a realistic character.

Outmaneuvered by Pamela's superior ability to interpret the subversive power of the Old Testament, Mr. B. seems unaware that the *Book of Esther* begins with an assertion of the relevance of the domestic household to the political realm. According to the biblical text, Ahasuerus casts off his legitimate wife, Queen Vashti, because she refused to appear when the king wanted to show her off to his people. Ahasuerus fears that "this deed of the queen shall come abroad unto all women, so that they shall despise their husbands in their eyes, when it shall be reported." Ahasuerus then decrees that Vashti should never see him again and that he will pick a new queen, with the intention that "when the king's decree which he shall make shall be published throughout all his empire, (for it is great,) all the wives shall give to their husbands honour, both to great and small."[9] By means of this allusion, Richardson insists on retrieving the traditional parallel between household and state, despite Mr. B.'s desire to adhere to an abstracted version of the social contract, from which household analogies have largely disappeared. In so doing, Richardson asserts the "reality" of an Old Testament domestic household against the abstractions of mid-century political theory. In other words, like Behn and Defoe, Richardson crafts "realistic" narrative scenes of domestic life drawn not by copying the details of some hypothetical apolitical reality, but through intertextual correctives to the omissions and oversights of high political theory.

Richardson's version of moderate political realism, like that of Behn and Defoe, corrects the oversights of high political theory and revises the caricatures of partisan tracts. By comparison to Pamela, who is neither a Whig rebel nor a passively obedient Tory wife, Mr. B. initially appears as almost the caricature of a tyrant, whether Walpolian or Jacobite. His usual method of navigating difficulties is to overpower the opposition; he marries Pamela only after she has repeatedly obstructed his attempts to rape her. Mr. B.'s reformation from tyrannical caricature to a more complex character occurs because Pamela dares to oppose his power in the domestic sphere. Just as the wife in Tyrrell's *Patriarcha non Monarcha* must be alert to the danger of "the Father of a Family" falling into "a mad or drunken fit,"[10] so Pamela must be alert to the danger that her husband could at any moment turn into the potentially tyrannical King Ahasuerus. Following the example of the biblical Esther, Pamela respectfully requests her husband to dine with her; she then invites him to her closet where she has arranged three chairs, which she describes as "the Bar, at which I am to take my Trial" (4:184). She then asks Mr. B. to be her "Accuser, as well as [her] Judge" (4:185), thus apparently deferring to his authority. However, having likened her trial bar to the one Mr. B. showed her in the House of Peers, "at which Causes are heard, and sometimes Peers are try'd" (4:185), Pamela establishes herself as his equal in marriage, or his political peer in a system in which peers are held accountable only to each other. Like Esther, she demonstrates her subtle understanding of the parallel between domestic disagreements and national politics.

As the "trial" begins, Mr. B. tries to insist that Pamela's head has "turned," or that she has forfeited her right to a full position of subject under the social contract through her ostensible loss of rational capacity; he thus functions here as caricature of a tyrant denying his subjects their basic rights as political subjects. In response, Pamela proves the soundness of her reason by insisting that he respond to her questions only with "Yes" or "No." By obliging her husband to confirm the validity of the rumors she has heard without responding to his demand for the names of her informants, Pamela protects the members of her parish who have risked their safety by revealing husband's apparently adulterous intentions. She thus follows the model of Esther who protected the safety of the rest of the Jewish people by pleading against Haman's decision to annihilate them. Like Esther, Pamela puts the good of her parishioners and informants above her own safety. She begs Mr. B. not to punish them for informing her of the truth; however, she does not plead in her own right to stop Mr. B. from proceeding as he intends. Rather than infuriating him by tears or protestation, she simply indicates that she understands why he would find the countess attractive; she then offers that she will give him up to her "*worthier* Rival" (4:191). Although this seems like an act of submission, in which Pamela subverts her own desires to Mr. B.'s more capricious will, in fact she is protecting herself by making certain that she will not be obliged, as she puts it, to "divide my interest in you, knowingly, with any Lady upon Earth" (4:193). Pamela refuses to submit her will to that of her husband in the matter of central importance to her, and she enacts this refusal by returning to the domestic analogies that were originally used to define the social contract during the conflicts of the 1680s.

Although she clearly does not intend to kill herself, Pamela reverts to the language of dramatic tragedy to convince Mr. B. of the seriousness of the romantic dalliance she suspects he is contemplating. Demonstrating that she is better able than her husband to read not only biblical narrative but his own secret desires, she puts him at his ease by acknowledging that she understands the awkward situation he is in: "I see your difficulties. You have gone too far to recede" (4:194).

Pamela here retains narrative control of the situation, in formal and political terms, by maintaining the right to put Mr. B.'s thoughts into words for him. She then borrows the language of "destiny" from classical tragedy to suggest that she might take her own life, even though she is not seriously considering this step: "If you can make it easy to your Conscience, I will wait with Patience my happier Destiny; and I will wish to live (if I can be convinced you wish me not to die) in order to pray for you, and to be a directress to the first education of my dearest baby" (4:194). Rather than envisioning "destiny" as the classical conception of fate at the hands of capricious gods, Pamela instead persuades Mr. B. that it is up to him to determine her fate, thus forcing him to acknowledge that he rules the household and she does not.

Richardson probably embraced a definition of "Liberty" such as that offered in the moderate treatise *A Dissertation on the Liberty of the Subject in Great Britain* (1737), which insists that even public officials are not exempt from the restraining concept of "public good." When Pamela insists that Mr. B. could not do justice to his position as husband, father, and member of Parliament were he to act in a capricious or selfish manner, she essentially recapitulates the following passage from the anonymous *Dissertation*:

> Every just and upright Man, who accepts of, and is employed in any Office of publick Trust, will, from the Nature of the Thing, consider himself as under an absolute Restraint from using the Power conferred upon him, to any other Purpose, than that of securing and promoting the publick Good, as it is distinguished from selfish and private Gain.[11]

Unlike the *Dissertation*, however, which relies mainly on the analogies of an efficient machine, "that artificial Spring which unites the Three Great, but independent Powers" (14), Richardson's text returns to the potentially more troublesome analogy of the domestic household in which the wife retains the right to resist an imperious husband. By persuading Mr. B., who is already a member of Parliament, to play the role of virtuous husband and good public servant in her new version of romance comedy, Pamela succeeds, like the two daughters in Behn's *The Dumb Virgin*, in rescripting the basis of dramatic tragedy so that it relies on the political virtue of individual members of Parliament. Her success in reforming Mr. B. also revises early eighteenth-century amatory fiction (such as Defoe's or Haywood's novels from the 1720s) by insisting on virtue and chastity for both heroes and heroines.

Appearing three years after *A Dissertation on the Liberty of the Subject* and one year after Hume's *Treatise of Human Nature* (1739–40), *Pamela* idealizes a "virtue" in many ways compatible with the abstract assertions of "liberty" typical of these politically moderate mid-eighteenth-century treatises. At the same time, however, the novel acknowledges that abstract platitudes about the public good do not necessarily prevent tyranny in the household. After Pamela has confronted Mr. B. with the example of the biblical Esther, Mr. B. finally ceases tyrannizing her and becomes humanized. Mr. B. is, in fact, drawn with less detail after Pamela's triumph over his potential adultery, since the novel turns away from their marital disagreement to Pamela's adaptation of Locke's theories of education. However, just as other novelistic characters are differentiated from partisan caricatures, so Mr. B. is humanized at the point when his tyranny need no longer be delineated, because he has ceased to practice it. Whether we view him ultimately as a Tory because he insists on his wife's not breast-feeding her children, as Toni Bowers has argued,[12] or a Whig, because he enables the "rise" of the more lowly born Pamela, Mr. B. becomes "human" when he renounces tyranny in the domestic sphere, and, as is hinted at in the "Conclusion," begins to take a more active, but presumably politically moderate, role in government.

Mr. B.'s gradual transformation from rake to husband to reformed husband is evident not only in how he treats his wife, child, servants, and country, but also in his attitude towards narrative disclosure. At the start of the novel, Mr. B.'s tyranny is signaled by his obsessive concern about his attempts to seduce Pamela becoming known to the public. As his character develops from predictable caricature to more humanized figure, Mr. B. becomes willing, even eager, to disclose both his and his wife's conduct to the world. After his initial reformation from rake to husband, he wants Pamela to share her narrative of captivity with friends and neighbors. During the period when he is apparently contemplating adultery, however, his reticence about his own activities increases and, rather than encouraging a policy of full disclosure, he keeps Pamela in the dark about his intrigues, intrigues about which she is informed by friends and servants. As soon as the trial scene has been concluded, Mr. B. once again permits, even encourages, Pamela's detailed narration of his behavior:

> If you write to Lady *Davers*, how the Matter has ended, let me see the Copy of it: And be very particular in *your*, or rather *my* Trial. It shall be a standing Lesson to me for my future Instruction; as it will be a fresh Demonstration of your Excellence, which every Hour I more and more admire. (4:200)

Mr. B.'s interest in having his story fully disclosed marks his emergence into a more developed moral and political character, at least by comparison with how we had first seen him, a caricature of tyrannical paranoia. It also signals the connection, for Richardson, between moral and political disclosure and the emergent convention of narrative realism. As the different characters stop fearing Mr. B.'s treachery, deception, or wrath, so the narrative itself becomes fully voiced, with Pamela and Mr. B.'s sister, Lady Davers, openly analyzing his past, present, and potential tyranny.

In the "Letter *to a* Lady" included in the appendix to *Sir Charles Grandison*, Richardson explains why he does not delineate every concluding detail of his multivolume "history." Unlike "a *single story*" which might conclude with some "great and decisive event; as a *Death*, or a *Marriage*," the last chapter of *Grandison* leaves most characters "with fair prospects" of everything ending happily although not every detail of every character's future is delineated.[13] By contrast, *Pamela*'s "Conclusion" leaves very little to the imagination, describing in detail everything from the continued virtue of Mr. B. to the happy marriage of Miss Goodwin and the particulars of Mr. Longman's last will and testament. This comprehensive survey is not exactly a "full" depiction of "life itself" but it is a response to an increasingly abstracted liberal political theory that no longer surveys the differences between different political individuals. By leaving no character unaccounted for—that is, by telling as full as possible a story of power relations within the domestic household and their relevance to political debate—Richardson helps develop the conventions of moderate political novelistic realism as he challenges mid-eighteenth-century liberal political theory to return to its original domestic analogies. Appropriately, his next novels stretch to even greater narrative length and incorporate the epistolary contributions of a greater number of different political viewpoints.

EPISTOLARY MODELS OF TORY AND WHIG VIRTUE

The bulk of twentieth-century criticism about *Clarissa: or, The History of a Young Lady* (1747–48) focused less on the political context of the novel than on Richardson's skill in describing character or on the post-structural demeanor of the text, although in recent years political interpretations of the text have increased.[14] One obstacle to interpreting the specific political discourses that permeate *Clarissa* is that even in some of the more sophisticated late twentieth-century criticism, it remained a commonplace to dismiss Anna Howe as more "an extension of Clarissa herself than . . . a separate individual."[15] However, viewing Anna as merely the psychological obverse of Clarissa's own personality prevents us from taking seriously the political content of the highly rational exchange between the two friends. Through the epistolary exchange between Clarissa Harlowe and her friend Anna Howe, Richardson offers a model for a rational exchange of ideas, with Clarissa representing virtuous Tory selfhood and Anna virtuous Whig selfhood. As in *Pamela*, Richardson contributes to the development of novelistic realism by reasserting the relevance of the contingent details of the domestic household to the increasingly abstract discourses of mid-eighteenth-century political treatises.

In his essay "Of Passive Obedience" (1752), David Hume attempts to mediate traditional disagreements between rights-based and obedience-based models of government by acknowledging the fairness of both models.[16] He refers to the familial basis of authority only once, when he refers to the absurdity of believing that "the consent of the fathers" can "bind the children, even to the most remote generations" (447). Thus he obscures the fact that most of the arguments against passive obedience since 1680 were grounded not in the rights of sons but in the rights of women to disobey tyrannical or abusive husbands. A decade and a half later, Adam Ferguson would refer to the family only once in his *History of Civil Society* (1767), and here he refers to a foreign seraglio. In striking contrast to such increasingly abstracted accounts of liberal political theory, Richardson and other eighteenth-century British novelists uphold the method of Tyrrell's *Bibliotheca Politica* and of Locke's increasingly popular *Two Treatises* by reasserting the metaphorical relationship between power relations in the family and power relations in the state.

Clarissa reprises an older formulation of the debate about obedience and authority, characterized specifically by a contrast between a patriarchal and a contractarian version of the domestic household. When Clarissa describes Lovelace as a tyrant, we hear echoes not only of Jacobite cabals surrounding the final attempt of 1745, as Morris Golden has argued,[17] but also echoes of earlier debates over social-contract theory, which were marked by discussions of tyranny in the household.[18] These two dependent women (one dependent on her parents and her abductor, one on her mother and her fiancé) actually rearticulate the political debates of 1688 through the language of the domestic analogies that had been commonplace in the 1680s but had largely disappeared from formal political treatises by the 1740s. The rationality with which these two women debate their different partisan positions provides a model for moderate political selfhood, both Whig and Tory, as well as a model for polite debate that moves beyond partisan name-calling. In other words, the narrative "reality" that Richardson is asserting is modeled on moderate political debate that contrasts with both the frenzied and passionate discourses of partisan disagreement and the decontextualized abstractions of mid-eighteenth-century political philosophy.

In the face of tyranny, Clarissa articulates an ideal of obedience traditionally espoused by proponents of absolute monarchy: "My duty," she explains, "will not permit me so far to suppose my Father arbitrary."[19] Although this is delivered in a speech full of irony, Clarissa does intend to follow the letter of patriarchal tradition— which means obeying her father but not her brother, James (perhaps an allusion to James Edward Stuart), who is increasingly insubordinate, asserting dominance even over their father. When she pleads to Lovelace, "permit me the freedom which is my birthright as an English subject" (934), Clarissa articulates a Tory, rather than a Whig, version of the ancient myth of English liberty, as Florian Stuber points out.[20] However, Clarissa's underlying belief in Tory patriarchy does not mean, as Stuber claims, that she "clings to an idea of what her father should be . . . no matter what he actually does" (565). She is aware that her father is unjust or she would not consider marrying Lovelace, but divine-right theory holds that the monarch is always right, even when he acts tyrannically. Her deferential language corresponds to two dicta in Robert Filmer's *Patriarcha*: "the Father of a family governs by no other law than by his own will" and "Kings keep the Laws, though not Bound by them."[21] In accordance with this rule, it would be treasonous for a daughter to give even the impression of disagreeing with her parents. After a negotiating session with Clarissa, in which they debate whether she should respond to one of Lovelace's letters, Mrs. Harlowe, pleased with her daughter's honesty and compliance, shows her appreciation by agreeing to hide the fact of her original disagreement: "It shall not be known that you have argued with me at all" (96). In this literal version of patriarchal divine right, even voicing differences with authority is considered treasonous.

By contrast, Anna Howe espouses the recognizable tenets of social-contract theory with such enthusiasm that she seems to have no doubt of their relevance to the dependent situations of herself and Clarissa. In the epistolary exchanges between the two friends, she voices the same objections to arbitrary authority that were voiced by contract theorists in their arguments to exclude James II from the throne in 1688 and that were alluded to in every subsequent statement of social-contract theory published in the eighteenth century. "AUTHORITY!" she declares, "What a full word is that in the mouth of a narrow-minded person, who happened to be born thirty years before one!" (85). Anna is willing to disobey her own mother and order a carriage herself to help Clarissa escape, rather than see her friend fall into Lovelace's clutches. Clarissa, however, refuses this seemingly reasonable offer on the grounds that it would force Anna to disobey her own mother, a disobedience for which Clarissa could not countenance being responsible. Yet Anna continues to challenge Clarissa's perception of her own family: "Another would call your Father a Tyrant, if I must not" (132–33).

The ideal of a loving, caring family—fundamental to a Lockean concept of the social contract—is evoked by Richardson not through the Harlowe family but through the final union between Anna Howe and her persistent lover, Hickman. Although Anna repeatedly insists on her "dislike of all men: Of him: Of matrimony" (1456), she eventually marries Hickman, following both Clarissa's advice and her own mother's wishes. In contrast to Clarissa's notions that family harmony can only be achieved through old-fashioned patriarchalism, Anna's marriage proves that her modern contractarian principles are the most plausible route to a literally equal union. The narrator tells us that "there is but *one will* between them; and that is generally *his* or *hers*, as either speak first upon any subject, be it what it will" (1492). In taking contract theory to its logical extreme, Anna Howe has managed to rewrite Genesis so that Locke's hypothetically updated version of the family (in which husband and wife share equal dominion in the household) actually applies to her own marriage. Their equal comfort in speaking their minds, or speaking "first upon any subject," also corresponds to Richardson's narrative preference for full disclosure, even though the novel does not offer us a detailed glimpse into their lives. While we do not get to know either Anna Howe or Hickman well, through the partial character-sketch Richardson provides we get a sense that they are both sensitive, thinking human beings who understand the need to listen to the voices and opinions of others around them, including Anna's mother and her friends.

In structuring the exchange between Clarissa and Anna as a quasi-political debate, Richardson prevents either the divine-right Tory or the contractarian Whig position from triumphing: each character's partisan stance demands the reader's respect. Although the plot, in which Clarissa escapes one tyrant only to fall into the clutches of another, underscores Richardson's strong opposition to tyranny, Richardson does not directly suggest that one partisan position more than another will necessarily prevent tyranny. In offering the eloquent epistolary exchange between Clarissa and Anna, Richardson demonstrates that proponents of two opposing, and politically resonant, views of household obligation can have a polite exchange of differences, just as he will show in *Sir Charles Grandison* that Anglicans, Methodists, and Catholics can agree to disagree without violence. *Clarissa*, like Richardson's other novels, is less about which side should win a partisan debate than about how the debate itself should take place. Clarissa and Anna write to each other in lucid and rational language that allows each to grasp and consider the other's position, even if neither ultimately persuades the other to change her partisan view. These young women represent for Richardson political and moral virtue, revealing in their private correspondence the admirable qualities he attributes to his own female literary correspondents, who "wd. do Credit to their Sex, & to the Commonwealth of Letters, did not their Modesty with-hold them from appearing in it."[22] For Richardson, this style of fully detailed epistolary exchange also offers a formula for narrative realism that allows a multiplicity of voices to be heard. Although Richardson ultimately seeks political harmony and narrative closure, narrative realism, for him, lies not in a simplified final "convergence" but in the detail of different narrative viewpoints that must all be heard. Rather than a simple partisan Whig empiricism, Richardson envisions an empiricism of different moderate views coexisting in tolerant harmony. The exchange between Clarissa and Anna offers a model for this type of coexistence, while the parallel exchange of letters between Lovelace and Belford falls short of this ideal, because Belford shows himself capable of a humanized interaction and exchange that Lovelace can never achieve.

By contrast to Clarissa and Anna's exchanges, the epistolary conversation between Lovelace and Belford seems one-sided, with Lovelace in control, inattentive to the concerns that Belford expresses about Lovelace's intentions. Whereas Clarissa and Anna seem to respond to each other's concerns, Lovelace ignores and dismisses Belford's caution. This style of narrative control helps render Lovelace a manipulative Walpolian figure, a plotting "Pretender,"[23] a belated Tory rake from Restoration drama, or simply a dissolute Whig gentleman unable to assert civic and moral responsibility. It has also been suggested that Lovelace was modeled after Philip, duke of Wharton (1698–1731), whose dissolute behavior and conversion to Catholicism and the Jacobite cause disgraced the staunch Whig patriotism of his father, Thomas, marquis of Wharton.[24] Whether representing a wayward Whig peer or a tyrannical prime minister, Lovelace positions himself as a maligned monarch, justifying his tyranny because the "letters that pass between these ladies" are "of a treasonable nature"[25] (573); on the other hand, he describes himself as outside the legitimate political spectrum, obliged to make elaborate "plots" to achieve his goals of power. As oblivious to his own tyranny as was Mr. B. before his reformation, Lovelace seems either unconcerned or unaware that holding Clarissa captive makes him her oppressor. He refers to *her* as a "tyranness" and describes himself as totally in her power: "I am so totally hers" (575). This romanticized language of oppression prevents Lovelace from acknowledging the actual power relations between them, either in terms of Clarissa's liberty or of his usurpation of it.

Lovelace's furious plotting against the woman he claims to love renders him, like Mr. B. during the initial portions of *Pamela*, at times more a caricature of a narcissistic tyrant than a fully human character. Early in the narrative, in a letter addressed to the Harlowe family's servant "Honest" Joseph Leman, Lovelace attempts to bribe Joseph to help him abduct Clarissa. Here Lovelace demonstrates his primary motive throughout the novel: to have control over how Clarissa's story is narrated. Lovelace is plotting not merely Clarissa's abduction, but a complex set of markers to make it appear to her family that she left willingly; he promises Leman that by both enabling Clarissa to escape and then by (belatedly) informing the family of the event, he will get credit for loyalty where it is no longer due. As Lovelace declares while explaining his strategy of political spin to the man he is training in double dealing: "You see, honest Joseph, I am always contriving to give you reputation" (384). This letter, marked by Lovelace's own honest admission of tyranny and treachery, certainly portrays a realistically detail portrait of a scheming manipulator. However, as the narrative progresses, Richardson ultimately allows Lovelace fewer occasions to represent himself in his own words and more occasions to be depicted by Clarissa, Belford, and other concerned friends and relations.

In contrast to Jane Austen's later depiction of Fitzwilliam Darcy, who is at first depicted through Elizabeth's biased initial perception of him but becomes more humanized as he is gradually depicted through his perspective and own words,[26] Lovelace becomes dehumanized as other characters are given the power to characterize him. Although clearly in control of the narration of his own schemes in his letter to Leman, we already saw Clarissa being given control of the narrative's depiction of Lovelace in the previous letter: "it is plain to me now, by all his behaviour, that he had as great a confidence in my weakness, as I had in my own strength" (381). Clarissa sums up

Lovelace's calculated strategy for ruining her even more precisely than he himself does. The first few paragraphs of a letter Lovelace writes to Belford shortly after raping Clarissa are devoted in fact to his relating Clarissa's own description of him, as "guilty wretch!—abandoned man!" (899). Lovelace even scrupulously relates how she corrects herself: "*Man* did I say?—Yet what name else can I? since the mortal worryings of the fiercest beast would have been more natural, and infinitely more welcome, than what you have acted by me" (899). After describing how shaken he is by her "voice," Lovelace continues to cite Clarissa as her language becomes more and more overtly political. He quotes her as finally demanding, "Whether in a country of liberty as *this*, where the sovereign of it must not be guilty of *your* wickedness; and where *you* neither durst have attempted it, had I one friend or relation to look upon me, I am to be kept here a prisoner, to sustain fresh injuries?" (901). While Lovelace was once eloquent on his own behalf, after his crime he relies on Clarissa's language to characterize him, a language that increasingly depicts him as the static caricature of a tyrant.

Lovelace again cites Clarissa verbatim as she moves from abstract political principles to their specific application in their present situation: "*That the man who has been the villain to me you have been, shall never make me his wife*" (901). Although Lovelace attempts to undermine the veracity of her depiction of him by asking "Does she not show me that she can willfully deceive, as well as I?" (905), he has already ceded control of his own narrative to her depiction of it. As the narrative concludes, Lovelace's voice is diminished: the letters from Belford take on increasing importance in the narrative; Belford even reframes Lovelace's prior self-depiction when he pleads with Colonel Morden not to avenge Lovelace's crime (1442). Belford also takes on a role of editor, analyzing for Lovelace the implications of the latter's desire to "revoke" a previous letter, a letter that Belford ultimately returns to Lovelace with the warning that he must not "destroy it" since "[t]he same dialect may one day come in fashion with you again" (1434). Belford becomes humanized as he demonstrates his ability to exchange ideas rationally with the other characters and contribute to the "Commonwealth of Letters" that Richardson's epistolary narrative represents.[27] He and Colonel Morden enter that commonwealth of rational exchange and debate that serves as Richardson's model for realistic narration, as they themselves exchange their admiration for Clarissa and Anna's narrative exchange, one that Morden describes as based in a remarkable friendship, a friendship cemented in difference: "Both excelling in *different ways*, in which neither sought to emulate the other" (1450).

This depiction of Clarissa and Anna's friendship evokes an image of humanized characters in open narrative exchange with others in different situations and contexts. By contrast, Lovelace is diminished as a character because he cannot acknowledge any sort of familial or community-oriented responsibility for his actions—whether following a model of Tory or Jacobite paternalism or Whig power-sharing. Lovelace describes Clarissa holding "up to Heaven, in a speechless agony, the innocent [marriage] licence (which she has in her own power); as the poor distressed Catalans held up their English treaty" (887). He is thus shown as sufficiently intelligent to reference his own tyranny in political terms, but he somehow he cannot visualize himself as a politically active individual, but only as the caricature of a tyrant, not oblivious of but indifferent to the legitimate evidence of his own tyranny.

Clarissa, although perhaps too virtuous to feel "real" to all readers, nevertheless is humanized through her wide-ranging epistolary exchanges through which she distinguishes herself from familiar mid-eighteenth-century representations of femininity, including both partisan stereotypes and classical ideals. Clarissa's honorable and chaste virtue provides a sharp contrast to the unflattering depictions of Jacobite women in many misogynist anti-Jacobite tracts from the mid-1740s. Clarissa's example certainly counters the misogynist mid-century impulse, evident in Fielding's *The Jacobite's Journal* (1747–48), to label any woman who discusses politics at her tea tables as outlaw, or Jacobite. In returning to the heroic model of Lucretia from earlier tracts such as *Female Excellency* (1688) or *The Female Orators* (1714), Richardson offers a virtuous model for politically alert femininity that contrasts sharply with the popular anti-Jacobite depictions of Jenny Cameron as self-centered and amoral. Clarissa, like the heroines of Behn's tragic novellas, is also rendered real by her difference from a virtuous heroine of classical and neo-classical dramatic tragedy.

Rather than simply stabbing herself, as Lovelace fears she might do and as Lucretia did after mutely publicizing her violation, Clarissa allows herself to die gradually, as if willing her own slow physical disintegration while she readies the legal tenets of her last will and testament. In his appendix to *Sir Charles Grandison*, Richardson explains that "in scenes of life . . . in which a *variety of interesting characters* is introduced, all events cannot be decided, unless, as in the History of *Tom Thumb the Great*, all the actors are killed in the last scene."[28] Distinguishing his works from Fielding's farcical dramatic tragedy *The Tragedy of Tragedies; or, The Life and Death of Tom*

Thumb the Great (1730), Richardson suggests how his prose fiction might return tragedy to its traditional concerns with the public good. This is not to suggest that Fielding was unconcerned with the public good (towards which end his persistent critique of Walpole was certainly intended), but that Richardson's contribution to the emergent genre of the novel provides a different model of political commentary, through a different paradigm for publicizing tragedy.

While Lovelace repeatedly stresses that Clarissa should save herself the shame of his rape of her becoming known, she insists on publicizing in her own way what, according to the legend of Lucretia, has always been both a deeply personal and an essentially political offense. During the eighteenth century, rape was perceived as the violation of a husband's unique right to his wife. Thus, had Clarissa taken Lovelace to court, as Anna Howe at first suggests, the crime would presumably have been articulated as a crime against Clarissa's father. Clarissa makes her experience public in a different way: she talks of her experience quite candidly to the strangers from whom she rents a room during the last period of her life; she writes to Lovelace's female cousins, making public his actions. Anna Howe and Lovelace both argue that Clarissa should stop publicizing her rape and simply marry her rapist, thus camouflaging Lovelace's offense through a ceremony that would, under eighteenth-century British law, legally render the crime null. Lovelace proposes that the tragic ending on which Clarissa insists could be avoided through a containment of it into either domestic comedy or romance when he asks, "Is not *the Catastrophe of every Story that ends in Wedlock accounted happy*, be the difficulties in progress to it ever so great?" (944). Lovelace and Anna Howe both wish to transform the highly political tragedy of Lucretia into the domestic romance of *Pamela*. In so doing, however, they overlook the importance of making public a violation whose political resonance must be acknowledged. Although, of course, few subsequent novelists would go to the narrative length Richardson attempted to demonstrate his attempt at "full" disclosure, Richardson's contribution to the emerging belief that realistic narration should provide a "full" disclosure of human exchange and debate ultimately derives from his political belief in moderate, rational debate between *different* partisan positions.

Clarissa finally scripts her own tragic version of nascent novelistic realism against the grain of romance convention, using the form of tragedy (traditionally about crises in the nation state) to prevent the domestic containment of a romance ending. Thus, her insistence on making public the details of her oppression also reasserts Richardson's belief that the reform of political virtue will not take place until participants in the political sphere acknowledge the public and moral connection between their actions in domestic life and their ideals of political behavior, until, in other words, political debate returns to the domestic analogies that once structured its discourse. The epistolary exchange between Clarissa and Anna Howe returns these analogies to political debate, as a "realistic" corrective to the abstractions of high political theory. This debate also allows Richardson to articulate a politics of exchange and moderation that refutes the limitations of any extreme partisan position.

MORAL VIRTUE AND
MODERATION POLITICS

If *Clarissa* provides a pessimistic rejoinder to *Pamela*'s cautious optimism, then *The History of Sir Charles Grandison* (1753–54) offers a new paradigm for addressing the irrational violence that Richardson saw as threatening the stability of both the political public sphere and the domestic household. Richardson extends the style of narrative exchange between the rational women in *Clarissa* to the conversational and epistolary patterns of the male characters in *Grandison*. The endless fascination the characters have for reading and rereading each other's epistles parallels the advice offered by the narrative: tolerance and patience. As Sir Charles Grandison remarks to his sister, "how could patience be patience, if it were not tried?" (2:108). Grandison's commitment to solving every conflict by thorough patient discussion and epistolary exchange rather than verbal abuse or violence represents not only a stylistic achievement significant to the development of formal realism, but also a political rebuttal to the narrowness of standard partisan positions. This is not to say that the idealized Grandison necessarily always feels "real" to readers. Like Clarissa, he is also perhaps too good to be true. However, this utopian hero comes to life as a realistic character when he breaks away from traditional models of male virtue himself and prompts the women around him to likewise revise their traditional models of feminine behavior.

We gain insight into both Richardson's model of political virtue and his narrative style through the letter that Grandison writes when refusing to meet Harriet's abductor, Sir Hargrave Pollexfen, in a duel: "I write a long letter, because I propose *only* to write" (1:208). Grandison's standard mode of response to what he terms "the vulgar notions of honor" (1:208–09) is to write or converse at length, explaining his somewhat unconventional position until he is understood.

Grandison insists that Pollexfen should "think himself obliged for this not unfriendly expostulation" (1:208). Although Pollexfen cannot immediately respond in a like manner, Grandison will not rest until they have shared a meal together in a community of Pollexfen's friends. Pollexfen, always ready to respond with violence rather than thoughtful dialogue, is less a "fully developed" character than an emblem of narrow-minded partisan bias. It is precisely this propensity to partisan haste and violence in mid-eighteenth-century British culture that Richardson seeks to repair through his depiction of an unconventional hero, one who refuses the familiar tropes of masculine "heroism." By challenging Grandison to a duel, Pollexfen asserts their bond as members of the same social class, operating under presumably similar abstract principles of honor and public good; even if Grandison refuses to operate under the principles of dueling, he acknowledges that he understands Pollexfen's meaning when the latter insists: "I demand from you the satisfaction due to a gentleman" (1:207). Once Sir Charles has broken through Hargrave's competitive façade and won over the latter's friends, it requires little effort for them to interact cordially and for the original animosity to dissolve. Acting as a polite but persistently Socratic thorn in the side of dueling rakes, Grandison's influence helps reform Pollexfen's set of friends by first acknowledging their version of masculinity and then challenging them to revise it.

Grandison breaks the traditional mold of masculinity not only by his ability to win over men of his own rank but in his capacity to form platonic friendships with a variety of women. When the reader first encounters him, Grandison seems a hero straight out of seventeenth-century French romance—chastely saving the unknown heroine, without actually putting his own sword to use (but boldly snapping in half that of his opponent). Still following the behavior of a typical romance hero, Sir Charles is cautious about declaring his love for the woman he admires until he has proved himself. Proving himself in this case, however, will not require feats on the battlefield, but delicate verbal posturing. Not until the middle of the second long volume does Grandison ever declare his intentions, and even then he does not quite acknowledge them, but rather only alludes to his situation obliquely: "Honour forbids me!—Yet honour bids me—Yet I cannot be unjust, ungenerous—selfish!" (2:132). The caution Grandison demonstrates in deference to Clementina is also the caution demanded of a new type of "realistic" narrative in which real-life obstacles, such as the ambiguous situation of a former fiancée, must be acknowledged and patiently negotiated. The endless delay in the plot development, however, allows the bond between Harriet and Sir Charles to become one of confidence before either allows it to develop into passion. Before he is free to ask for her hand in marriage, Grandison asserts his right to her friendship: "As I am not conscious of being unworthy of your friendship, I will *suppose* it; and farther talk to you of all my affairs and engagements" (2:301). This grounding in platonic friendship should help ensure that when Charles and Harriet finally do wed, their relationship will more closely resemble the joint dominion that Tyrrell and Locke originally scripted in their political treatises rather than the asymmetrical bond between traditional romance hero and heroine. However, unlike previous Whig uses of the household analogy, in which the wife is elevated to joint sovereign but never encouraged to deploy her power, Richardson here seems to be taking seriously the ideal of shared dominion between husband and wife. As in his first two novels, Richardson here again offers the original domestic analogies of the social contract as realistic corrective to the abstractions of mid-eighteenth-century political theory and to the flattening conventions (in both political and romantic discourse) of gender difference.

In response to traditional alignments of masculine valor with physical prowess, Richardson defines a hero who refuses to fight a duel and who attempts to befriend every enemy. With women, Grandison is as open and honest as possible and expects complete honesty and as full disclosure as possible in return: after sharing hundreds of pages of his own letters to Dr. Bartlett with Harriet, he then asks to read her letters home in return. Having recast the standard vision of male friendship (by becoming friends with all the men who attempt his life) and recast the male–female bond as one of real rational friendship, Grandison further insists that women learn to treat each other differently under the bonds of female friendship. Asking his sisters to accept Harriet as their sister requires no effort on their parts; obliging them to treat their father's mistress in a just and respectful manner proves a harder trial, but one they eventually accept. Grandison's necessarily cautious behavior towards Harriet likewise obliges her to deviate from standard modes of interaction with other women. In the eighteenth century, it was generally considered immodest, even unfeminine, on a woman's part to declare a preference for a man before he had acknowledged a preference for her. However, Harriet chooses honesty and openness over excessive modesty as she acknowledges her feelings for Sir Charles to her own family, then to his sisters, and finally to Lady D., mother of Lord D., who wishes to court Harriet.

Although in his first two novels Richardson's female characters serve as models for moral political behavior and rational epistolary exchange and narration, in *Grandison*, the eponymous hero needs no instruction but serves as a model for everyone, both male and female, with whom he comes into contact. The honesty, openness, and patience Grandison practices in the public and political sphere, moreover, offers unexpected benefits in the moral and domestic sphere. Following Grandison's example, Harriet is able to be open and honest with Lady D. when the subject of her attachment to Sir Charles is broached. In acknowledging the difficult and "affecting" truth that Sir Charles has not yet proposed to her, but that nevertheless her heart is "*already* a wedded heart" (4:289), Harriet follows Charles's example of worrying less about conventional shame or embarrassment (she for being thought forward in acknowledging her love for Grandison, he for being thought cowardly in not responding to the challenge of a duel) than about causing as little disruption as possible to others. Lady D. gratefully acknowledges the heartache that Miss Byron has spared her son: "Had you had the least lurking inclination to coquetry, and could have taken pride in conquests, he might have been an undone man" (2:289). In setting an example for open, rational dealing between women, Richardson challenges traditional images of female rivalry, including the cunning with which women have traditionally been expected to outwit each other in their quiet maneuvers to snare a man. He thus links the narrative style of apparently "full" disclosure (or as close an image of it as could be managed in several thousand pages of letters) to new paradigms for both gender relations and politics.

In insisting on openness and honesty in all dealings with all people, Richardson challenges his readers to radically alter not only their view of domestic, interpersonal relations, but also their conception of national politics. Sir Charles's loyalty to the House of Hanover is made clear through his insistent Protestantism and his embarrassment in receiving congratulations while in Italy and France during Charles Edward Stuart's early successes in 1745. Beyond that, whether Grandison is Whig or Tory seems immaterial, because his manner of dealing with others is so open and tolerant that whatever partisan position he might hold, he would never make someone in another camp feel alienated. Grandison's example also suggests how open, honest dealings in personal affairs might provide political debate that pushes the boundaries of conventional partisan exchange.

By the morning of his wedding to Harriet, Sir Charles had already established himself so effectively as "The Domestic man, The chearful

Friend, The kind Master, The enlivening Companion, The polite Neighbour, The tender Husband" that his wife-to-be insists that his life is living proof that "the private station" is "that of true happiness" (3:281). His skills in the "private" sphere (a sphere that includes multiple "beneficent schemes" (3:438) for his tenants and neighbors) have naturally drawn the attention of "some gentlemen of prime consideration in the county" who would support him in the next election (3:439). However, the same modesty, openness, and tolerance that govern his affairs in the "private" realm make him wary of the narrow partisan interests demanded by the political sphere. As he explains to his neighbors, "We young men . . . are apt to be warm: When we have not studied a point thoroughly, we act upon hasty conclusions, and sometimes support, sometimes oppose on insufficient grounds. I would not be under *Engagements* to any party"(3:439). The openness on which Grandison has insisted in his interactions with every other character in the novel may here be linked to an open tolerance of a range of political views, rather than to a narrow bias toward one party. We may understand such attempts at full disclosure as not merely the detail of prescriptive Whig empiricism, but an empiricism through which Richardson attempts to embrace a range of moderate political views.

Sir Charles's cautious interest in politics, following the "natural" interests of his birth, aligns him with a moderate mid-century Whig or Tory political position. In marrying the English (Protestant) Harriet Byron rather than the Italian (Catholic) Clementina, Sir Charles also sets an example for the exiled Stuart claimants to the throne, who continued to marry foreign-born Catholics. In this light, Grandison might be read as "a corrective and hopeful image (if from the Never-Never Land of speculation) of what the true Tory Prince should look like," as Margaret Anne Doody observes.[29] On the other hand, despite his cautious prudence, Sir Charles also challenges certain familiar discursive models for political behavior. Unlike the abstracted mid-eighteenth-century versions of the social contract articulated by such moderate Tories as David Hume and Henry Bolingbroke, Richardson insists upon the moral and political centrality of the household. The central point made by Richardson's lengthy narrative is that no man should consider entering politics until he has mastered the art of being a virtuous son, brother, husband, and neighbor. In other words, virtuous behavior in one's "private" life must provide the pattern for political action capable of moving beyond partisan squabbling. The rational platonic friendship that develops between Harriet and Charles before their marriage is consistent with the Lockean scenario of joint dominion in the household once associated with the Whig cause, which Grandison returns to the abstract mid-eighteenth-century discourses of high politics. In so doing, Sir Charles also refutes misogynistic images of women from partisan propaganda. For example, his respectful treatment of Clementina (likely named for Clementina, James Edward Stuart's Polish wife, who spent her last years in a nunnery)[30] serves as a corrective to the unflattering images of Jenny Cameron so familiar to the 1740s reading public. Richardson also refigures women's role in politics: rather than the apolitical tea-drinkers of Fielding's *The Jacobite's Journal*, Richardson's female characters (Harriet, Charles's sisters, Emily, Lady D., and eventually Clementina) serve as honest and rational advisers and managers to each other and to those around them.

In rewriting traditional scenarios of friendship between men, between women, and between men and women, Richardson is supporting a moderate political stance, one somewhere between Whig and Tory, but tolerant of other partisan positions. His novels thus respond to the quagmire of partisan name-calling, which intensified during and after the Jacobite rising of 1745, by offering a more fundamental conception of politics—one that reminds citizens of their simultaneous moral responsibilities in both the domestic and the political spheres. This conception of political responsibility is, moreover, connected to an ideal of narrative responsibility, demonstrated by a novel in which the most fully developed characters themselves come to demand as much "transparency" as possible in their letters and conversation because they see it as indispensable to moral political and social interactions. Richardson's lengthy narrative attempts at the "full" disclosure we now associate with formal realism thus represent a response to partisan political debates. This focus on transparency, however, ultimately portrays a moralizing and humanizing image of life itself, easily understood as apolitical.

Richardson's novels thus help us understand how by the mid- to late eighteenth century a genre that emerged within the crucible of partisan conflict would come to be viewed in the humanizing contexts of domestic morality and individualist psychology. In much the same way, Eliza Haywood's approach to narrative realism derives from her own partisan engagement with the political discourses of her day. Haywood, like Richardson, would be also judged (albeit more harshly) in moral terms, although her partisan sympathies would ultimately confound critics who insisted on viewing her increasingly sophisticated studies of Jacobite character development as merely apolitical romance.

CHAPTER 5

Jacobite Ideology and Eliza Haywood's Response to Whig Realism

Although an immensely popular author in her own time and a remarkably inventive narrative stylist who helped shape novelistic writing throughout the eighteenth century,[1] Eliza Haywood (c. 1693–1756) fell from favor in the nineteenth century, in part because her works were judged licentious.[2] Her early twentieth-century biographer only contributed to her fallen reputation by conflating the scandalous romances of her early writings with the story of her own life.[3] The perception of her as a writer of licentious romance ultimately helped to define her as both apolitical and unimportant to the development of the "realistic" novel. In order to correct both of these common misapprehensions of Haywood's work, I believe that we must understand the specific political discourses that shaped the Tory and Jacobite versions of realism that she authored.

Traditional Whig histories of realism generally presume a tacit connection between anti-Jacobite politics and realistic narrative. As Margaret Anne Doody has pointed out, in *The Female Quixote* (1752) Charlotte Lennox stages not only the suppression of romance conventions but also the simultaneous suppression of the romantic myths of the Jacobite cause.[4] By dramatizing the heroine's recovery from the delusions of romance, *The Female Quixote* calls our attention to the narrative sway of different competing partisan realisms even as it demonstrates the apparent inevitability of their subordination to a prescriptive realism consistent with the discourses of mid-eighteenth-century Whig or anti-Jacobite Tory politics. Haywood's final novel, *The History of Jemmy and Jenny Jessamy* (1753), which appeared the year after *The Female Quixote*, may be read as a response to Lennox's acceptance of Whig prescriptive realism. Moreover, as this chapter demonstrates, Haywood's contributions to the development of narrative realism across her career derive from the way she recasts Whig versions of selfhood and virtue into differently "realistic" Tory and Jacobite versions.

Having published her first novel in 1719, the year Defoe published *Robinson Crusoe*, and her last novel in 1753, the year Richardson's *Sir Charles Grandison* appeared, Eliza Haywood was still considered important enough that three decades after her death two of her novels were included in the twenty-three-volume collection *The Novelist's Magazine* (1780–89). She had fallen from favor somewhat by the early nineteenth century: in the introduction to her canon-shaping fifty-volume edition *The British Novelists* (1810), Anna Barbauld describes Haywood's mature novels in complimentary terms, but she does not include any of Haywood's works in that edition. By the early twentieth century, scholars generally dismissed Haywood's work as licentious, apolitical, and unimportant to the formal evolution of the British novel.[5] Recent criticism has moved into new directions by analyzing Haywood's work in terms of gender politics, party politics, and mercantilist policy.[6] However, whereas a novelist such as Fielding has been taken seriously by scholars in part because of his political interests, the political interventions of female writers from Behn to Haywood have frequently been seen as unrelated to their literary accomplishments. Haywood's centrality to the development of the British novel cannot be understood, I argue, until the link between her partisan position and her significant contributions to the formal techniques of narrative realism is understood.

One reason why Haywood's pro-Stuart sympathies have been overlooked may be that in attempting to rescript the partisan tropes used to define Jacobitism, she replaces the usual references to factionalism, cabal, and intrigue with the romantic discourses of honor, loyalty, and devotion. Her glowing descriptions of pro-Stuart loyalists might be unrecognizable (and so perhaps seem "unrealistic") to scholars accustomed to Whig depictions of Jacobites as monstrous, sexually promiscuous zealots. It is also the case that Haywood's Jacobitism took on different manifestations over the three-and-a-half decades of her career as a professional writer, from 1719 to 1756. After James Edward Stuart's embarrassing estrangement from his wife in the mid 1720s, many otherwise loyal Jacobites lost patience with him.[7] Not surprisingly, Haywood's novels from the 1720s evince a political ideology consistent with loyalty, chivalry, and respect for authority, although she makes few specific references to Stuart leaders or Jacobite heroes. Her novel *The Adventures of Eovaai, Princess of Ijaveo*

(1736) offers an unmistakable critique of Walpole, and although the work offers little overt evidence of a preference for the Stuarts, it nevertheless deploys romantic images typical of Jacobite mythology as an antidote to what Haywood obviously perceived as the dangerous illusions of Walpole's regime. Thus we must understand her continued deployment of certain romance conventions during the 1740s and 1750s as part of her continued support for the Stuart cause, rather than as an aesthetic inability to move beyond the genre of romance.[8]

Only in the 1740s, when it had become clear to Jacobite supporters that they might pin their hopes on Charles Edward Stuart, did Haywood take a more direct approach to pro-Stuart propaganda. The protagonist of *The Fortunate Foundlings* (1744), a politically resonant novel in which James Edward Stuart actually appears as a character, demonstrates his courage by joining the cause of the exiled Stuarts; Horatio's example then serves as a model for other characters in the novel. Haywood's short-lived periodical *The Parrot* (1746) provides a scathing critique of the severe punishment exacted against the leaders of the 1745 rising.[9] Although most scholars have assumed that Haywood turned away from political writing after her 1749 arrest, *The History of Jemmy and Jenny Jessamy* (1753), whose very title reveals a connection to the exiled hero of Jacobite ballads, further elaborates Haywood's paradigm for pro-Stuart loyalty. Moreover, Haywood's political sympathies are also evident in the conduct books that she wrote during the last years of her life, *The Wife* (1755) and *The Husband* (1756).[10]

In her conduct books, her political journalism, and her several dozen novels and novellas, Haywood tirelessly refigures the standard political stereotypes of her day. Like Behn and Defoe, Haywood interrogates the standard Whig versions of the abstract political individual.[11] Like Richardson, Haywood explores the conundrum of male political virtue, although she explicitly rejects the cautious, moderation politics of either Mr. B. or Sir Charles Grandison. Haywood's true heroes— few and far between in an oeuvre in which ambitious mercenary scoundrels far outnumber admirable men—are bolder, and more explicitly partisan, than Grandison.

This chapter begins with an analysis of Haywood's lengthy pro-Jacobite pamphlet *A Letter . . . to a Particular Friend* (1750), a work of partisan propaganda whose complex narrative frame and nuanced depiction of characters demonstrate the strong interconnections between political and novelistic discourse in Haywood's writing. The next sections of this chapter trace the techniques of character development and narrative voicing that Haywood used to assert her own partisan vision of reality in her early Tory fiction, in her anti-Walpole satire, and in her mature Jacobite novels. The real scandal of Haywood's work, I argue, was caused less by the sexual licentiousness of her early fiction than by her challenge to the increasingly dominant conventions of novelistic Whig realism.

JACOBITE IDEOLOGY AND
NARRATIVE REALISM

The increasing formal sophistication of the eighteenth-century novel depended not only on the development of "realistic" characters in the main plot but also on the increasing complexity of narrative voicing and point of view, which are in turn linked to the reader's perception of the narrator as a fully developed character. Fielding has long been commended for the authority and irony of his novelistic narrators, while Eliza Haywood has traditionally been dismissed as merely writing formulaic fiction. As Andrea Austin has pointed out, however, "parodic works by women are often unrecognized or misread," and Haywood's capacity for both parody and irony has generally gone unnoticed by modern scholars.[12] Following Austin's lead, I propose that we can understand Haywood's contributions to novelistic realism only when we understand her sophisticated and ironic narrative voicing. This technique is evident in a work of Jacobite political propaganda, published in late 1749, for which Haywood was taken into custody for seditious libel, entitled *A Letter From H----G----g, Esq.; One of the Gentlemen of the Bed Chamber to the Young Chevalier, and the only Person of his own Retinue that attended him from Avignon, in his late Journey through Germany, and elsewhere; Containing Many remarkable and affecting Occurrences which happened to the P——during the Course of his mysterious Progress. To a Particular Friend.*

In *A Letter*, Haywood reveals neither the name of the friend to whom this H----G----g (believed to be the Jacobite conspirator Henry Goring)[13] is writing, nor her own relationship to Goring or his friend. She explains in the preface that she received the letter only as a mistake, because her own name differed by just a single consonant from that of the intended recipient, who had recently left the lodging where she is now staying. The conundrum of the intended recipient's name seems more a distraction than a clue, a narrative diversion intended to reinforce the fact that Haywood is not going to let us know who her narrative persona represents or for whom the letter was intended. However, the examiner presumably would care less about the intended recipient's identity than that of the actual recipient,

Haywood's own editorial persona, who in the preface takes note of her perceived duty to "gratify the Curiosity of the Town, which I observe has been raised pretty high on account of that adventrous Wanderer."[14] Whether or not in 1751, six years after the failure of the 1745 rising, the British population cared anything about the whereabouts of Charles Edward Stuart, Haywood seemed determined that it should. She expresses concern about publishing something that "was wrote only to oblige a much trusted and valued Friend, and never intended for the Press" (iii), but she finally decides that the "Regard owing from me to the *Publick* . . . [is] overbalanced by the Fears of displeasing any particular Gentleman, especially one who is known to me only by Name and Character, and whom it is not likely I shall ever be better acquainted with" (iv). The text itself addresses "a Particular Friend" and focuses on the problem of discerning which friends Charles Edward Stuart can trust with his secrets and which he cannot; Haywood thereby indicates that the narrator is *not* a friend of "the P——" and not likely to become better acquainted with him, but will spread his secrets. Thus camouflaged as someone who would serve the public good by revealing the whereabouts of Charles Edward Stuart after his exile from France, Haywood offers not useful geographical details but a sequence of anecdotes that reveal the courage, royal demeanor, and self-restraint of her hero. She thus satisfies the "regard" (or friendship) she believes she owes to the "Publick" by putting a positive spin on the "Young Chevalier." Moreover, in so doing, Haywood helps to develop a style of ironic narration important to the development of eighteenth-century narrative realism.

Whether he is displaying good manners and deference to invited guests, or virtuously saving an attractive young neighbor from a fire without attempting to ravish her, the "Young Chevalier" portrayed by H. G.'s letter demonstrates "Constancy of Mind, and the absolute Command he has over all his Passions" (18), traits that belie standard anti-Stuart propaganda in which Jacobites are hot-blooded and reckless. In refuting these stereotypes, Haywood focuses on Charles Edward Stuart's chivalrous restraint. Explaining why he did not take advantage of the young woman, Stuart sounds like a hero of romance, insisting on his virility, without denying his desire to protect the vulnerable:

> *I am no Stoick*, answered the P——, *but I have always been taught that Pleasures, how* pardonable *soever they may be in themselves, become* highly criminal *when indulged to the Prejudice of another . . . It would have been an Action unworthy of my real Character, under a feigned Name, to rob her of her Innocence;—to ruin, and then to abandon her for ever.* (25)

Whereas this passage may seem to describe a merely conventional romance hero rather than a more particularized character, one quality associated with the exiled Stuarts in eighteenth-century mythology was their inherent recognizability even when disguised, as Deidre Lynch has noted.[15] Charles Edward Stuart's reference to his "real Character" thus conveys a short-hand reminder (especially for his loyal followers) of his integrity and humanity; in political terms, this passing comment renders him more "real" (and, for those paying attention, more clearly the "real sovereign") than might a more detailed description.

To the extent that by 1750 Jacobite supporters had lost faith in the viability of their cause and lost interest in the whereabouts of their leader, Haywood's *A Letter* seems designed to publicize the possibility of another Jacobite landing on British soil even as it delineates Charles Edward Stuart's fitness for the task of governing. In Goring's account, "the P——" shows himself to be a master of philosophic asceticism. When faced with a delay in his plans to board a certain ship (we are not told his intended destination but are left to wonder whether it might be Scotland), he passes his time tranquilly by reading, an activity often associated with a depth of "true feeling" in novelistic protagonists. Goring does not provide specific, strategic details of Charles Edward Stuart's plans, but merely notes that the delay in getting the ship ready "threatened the Ruin of an Affair, which I will venture to inform you was of the most Importance he had ever been engaged in, since his glorious, though unfortunate Expedition into *Scotland*" (37). As we come to realize, the most important confidence that Goring conveys to his "particular friend" consists not in the details of this failed launch, but in the idea that another crossing to Scotland is possible. While waiting for repairs to his ship, the Stuart hero reads works of political philosophy, citing truisms about ruling sovereigns, such as "*the Dignity they enjoy is not given for their own Sakes, but that of others*" (38). Merging a traditional Jacobite respect for a monarch's dignity with a moderate mid-century Tory appropriation of the term "public good," the words that Goring ascribes to "the P——" echo Bolingbroke's vision of a patriot king, except that in this case the king most fitted to the role is from the House of Stuart, not the House of Hanover.

Having already admitted to breaking the seal of a letter addressed to someone else, the narrator then develops a short treatise on the nature of confidence itself. According to Haywood's *A Letter*, H. G. becomes sole confidant to "the P——" because, as the latter explains:

I have found that of late, not only what I do, but even the very Words I speak, have been reported through all the Courts in Europe, to the great

Detriment of my Affairs . . . As a Matter of the utmost important Nature is now upon the Tapis, I am determined not to be betrayed in it, or to know at least by whom I am so.—— I shall therefore confide but in one Person, and that one shall be you. (9)

Charles Edward Stuart's unexpected confidence in Goring moves the latter to observe: "I was perfectly confounded at so unlooked for, so unhoped for a Condescension——I threw myself at his Feet, I embraced him and kissed the Hand, which he graciously stretched out to raise me, with the most unfeigned and warmest Transports of a duteous Love, Loyalty and Gratitude, but could find no Words suitable to express my Thanks" (9). Against a political paradigm of friendship between abstract subjects whose supposedly universal humanism belies their particular status as Whigs or anti-Jacobite Tories,[16] Haywood reasserts a romantic notion of chivalric friendship between loyal adherents to a political cause that is excluded from the abstract "universals" of Whig political discourse.

Haywood is careful to avoid associating the Jacobite cause with any hint of irrationality or partisan fervor, the terms through which Jacobitism had so long been dismissed as mere factionalism. Charles Edward Stuart's political principles, as H. G. describes them, echo the rational abstractions of the hegemonic anti-Jacobite discourses of the day. Although not going so far as to use the language of "liberty," Haywood's hero adopts the dominant discourses against tyranny by insisting that he could not engage in any tyrannical action: "*I would not,* said he, *presume too far on the Strength of my own Resolution, but I think it is not in my Nature, either to do, or to permit to be done, any Thing oppressive or unjust, even to the meanest Subject*" (38). This assurance against tyranny relies neither on Whig discourses of "liberty" nor on Hume's or Bolingbroke's more cautious Tory version of the social contract, but on a Jacobite faith in the natural goodness of the individual monarch to guarantee not universal liberty to a hypothetical fraternity of abstract individuals, but universal protection to dependent subjects with a range of contingent needs.

Haywood's image of Jacobitism, unlike the dominant image of it in mid-eighteenth-century political writings, is a Jacobitism not of sedition or rebellion but of quiet conviction and patience. Daniel Szechi has described a strain of what he terms "cosmic" Jacobitism which relied on an optimistic faith that God supported the Stuart cause—and that no matter how many trials divine providence put its supporters through, the cause would triumph when God was ready.[17] Haywood certainly shared the patient forbearance of this Jacobitism, and *A Letter* functions as propaganda that might assist divine providence in helping the Stuarts. Haywood's main objective in this work seems to be to convince the British populace that the "Young Chevalier" would never seek to impose his rule on an unwilling populace. According to Haywood's account, when reminded that should he fail to marry and produce an heir, the next in line to the Stuart throne would be the king of Sardinia, Charles Edward Stuart acknowledges the pointlessness of seeking a Stuart restoration against popular resistance, even as he compliments the British valor and courage that helped defeat previous Jacobite efforts: "*I will never believe that the People of* England, *who have so vigorously opposed all the Efforts, both of my* R——Father *and myself, in Support of the Family they have made Choice of to reign over them, will be less warm in repelling an Invasion of any other Claimant whatsoever*" (47).

Although Goring often seems to emphasize Charles Edward Stuart's military valor, he also simultaneously downplays the risk that blood will be spilt again. The "Young Chevalier" admits that he knows he would fail without popular support; he then suggests that he would make a future attempt for the throne only if he is confident of the support of a majority of the English population:

> *And if the Bulk of the Nation, that is, the Nobility and Gentry, whose Example influences the Nation, should grow desirous of a Change, and be ready to repeal what they have done, I am not so old as to despair enjoying in my own Person the Fruits of such a Change, to which the Success of my present Enterprise can be no Manner of Impediment.* (47)

This passage suggests that Charles Edward Stuart's current strategy, or at least Haywood's version of it, is to wait for the British populace to request his return before making another attempt on the throne. This text here also suggests a segue between Stuart's ostensible political plans and his romantic agenda. The "present enterprise" to which he refers seems not to be an attempt on the throne, despite the allusions to the 1745 rising, but a possible engagement to a Polish princess.

Although standard historical sources suggest that Charles Edward Stuart was not seriously considering an alliance with Poland,[18] Haywood may have believed he was or wished that he were considering this marriage proposal. Through H. G.'s supposedly confidential letter, Haywood apparently attempts to dispel any misinterpretation of the "Young Chevalier" 's sexual preferences that may have arisen because of his reputed "Disinclination to Marriage" by assuring her readers that "he loves, and is beloved . . . by a Princess of the highest and most pure Descent" (45). Reinforcing the overlap between amorous virility and political prowess, Goring plays on the double meanings of the word "affair," assuring his "Particular Friend" that "the grand Affair, in which he is now Engaged . . . is not of that Kind which you and many of his Friends have all along believed" (48), that is, another military invasion. Goring insists, rather, that Stuart is "entertaining other Views" for the moment, which "are not inconsistent with it [his future political goals] nor beneath the dignity of his birth" (48). Goring also attempts to convince the recipient of his letter that in contrast to the extravagance for which the House of Hanover was known, Charles Edward Stuart would not waste his followers' energy and resources without a purpose. Goring asserts that "the P——took not such fatiguing Journeys . . . merely to amuse the World, or . . . for any other of those mean and frivolous Views which his Enemies would have believed, but for Ends truly noble and worthy of himself" (48), that is, worthy of his royal pretensions. Through this style of telling by not telling—of communicating political loyalty through a subtle form of ellipsis—Haywood (though H. G.'s epistolary narrative) offers a new style of narration that connects readers to her version of "reality" (and to the authenticity of Charles Edward Stuart's desire to rule if called upon) through acts of concealment rather than through claims of transparency.

Publishing this hagiographic account, with its coyly concealed statements of support for "the P——," represents a daringly open act of public support for the Jacobite cause and one that ultimately caused Haywood, her maid servant, and five booksellers to be examined by a state officer between December 1749 and January 1750. The final extratextual irony surrounding a text about loyalty and disguise in political discourse is that neither Haywood nor her maid, Hannah Streddon, ever signed their testimonies defending themselves against the charges of seditious libel.[19] In their unsigned statements, both Haywood and Streddon deny any knowledge of the authorship of *A Letter*, and Haywood even goes so far as to suggest that although she has been an author for many years, she has never written anything "in a political way."[20] Like the editorial persona in her preface, who breaks a small confidence (by opening a letter from H. G. addressed not to her, but to his "Particular Friend") in order to keep a larger one (her loyalty to the Jacobite cause), Haywood denies the truth of her political loyalty in the course of being examined, but will not deny on paper a fidelity that is evident in many of her published works.

In contrast to the "Prescriptive Realism"—the "fidelity to a very close physical and social reality"—that Doody associates with the influence of "Whig mercantilism,"[21] Haywood establishes a sophisticated approach to narrative realism that involves depicting less rather than more detail, and hinting at truths that she intentionally keeps obscured. Haywood is clearly working against the Whig Enlightenment ideal of apparently objective, empirical depiction of evidence so visible in the ideal of "transparency" or "full" disclosure promoted in Richardson's novels. The complex narrative layering in *A Letter . . . to a Particular Friend* suggests a very different ideal of realism, one that was frequently illegible to subsequent critics who dismissed her works as "romance" and then did not discern her technical innovations.

An obviously Tory perspective is evident in Haywood's earliest novels, which are also her least developed stylistically. Her anti-Walpolian but not necessarily pro-Jacobite *Eovaai*, which I examine in the next section, demonstrates how political caution shapes the complexity of her narrative framing. As her political views become more obviously Jacobite during the 1740s and 1750s, her novels also develop in complexity. In *The Fortunate Foundlings* (1744) and *The History of Jemmy and Jenny Jessamy* (1753), which I examine in the last two sections of this chapter, Haywood reveals a covert political agenda, one that dares not speak its name directly, but will shape and structure her subtle narrative positioning as well as her insistent depiction of Jacobite virtue, both male and female, as a normative model for "realistic" character.

TORY POLITICS AND PATERNALISM IN HAYWOOD'S EARLY FICTION

Haywood's vision of Tory virtue has been described a "collusive resistance" between heroines and their lovers.[22] According to this paradigm, Tory agency is more covert and more complex than Whig individualism, especially when scripted through the guise of female desire. At an even more basic level, I argue, we may recognize Haywood's critique of Whig individualism simply through her depictions of the power struggles between daughters and fathers. In *Idalia: or, the Unfortunate Mistress* (1723), for example, Haywood describes the major character flaw of her eponymous heroine: "The Greatness of her Spirit (which from her Childhood had been untameable, or was render'd so thro the too great Indulgence of her doating Parents) made her unable to endure Controll, disdainful of Advice, and peremptory in following her own *Will*."[23] Haywood bluntly predicts the inevitable conclusion of this personality trait: "The Consequence of such a Disposition could not be expected to be very fortunate" (3).

She later describes the unfortunate, but unsurprising, results of Idalia's coquetry: "In the midst of Shrieks and Tremblings, Cries, Curses, Swoonings, the impatient *Ferdinand* perpetrated his Intent, and finished her undoing" (17).

The explicitness of Haywood's moral warnings in her 1720s fiction might have seemed licentious to nineteenth-century critics, compared, say, with Jane Austen's more elliptical references to Lydia Bennet's elopement in *Pride and Prejudice* (1813). Yet the major force of Haywood's moralizing seems directed less against premarital sex (although she describes its harsh material consequences in no uncertain terms) than against what she would view as the Whig character flaw of self-will. Following the model of Idalia, the eponymous heroine of *Lasselia: or the Self-Abandon'd* (1723) makes a sequence of predictable mistakes after her parents' deaths because her guardian aunt "gave her so much the liberty of acting as she pleas'd."[24] The heroine of *The Rash Resolve: or, the Untimely Discovery* (1724) also succumbs to what Haywood describes as "the only Fault she was guilty of . . . Self-Will."[25] One of the two heroines of *The British Recluse: or, The Secret History of Cleomira* (1722) succumbs to Bellamy's charms because a neighbor convinces her that her widowed mother does her the "Injustice" of curtailing her "belov'd Liberty";[26] the other falls prey to his charms only after the death of her father, as otherwise "*Obedience* to him" (126) would have ensured that she marry the aptly named Worthy.

In all of Haywood's novels, obedience to parents is shown as essential to happiness. If parents and children at first disagree, Haywood insists that children somehow gain parental approval before pursuing any serious course of action, and especially before marrying. In Haywood's novels from the 1720s, heroines (and anti-heroines) who have been abandoned or orphaned by their actual father or else who rush into a marriage against his wishes typically suffer a variety of dreadful scenarios. The two heroines of *The British Recluse* are obliged to take refuge in their joint anguish over being jilted by the same man; however, by allowing them to live tranquilly together, rather than dying from grief or shame, Haywood offers a new model for tragic heroines. The heroine of *Lasselia* ends her life in a convent; the protagonist of *Idalia* is left ruined and unmarried. The heroine of *The Mercenary Lover* (1726) ends up murdered by the brother-in-law who impregnated her. The eponymous heroine of *Cleomilia: or, The Generous Mistress* (1726) is caught between love for one man and a secret marriage to another, as are the heroines of *The Life of Madame de Villesache* (1727) and *Dalinda: or, The Double Marriage* (1749).

An overly willful heroine might also end up dead from grief and shame, as in *The Secret History of the Present Intrigues of the Court of Caramania* (1727), or murdered by her estranged husband, as in *Madame de Villesache*. The other model Haywood offers to avoid filial disobedience is for children to persuade their parents to change their minds, as occurs in her translation of *The Disguis'd Prince: or, The Beautiful Parisian* (1728). In her final novel, *The History of Jemmy and Jenny Jessamy* (1753), Haywood circumvents the problem of filial disobedience by having the wishes of hero and heroine felicitously concur with the wishes of both of their parents.

In the plots of her early novels, Haywood also makes a subtle but crucial distinction between real and inauthentic paternity. Daughters who are most at risk are either those without proper guardianship, as is the case of the joint heiresses in *The Mercenary Lover*, or those who are left under the improper, even tyrannical dominion of a mercenary uncle, as in *The Distress'd Orphan; or, Love in a Madhouse* (1726) or of a mercenary grandmother, as in *Dalinda*. Actual paternity, obviously politically resonant to those who would have preferred an uninterrupted line of Stuart monarchs, is usually represented by fathers such as Bonnin in *The Disguis'd Prince* or Dorilaus in *The Fortunate Foundlings* (1744), who are capable of recognizing and then correcting an earlier mistake.

As is evident in this brief survey of plots, Haywood's overall message about obedience to authority does not change dramatically across her career. Her novels demonstrate a Tory position throughout, and her works from the 1740s and 1750s reveal a distinctly Jacobite ideology. Moreover, the increasing subtlety in her narrative technique seems to derive from her increasingly pointed support for the exiled Stuarts. Her early works privilege a Tory over a Whig version of selfhood, but the novels are short and both her characters and her narrators are less developed than in her later works. In *The Disguis'd Prince*, for example, no allusions are made to any of the exiled Stuarts, but the heroine manages through deference, obedience, and patience to persuade her father to accept her marital choice. Not surprisingly, these are exactly the same qualities that Haywood will recommend to Jacobite supporters two decades later in *A Letter . . . to a Particular Friend*. The *Disguis'd Prince* is a simple moral tale, whose message about Tory virtue is self-evident, and whose narration is straightforward. By contrast, in *A Letter*, Haywood is obliged to create a complex interlocking narrative, with several ambiguous narrative personae and a protagonist who must demonstrate his authenticity despite his disguise. Haywood's prose thus develop increasing narrative sophistication as her political agenda, however covertly expressed, becomes more explicit.

The Adventures of Eovaai, Princess of Ijaveo (1736), her most direct satire of a political figure, marks Haywood's first experimentation with a complexly layered set of narrative personae. Although pointedly anti-Walpole, the text does not necessarily indicate support for the exiled Stuarts, but suggests a sympathy for Frederick, prince of Wales (George II's eldest son), in whose honor Haywood had written the play *Frederick, Duke of Brunswick-Lunenburgh* (1729).[27] The story itself reverses the standard representation of Jacobites as under the spell of romantic delusion by casting Ochihatou, the Walpolian villain, in the role of magician. This "*Pre-Adamitical* History," which ostensibly takes place in the Year 13799, according to native chronology (or 4237 by European record-keeping), provides a rich political debate, made more complicated by the editorial comments of the anonymous translator and the footnotes describing arguments about the text by earlier commentators.[28] For example, King Eojaeu reminds his daughter before he dies that "you are no less bound by *Laws*, than the meanest of your Subjects" (4), thus voicing a standard mid-eighteenth-century Whig political position. However, he modifies the Whig position even as he offers it, changing the familiar Whig motto *Vox Populi est Vox Dei* into the more cautious recommendation: "the publick *Opinion* ought to have some weight" (5). Later, when visiting the commonwealth of Akbar, the young princess finds herself thinking that "if she were not a Convert to all the Republican Principles, she at least thought some of them so highly reasonable, that she resolved, if she was ever happy enough to regain her Crown, she wou'd make them Part of the Constitution" (127).

The "translator" of this pseudo-Oriental tale observes in a footnote that "Liberty" may be the true translation of the word "Akbar," the ruling light of the republican nation Eovaai visits. However, Haywood's "translator" refuses to rule definitively on the meaning of the word because she claims to be "a Stranger . . . and in a Place where Monarchical Government is established" (107). The political import of this coy self-representation, however, is undercut when, after the princess's meditation on republican principles, the narrator (not the translator) exclaims, "How fluctuating is Human Nature! How variable its Inclinations! How little able to withstand the Force of Persuasion and Example!" (127). The narrator's mocking tone undermines the seriousness we can accord to Eovaai's momentary fascination with republican principles. We thus observe a fascinating interplay between translator and narrator, similar to the ironic narrative play effected by the supposed recipient of *A Letter . . . to a Particular Friend*. The action and plot provide yet a third layer of commentary: the resolution of two monarchies equitably "united" through marriage defies the standard anti-Jacobite vision of foreign domination that a Stuart restoration would supposedly necessitate. Haywood's model of narrative interplay derives from a conversational exchange of ideas and viewpoints rather than a dominant single view. Although the novel is not necessarily pro-Stuart, the multiple narrative viewpoints are consistent with what Murray Pittock describes as the "limited common purpose" sought by those who envisioned a "Jacobite Britain of multiple kingdoms."[29]

Princess Eovaai escapes the clutches of the tyrannical prime minister and finds some respite in exile outside the country, much like the exiled Stuart claimants to the throne; she manages to win her kingdom back only with the heroic intervention of Adelhu, king of neighboring Hypotofa. Haywood's narrator describes the kingdoms, once united after Eovaai and Adelhu's marriage, as "the most powerful, most opulent, and most happy Monarchies in the World" (224). Haywood crafts her own version of a chivalrous romance ending—Adelhu's heroic prevention of Ochihatou's rape of Eovaai—as antidote against the deceptively romantic spells of enchantment with which Ochihatou had ensnared Eovaai and the kingdom. Although by the 1730s the Jacobite cause would have been viewed by many as a romantic fable, Haywood here shows how the domineering Whig politics of Robert Walpole represent a further departure from reality, rather than a more realistic representation of it.

Like most of Haywood's novels from the 1720s, *Eovaai* depicts undeveloped characters who are either wholly good (Eovaai, her father, and her eventual husband) or wholly evil (Ochihatou), and yet we also discern the development of sophisticated layers of narrative personae, in the guise of an ancient author, subsequent commentators, and a recent translator. Haywood would appear on stage in Fielding's 1737 production of *The Historical Register for the Year 1736* (the far-cical anti-Walpole production that ultimately prompted passage of the Licensing Act), yet by having written *Eovaai* the previous year, she had already initiated the transition Fielding would soon make from providing partisan commentary on the stage to embedding it in a comic epic in prose. Whereas Fielding refuted the conventions of romance by including parodic stereotypes of Jacobite figures in his novels and so helping to establish anti-Jacobitism as part of the normative political discourses of novelistic realism, Haywood, in her mature fiction from the 1740s and 1750s, converted romance conventions into a narrative realism defined by an increasingly explicit, although always veiled, support for the Jacobite cause.

Models of Virtue in Haywood's Mature Fiction

Just as she refuses to reveal any concrete details either about her own narrator's identity or about the intended recipient of the original missive in *A Letter . . . to a Particular Friend*, so in *The Fortunate Foundlings* (1744), a novel written during a period when Jacobite plots were suspected everywhere, Haywood never directly acknowledges the political bias either of her own narrative persona or that of her protagonist, whom she describes only as "a gentleman, whose real name we think proper to conceal under that of Dorilaus."[30] Setting the scene "in the ever memorable year 1688," Haywood reveals only that in returning "from visiting most of the polite courts of Europe," Dorilaus intentionally stayed away from London "to avoid interesting himself on either side" of the question of whether "the throne were vacated or not, by the sudden departure of the unfortunate king James" (1). After this single allusion to the political context that defines the events of the novel, Haywood then turns to the heart of the story, which begins with a pair of twin infants left in Dorilaus's garden, never explaining why Dorilaus so carefully avoided the political upheavals of 1688.

As far as we can tell from the early pages of the novel, Haywood's narrator seems to approve of her protagonist's behavior. The note that is left with the infants sets the scene by offering Dorilaus the chance to fulfill the duties of aristocratic heroism:

> Irresistible destiny abandons these helpless infants to your care.—They are twins, begot by the same father, and born of the same mother, and of a blood not unworthy the protection they stand in need of; which if you vouchsafe to afford, they will have no cause to regret the misfortune of their birth, or accuse the authors of their being. (3)

In responding to the needs of the foundlings, Dorilaus acts in a manner appropriate to a ruling class that has not forgotten its obligations to the vulnerable: "the children wanted immediate succour, and he hesitated not a moment whether it would become him to bestow it: he took the basket up himself" (3). Articulating a traditional Tory belief in noblesse oblige consistent with his chivalrous impulses, Dorilaus observes that "whatever stands in need of protection, merits protection from those who have the power to give it" (3). Apparently in agreement with her protagonist in this matter, Haywood adds, "This was his way of thinking, and in pursuance of these generous sentiments he always acted" (3). As if offering further proof of his Tory chivalry, Haywood describes Dorilaus's attention to Horatio and Louisa as the affection of a real father: "he began to regard them with a tenderness little inferior to paternal" (5).

Despite his paternalistic chivalry, Dorilaus later appears to fall short of the Tory ideal of courageous manhood when he tries to persuade the adolescent Horatio not to join the army but to pursue a university degree instead. When asking Dorilaus's permission to join the army, Horatio seems motivated by his own inner principles, while Dorilaus appears motivated by fear rather than courage. Horatio is deferential to Dorilaus and respectfully acknowledges the older man's paternal patronage: "Think me not, sir . . . too presuming in this request I am about to make you.—I know all that I am is yours.—That I am the creature of your bounty and that, without being a father, you have done more for me than many of those, who are so, do for their most favourite sons.—I know also that you are the best judge of what is fit for me" (7). However, like Bonnin's dutiful daughter in *The Disguis'd Prince*, who recognizes her father's more prudent judgment in choosing her husband yet finds herself unable to obey his commands, Horatio gently but firmly continues to press for the right to join the army.

Horatio's desire to "repair the obscurity" (7) of his birth by succeeding in the army might be read as an example of Whig individualism, an impulse to follow Robinson Crusoe's path in disobeying his father and trying to raise himself above the station into which he was born. We almost expect Horatio to be humbled by the worthy Dorilaus and eventually agree to follow his foster father's wishes. However, it again becomes clear that Haywood is modifying, rather than reaffirming, standard political tropes and stereotypes. Rather than representing Horatio's decision as Whig individualism, she casts it as loyalty to a higher cause and in doing so calls Dorilaus's caution into question. Dorilaus's inability to understand Horatio's desire to take a risk, coupled with his own earlier disinclination to take sides in the events of 1688, ultimately makes him seem less heroic than his son. Eventually, Dorilaus allows Horatio to pursue a military career even though he does not yet fully understand the import of what his adopted son intends; the former finally gives his permission because he considers "so strong a propensity as something supernatural" (8). Although Whig propaganda often denigrated the Jacobite cause by associating it with supernaturalism, Dorilaus's comment seems to represent political naïveté rather than any definite partisan response to the intensity of his son's desire.

After being captured in battle by a French baron, Horatio is brought to the English court in exile at St. Germain where he pledges loyalty to the "Chevalier St. George" (i.e., James Edward Stuart, the "Old Pretender") and eventually gains a commission in the army of Charles XII of Sweden. We realize at this point that the "supernatural" impulse that directed Horatio was the "guiding light" of the Jacobite cause, which Haywood depicts favorably. We also realize that the missing piece in Dorilaus's personal character is his lack of a definite political commitment.[31] Revising the image of the zealous partisan Jacobite familiar from mid-century Whig discourse, Haywood shows Horatio's polite and deferential manner winning him loyalty and recognition in the exiled Stuart court, which itself is described as a model of civilized virtue. Meanwhile, it is the politically uncommitted Dorilaus who risks crossing the line into inappropriate, even tyrannical behavior. Although Dorilaus is apparently a confirmed bachelor at the start of the novel, as soon as Horatio joins the army Dorilaus develops a disturbing passion for his foster daughter. When Dorilaus first mentions marriage to Louisa, without as yet suggesting himself as her husband, he borrows the language of chivalrous protection: "the care I have taken of you would not be complete unless I saw you well settled in the world.—I have therefore provided a husband for you, and such a one as I think you can have no reasonable objection to" (15). Following the pattern of dutiful Jacobite daughter, Louisa's automatic response reflects gratitude for his concern and deference to his wishes, tempered with caution: "I hope . . . you will not oblige me to act with too much precipitation in an affair on which the happiness or misery of my whole future life depends" (15). Even as he compliments her on her prudent way of thinking, however, Dorilaus does not seem to realize that his own intentions toward her represent not chivalrous protection but a threat to her well-being.

When Dorilaus tells Louisa to consider "the affection you bore me, as a faithful friend, and the protector of your innocence" (18), Louisa is unable to speak at all at first, for fear "lest what she should say would either lose his friendship or encourage his passion" (15). Although she would like to express the loyalty and gratitude she feels to him as a father and a protector, Louisa realizes that Dorilaus's actions contradict his chivalrous vocabulary. Her only response is to exclaim at the incomprehensibility of his suggestion: "Oh! Sir, cried she, how is it possible for me to make any answer to so strange a proposition!" (18). Insisting on the horror of rupturing a bond of filial affection, which comprehends a mutual sense of obligation, Haywood's narrator explains, "never had the most dutiful child loved the tenderest of fathers more than she did Dorilaus; but then it was only a filial affection, and the very thoughts of his regarding her with that sort of passion . . . had something in them terribly alarming" (19). While in other novels Haywood makes clear the danger of a daughter or son too enamoured of the Whig ideal of "liberty," she is careful never to describe Horatio's or Louisa's disagreements with their guardian in terms of a desire for independence. In this case, it is Dorilaus who attempts to disguise his own Whig impulse, as Haywood perceives it, for personal gratification under the rubric of paternal benevolence. It is up to Louisa to show the same virtuous spirit that her brother demonstrates: she saves herself, her father, and the family name by running away from home, a courageous act not usually associated with the Tory model of daughterly obedience.

Unlike Defoe's Robinson Crusoe, who follows Whig principles in assuming that his duty to his parents diminishes once he is old enough to leave home, Haywood places no limit on the period of mutual obligation between children and parents. Moreover, she refuses to accept any notion of individual success that contravenes the good of the whole family. Although Louisa flees home after Dorilaus makes a physical advance towards her, she never speaks ill of him or acts in any way that would hurt the family's reputation. When employed as a lady's companion in France and Italy after escaping from home, she dutifully writes to Dorilaus to assure him that "in spight of my enforc'd disobedience . . . heaven has raised me a protectress in a lady of quality" (48). When Louisa falls in love with a worthy young man who would like to marry her, she refuses to respond to him until she can obtain her father's permission.

Because she has been in self-enforced exile from Dorilaus and because her suitor, du Plessis, must return to his regiment, Louisa places herself in the protection of a convent after an Italian count repeatedly attempts to rape her. However, when the nuns attempt to trick her into taking permanent vows, we are taught that no matter how sensible and independent a young woman may seem, there is no protection comparable to that of an authentic father figure who remembers his duty. This position is comparable to that taken by Clarissa Harlowe, who believes in daughterly obedience even when she feels morally obliged to disobey her father. Whereas for Richardson novelistic realism meant scripting a tragic narrative in which the Tory Clarissa is ultimately sacrificed to a stubborn father's inability to change his mind, Haywood's Jacobite ideology allows her to envision a different version of reality, in which virtuous fathers correct their actions once they finally accept the true spirit of Jacobite faith. Uninvolved (on either side) in the crucial events of 1688, away in Ireland when Horatio is taken prisoner in France, and unavailable for Louisa when she most needs a father's protection, Dorilaus cannot be relied on to take full responsibility for either his parental or his political duties. His children, however, ultimately help him correct this weakness, which is clearly, in the novel, both a "moral" and a political failing. Having fled the incestuous passion of a man whom she had always viewed as a father, Louisa proves to have acted with prescience when it turns out that Dorilaus is in fact her real father, as he acknowledges when they are finally reunited: "It was heaven . . . that inspired you with that abhorrence of my offers, which, had you accepted, we must both have been eternally undone! You are my daughter, Louisa! . . . my own natural daughter . . . Rise then, and take a father's blessing" (317). At this moment, Dorilaus acknowledges his paternal responsibilities, granting Louisa a dowry appropriate to her suitor's station and offering his blessing not only on her marriage but on the marriage of Horatio and Charlotta. The text makes clear, however, that the credit for Dorilaus's transformation from irresponsible to responsible parent belongs not merely to "heaven" but to the political transformation that his children helped him achieve. Only after Horatio has demonstrated his military loyalty to Stuart interests and Louisa has become engaged to a Frenchman connected to the Stuart Court at St. Germain does Dorilaus decide to sell his estate in England and take up permanent residence in France. Dorilaus's expatriation, which marks his first public act of political allegiance to the cause to which his son has already sworn loyalty, thus coincides with his understanding and acceptance of his responsibilities as true head of his family.

Dorilaus's evolution represents a stylistic achievement for Haywood, whose earlier male characters were either static caricatures of Whig rakes or worthy, if undeveloped, Tory gentlemen. Dorilaus's emotional and political development, however, is difficult to fit into a traditional account of psychological narrative "realism." Readers accustomed to the detailed psychological accounting of Samuel Richardson, for example, may ask why Dorilaus never connects the appearance of the infants on his doorstep to his affair nine months earlier with a young woman of good family who was already promised to an Irish aristocrat. Much later in life, when he has finally been told of the orphans' parentage, he explains to his children that his memory lapse represented a conscious decision to block out the memory of their mother: "as I never expected to see her any more, I endeavoured not to preserve a remembrance which would only have given me disquiet . . . I soon forgot both the pleasure and the pain I had experienced in this as well as some other little sallies of my unthinking youth" (323).

The young woman whom Dorilaus left behind, being unable to forget so easily an affair that had left such tangible evidence, contrived, with the help of her maid, to give birth secretly and then have the maid deposit the infants on Dorilaus's doorstep while she returned to marry the man to whom she had long been engaged. Not wanting to risk news of her previous escapade disturbing the peace of her new husband, Mathilde conveys the fact of his paternity to Dorilaus only on her deathbed, after the children have come of age. While the mother's actions may be plausible, Dorilaus's apparent amnesia about his love affair does not ring true according to the norms of either what has come to be called Whig prescriptive realism on of more traditional romance. To follow romance conventions, Dorilaus should have married Mathilde himself or else spent the rest of his life grieving for having lost his first true love; according to the norms of psychological realism, Dorilaus should have demonstrated some recollection of and possibly guilt over his youthful treatment of his lover. Haywood here inscribes a Jacobite version of virtuous selfhood by reworking the tropes of partisan discourse. Rather than make Dorilaus conform to the stereotype of hot-blooded Jacobite by challenging Mathilde's previous engagement, Haywood has him accept the equally noble fate of renouncing his passion and attempting to forget. Unfortunately, his forgetting is too complete, since it causes him to misinterpret his parental responsibilities toward the offspring he does not suspect might be his own.

In a subsequent foundling narrative, Henry Fielding makes Tom Jones Squire Allworthy's illegitimate nephew rather than his natural child. On the other hand, Fielding is less concerned than Haywood with the issue of paternal lineage, nor is he obviously challenging standard Whig representations of Whig and Jacobite characters. Allworthy acts as a predictable country Whig squire, who means well although he sometimes loses his patience; he seems a realistic character less because of any detailed character development than because he functions in contrast to the flat Jacobite caricature of Squire Western. For Haywood to convey her Jacobite preference, however, she must rework traditional partisan representations of both Whigs and Jacobites.[32] When Dorilaus acknowledges the memory lapse that explains his paternity, he seems, in retrospect, to have been both implausibly naïve and plausibly unable to acknowledge an awkward reality. More complex than Richardson's later peacemaking Grandison, Dorilaus represents a whole range of politically ambivalent positions—from a Jacobite who will drink a toast to the "king over the water" but not fight for him, to a moderate anti-Jacobite Tory who has forgotten his paternal responsibilities after absorbing the dominant (Whig) discourses of individual liberty. By thus blending the characteristics of various standard political stereotypes, Haywood manages to capture the political ambivalence that must have been extremely common during this period, and possibly one of the reasons for the ultimate failure of the 1745 rising. Dorilaus's model of reformed heroism also sends a "cosmic" message to Jacobite supporters—that it is never too late to rekindle the flame. This trajectory of political and psychological development does not necessarily match conventions of novelistic character familiar to the inheritors of a Whig version of history and so may not feel "real" to readers in subsequent eras. Nevertheless, Dorilaus represents a significant technical achievement important to the development of a narrative realism that depicts particular "individuals" rather than predictable character types.

In *The Fortunate Foundlings*, Haywood conveys her increasingly pointed political views not only through increasingly subtle character development but through careful narrative circumlocution and political irony legible to those attentive to it. This is the first of her works in which one of the exiled Stuarts—James Edward Stuart—actually appears as a character. Horatio's friendship with the Chevalier St. George, during the first decades of the eighteenth century, while both are young men, clearly establishes the link between friendship and political loyalty. Captured and taken to the court at St. Germain, Horatio is made an attendant to the Chevalier St. George, in part because they are both the same age, both born in what Haywood describes as "the ever memorable year 1688" (1), but their bond is not merely that of friends or contemporaries. Unlike the liberal Whig scenario of affective or fraternal humanism, in which rational men exchange ideas with others whom they view as equal, Horatio's loyalty to James Edward Stuart exists because of the inequality, rather than the similarity, between their positions.

When Horatio loses at chess, a rare event, the Chevalier notes "How is this, Horatio, . . . you used to play better than I, but now I have the advantage of you." Always deferential, Horatio responds, " 'May you always have it, . . . over all who pretend to oppose you.' " Hinting at his desire to garner some military expertise under the tutelage of Charles XII of Sweden, Horatio adds,

> Chess is a kind of emblem of war, where policy should go hand in hand with courage; and there is a great master in that art, whom if I were some time to serve under, I flatter myself that I should be able to know how to

move my men with better success than I have done tonight; but then my
skill should be employed only against such as are your enemies. (130)

This eloquent statement of loyalty avoids mention of anyone specifically
by name, in accordance with Jacobite rhetorical conventions. Horatio
continues, "if a day should come when you, sir, shall attempt the
prize, how fortunate would it be for me to have learned to serve you
as I am obliged by much more than my duty, by the most natural and
inviolable attachment of my heart" (130). Reaffirming the link
between love and political loyalty, James responds, "I believe,
indeed . . . you love me enough to fight in my cause whenever occasion
offers; in the mean time play as well as you can against me at
St. Germains" (130).

Offering advice to other Jacobite supporters through the example
of her virtuous young hero, Haywood suggests that it is not enough
to voice support or to drink a toast to the "king over the water";
instead they must prepare themselves strategically and militarily—
prescient advice, as it turned out, since the Jacobites would have difficulty raising military support from regions south of the Midlands
during the 1745 rising. Setting the main events of her 1744 novel in
an unidentified year during the early part of the century, when James
Edward Stuart (no longer a political threat by the 1740s) was still a
young man, Haywood technically could deny the claim that her novel
touched on the contemporary cause of Charles Edward Stuart. At the
same time, her approval of Charles XII's military endeavors makes her
Jacobite loyalty unmistakable to supporters of the cause.[33] Haywood
(or her publisher) might have been attempting to avoid political trouble
by presenting the text as a novel about the personal experiences of
society figures, advertising it on the title page as "Being the Genuine
History of *Colonel M*——*rs, and his Sister, Madam* du *P*——*y, the
Issue of the Hon.* Ch——es M——rs, *Son of the late Duke of* R— L—D.
Containing Many wonderful Accidents that befel them in their
Travels, and interspersed with the Characters and Adventures of
Several Persons of *Condition*, in the most polite Courts of *Europe*."
Given the difficulties that ensued from her more politically pointed
title page for *A Letter . . . to a Particular Friend*, it was probably prudent
to camouflage her outlawed political partiality under a title page
suggesting a narrative of society gossip.

Haywood disguises her partisan bias by linking the text to a
humanizing sphere of moral virtue, claiming on the title page that the
work is "*calculated for the Entertainment and Improvement of the
Youth of both Sexes*." She also indicates that the novel is the real-life

account of two of the grandchildren of the late duke of Rutland, an actual historical figure who had carried the Queen's sceptre in 1679 but followed the Parliamentarian impulses of his ancestors and became a strong supporter of the Whig and Williamite cause during the events of 1688. Closer examination of the names of the persons whose lives she supposedly describes, however, suggests that Haywood is in fact slighting the legitimate Whig branch of this ancient family in preference for a less legitimate side branch. John Manners, ninth earl and first duke of Rutland (1638–1711), did have two legitimate sons, but these were borne by his third wife, whom he did not marry until 1674, so neither would have been of age in 1688 to have fathered the eponymous foundlings. In any case, the line of descent from the first duke of Rutland, to his great-grandson, John, marquis of Granby, who would raise forces against the Jacobites in 1745, was so firmly anti-Jacobite that there is no logical link to Haywood's depiction of Horatio and Dorilaus, except as camouflage to deter government censors who might have been scanning title pages rather than reading texts in full.

It is more likely that the Hon. Ch——es M——rs, represented by Dorilaus, was a son by the duke of Rutland's first wife, Lady Anne Pierrepoint, whom he married in 1658 but divorced in 1670. If such a son had been born to a woman whose husband subsequently divorced her (presumably for adultery or a plausible appearance thereof) he would likely have been, as Dorilaus describes himself, "by some imprudencies on the one side, and injustice on the other . . . deprived of that title which [his] ancestors for a long suc-cession of years had enjoyed" (321), which would explain why he is not mentioned in standard biographical sources; chronologically such a figure would have been of the right age to have been a "confirmed bachelor" by 1688, as Dorilaus is described. As the son of Anne Pierrepont, daughter of Henry, marquis of Dorchester, this person might have had an estate through his mother's branch of the family, as Dorilaus suggests. Whether Dorilaus represents a real or imaginary figure, however, it is striking that Haywood uses him and his natural son, Horatio (the *Colonel* M——rs of the title page), to reinforce a paradigm of loyalty, virtue, and courage. By suggesting that the illegitimate branch, represented by the ambivalent figure of Dorilaus, could redeem itself and regain its stature and reputation through Horatio's Jacobite valor and courage, Haywood casts aspersions on the Whig branch of the family, even as she cashes in on its political respectability through her titular allusion to the late duke. This interplay between text and title page, which allows Haywood simultaneously to admit and disguise her own political position, mirrors the novel's complex narrative voicing, in which Haywood's narrator claims omniscience and objectivity even as her novel promotes a subjective and partisan position. Haywood here creates a narrative persona capable of the same kind of narrative control deployed by Jane Austen, whose use of free indirect discourse and other techniques often lead us to admire a given character before we learn that he or she is deficient in some moral quality. Haywood's contributions to the formal complexity of the mid-eighteenth-century novel thus lie not in the complete or literal quality of her descriptions but in the inventive ways in which she rewrites prescriptive Whig versions of "humanized" selfhood and ironically disguises the partisan nature of her own narrative personae.

Difference through Sameness

Although acknowledging that *The History of Jemmy and Jenny Jessamy* (1753) is "much superior to those wretched romances mentioned in our catalogue for last month," *The Monthly Review* objected that "there is no plot" and that the "incidents" that do occur do not seem "natural" but feel "either trivial, or forced, or improbable."[34] *The Monthly Review*, a Whig publication founded by the Nonconformist bookseller Ralph Griffiths, had dismissed Haywood's earlier novel *Dalinda* (1749), because its plausibility—that is, its connection to a real-life scandal—rendered it morally deficient.[35] The review of *Jemmy and Jenny Jessamy* acknowledges that the heroine is "more interesting" than the eponymous heroine of Haywood's *The History of Miss Betsy Thoughtless* (1751). However, this does not seem to compensate for the novel's apparent lack of plot. The continued popularity of this work over the next few decades, however, suggests that Haywood's readers may have appreciated her subordination of plot to character.[36]

For Haywood, who had spent more than three decades crafting plot-driven tales of adventure and sexual intrigue, focusing on character development allowed her to reexamine the crucial issue of discerning friend from foe. The skill of discernment—a talent that itself helps to distinguish "realistic" and sympathetic characters from undiscerning comic caricatures in the novels of Jane Austen—is a skill with obvious political resonance, as Haywood had already suggested in her lengthy treatment of how the "Young Chevalier" decides to confide his trust in *A Letter . . . to a Particular Friend*.

In her early fiction, Haywood's male characters are either clearly good or clearly evil; plots typically focus on the heroine's ability to discern the virtuous Tory or Jacobite gentleman from the unscrupulous

Whig rake. In other words the female characters are more developed than the male characters in Haywood's novels from the 1720s and 1730s, providing further evidence for Nancy Armstrong's claim that the characteristics of the modern individual were first articulated through characteristics of virtuous femininity.[37] Whereas the male characters in Haywood's early novels typically display little ability to grow or develop, often even the most self-willed of her early heroines either evolve to become models of reformed piety, or else, like the protagonists of *Fantomina* and *Anti-Pamela*, they demonstrate an ability to manipulate moral conventions so as to critique standard Enlightenment models of the self. In *The Fortunate Foundlings*, Haywood breaks her pattern of stock male characters with Dorilaus, a complex and dynamic male character, who evolves into a virtuous Jacobite before he can become a worthy father to his children. However, in *Dalinda* (1749) the suspense is once again over whether or not the eponymous heroine will learn to resist her adulterous (and bigamous) passion for her mercenary (Whig) cousin and recognize the real worth of (Tory) Leander, just as in *The History of Miss Betsy Thoughtless* the focus is on whether Betsy will recognize the value of the chivalrous Trueworth, rather than satisfying her youthful, self-willed ambitions of flattery and coquetry.

In *The History of Jemmy and Jenny Jessamy*, Haywood reinvokes the paradigm of seventeenth-century French romance, in which heroes must go to great lengths to prove themselves worthy of the women to whom they pledge loyalty. She thus returns to the pattern of *The Fortunate Foundlings*, which emphasizes the hero's, rather than the heroine's need for moral reform. Creating a valiant romance hero who, unlike Grandison, is not reluctant to fight a duel or face a life of European exile, Haywood asserts the desirability of a Jacobite hero just one year after Charlotte Lennox's merciless mockery of what Doody has described as "the too romantic cause of the Jacobites" in *The Female Quixote*.[38] Unswerving loyalty to what looks like a lost cause might have been tedious for some readers, as the critique in *The Monthly Review* suggests. Haywood nevertheless puts character development over suspense as she develops a Jacobite counter-narrative to Richardson's even more protracted depiction of Grandison's moderate political virtue. The novel's persistent popularity, demonstrated by its subsequent inclusion in *The Novelist's Magazine* (1780–89), suggests, moreover, that many readers appreciated this focus on character development.

Intermarriage between two branches of the same ancient family clearly represents more than a union between two individuals in *The*

History of Jemmy and Jenny Jessamy, a novel whose plot centers on the question of how long two cousins, betrothed from birth, will wait to carry out the preordained plans for their union. The narrator's suggestion that it would require too much effort "in examining old records, memorandums, and church registers"[39] to trace the precise connections between the two male lines of the Jessamy family reminds us that tracing the minutiae of genealogies is a quintessential Jacobite pastime. Yet Haywood once again manages to disguise her political sympathy: her narrator seemingly cannot be bothered with the effort or expense required to trace the lineage, presumably because the authenticity of the connection is never in any doubt. By contrast to tedious efforts of Jacobite antiquarians to prove sovereign right through genealogy, Haywood's more cosmic Jacobitism assumes the authenticity of the Jacobite claim and then examines the temperament necessary to ensure the success of the floundering political cause. Thus Haywood emphasizes "the perfect friendship" that existed between Jenny's and Jemmy's fathers, a friendship that both desired should "continue beyond the grave" (1:2) Such a friendship clearly also represents a shared political ideology and a faith in a cause that had already survived through several generations of Stuarts in exile.

As in *A Letter . . . to a Particular Friend*, real friendship is something sacred and enduring; however, it is also something that Haywood insists should not be forced. In arranging the future marriage between their young children, Jenny's and Jemmy's fathers decide that it should not take place if either "should have any objection to such an union" (1:2). Despite this suggestion that personal choice should figure into the marriage bond, Haywood distinguishes a choice carefully inculcated by proper nurturing from a choice governed by mere caprice or self-will. The narrator notes that Jenny and Jemmy's parents took care "to excite in the children a mutual affection for each other, and to make the name of love familiar to them long before they knew what was meant by the words, much less could have any notion of the passion" (1:2).

Refusing the trope of love at first sight, which she evokes vividly in her early fiction, Haywood insists here that enduring love, like any other kind of affection, duty, or responsibility, requires practice and experience to become "a kind of second nature" (1:4). Given the steps taken by their parents to ensure their mutual affection, it should not be surprising that neither Jenny nor Jemmy was "possess'd of any strong passions; and though the affection they had for each other was truly tender and sincere, yet neither of them felt those impatiencies, — those anxieties, — those transporting hopes, — those distracting fears, — those causeless jealousies . . . they were happy when they met, but not uneasy when they parted" (1:42). This passage offers an interesting counterpoint to Haywood's own earlier overblown descriptions of love, and her narrator emphasizes the difference between the old and new models: "*I am ready to confess, that according to the receiv'd notions of love, there was a seeming inconsistency in this conduct, and had more the appearance of a cold indifference than the warm glow of mutual inclinations*" (1:43). Haywood nevertheless insists not only "that that they did love each other" but that this will be "demonstrated by proof much more unquestionable than all those extravagancies; — those raging flights commonly look'd upon as infallible tokens of the passion" (1:43). Consistent with her discussion of novel-writing in *The Female Spectator* (1744–46), in which she insists that she "can by no means approve of such Definitions of that Passion as we generally find in Romances, Novels, and Plays," that is the "vindictive Fury, and the Rage of *Mars*,"[40] her last novel demonstrates that "realistic" love, like loyalty to the Jacobite cause, should run deeper and endure longer than quick-burning passion.[41]

As if to signal its departure from conventions of narrative suspense that her own earlier novels had helped to solidify, Haywood's final novel begins with something of an anti-dénouement: Jemmy has come of age, both he and Jenny are possessed of ample fortunes, both their fathers have died, and there is no impediment to their marrying immediately. The novel thus commences where most novels end, with all obstacles to marriage being swept away and Jemmy suggesting that they call for a parson. In this early scene Jenny surprises Jemmy, with whom she usually sees eye-to-eye, by contradicting his assumption that all there is left for them to do is to go ahead with the plans their fathers made for them at birth. She insists, "for my part I am of a quite different opinion, and think there is a great deal for us both to do before we come to the words, — to have and to hold" (1:46). In contrast to Richardson's Harriet Byron, who manages to postpone her marriage to Grandison for only about a fortnight after all the obstacles are resolved, Jenny Jessamy insists that she and Jemmy must first "know a little more of the world and of ourselves before we enter into serious matrimony" in order to be certain "of never repenting the engagements we are about to enter into" (1:47).

Once Jenny suggests this delay, Jemmy quickly agrees, apparently recognizing that he is not yet ready to accept the paternal responsibilities that will come with marriage: "you are in the right; — I should not much like, methinks, to be quite so soon the father of a family" (1:47). Although some aspects of the novel may have seemed

"improbable" to one contemporary reviewer, this frank conversation—
so unlike the romantic repartee of other courtship novels—bluntly
acknowledges the probable real-life consequences of marrying too
young: having children when too young. The lesson in Haywood's
"realistic" deviation from the standard marriage plot is also typical of
her partisan version of paternal morality: fatherhood entails an inviolable
obligation, and men who are not yet ready, such as Dorilaus, risk
harming their children. Rather than suggesting, as Richardson does,
that men as virtuous as Charles Grandison could exist, Haywood
offers a Jacobite vision of reality in which paternal virtue and political
loyalty are not wholly innate (or else the Jacobite cause would already
have triumphed), but must be carefully nurtured and continually rein-
vigorated. Such a vision of character may seem more "romantic" than
"realistic" but Haywood is clearly offering a version of "reality" in
which political loyalty or character (both in fiction and in life) must be
developed slowly and gradually, although such a Jacobite vision might
not have been perceived as "realistic" by all readers—either in her own
time—or in subsequent eras.

In the end, the measured feelings that Jenny and Jemmy demonstrate for each other intensify through a sequence of crises set into
motion by rumors casting into question Jemmy's loyalty to Jenny.
Throughout these crises, Jenny proves a model of patience and tranquillity, demonstrating an underlying faith in Jemmy's devotion that
allows her to conquer her initial convulsions of "Grief and indignation"
(2:54) while she waits for the false rumors to be disproved. Just at a
point in the narrative when readers might expect that the crisis will be
explained, Haywood increases the suspense by interjecting a moral
political commentary, which delays her narration of the resolution. In
this narrative interlude, Haywood first asserts her own objectivity: "As
I have no view to self-interest in this work,—no time-server, no
patron to please, it may be depended on that I shall present my hero
such as he truly is, and not like some political historians of modern
date, attempt to mislead the judgment by any false glosses or misrep-
resentations of facts" (2:197). Haywood is clearly writing from the
position of Jacobite sympathy, and she reverses the dominant Whig
(or anti-Jacobite Tory) versions of political history by casting the
Jacobite position as objective and the Whig as subjective or partisan:

> The writers I have been speaking of, will not allow the person on whom
> fortune has not vouchsafed to smile any one virtue or good quality;—
> he must be all black, without a single speck of white . . . what false steps
> he may have been guilty of are ascribed to his own innate propensity to

evil, not to any inadvertency, nor to the wicked insinuations of those on whom he may unhappily have depended, and who perhaps have found their interest in pushing him on things purposely to betray and ruin him. (2:197–98)

In linking her readers' suspicions about Jemmy to the suspicions raised by certain mainstream political historians about another "person," who remains unnamed, Haywood leaves no doubt that the Jemmy of the novel doubles for the Jemmy familiar in popular Jacobite political ballads: the "Pretender," in this case, young Charles Edward Stuart, rather than his father the "Old Pretender" (James Edward Stuart).

Before returning to the main plot and eventually assuring the reader of Jemmy's fidelity, Haywood concludes this brief narrative interlude by observing that "there is one who bravely and almost alone, has courage to enter the lists of battle against an host of adversaries, and attempts to rescue injured innocence from the claws of cruel and all-devouring scandal; may his honest endeavours meet the success they merit, and in spite of prejudice and partiality open the eyes of too long hoodwink'd reason" (2:198–99). Eventually returning to Jemmy's story, Haywood notes, using language that could just as easily apply to the maligned Stuart claimants to the throne, "It is high time therefore to let his actions speak for themselves; and if they cannot shew him so wholly blameless . . . from the fruits of youth and nature, they will at least defend his character from the more gross imputations of perfidiousness, ingratitude, and deceit" (2:197). Echoing the passage in *A Letter . . . to a Particular Friend* in which Charles Edward Stuart's inherent virtue is revealed even when he is travelling incognito, Haywood here again shows her preference for depicting character through a few carefully chosen actions rather than minute descriptions of her characters' every thought. Haywood's approach to realism, developed for her own partisan reasons, is one that Wayne Booth would subsequently describe as knowing which details to include and which to exclude.[42]

The novels that Haywood wrote in the last decade of her career demonstrate that any claim to narrative objectivity is necessarily subjective, or partisan. These works calls into question not only the possibility of narrative neutrality but also the ostensible objectivity that characterizes both Whig political history and Whig prescriptive realism. The apparently objective accounts of Jemmy's behavior, which seem to offer empirical proof of his unfaithfulness, will eventually be proven wrong. Jenny's seemingly naïve belief in her fiancé's fidelity is not mocked as romantic delusion, as is the heroine's quirky romantic vision in Lennox's *Female Quixote*, but given as evidence for her own virtue and consistency. And as the narrative unfolds, Jemmy is eventually shown to be innocent of the charges of infidelity. Similarly, the narrator's own persistent (and cosmically Jacobite) faith in "one who bravely and almost alone, has courage to enter the lists of battle against an host of adversaries" (2:198) is cast as a more rational political position than that of those who would mock this noble figure or his cause.

Haywood's brief allusion to her own political sympathy, conveyed with characteristic delicacy, is ironically reinforced later in the novel when Jenny is asked to solve a dispute between a husband and wife who are arguing over whether their child should be named Charlot or Wilhelmina; the wife fears that the child will be thought "papist" and "jacobite" if named Charlot, while the husband fears that Wilhelmina sounds foreign. Jenny diplomatically suggests that both names are equally English: "how can Charlot be accounted papish?— or Wilhelmina, outlandish.—The one, as I take it, being the feminine of Charles and the other of William, which are both English, and also good protestant names" (3:213). Jenny thus adds a certain credibility to the "Englishness" of the ousted Stuarts, even as she subtly alludes to Charles Edwards Stuart's strategic conversion to Anglicanism in 1750; thus she also links Stuart to the rather un-English Protestant King William of the Revolution settlement. And although Jenny seems to ridicule the couple's anxiety about the partisan import of the name they give their daughter, she finally resolves the dispute herself by slyly insisting that as godmother she should be allowed to name the child. She suggests that she should be able to name it after her "Jemmy," who is currently in exile in France: "in compliment to a person who is much nearer to me than any Charles or William in the world, I shall call it Jemima" (3:216). The unsuspecting couple, apparently unversed in Jacobite ballads, despite the continued popularity of such songs into the middle of the century,[43] seem oblivious to her partisan ploy.

Jenny, who serves as a female model of Jacobite courage and patience, has never truly doubted Jemmy's loyalty, but she is relieved to find that the false rumors of his intrigue with Miss Chit were spread by his quondam friend, Belpine, in an effort to break off the Jessamy cousins' engagement so that Belpine could pursue Jenny himself. When Jemmy learns of Belpine's treachery, he at once challenges him to a duel, and then Jemmy, fearing that he has killed his rival, flees to France to escape arrest. Here Haywood strategically juggles several different representations of Jacobitism. On the one hand, she has attempted throughout her work to challenge the cliché that Jacobites are overly emotional or reckless; on the other hand, she must refute the prevalent image (especially common after 1745) that they were impotent, more inclined to drink toasts than to prove themselves in battle, and over-run by their "Amazonian" wives. Jemmy thus fights the duel with Belpine to prove his courage and manhood. This act distinguishes Jemmy's courage from Lennox's version of bloodless Whig heroism in *The Female Quixote* (the hero never fights a duel for his heroine) or Richardson's version of virtuous, bloodless heroism in *Sir Charles Grandison* (Grandison generally refuses duels).

In order to avoid being cast as the partisan cliché of a reckless, violent Jacobite, however, it is important that Jemmy assert his courage without actually killing his rival. The only reason why he must spend several months' exile in France is that the unscrupulous Belpine has tried to trick him by exaggerating the severity of his wounds and attempting to keep Jemmy in exile, so that he might again attempt to court Jenny himself. In keeping with his mercenary (for Haywood, presumably Whig) nature, Belpine is more interested in Jenny's person and estate than in her virtue. The interlude on the Continent, however, allows Haywood to depict France in positive terms, befitting her Jacobite sympathies, and to reinforce her depiction of Jenny as a model of patient, feminine loyalty as she waits for Jemmy's return. Jenny thus stands in stark contrast to the lascivious representations of the Jacobite heroine Jenny Cameron in such conventional works of anti-Jacobite propaganda as *A Brief Account of the Life and Family of Miss Jenny Cameron* (1746), mentioned in chapter 1.

Belpine, who represents ambitious Whig individualism, understands nothing of true Jacobite loyalty, which Jenny embodies in its most patient form: she is of course prepared to join Jemmy in exile in France. The narrator's language in describing her sacrifice leaves no doubt as to her admiration for

> the love, the constancy, — the generosity, of this amiable lady, who at her years could so readily renounce her native country, kindred, and all the amusements to which her youth had been accustomed, and resolve to live in a perpetual banishment, if by the death of Belpine, the man ordain'd to be her husband in his more prosperous circumstances, should now be reduced to the condition of an exile. (3:109–10)

Jenny becomes a model of loyalty for British Jacobites who, by 1753, might well have lost faith in the cause. When Jemmy signs his entire estate over to her, even before their marriage has taken place, to secure his property for them should he face trial, Jenny also becomes a symbol of the women whose husbands were forced into exile after the 1715 rising. Just as the Scottish women who were left behind in 1715 had to manage the family holdings wisely and simultaneously plea for their husbands' return,[44] Jenny proves herself worthy and prudent when she immediately draws up a will so that should she die before their marriage can take place her estate would revert to Jemmy.

By proposing these financial dealings between her Jacobite hero and heroine, in which husband and wife are equal players, Haywood, as Behn had before her, refutes the standard patriarchal domestic analogies traditionally associated with a pro-Stuart position. Like Defoe and Richardson, she also implicitly interrogates increasingly abstract Whig and Tory political theory that has lost its connections to the joint household dominion suggested by the domestic analogy originally used to describe the Whig social contract.

When it becomes evident that Belpine has been faking the seriousness of his wounds, Jenny surprises Jemmy by joining him in France, where they enjoy a pleasant interlude of sightseeing before returning to England. The restless struggle of the ambitious Belpine provides a point of contrast for what Jenny and Jemmy will enjoy "in calm retirement," that is, "the more pure and lasting sweets of a well govern'd and perfect tenderness" (3:311). Always maintaining the link between government of self and government of the kingdom, Haywood returns the united lovers to England, where they celebrate their union in Westminster Abbey, the spot where traditionally kings and queens of England have assumed the throne. Resolving a novel of so few surprises with the least surprising of conclusions, Haywood makes one of her strongest political statements through a narrative that might seem her most conventional domestic romance. Yet, it is through such sophisticated narrative reassertion of romance tropes that she refutes the partisan empiricism of Whig prescriptive realism.

The History of Jemmy and Jenny Jessamy remained popular into the nineteenth century and, along with *The History of Miss Betsy Thoughtless,* came to represent for future critics Haywood's morally respectable mature fiction. Haywood would nevertheless become viewed, as would the pro-Stuart Aphra Behn, as a lesser predecessor to Jane Austen, always falling short of Austen's technical skill in character development and ironic social commentary. However, when we resituate Haywood's use of romance conventions against the backdrop of mid-eighteenth-century novelistic realism, we recognize the subtlety of her characterization, the complexity of her narrative voice, and the irony with which she inverts the standard narratives of Whig individualism. Haywood's deft use of irony also foreshadows Austen's own ironic voicing in novels written after the political upheavals of the French Revolution. These narrative innovations, moreover, situate her within the canon of early British novelists who developed techniques of "realistic" narration by challenging both the particular details of partisan propaganda and the abstractions of high political theory.

To the extent that the eighteenth-century British novel has largely been written by inheritors of a Whig version of history, it is not surprising that Haywood's Jacobite version of realism has been, until recently, illegible to literary historians or that her ironic narrative voice has been overlooked by many of her subsequent readers. When read with attention to their narrative distance from Whig and anti-Jacobite Tory realisms, however, Haywood's novels demand that we acknowledge the many counter-histories of individualism inscribed in the evolution of formal realism and the emergence of the British novel.

Conclusion: Partisan Realisms and Canon Formation

In "On the Origin and Progress of Novel-writing," an influential, canon-shaping essay that introduces her multivolume anthology *The British Novelists* (1810), Anna Barbauld divides Haywood's oeuvre into two parts: "her earlier novels" which she describes as "in the style of Mrs. Behn's (that is, "licentious . . . also fallen") and "her later works," which she acknowledges are "by no means void of merit."[1] In other words, within a half century of Haywood's death in 1756, her reputation, which was already in peril when the Whig *Monthly Review* dismissed her as merely the author of "novels" and "other romantic performances" in its response to her arrest for writing *A Letter . . . to a Particular Friend*,[2] hinged on the single question of sexual morals. Although Barbauld describes Haywood as a "very prolific genius" (401), her "merit" or skill as a writer, along with her contribution to the structural evolution of the novel, remains obscured because the moral "merit" of her later works must atone for the dubious morality of her early writings.

By contrast to her treatment of Haywood, Barbauld ignores the licentiousness of Daniel Defoe's heroines and praises his invention of a formal quality she characterizes as "natural painting" (350). Barbauld's notion of what is "natural" in narrative representation paves the way for Watt's subsequent definition of formal realism as "a full and authentic report of human experience."[3] Haywood, of course, does not necessarily provide the wealth of specific details that Watt associates with a full empirical account of experience. However, as we could see in *A Letter . . . to a Particular Friend*, Haywood's characters break the molds of early and mid-eighteenth-century political propaganda to naturalize a Jacobite version of "reality" through a counternarrative of individualism that defied standard Whig versions of selfhood.

Although Barbauld was somewhat sympathetic to the French pursuit of liberty and objected publicly to England's long war against France,[4] she nevertheless demonstrates a standard early nineteenth-century distrust of French romances. Barbauld suggests that inferior novelists in general paint "the passion of love . . . too high, and represent its influence beyond what it will be found in real life" (46). Objecting to romances that depict love in overly heroic terms, Barbauld privileges novelists who "soften and refine" the passion. We thus understand her appreciation for Haywood's later works, in which the rationally uplifting effects of mature and refined love are emphasized over the dangers of rash passion, which are the focus of Haywood's early works. Nevertheless, her appreciation for Haywood's later works did not persuade her to include any in her edition of British novels, even though two of Haywood's works had been included in an earlier serialized anthology of novels, *The Novelist's Magazine* (1780–89).

In diminishing the tradition of heroic romance, Barbauld also objects to a genre that was associated at different times with both the Jacobite and Jacobin causes. This does not indicate that she necessarily sought an apolitical model for literature: Barbauld herself was known for her forceful political writings against the slave trade and in support of the revocation of the Test Acts. Nevertheless, by judging novels according to their ability to turn the nation's habits "towards domestic life and matrimonial happiness," Barbauld's "On the Origin and Progress" reinforces the critical tendency, already visible in *The Monthly Review*'s assessment of Haywood, to praise fiction for its supposed distance from partisan politics. Barbauld's comments also tend to reify the difference between romance and what Doody terms Whig prescriptive realism and to obscure the political underpinnings of that realism.

Writing in the wake of the British backlash against the French Revolution, Barbauld criticizes the narrative "absurdities" created by the efforts of Jacobin novelist Thomas Holcroft "to recommend . . . those systems of philosophy or politics which have raised so much ferment of late years" (415). Just as in 1810 most of the British population had come to view progressive Jacobinism as dangerously extreme, so in the middle of the eighteenth century reactionary Jacobitism was outside the acceptable range of voices in the political spectrum. I propose that the reason that Haywood's work, like that of the pro-Stuart Behn, was denigrated by critics during the mid- to late eighteenth century had less to do with the explicitness of her cautionary sexual tales (for certainly Defoe offered just as explicit detail in his fictional lives of criminals and prostitutes), than in her protest against the concepts of "self will" and "liberty," which were so central to Whig versions of selfhood.

The belief that art should mirror nature was not a new one for readers or theater-goers in the neo-classical age. When eighteenth-century novelists and reviewers judged the novel according to its ability to paint "nature," they were helping elevate the novel to the rank of serious, or classical, literature through their focus on its realistic depiction of "life." Similarly, their claims for the moral import of the novel were also part of raising its cultural stature, although the morality and the formal realism of a work were frequently assumed to be indistinguishable.[5] When *The Monthly Review* criticized Haywood's plots for being "forced" or "improbable,"[6] it was helping improve the status of the novel at the expense one of the genre's most important early practitioners. The commentary in *The Monthly Review* also helped to contribute to the subsequent perception of "the novel" as ultimately concerned with transcendental human and moral truths while "the political novel" might be viewed as a sub-genre, less concerned with natural or realistic depictions of human life.[7] However, this does not mean that the most eighteenth- or early nineteenth-century readers would have made such a distinction or would have found politically motivated writing unnatural or unrealistic.

Anna Barbauld's "On the Origin and Progress of Novel-Writing" was not the first history of the novel, but as the introductory essay to the fifty-volume collection *The British Novelists* (1810), the first twenty-one volumes of which established Richardson, Defoe, and Fielding as the most important early British novelists,[8] it had an important influence on subsequent constructions of the eighteenth-century literary canon. Following Clara Reeve's *The Progress of Romance* (1785), which defended the novel as morally appropriate domestic entertainment, "On the Origin and Progress" set the stage for Hazlitt's *Lectures on the English Comic Writers* (1819), which, as William Warner explains, links the rise of the novel to British nationalist ideals of liberty and individualism.[9] Barbauld suggests that the novel improves both domestic (or household) virtue and the domestic (or national) "taste." Through its simultaneous focus on both the moral and national resonance of the novel, this essay helps us understand how a genre originally steeped in partisan discourse would come to be viewed in largely moral and aesthetic terms.

When, in her introduction to Fielding in *The British Novelists*, Anna Barbauld refers to Fielding's accurate or "very natural" description of Squire Western as "a bitter Jacobite, as almost all the country squires of that time were," and of Squire Allworthy's sister as "a staunch whig, a politician in petticoats . . . not disposed . . .'to take her tea without a stratagem,' "[10] it is clear that such partisan caricatures certainly seemed to Barbauld an accurate description of "what we see every day exemplified in real life" (421). Whether such political caricatures actually were familiar from real life—and, of course, Barbauld (who was born in 1743) could only draw on childhood memories of actual Whigs or Jacobites from the 1740s—they certainly would have been familiar from other textual representations, including popular songs and ballads.[11] Barbauld, however, was less concerned with proving the verisimilitude of these character descriptions than in asserting their value to moral instruction. In Barbauld's interpretation of *Tom Jones*, Squire Western and Bridget Allworthy represent "wrong modes" of "managing" or educating Western's daughter, Sophia. Thus, Fielding juxtaposes these amusingly partisan caricatures with an implicitly more desirable, and potentially more natural, selfhood, which is neither misguidedly Whig nor Jacobite, but presumably somewhere between these two extremes. We might conclude from this that Barbauld's preferred model of moral selfhood was nonpartisan, or even apolitical. However, we should remember that Barbauld's own political strategy, as a Dissenter and an opponent of the Test Act, was, like other political writers of her era, to cast her own political points in the light of a moderate, depoliticized ideal of individual selfhood.

In her *Address to the Opposers of the Repeal of the Corporation and Test Acts* (1790), Barbauld insists that it is not "as Dissenters we wish to enter the lists [of civil office-holders]; we wish to bury every name of distinction in the common appellation of Citizen."[12] Borrowing the same political strategies of the novelists she analyses, Barbauld casts the liberal Dissenting self as moderate, disinclined to proselytize within the Church of England and above all nonpartisan. "If we are a party," she points out, "remember it is you who force us to be so" (270). Over and over again she insists on the rationality and humanism of the Dissenters' aims and their nonpartisan attachment to "our King and our Country" (270). Above all, she presents her fellow Dissenters as moderate humanists, more interested in the public good than in their own partisan goals.

Responding to the national call for a day of fasting in support of the war against France, which she opposes, Barbauld again casts her political position as merely rational, individualist humanism. In *Sins of Government, Sins of the Nation; or, a Discourse for the Fast* (1793), she translates the call for a national fast in support of the war effort into an opportunity for individuals to consider for themselves, as moral and rational beings, whether or not they favor the war with France. She reminds her readers that national or "public acts," such as declarations of war, are, in essence, "all *our own* acts; and that, for every violation of integrity, justice, or humanity in public affairs, it is incumbent upon every one of us, to humble himself personally before the tribunal of Almighty God" (299). Barbauld turns the government's call for a fast into an opportunity for individuals to judge the government's policies for themselves, and possibly even dismiss with them.

Refuting Edmund Burke's suggestion in his *Reflections on the Revolution in France* (1790) that reform necessarily incites the factional aggression of the masses, Barbauld insists that true reformers (presumably including herself and other like-minded liberals) likewise "contemn a *swinish multitude*" (304). Rather than overthrowing the status quo, these real reformers "attack the prejudices, and to rectify, if they can, the systems of their countrymen, but, in the mean time, to acquiesce in them" (304). Without promoting the extreme social overhaul of the French Revolution, Barbauld casts her own position as nonideological and antisystem and portrays the Dissenting reformer as a rational, enlightened citizen more interested in the public good than in any particular partisan goal.

Once we understand Barbauld's rhetorical strategy in her political writing, it is instructive to return to her introductory essay to *The British Novelists* with a new eye. Although Barbauld's references to Haywood's work seem to align the genre of the novel with an apolitical ideal of selfhood, we now see that this apparent interest in the rational, moral domestic self is a subtle means of challenging citizens, if not to oppose, at least to consider for themselves whether they agree with their government's decision to wage war or tolerate slavery. She criticizes the novelist Thomas Holcroft's "absurd" depiction, in *Anna St. Ives*, of a heroine "gravely considering, in the disposal of her hand, how she shall promote the greatest possible good of the system" (415). However, this does not mean that Barbauld herself is uninterested in promoting such a utopian vision of public good. In the last line of her *Address to the Opposers*, she expresses her dream for a world in which, "the name of *Dissenter* shall no more be heard of, than that of *Romanist* or *Episcopalian*, when nothing shall be venerable but truth, and nothing valued but utility" (281). She clearly has utopian dreams for the nation state of Britain, which might be described in terms of the philosophy or system of utilitarianism. However, she would prefer that these be conveyed through fiction that conforms to her Dissenting notions of moral propriety.

Much of Barbauld's "On the Origins and Progress of Novel Writing" is devoted to promoting the novel as a morally useful genre and an appropriate entertainment for the domestic households of Britain. Authors such as Behn and Haywood, although acknowledged as talented, are judged on their ability to conform to an early nineteenth-century moral ideal. In distinguishing the morally proper novel from its more frivolous counterpart, Barbauld follows the example of *The Monthly Review* in its dismissal of novelists such as Haywood when she explains: "Our national taste and habits are still turned towards domestic life and matrimonial happiness, and the chief harm done by a circulating library is occasioned by the frivolity of its furniture, and the loss of time incurred" (414). Through comments like this, Barbauld's essay helps construct the novel as an apolitical genre, whose central purpose should be to promote moral good. From this perspective, we may see how twentieth-century social critics, such as Jürgen Habermas, would ultimately understand the novel as part of a separate literary public sphere whose influence on the political public sphere was more in its ability to promote a feeling of humanizing unity among readers than its ability to make a partisan political statement.[13]

However, Barbauld herself was far from seeing the novel as an apolitical entity. Although she criticized Holcroft for his unrealistic depiction of a heroine overly interested in systems, this may have been because she seemed to believe that the novel could have a stronger effect on the public good than statements of political policy or descriptions of political systems. The final lines of the essay sum up her faith in the novel's power as a political tool. Citing Fletcher of Saltoun's remark, "Let me make the ballads of a nation, and I care not who makes the laws," Barbauld asks, "might it not be said with as much propriety, Let me make the novels of a country and let who will make the systems?" (416).[14]

Given Barbauld's subtle understanding of the political power of the genre, we may well ask why it was that she never acknowledged the importance of writers such as Behn and Haywood to the novel's history. In the first place, the very tendency of novelists to humanize and universalize their partisan paradigms of selfhood meant that their political positions would be lost to history in fairly short order. The more humanized the characters, the more likely they would be viewed as natural or realistic and the more likely their political position would be illegible to future readers. Although the amusing partisan caricature of Squire Western was still identifiable to Barbauld, Jenny Jessamy's more subtle approbation of the Jacobite cause would have been less obvious than her moral purity to early nineteenth-century readers.

Even when the contingent details of partisan selfhood were discernible to future generations, they were likely to be appropriated to the different political concerns of a later period. Thus for Barbauld, the figure of Squire Western is merely amusing: his Jacobite sympathies are not something that she takes seriously. Barbauld suggests that the Jacobite cause itself, for which much blood was shed during the period when Fielding was writing *Tom Jones* (1749), was quaintly innocuous and certainly less threatening to the national well-being than Britain's avaricious imperialism. From Barbauld's early nineteenth-century vantage, the "nearly extinct" Jacobite squires had previously flourished during a period when the earnings from their landed estates had "sufficed them to reside among their tenants and dependants in rustic consequence" (421). This isolated life on the estate is for Barbauld much less threatening than "the increasing demands of luxury" in her own era, which she believes, "have occasioned of seeking an increase of fortune in the busy and active scenes of life" (421). She mourns the decline of the landed estates under the governance of the moneyed classes and distrusts the spread of empire that such a thirst for luxury entails. Offering a wry anti-imperialist commentary through her analysis of the Jacobite caricatures in *Tom Jones*, she observes, "It is probable there are more of his majesty's subjects at this moment hunting the tiger or the wild boar in India, than there are hunting foxes at home" (421).

Barbauld's early nineteenth-century liberal and moralizing interpretation of Fielding's 1749 novel reminds us how, as time passes, the contingent meaning of partisan detail will be erased or reassigned. Not surprisingly, the political nuance of Behn's novels, over a century old by the time Barbauld was writing her history, were less visible than the bawdy detail of her Restoration humor. Defoe is admired merely for his "natural painting" rather than for his subtle analysis of the Whig social contract. Richardson is preferred to Fielding because he "elevates" his female characters, while Fielding "uniformly keeps [his] down" (423). Haywood becomes a "prolific genius" whose marginal value stems from the moral propriety of her later novels rather than from the immense contribution she made to the formal evolution of the novel over the three-and-a-half decades of her career as a novelist. Through this focus on "natural," trans-historical morality, the contingent partisan concerns in these texts become obscured to future generations by a critic who herself appreciated the novel's political power.

Like scaffolding necessary to the development of narrative realism, the partisan underpinnings of the novel were reinterpreted by subsequent readers and critics with particular moral and aesthetic concerns. In other words, the early eighteenth-century novel's contributions to emergent debates about the role of the civic individual became illegible through the very humanizing language novelists used to depict their own partisan positions. Not surprisingly, narrative realism would ultimately be linked to a transcendental depiction of life writ large and not seen as a contingent response to certain partisan representations of selfhood. If Grub Street and the eighteenth-century coffee house helped develop the power of the individual citizen's political voice, it was the novel that allowed us to perceive this voice as a natural part of our own humanity. Although the partisan arguments that helped to shape the formal structure of eighteenth-century realism became obscured by the universalizing rhetoric used to convey them, the novel's potentially humanizing discourses retained their underlying political power and would ultimately develop into new forms of political and social "realism" as the genre confronted new social conflicts and cultural tensions in subsequent centuries.

NOTES

INTRODUCTION: REALISM AND THE RISE OF THE NOVEL

1. John Richetti, "Ideas and Voices: The New Novel in Eighteenth-Century England," *Eighteenth-Century Fiction* 12 (January–April 2000): 327–44.
2. Ian Watt, *The Rise of the Novel: Studies in Defoe, Richardson, and Fielding* (Berkeley and Los Angeles: University of California Press, 1957), 92, 32, 31.
3. During the 1960s and 1970s, New Critics regularly disagreed with Watt over such formal issues as the degree to which the early novel had really broken from the genre of romance. Watt himself provides a witty overview of some of the early objections to his work in "Serious Reflections on *The Rise of the Novel*," in *Towards a Poetics of Fiction*, ed. Mark Spilka (Bloomington: Indiana University Press, 1977), 90–103. See also Ian Watt, "Flat-Footed and Fly-Blown: The Realities of Realism," *Eighteenth-Century Fiction* 12 (January–April 2000): 147–166. This reception of Watt's work may be explained by the influence of New Criticism in the cold-war era. Such criticism, as Terry Eagleton explains, "drove you less to oppose McCarthyism or further civil rights than to experience such pressures as merely partial, no doubt harmoniously balanced somewhere else in the world by their complementary opposites." See *Literary Theory: An Introduction* (Minneapolis: University of Minnesota Press, 1983), 50.
4. When Watt identifies Robinson Crusoe's "original sin" as "the dynamic tendency of capitalism itself" (Watt, *Rise of the Novel*, 65), he suggests the link that Georg Lukács asserted between narrative realism and "the contradictorily progressive character of capitalist development." See *Studies in European Realism* (New York: Grosset & Dunlap, 1964), 13. Elsewhere, Watt refers directly to Lukács's *Die Theorie des Romans* (Berlin, 1920), 84 (Watt, *Rise of the Novel*, 84). Rather than directly pursuing Lukács's larger ideological goal of "helping to combat the sociological and aesthetic prejudices which have prevented many gifted authors from giving their best to mankind" (19), Watt focuses on the history of "bourgeois" British realism, leaving the future of progressive

realism to others. Raymond Williams subsequently describes the need for "a new realism" in *The Long Revolution* (New York: Columbia University Press, 1961), 289. Stephen Heath sees realism as "a utopia of writing and reality." See "Realism, Modernism, and 'Language-Consciousness,' " in *Realism in European Literature*, ed. Nicholas Boyle and Martin Swales (Cambridge: Cambridge University Press, 1986), 120. Harry E. Shaw provides an overview of the ideological tensions in the competing analyses of nineteenth-century narrative realism, especially regarding its potential for presenting a "totalizing" image of reality, in *Narrating Reality: Austen, Scott, Eliot* (Ithaca and London: Cornell University Press, 1999). Such concerns about realism's potential for totalizing have not yet fully permeated mainstream eighteenth-century literary scholarship, however.

5. Michael McKeon's *The Origins of the English Novel 1660–1740* (Baltimore: Johns Hopkins University Press, 1987) allows us to understand the emergence of verisimilitude in the historical context of the evolving dialectical relations between aristocratic and progressive ideologies. However, his work has not yet prompted much new scholarship on the category of formal realism per se, nor does he account for the fact that some of the discourses he associates with generalized aristocratic ideology might derive more specifically from particular partisan debates. First-wave feminist scholars tended to emphasize the similarities between the works of canonical male novelists and those of their rediscovered sisters without challenging the traditional category of narrative realism. Dale Spender establishes the sheer number of women writing novels in *Mothers of the Novel* (New York: Pandora, 1986). Jane Spencer emphasizes the similarities between Richardson's work and that of many female novelists in *The Rise of the Woman Novelist: From Aphra Behn to Jane Austen* (Oxford: Basil Blackwell, 1986), 140–42. Janet Todd suggests that "The novel that women wrote . . . did not pursue verisimilitude for its own sake" in her highly informative study of early woman writers. See *The Sign of Angellica: Women, Writing, and Fiction, 1660–1800* (New York: Columbia University Press, 1989), 139. Subsequent feminist scholarship on the rise of the novel has focused on revising Watt's category of the individual, rather than his analysis of formal structure. Nancy Armstrong provocatively suggests that the novel helped to establish the domestic woman, rather than the bourgeois man, as the embodiment of the modern individual in *Desire and Domestic Fiction: A Political History of the Novel* (New York: Oxford University Press, 1987). In *Nobody's Story: The Vanishing Acts of Women Writers in the Marketplace, 1670–1820* (Berkeley and Los Angeles: University of California Press, 1994), Catherine Gallagher delineates the narrative and social power that women writers derived from gendered self-representation. Ros Ballaster, Toni Bowers, and Jill Campbell have pursued the question of how early novelists deployed different gendered categories of the individual for partisan political pur

poses. See Ros Ballaster, *Seductive Forms: Women's Amatory Fiction from 1684 to 1740* (Oxford: Clarendon Press, 1992); Toni Bowers, *The Politics of Motherhood: British Writing and Culture 1680–1760* (Cambridge: Cambridge University Press, 1996); Jill Campbell, *Natural Masques: Gender and Identity in Fielding's Plays and Novels* (Stanford: Stanford University Press, 1995). Ruth Perry's *Novel Relations: The Transformation of Kinship in English Literature and Culture, 1748–1818* (Cambridge: Cambridge University Press, 2004) adds much to our understanding of a significant cultural shift in the way family relations were perceived and negotiated in the second half of the eighteenth century, but does not directly address the category of narrative realism.

6. See J. A. Downie, "Mary Davys's 'Probable Feign'd Stories' and Critical Shibboleths about 'The Rise of the Novel,' " *Eighteenth-Century Fiction* 12 (January–April 2000): 325.

7. Michael Seidel, "The Man Who Came to Dinner: Ian Watt and the Theory of Formal Realism," *Eighteenth-Century Fiction* 12 (January–April 2000): 194. See also J. Paul Hunter's comments on the dangers of placing too much emphasis on realism as the primary distinguishing feature of the novel in *Before Novels: The Cultural Contexts of Eighteenth-Century English Fiction* (New York: W. W. Norton, 1990), 22–23. Toni Bowers offers cautionary advice about the "privileged category 'novel' " which defines itself against works excluded by "gender and genre hierarchies" See "Sex, Lies, and Invisibility: Amatory Fiction from the Restoration to Mid-Century," in *The Columbia History of the British Novel*, ed. John Richetti et al. (New York: Columbia University Press, 1994), 50.

8. In fairness, realism continued to generate scholarly consideration after Watt published his *Rise of the Novel*, even though its central position in scholarly histories of the British novel diminished. See, for example, Michael Holquist and Walter Reed, "Six Theses on the Novel—and Some Metaphors," *New Literary History* 11:3 (1980): 413–423; Marshall Brown, "The Logic of Realism: A Hegelian Approach," *PMLA* 96:2 (March 1981): 224–241; Elizabeth Deeds Ermarth, *Realism and Consensus in the English Novel* (Princeton: Princeton University Press, 1983).

9. William B. Warner, *Licensing Entertainment: The Elevation of Novel Reading in Britain, 1684–1750* (Berkeley and Los Angeles: University of California Press, 1998), 34.

10. See note 1 above. In *The Cambridge Companion to the Eighteenth-Century Novel* (Cambridge: Cambridge University Press, 1996), Richetti characterizes "the realistic novel" as "a very self-conscious revision and strict reformation of what its authors tend to define as unacceptably loose attitudes toward the referentiality of narrative in relation to the actualities of experiences, as the Enlightenment came to define that elusive category" (2).

11. His *Popular Fiction Before Richardson* (Oxford: Clarendon Press, 1969) was a pioneering work, although he routinely relegates women writers to the second tier. More recently, Richetti has contributed to the study of early women novelists by co-editing, with Paula Backscheider, the anthology *Popular Fiction by Women 1660–1730* (Oxford: Oxford University Press, 1996).

12. Deborah Ross, *The Excellence of Falsehood: Romance, Realism, and Women's Contribution to the Novel* (Lexington: The University Press of Kentucky, 1991), 12.

13. "The Novel's Gendered Space" in *Revising Women: Eighteenth-Century "Women's Fiction" and Social Engagement*, ed. Paula Backscheider (Baltimore: Johns Hopkins University Press, 2000), 1. All italics in the text quoted throughout this book have been reproduced as in the original, unless where specified otherwise.

14. In *The English Novel in History 1700–1780* (London and New York: Routledge, 1999), Richetti devotes one chapter to the "amatory fiction" of Behn, Manley, and Haywood and another to the "women novelists" of the mid-eighteenth century, while Defoe, Richardson, Fielding, and Smollett are each accorded a chapter of their own. Similarly, in *The Cambridge Companion to the Eighteenth-Century Novel*, six individual male novelists and Fanny Burney are accorded seven separate chapters, while all other "women writers" are lumped into a single chapter. In both of these influential texts, the works of women novelists become relegated to a subcategory on par with the subcategory of the "sentimental" novel, which is likewise accorded a separate chapter in each volume.

15. Backscheider, "The Novel's Gendered Space," 12.

16. J. A. Downie appropriately cautions scholars against using either the term "rise" or the term "novel" during this period since "the novel was still in the process of being made." See "The Making of the English Novel," *Eighteenth-Century Fiction* 9:3 (April 1997): 264. In discussing the instability of the term "novel" during this period he points out how it was frequently used interchangeably with "romance" (257–60).

17. In analyzing the category of "amatory fiction," one perhaps as susceptible to marginalization as that of "romance," Toni Bowers cautions critics to "ask why we define 'good' literature as we do, how our assumptions about literary value still work to valorize some voices and exclude others, and how our capacities for pleasure might be augmented by respectful engagement with works we have been trained to resist or dismiss." See "Sex, Lies, and Invisibility: Amatory Fiction from the Restoration to Mid-Century," 70.

18. Watt, *Rise of the Novel*, 11–34.

19. Booth objects to Watt's complaint, in privileging Richardson over Fielding, that Fielding's "authorial intrusion . . . tends to dismiss the authenticity of the narrative." See *The Rhetoric of Fiction* (Chicago and

London: University of Chicago Press, 1961), 42; Booth is citing Watt's *Rise of the Novel*, 285.

20. Booth (41) is citing Watt's *Rise of the Novel*, 32.

21. Deidre Shauna Lynch, *The Economy of Character: Novels, Market Culture, and the Business of Inner Meaning* (Chicago: University of Chicago Press, 1998), 69.

22. I am drawing here on Marilyn Butler's analysis of the anti-Jacobin elements in Austen's fiction. See *Jane Austen and the War of Ideas* (Oxford: Clarendon Press, 1975), 197–213. For an explanation of how our perception of Darcy evolves through a subtle shift in narrative perspective (a technique that renders him more "human"), see Susan Fraiman's analysis of *Pride and Prejudice* in *Unbecoming Women: British Women Writers and the Novel of Development* (New York: Columbia University Press, 1993), 69–87.

23. Watt, *Rise of the Novel*, 16.

24. Anthony Ashley Cooper, third Earl Shaftesbury, *Sensus Communis, an Essay on the Freedom of Wit and Humour in a Letter to a Friend* in *Characteristics of Men, Manners, Opinions, Times*, ed. Lawrence E. Klein (Cambridge: Cambridge University Press, 1999), 66. Portions of these passages (from a different edition of Shaftesbury) are cited in Watt, *Rise of the Novel*, 16.

25. Ermarth, *Realism and Consensus*, 33.

26. J. A. Downie, "Mary Davys's 'Probable Feign'd Stories' ": 312–13.

27. Richard Ashcraft and M. M. Goldsmith, "Locke, Revolution Principles, and the Formation of Whig Ideology," *Historical Journal* 26:4 (1983): 773–800.

28. Linda Colley, *In Defiance of Oligarchy: The Tory Party 1714–60* (Cambridge: Cambridge University Press, 1982); J. C. D. Clark, *English Society 1688–1832* (Cambridge: Cambridge University Press, 1985).

29. Geoffrey Holmes, *British Politics in the Age of Anne* (New York: St. Martin's, 1967), 21.

30. Jerry Beasley, *Novels of the 1740s* (Athens: University of Georgia Press, 1982), 13.

31. Margaret Anne Doody, *The True Story of the Novel* (New Brunswick: Rutgers University Press, 1996), 286, 294.

32. For further details about the association of Jacobitism with romance, see also Margaret Anne Doody's introduction to Charlotte Lennox's *The Female Quixote or The Adventures of Arabella*, ed. Margaret Dalziel (Oxford and New York: Oxford University Press, 1989), xviii.

33. Connecting the rise of the novel to partisan political history is not a new idea, although such a partisan history has not specifically been connected to the development of narrative realism. In *Factual Fictions: The Origins of the English Novel* (New York: Columbia University Press, 1983), Lennard Davis's study of the effect of censorship laws on the novel's development helps set the stage for a partisan analysis of the novel's formal history. Ros Ballaster's *Seductive*

Forms and Toni Bowers's *Politics of Motherhood* demonstrate how to decode the partisan political ground of amatory fiction. Their work, alongside that of Christopher Flint, has also helped break previous assumptions about the early novel as primarily a Whig phenomenon. See Flint's *Family Fictions: Narrative and Domestic Relations in Britain, 1688–1798* (Stanford: Stanford University Press, 1998).

34. Scholars of eighteenth-century literature have long recognized the deeply political nature of Restoration drama and Augustan satire, although formalist literary study emphasized the "literariness" of such texts, just as New Criticism has emphasized their universal human truths. William Warner, who eschews the literary category of the novel, nevertheless cautions us to read Behn's *Love Letters Between a Nobleman and His Sister* as a "political intervention" rather than as a novel "of a literary type." See *Licensing Entertainment*, 52.

35. In *The Structural Transformation of the Public Sphere*, trans. Thomas Burger (Hermann Luchterhand Verlag, 1962; Cambridge: MIT Press, 1989), Jürgen Habermas predictably relies on 1950s and 1960s conceptions of literature. In Habermas's analysis, Richardson's *Clarissa* demonstrates an historical and cultural context in which author and reader together wept over the events in the novel, a context that created the "family's self-image as a sphere of humanity-generating closeness" (48) necessary to bind together the men who had a voice in the political public sphere. Thus, for Habermas, "the humanity of the literary public sphere served to increase the effectiveness of the public sphere in the political realm" insofar as "political emancipation" was understood as "human emancipation" (56). Such an assertion about the liberating effects of the bourgeois public sphere's humanist claims is complicated, however, by the example of novelists who never claimed to be writing either from or about the supposedly "universal" position of the Whig bourgeois male. It also presupposes that the novel was a genre more closely connected to apolitical humanist morality than to partisan political debate. See my "Clarissa's Treasonable Correspondence: Gender, Epistolary Politics, and the Public Sphere," *Eighteenth-Century Fiction* 10:3 (April 1998): 269–287; and my "It's Not Easy Being Green: Gender and Friendship in Eliza Haywood's Political Periodicals," *Eighteenth-Century Studies* 32:2 (Winter 1998–99): 199–214. Paula Backscheider sees the public sphere as a "liminal space . . . in which new knowledge is produced"; novels thus "negate the boundaries" between what is understood to be public and what is understood to be private. See her "Introduction" to a special issue of *Prose Studies*, "The Intersections of the Public and Private Sphere in Early Modern England," ed. Paula R. Backscheider and Timothy Dykstal, *Prose Studies* 18:3 (December 1995): 13–15. Backscheider also paraphrases Habermas's more recent observation in *The Philosophical Discourse of Modernity*, that "some literature is both 'world-discovering' and problem-solving' " (15).

36. Anna Letitia Barbauld, "On the Origin and Progress of Novel-Writing," reprinted in *Anna Letitia Barbauld: Selected Poetry and Prose,* ed. William McCarthy and Elizabeth Kraft (Peterborough, Ontario: Broadview Press, 2002), 350.

37. For Watt, these developments included the rise of capitalism and Protestantism; for McKeon, the dialectical emergence of bourgeois ideology; for Armstrong, the emergence of the domestic woman.

38. In *Family Fictions,* Christopher Flint describes the early British novel as promoting a more conservative version of individualism and conformity than was previously assumed. Toni Bowers has spoken on Tory ideology in early eighteenth-century novels at several conferences and refers to some of these ideas in "Collusive Resistance: Sexual Agency and Partisan Politics in *Love in Excess,*" in *The Passionate Fictions of Eliza Haywood,* ed. Kirsten T. Saxton and Rebecca P. Bocchicchio (Lexington: University of Kentucky Press, 2000), 48–68.

39. Paula McDowell, *The Women of Grub Street: Press, Politics, and Gender in the London Literary Marketplace 1678–1730* (Oxford: Clarendon Press, 1998), 4.

40. J. A. Downie, *Robert Harley and the Press: Propaganda and Public Opinion in the Age of Swift and Defoe* (Cambridge: Cambridge University Press, 1979), 1. Downie emphasizes that Robert Harley, in particular, enabled the press "to be controlled by government without the imposition of a strict system of censorship" (130).

41. Davis, *Factual Fictions,* 96.

42. Campbell, *Natural Masques,* 163.

43. Another factor explaining the continued misogyny of anti-Jacobite pamphlets could be the actual economic circumstance of the wives of those Jacobites arrested in 1715. While their husbands were stripped of their material possessions and exiled to France, the Jacobite wives retained control of their dowries and became in essence the legal and economic heads of household in their husbands' absence. See Daniel Szechi's " 'Cam Ye O'er Frae France?' Exile and the Mind of Scottish Jacobitism, 1716–1727," *Journal of British Studies* 37:4 (October 1998): 357–90. See also his *The Jacobites, Britain, and Europe, 1688–1788* (Manchester: Manchester University Press, 1994).

44. Here I am necessarily drawing on a Foucauldian idea of discourse. However, I do not assume that the novel itself functioned as a "discourse," as Lennard Davis has argued (*Factual Fictions,* 7); rather, I see the early British novel as a discursive field in which various political and social discourses were put into play. As Michel Foucault explains, every statement exists within an "enunciative field in which it has a place and a status, which arranges for its possible relations with the past, and which opens up for it a possible future." See *The Archaeology of Knowledge,* trans. A. M. Sheridan Smith (New York: Pantheon Books, 1972), 99. He also explains that any given statement takes on a different meaning, depending on the "material status of the

statement," or the context in which it is uttered: "it does not constitute the same statement if it is spoken by someone in the course of conversation, or printed in a novel; if it was written one day centuries ago, and if it now reappears in an oral formulation" (100).

45. See Carole Pateman, *The Sexual Contract* (Stanford: Stanford University Press, 1988) and Susan Moller Okin, "Humanist Liberalism" in *Liberalism and the Moral Life*, ed. Nancy L. Rosenblum (Cambridge: Harvard University Press, 1989), 39–53.

46. Mary Astell's preface to the third edition of *Reflections on Marriage* (London, 1706) in *The First English Feminist*, ed. Bridget Hill (New York: St. Martins Press, 1986), 76. (In the third edition Astell removed *Some* from her original title.) After the Revolution of 1688–89, early English feminist writers Mary Astell and Margaret Cavendish, both staunch Tories, expressed serious reservations about the advantages to women of power being shared between men, rather than concentrated in the single person of the king. See Ruth Perry, "Mary Astell and the Feminist Critique of Possessive Individualism," *Eighteenth-Century Studies* 23:4 (1990): 444–57. See also Catherine Gallagher, "Embracing the Absolute: The Politics of the Female Subject in Seventeenth-Century England," *Genders* 1 (1988): 24–39.

47. Joan Wallach Scott, *Gender and the Politics of History* (New York: Columbia University Press, 1988), 25.

48. Armstrong, *Desire and Domestic Fiction*, 36.

49. See *Simeon and Levi: or, Jacobite Villany and French-Treachery, Hand in Hand* (London: n.p., 1696), *The True Picture of a Modern Tory: In a Dialogue, between Jack and Ned* (London: n.p., 1702), and *A Seasonal Warning Against Jacobites and Papists in Favour of the Pretender* (London: printed for J. Baker, 1712).

50. The *Jacobite Curse, or, Excommunication of King George and His Subjects* (Glasgow: printed by Hugh Brown, 1714); *The History of the Jacobite Clubs* (London: printed for J. Baker, 1712); *The Counsel to the True English; or, A Word of Advice to the Jacobites* (London: printed for S. Manship, 1691).

51. We might see a parallel here between what I am suggesting about novelistic realism and the "principle of opacity" that Stephen Greenblatt identifies in Shakespeare's dramatic writings—an opacity he attributes in part to a political caution that allowed him to depict the full range of humanity without his company ever falling "from its position as the King's Men." See *Will in the World: How Shakespeare Became Shakespeare* (New York: W. W. Norton, 2004), 355.

52. John Richetti insists that Eliza Haywood's early novels depict "tumultuous emotions," not ideas or developed characters. A selected passage in *Robinson Crusoe*, in contrast, reveals both depth of character and a "dialogic" engagement with the moral issues of cannibalism and colonialism. Yet, had Richetti chosen a passage from Haywood's *The Adventures of Eovaai*, for example, he could not have ignored her

narrator's and heroine's "dialogic" engagement with the "ideas" of tyranny, republicanism, and the social contract, many of the same themes addressed by Crusoe when he becomes "monarch" of his desert island.

1 POLITICAL SELFHOOD AND NOVELISTIC CHARACTER

1. Edmund Burke, for example, resorts to the image of the vulnerable Marie Antoinette and her children in his *Reflections on the Revolution in France*, especially in part 5, chapter 2, "Of the Outrage against the Royal Family, Aristocracy, and the Clergy." See *Reflections on the Revolution in France*, ed. Thomas H. D. Mahoney (New York: The Liberal Arts Press, 1955), 79–85.

2. Over the slaves, the rule of the household head is absolute (*despotikē*); over the children, his rule is monarchical (*basilikē*), since their reasoning faculties are undeveloped; over the wife his rule is constitutional (*politikē*), since her reasoning power is without authority. See Constance Jordan, "The Household and the State: Transformations in the Representation of an Analogy from Aristotle to James I," *Modern Language Quarterly* 54:3 (September 1993): 310–11.

3. *The Trew Lawe of Free Monarchies* (66) cited in Jordan's "The Household and the State": 309.

4. Peter Laslett remarks in his introduction to Filmer's *Patriarcha* that while the family was at this time a solid feature of society, more so than in medieval times, it may well have been fending off decline at the moment that Filmer defends it so emphatically. See *Patriarcha and Other Political Works of Sir Robert Filmer*, ed. Peter Laslett (Oxford: Basil Blackwell, 1949), 20–29. Laslett also suggests that there was "something faintly ridiculous . . . even by the year 1679" about Filmer's argument. See his introduction to Locke's *Two Treatises of Government*, ed. Peter Laslett (Cambridge: Cambridge University Press, 1988), 71. Richard Ashcraft emphasizes in *Revolutionary Politics and Locke's Two Treatises of Government* (Princeton: Princeton University Press, 1986) that the Tories did not need Filmer, but were "quite content to defend the king's authority through the citation of a few specific passages from the Bible" (187). However, Filmer's treatise, in its painstaking proofs through his peculiar interpretation of Genesis, was readily available; it would also become a convenient target for contract theorists.

5. Laslett suggests that Locke and Tyrrell may have written portions of their treatises at the same time, while staying at the same country retreat, although Locke did not mention his to Tyrrell and waited until the Exclusion crisis reached its culmination before publishing it anonymously. See the introduction to Laslett's edition of Locke's *Two Treatises*, 63–66.

6. James Tyrrell, *Patriarcha non Monarcha, The Patriarch Unmonarched; Being Observations on a late Treatise & Divers Other Miscellanies Published Under the Name of Sir Robert Filmer Baronet* (London: printed for Richard Janeway, 1681), 110–11.

7. James Tyrrell, *Bibliotheca Politica or an Enquiry into the Ancient Constitution of the English Government, in Thirteen Dialogues* (London: printed for R. Baldwin, 1694), 13.

8. Jonathan Scott persuasively argues that what we understand as crises of "exclusion" were rather crises about arbitrary government and Catholicism, of which the so-called Exclusion crisis was but a symptom. See *Algernon Sidney and the Restoration Crisis, 1677–1683* (Cambridge: Cambridge University Press, 1991), 1–80. I continue to use the term "Exclusion crisis" or "crises" to denote the various attempts to pass Exclusion bills because Scott's proposed term "Restoration Crisis" would be less comprehensible to readers. For more on the significance of the Exclusion crises, see also Howard Nenner, *The Right to Be King: The Succession to the Crown of England 1603–1714* (Chapel Hill: The University of North Carolina Press, 1995), 95–258.

9. John Locke, *Two Treatises of Government*, ed. Peter Laslett, paragraph 38. Future references to this work are by paragraph number.

10. *The Fundamental Constitution of the English Government* (London: printed by J. D. for the Author, 1690), 102.

11. *The Original Power of the Collective Body of the People of England, Examined and Asserted* (London: n.p., 1702), 9.

12. *A Brief Justification of the Prince of Orange's Descent into England and of the Kingdom's Late Recourse to Arms* (London: printed for J. S. and sold by Richard Baldwin,1689), 35. For related nineteenth- and twentieth-century references to women as too virtuous to vote, see Suzanne Marilley's *Woman Suffrage and the Origins of Liberal Feminism 1820–1920* (Cambridge: Harvard University Press, 1996).

13. Algernon Sidney, *Discourses Concerning Government* 2nd edn. (London: n. p., 1698), 40.

14. Samuel Richardson, *Clarissa, or the History of a Young Lady*, ed. Angus Ross (London: Penguin Books, 1985), 934.

15. Richard Ashcraft argues in *Revolutionary Politics* that one of the reasons that Locke's treatises were ultimately understood as less radical than he believes they were is that Locke's *Essay on Human Understanding* led readers to picture him more as an apolitical philosopher than a political partisan, despite the distinctly radical arguments contained in his *Two Treatises of Government*. See *Revolutionary Politics* 56–74, 75–127, and 299–37. However, at a moment when gender difference was routinely invoked as a rhetorical strategy in marginalizing other excluded political groups, Locke still did not fully include women in his category of the universal political individual. Teresa Brennan and Carole Pateman, in " 'Mere Auxiliaries to the Commonwealth': Women and the Origins of Liberalism,"

Political Studies 27 (1979): 183–200, assert that Locke was well aware that "there was a problem about the position of married women" but that he capitulated to the old-school patriarchalists on this point (187).

16. Martyn P. Thompson explains that Locke's *Two Treatises* "did eventually become a very successful work" although it was not read widely enough to have received any critical responses until 1703. See "The Reception of Locke's *Two Treatises of Government* 1690–1705," *Political Studies* 24:2 (1976): 184–91.

17. See "Locke, Revolution Principles, and the Formation of Whig Ideology," 789 (see note 27 to my introduction).

18. *The Judgement of Whole Kingdoms and Nations* (London, 1710; New York and London: Garland facsimile reprint, 1979), 45–55.

19. [William Keith], *A Dissertation on the Liberty of the Subject in Great Britain* (London: printed for J. Roberts, 1737), 7.

20. Henry St. John, Viscount Bolingbroke, *The Idea of a Patriot King*, ed. Sydney W. Jackman (Indianapolis: Bobbs Merrill, 1965), 14.

21. Adam Potkay, in his analysis of Hume's ambivalent attitudes toward rhetorical eloquence, suggests that "Hume's advocacy of classical eloquence may be read as a skeptical and conservative critique of Locke's liberalism." See *The Fate of Eloquence in the Age of Hume* (Ithaca: Cornell University Press, 1994), 58. Duncan Forbes clarifies that Hume's conservatism should not be confused with the more radically conservative reaction of Jacobitism. He explains that "it was . . . a post-revolutionary, establishment political philosophy: its object was to give the established regime, the Revolution Settlement, the Hanoverian succession, the respectable intellectual foundation which, in the 'fashionable system' it had not got." See *Hume's Philosophical Politics* (Cambridge: Cambridge University Press, 1975), 91.

22. David Hume, *The Philosophical Works*, ed. Thomas Hill Green and Thomas Hodge Grose, 4 vols. (Darmstadt: Scientia Verlag Aalen, 1964), 3:444.

23. David Hume, *A Treatise of Human Nature*, ed. L. A. Selby-Bigge (Oxford: Clarendon Press, 1978), 495.

24. Hume, of course, does not eliminate women entirely from his philosophy. Adam Potkay describes how Hume approves of women's civilizing influence on polite discourse. Hume apparently appreciates the "sweetness" and "amiability" that women bring to society, which, while diametrically opposed to the political forces of the public sphere, nevertheless were necessary to it (*Fate of Eloquence*, 74–86). Potkay suggests that Hume was trying to expand on Bolingbroke's traditional base of support by addressing himself to "women as well as men; to rising professionals as well as landed proprietors; to the Scottish and French nations as well as the English; to citizens of the world as well as compatriots" (86). Potkay does not examine, however, whether in speaking to all these different groups, Hume intended that they all should be considered equal citizens under law.

25. In pointing to the way in which Hume's essays define a highly abstracted citizen-individual, I am using "abstraction" differently than is usual in Hume criticism. M. A. Box, for example, in dividing Hume's writings between first- and second-order levels of philosophical abstraction, or abstruseness, appropriately locates Hume's political discourses as "all first-order questions of fact. (Does the British government, for example, incline more to absolute monarchy or to a republic? What are the first principles of government?)." See *The Suasive Art of David Hume* (Princeton: Princeton University Press, 1990), 159.

26. As Annabel Patterson has demonstrated, American colonists drew direct inspiration for their assertion of independence from key texts written in justification of the Revolution of 1688–89. She demonstrates how eighteenth-century "secret histories" provided a counter-narrative to official histories and thus helped promote the premises of early liberalism by depicting the horrors of tyranny. Patterson distinguishes anecdotes about abuses of power under the Stuart monarchs from sexual anecdotes in politicized scandal chronicles apparently more concerned with sexual titillation than liberal politics, such as Haywood's "pulpy" *Present Intrigues of the Court of Caramania* (1727). See *Early Modern Liberalism* (Cambridge: Cambridge University Press, 1997), 185–86. While I agree with Patterson about the role of Whig counter-histories and memoirs in the spread of liberal political theory, I believe that a different sort of anecdote—familial and fictional—was needed to interrogate the abstract political notions of liberty and equal rights, which did not yet have universal application.

27. See for example Charles Davenant's *The True Picture of a Modern Whig Set Forth in a Dialogue between Mr. Whiglove and Mr. Double* (London: n. p. 1701) and *Tom Double Return'd: Or, the True Picture of a Modern Whig Set Forth in a Second Dialogue Between Mr. Whiglove & Mr. Double* (London: n. p.,1702). See also J. A. Downie's discussion of these pamphlets in *Robert Harley and the Press*, 49–54.

28. See note 49 to my introduction.

29. See note 50 to my introduction.

30. For a fuller discussion of the figure of "Faction" in political propaganda during the reign of Queen Anne, see Ruth Herman, *The Business of a Woman: The Political Writings of Delarivier Manley* (Newark and London: University of Delaware Press, 2003), 52.

31. In a similar way, the categories of rake, cuckold, and licentious woman were invoked by both pro- and anti-Stuart sides in Restoration drama. See Susan J. Owen, *Restoration Theatre and Crisis* (Oxford: Clarendon Press, 1996).

32. George Logan's laboriously repetitive *A Treatise on Government; Shewing That the Right of the Kings of Scotland to the Crown was not Strictly and Absolutely Hereditary* (Edinburgh: printed for the booksellers here and at Glasgow, 1746) is a paradigmatic example of this

historically sound, if not philosophically profound, refutation of Jacobite claims to the throne.

33. *A Comparison of the Spirit of the* Whigs *and* Jacobites: *Being the Substance of a Discourse Delivered to An Audience of Gentlemen in* Edinburgh, *December 24, 1745* (Edinburgh: printed by R. Fleming, 1746), 8.

34. [James Montgomery], *Great Britain's Just Complaint For Her Late* Measures, *Present* Sufferings, *And the Future* Miseries *She Is Exposed To* ([London],1692).

35. *An Attempt towards a Natural History of the Hanover Rat* (London: printed for M. Cooper, 1744).

36. I do not assume that Toryism was necessarily the most powerful form of proto-feminism during this period, as some earlier scholars have done. For a refutation of this familiar claim, see Susan J. Owen's "Sexual Politics and Party Politics in Behn's Drama, 1678–83," *Aphra Behn Studies*, ed. Janet Todd (Cambridge: Cambridge University Press, 1996), 15–29.

37. See *Female Excellency, or the Ladies Glory* (London: Nath. Crouch, 1688), sig. A3; this work is ascribed on the title page to R. B.—that is, Richard or Robert Burton, the pen name of the bookseller Nathaniel Crouch.

38. Jill Campbell has described the misogyny of 1740s anti-Jacobite rhetoric as part of a Whig attempt to deflect attention from the potentially empowering effect their own theories of government structure might have on women. Despite the potentially empowering domestic analogies in Whig political treatises, however, it is clear that misogyny was noticeable in polemical anti-Stuart writings as early as Settle's dramatic tragedy *The Female Prelate* (1680). See Campbell, *Natural Masques*, 145.

39. *The Anatomy of a Jacobite-Tory: In a Dialogue between Whig and Tory, Occasioned by the Act for Recognizing King William and Queen Mary* (London: Richard Baldwin, 1690); *An Excellent New Song Call'd, The Female Duel; or, The Victorious Williamite Lady, Who was challeng'd to Fight a Duel by a Jacobite Lady* ([London]: printed and sold by P. Pelcomb, [1700]).

40. Sacheverell was impeached (and eventually prevented from preaching for three years) by the Whigs on charges that this sermon was seditious; the mob that protested his impeachment ironically challenged, by their very uprising, the premise of passive obedience that his sermon upheld and that the protesters believed themselves to be supporting. Geoffrey Holmes quotes a letter from Abigail to Edward Harley: "Even Sacheverell himself [was] no doubt conscious that the violent insurrection of his supporters was 'an odd way of defending passive obedience and non-resistance.'" See *The Trial of Doctor Sacheverell* (London: Eyre Methuen, 1973), 175.

41. [John Toland], *The Jacobitism Perjury and Popery of High-Church-Priests* (London: printed for J. Baker, 1710), 14.

42. [John Shute Barrington], *A Dissuasive from Jacobitism: Shewing in general What the Nation is to expect from a Popish King; and in particular, from the Pretender* (London: printed for John Baker, 1713), 8.

43. "Come if You Dare" (London: printed for P. Clifton, 1714).

44. *The Jacobite Curse, or Excommunication of King George and His Subjects* (Glasgow: printed by Hugh Brown, 1714), 9.

45. Henry Fielding, *The Jacobite's Journal and Related Writings*, W. B. Coley, ed. (Middletown, CT: Wesleyan University Press; Oxford: Oxford University Press, 1975), 99.

46. The Jacobite fascination with lineage did have some foundation in truth, as Paul Kléber Monod suggests in *Jacobitism and the English People 1688–1788* (Cambridge: Cambridge University Press, 1989), 73–92.

47. *The Female Rebels: Being Some Remarkable Incidents of the Lives, Characters and Families of the Titular Duke and Dutchess of* Perth, *the Lord and Lady* Ogilvie, *and of* Miss Florence M'Donald (Edinburgh; reprinted London: sold by L. Gilliver, Mrs. Dodd, and G. Woodfall, 1747).

48. *The* Highlanders Salivated, *or the Loyal Association OF* M——ll K—— g's *Midnight Club: with The serious Address of the Ladies of* Drury, *to the Batter'd Strolling Nymphs of their Community* (London: printed for M. Cooper, 1746), 17.

49. See Annabel Patterson, *Early Modern Liberalism*, 153–231.

50. Sig. A6, quoted in Patterson, *Early Modern Liberalism*, 158.

51. In a key passage, the anonymous author suggests that "the King of Tamaran [Charles II] took his Crown from his head to put it on Hattigé's [Palmer's]." See *Hattigé: or the Amours of the King of Tamaran. A Novel* (Amsterdam, 1680), 22.

52. *The New Atalantis* is undoubtedly Manley's work; *The Secret History of Queen Zarah* may not have been written by Manley, although it has long been ascribed to her. See J. A. Downie's "What if Delarivier Manley did *Not* Write *The Secret History of Queen Zarah?*" *The Library*, 7th series 5:3 (September 2004): 247–64. If, as is certainly possible, the work was written by Joseph Browne, not Manley, it still provides an example of the style of partisan discourse typical of secret histories from this period.

53. For a more detailed account of Manley's work as a political anecdotographer and proto-novelist see the general introduction to *The Selected Works of Delarivier Manley*, ed. Rachel Carnell and Ruth Herman, 5 vols. (London: Pickering & Chatto, 2005), 1:14–26.

54. Archibald Arbuthnot, *Memoirs of the Remarkable Life and Surprizing Adventures of Miss Jenny Cameron, A Lady, who by her Attachment to the Person and Cause of the young Pretender, Has Render'd Herself Famous by her Exploits in his Service* (London: printed and sold by R. Walker, 1746), 27.

55. In other visual images of Cameron from the period, she is dressed as a man, sometimes bearing a sword, sometimes wearing tightly fitting

male clothing in Highland plaid, so as to emphasize both her masculinity and her promiscuity. Here she is sitting by a window, next to a vase of flowers, wearing an elegant, tight-fitting gown.

56. Richetti, "Ideas and Voices," 328.

57. Campbell, *Natural Masques*, 137–59.

58. See note 45 above.

59. See note 44 in my introduction for the reference to Foucault. Mikhail Bakhtin's analysis of the novel in terms of a "*system* of languages that mutually and ideologically interanimate each other," is developed in *The Dialogic Imagination: Four Essays by M. M. Bakhtin*, trans. Caryl Emerson and Michael Holquist, ed. Holquist (Austin: University of Texas Press, 1981), 47.

60. See note 31 to my introduction.

61. See my conclusion for a discussion of the exclusion of Haywood's works from Anna Barbauld's canon-shaping *The British Novelists* (1810).

2 Tory Ideology and Aphra Behn's Turn to the Novel

1. *The Works of Aphra Behn*, 7 vols., ed. Janet Todd (Columbus: Ohio State University Press, 1992–95), 5:163. All of Behn's works will be cited from this edition. In the previous paragraph, she explains: "I think a Play the best divertisement that wise men have; but I do also think them nothing so, who do discourse as formalie about the rules of it, as if 'twere the grand affair of humane life" (5:162).

2. In editorial comments, Janet Todd speculates that Behn may have enjoyed translation because it allowed her to publish in areas of philosophy, science, and religion that were not otherwise open to women and which she avoided in her poetry (*The Works of Aphra Behn*, 4:ix).

3. In Janet Todd's edition of Behn's works, novels and novellas comprise two out of seven volumes.

4. Rose Zimbardo explains Behn's turn to the novel as deriving from her increasing preference for "analytico-referential discourse." Laura Brown describes her prose fiction as allowing her to transcend "the clear evaluative hierarchy" of heroic tragedy, and Paula Backscheider observes that Behn found a "new means of expression" for the new ways of viewing "men, women, and social relationships" that arose during the 1680s. See Rose Zimbardo, "Aphra Behn: A Dramatist in Search of the Novel," *Studies in Eighteenth-Century Culture* 19 (1989): 279; Laura Brown, *English Dramatic Form English Dramatic Form 1660–1760: An Essay in Generic History* (New Haven: Yale University Press, 1981), 26; Paula Backscheider, *Spectacular Politics: Theatrical Power and Mass Culture in Early Modern Europe* (Baltimore: Johns Hopkins University Press, 1993), 117. In her

edition of Behn's works, Janet Todd does not necessarily insist on defining Behn's role in the origins of the novel (in fact, she refers to most of Behn's shorter prose works simply as "short stories"). Todd does, however, suggest that because two of Behn's plays produced during the last three years of her life were quite successful, Behn might have turned to prose not merely from financial necessity but rather "because she enjoyed it." See *The Works of Aphra Behn*, 3:xi.

5. See her dedication to *The Luckey Chance* in *The Works of Aphra Behn* (7:213). Behn also understood the dangers of the political implications of her work: In 1682, despite her well-known loyalty to Charles II, Behn was arrested by the court for implicitly criticizing, in her prologue to the anonymous play *Romulus and Hersilia*, the Duke of Monmouth's disloyalty to his father.

6. I am referring to the nineteen plays included in Janet Todd's edition of Behn's works and the lost play, *Like Father, Like Son; or the Mistaken Brothers* (probably produced March 1682), which Derek Hughes lists as a comedy; see *The Theatre of Aphra Behn* (New York: Palgrave, 2001), 108, 211 n. 39.

7. For the purposes of this category, I divide the novels according to their endings—usually either deaths or marriage—and class as tragedy those ending in death or in multiple deaths and as comedy those ending in marriage. According to these criteria, the comedies include: *The Adventures of the Black Lady* (1698), *Memoirs of the Court of the King of Bantam* (1698), *The Unfortunate Happy Lady* (1698), *The Wandering Beauty* (1698), *The Unhappy Mistake* (1698), *The Fair Jilt* (1688), *The Lucky Mistake* (1688). Behn's novelistic tragedies include: *Love Letters Between a Nobleman and his Sister* (1684–87), *The Unfortunate Bride: or, the Blind Lady a Beauty* (1698), *The Dumb Virgin: or, The Force of Imagination* (1698), *The History of the Nun: or, The Fair Vow-Breaker* (1688), *The Nun: or, The Perjured Beauty* (1688), *Agnes de Castro: or, the Force of Generous Love* (1688), *Oroonoko; or, The Royal Slave* (1688). The novels that appeared posthumously may have been written sometime between 1682, when the amalgamation of the Duke's and King's Companies reduced the demand for new plays, and before her death in 1698, but the precise dates of composition are unknown. See Janet Todd's Textual Introduction to volume 3 of her edition of Behn's *The Works of Aphra Behn* (3:x–xi). I do not class either as comedy or tragedy the extremely brief *Love Letters*, which was included in the posthumous *Histories, Novels, and Translations* (London, 1698) as an ostensibly autobiographical supplement. As there is no resolution provided in the few letters, there is no way of categorizing them as either comic or tragic, although the heroine's desperate pleadings to her lover intimate that, had it been finished as an epistolary novella, it might have ended tragically.

8. *The Works of John Dryden*, 20 vols. (Berkeley and Los Angeles: University of California Press, 1956–2000), 13:231. Subsequent

references to Dryden's dramatic works are to this edition, by act and scene number.

9. J. Douglas Canfield argues that in most political tragedies written between the period of the first Exclusion crisis and the Revolution of 1688–89, "the royalist code of loyalty to a rightful monarch, however weak or indulgent, wrong or unfortunate, is strenuously maintained." See "Royalism's Last Dramatic Stand: English Political Tragedy, 1679–89," *Studies in Philology* 82:2 (Spring 1985): 234–263, 238. Susan J. Owen has complicated Canfield's history by suggesting that there certainly were Whig plays during this period, although their rhetoric of "Loyal Protestantism" has frequently been misinterpreted as Tory. Nevertheless, she agrees with Canfield when she asserts: "In the divided society of the 1660s, in which Stuart ideology has to be reconstructed and reinstated after the rupture of the interregnum, the royalist heroic play represents an attempt to paper over ideological cracks. It is an attempt which, in its very artifice, reveals the constructed nature of late Stuart ideology" (*Restoration Theatre and Crisis*, 19).

10. *All for Love*, V.I.510–11.

11. Such representations were also common in earlier Tudor and Stuart plays, of course. However, as Susan Staves explains, "It is not that the resistance of domestic inferiors is dramatized after the Restoration and not earlier, but rather that the justifications for patriarchal authority are weaker and the resistance is more often politically self-conscious." See *Players' Scepters: Fictions of Authority in the Restoration* (Lincoln: University of Nebraska Press, 1979), 134.

12. Hughes, *The Theatre of Aphra Behn*, 133.

13. As Susan J. Owen explains in *Restoration Theatre and Crisis*, representations of sexual libertinage were used by both sides of the political divide: Whigs used it to allude to the constant extramarital intrigues of both Charles II and James II; Tories used it, albeit gingerly, given its potential ability to backlash against them, to slander the Whigs, frequently by suggesting that Whig leaders are impotent libertines by comparison to the sexually attractive Tory rakes. On this topic, see also J. Douglas Canfield, "Tupping Your Rival's Women: Cit-Cuckolding as Class Warfare in Restoration Comedy," in *Broken Boundaries: Women and Feminism in Restoration Drama*, ed. Katherine M. Quinsey (Lexington: University of Kentucky Press, 1996), 113–28, and Robert Markley, " 'Be impudent, be saucy, forward, bold, touzing, and leud': The Politics of Masculine Sexuality and Feminine Desire in Behn's Tory Comedies," in *Cultural Readings of Restoration and Eighteenth-Century English Theater*, ed. J. Douglas Canfield and Deborah Payne (Athens: University of Georgia Press, 1995), 114–40.

14. Hughes, *The Theatre of Aphra Behn*, 156–57.

15. This should not lead us to assume that Behn was uninterested in Monmouth's political career. In " 'For when the act is done and finish't cleane, / what should the poet doe, but shift the scene?': Propaganda,

professionalism and Aphra Behn," in *Aphra Behn studies*, ed. Janet Todd (Cambridge: Cambridge University Press, 1996), Virginia Crompton explains that ballads written between 1672 and 1685 demonstrate "Behn's sustained interest in Monmouth's ambiguous political position" (134).

16. See note 5 above. As Paula Backscheider has pointed out, Behn maintained her Tory critique of Monmouth, but chose not to make it the centerpiece of her novel: by focusing instead on the amorous intrigues of Grey and the Berkeley sisters, Behn "avoided dangerous reflections on Monmouth and other powerful men" even as she criticized the opposition to James II's succession (*Spectacular Politics*, 110).

17. Janet Todd suggests that Philander "*poses* as a Whig," in his rebellious stance, but is "in fact an unprincipled and power-hungry individualist, resenting the sexual affront of Monmouth while taking no heroic action, and disliking the rule of anyone, whether legitimate king or 'bastard.' " See *The Secret Life of Aphra Behn* (London: Pandora, 2000), 307. This description of self-serving individual, however, embodies the Tory caricature of Whiggism.

18. Todd, *Secret Life*, 386–92.

19. Behn's *Love Letters* has been described by Paula Backscheider as a "new means of expression" in which she was grappling with a "new political order" (*Spectacular Politics*, 117). In this section, Backscheider refers to McKeon's *Origins of the English Novel*, 20. In Backscheider's account, it is "dialogic and open-ended," a novel that "could capture ambiguities and contradictions and construct a psychological realism that pleased people"(122). This "psychological realism," I would insist, does not derive from a depiction of transhistorical psychological "truths" but stems from Behn's manipulation of the techniques of partisan propaganda.

20. This comparison is made by Behn's narrator in *The Dumb Virgin* (Todd, *The Works of Aphra Behn*, 3:359).

21. One of the few twentieth-century critics who have noticed the relationship of Behn's *The Dumb Virgin* to *Oedipus*, Frederick Link, suggests that Behn's attempts to give the events a credible context of seventeenth-century Venice fail because "the events belong to psychological rather than to objective history." See *Aphra Behn* (New York: Twayne, 1968), 149. In falling into the trap of ahistorical psychologizing, Link misses the way that Behn redefines the classical political tragedy to critique the specific cultural paradigms of her era. More recently, Janet Todd notes the link to Oedipus and also points out the political importance of the figure of Dangerfield. See *Secret Life*, 251–52.

22. "Je l'aimais en amant, je l'aime encore en frère." ("I used to love him as a lover, I love him still as a brother.") See Pierre Corneille, *Oeuvres Complètes* (Paris: Editions du Seuil, 1963), 580.

23. In editorial comments in her edition of Behn's works, Janet Todd points out that the name "Dangerfield" might easily refer to Thomas

Dangerfield, notorious for his part in the Meal-Tub Plot, a plot similar to the supposed Popish Plot, but instead a conspiracy among Protestants (3:336).

24. See Janet Todd, *Secret Life*, 251; she is citing Behn's *The Dumb Virgin*, 3:359–360. Todd corrects previous scholarly speculation that Behn may have been raised Catholic, but points out Behn's general sympathy for Catholics and her religious tolerance (*Secret Life*, 266, 369, and 439 n. 35.)

25. As Paula Backscheider has observed, rape scenes in Behn's comic drama undermine otherwise heroic male figures; she also points us to Behn's interest in transgressive, if not always morally heroic, female characters (*Spectacular Politics*, 90–91).

26. Although many undergraduates find that little feels real to their modern-day expectations for a novel, there are always some students who point to the sisterly rivalry as the most believable emotion depicted in the story; this perception of course does not vindicate the realism of this detail as much as it demonstrates the persistent cultural assumption (then and now) that sisterly rivalry is a defining feature of familial relations.

27. Ros Ballaster interprets Belvideera's final act as "a both a gesture of submission to patriarchal power, by mediating the passage of familial wealth between her father and uncle, and of resistance, by refusing to participate any longer in a specularizing and objectifying male homosocial economy. Where she previously used voice and wit to negotiate that world, she now uses silence and virginity to deny it." See " 'Pretences of State': Aphra Behn and the Female Plot," in *Rereading Aphra Behn*, ed. Heidi Hutner (Charlottesville: University of Virginia Press, 1993), 198.

28. In *Reconstructing Aphra: A Social Biography of Aphra Behn* (New York: Dial Press, 1980), Angeline Goreau suggests that there was an inconsistency between her politics and her patriarchalism (252); subsequent feminist criticism saw early patriarchy as providing a space for proto-feminism, a view that Susan J. Owen dismisses in "Sexual Politics and Party Politics in Behn's Drama, 1678–83," in *Aphra Behn Studies*, ed. Janet Todd (Cambridge: Cambridge University Press, 1996). Owen explains that "the idea that late Stuart ideology created a liberating space for women is as false as the school child's notion of the jolly cavalier, but it persists in part because studies of Behn's sexual politics have placed her in relation to other women writers rather than thoroughly examining her relationship to her own society" (15).

29. In *Restoration Tragedy: Form and the Process of Change* (Madison: University of Wisconsin Press, 1967; reprint, Westport Connecticut: Greenwood Press, 1978), Eric Rothstein explains that "One becomes more skeptical about the mangling of heroines, if only because the sexual interest [sic] of seeing wounded or recently raped women must have acted against the more respectable profession of the tragedies," 155.

30. As Susan J. Owen points out in *Restoration Theatre and Crisis*, Southerne's plays, from the early 1680s, including *The Loyal Brother*, articulate a standard pro-Stuart ideology (122 n. 26), although his politics seem to shift after 1688, according to his patrons, a fact that does not change the way he depicts female characters. See Robert Jordan and Harold Love, Introduction to *The Works of Thomas Southerne* (Oxford: Oxford University Press, 1988), xi–xliv.

31. Backscheider, *Spectacular Politics*, 93.

32. In *The Passionate Shepherdess* (London: Methuen, 1989), Maureen Duffy makes the case for James, Duke of York before his accession to the crown (275); in "Aphra Behn's *Oroonoko*: Occasion and Accomplishment," paper read at Clark Library Seminars, UCLA, May 11, 1974, George Guffy makes the case for James II; in "The Romance of Empire: *Oroonoko* and the Trade in Slaves," in *The New Eighteenth Century*, ed. Laura Brown and Felicity Nussbaum (New York: Methuen, 1987), 59–60, Laura Brown argues for Charles I. Brown locates "the contradictions of colonialist ideology" in Behn's juxtaposition of a narrative of heroic romance with her historically accurate treatment of slave revolts (61). In 1688, however, Behn was probably concerned more specifically with how those who were threatening to force James II into exile would guarantee liberty to the citizens of England. While Brown argues for the importance of Behn's manipulation of romance conventions, I insist on the importance of Behn's manipulation of the genre of dramatic tragedy as well.

33. Ros Ballaster identifies a parallel between the powerlessness of the female narrator and that of the enslaved prince. See *Seductive Forms*, 96.

34. Todd, *The Works of Aphra Behn*, 7:216.

35. Todd, *Secret Life*, 393.

36. Todd, *Secret Life*, 393.

37. See Jacqueline Pearson's "The History of *The History of the Nun*," in Heidi Hutner, ed. *Rereading Aphra Behn*, 234–52, for a further discussion of the changes to Behn's novella made by subsequent dramatic adaptations.

38. William was encouraged in a secret letter sent in June of 1688. As someone who was well connected in the political world of the theater and had possibly worked as a royalist agent in Holland during the last years of the Interregnum, Behn is likely to have been among those who might have anticipated William's landing, although she would have opposed it.

39. As Janet Todd notes, Isabella's honorable demeanor in the face of death contrasted sharply to the actions of Monmouth, when facing his own execution for treason. See *Secret Life*, 392.

40. Tragicomedy was the genre with which Behn started her career in the early 1670s, but it was falling out of fashion on stage by the mid 1670s.

41. Todd, *Secret Life*, 113.

42. Christopher Flint believes that Behn approaches narrative realism, with skepticism since "her romantic inventions challenge the boundaries imposed by the realistic story" (*Family Fictions* 82). However, Flint here is aligning realism with "everyday life and, by extension, domestic ideology"; thus "it is the romance element, uncharacteristically, that appears to have provided the destabilizing effect usually attributed to realism" (82). Flint explains Behn's formal innovations in terms of the way she "uses romance and scandal to evoke female discontent with a culture directed by ineffective or incompatible codes of domestic behavior" (83). However, when we put this novel back into the context of partisan political discourses and the conventions of Restoration drama, we see that there is no single "domestic ideology" at this period but different partisan representations of the domestic household. I would argue that its nascent realism is defined as much in contrast to Restoration drama and partisan political propaganda as to the conventions of French heroic romance. Michael McKeon suggests that *The Fair Jilt* "incorporates, within its critique of aristocratic ideology, a self-conscious defense against the anticipated countercritique of conservative ideology" (*Origins of the English Novel*, 259).

43. Flint, *Family Fictions*, 101.

44. In her introduction to *The Fair Jilt*, Janet Todd quotes the description of Tarquini's incomplete execution, in which the sword glanced off a knot in the handkerchief that had been tied about his head, from the *London Gazette* for the week of 28–31 of May 1666 (*Works of Aphra Behn*, 3:2). See also *Secret Life*, 111–12.

45. Todd, *Secret Life*, 111.

46. See note 37 to chapter 1.

47. [Crouch], *Female Excellency, or the Ladies Glory*, 80.

48. In 1674, Crouch apprenticed Elizabeth Guard, of Sussex, although there is no evidence as to when or whether she completed her apprenticeship (*Oxford Dictionary of National Biography*, s. v. Nathaniel Crouch).

49. I agree with Flint's observation that through the character of Miranda, Behn "dramatically reverses the assumption that women represent private experience" (*Family Fictions*, 97). However, because Restoration drama routinely represented an overlap between domestic power and political power, the "assumption" he refers to is an ex–post facto one.

3 DANIEL DEFOE AND THE WHIG IDEAL OF SELFHOOD

1. Homer Obed Brown refers to Defoe's relatively late entry into the modern canon of eighteenth-century novel in "The Institution of the English Novel: Defoe's Contribution," *Novel: A Forum on Fiction* 29:3 (Spring 1996): 299–318.

2. Maximillian Novak concedes the realistic detail of Defoe's narratives, but insists that their greatness lies in their development of the mythic individual. See *Realism, Myth, and History in Defoe's Fiction* (Lincoln: University of Nebraska Press, 1983). John Richetti focuses on the imaginative energy of Defoe's narratives in *Defoe's Narratives: Situations and Structures* (Oxford: Clarendon Press, 1975).

3. Brown, "The Institution of the English Novel," 306–07.

4. While this traditional explanation may be sufficient, new light is shed on Defoe's partisan position, and the possibility of his deceiving his Whig rather than his Tory pay-masters by 1718, in *A Political Biography of Daniel Defoe* by P. N. Furbank and R. W. Owens (Pickering & Chatto, 2006), 159–71.

5. Manuel Schonhorn, *Defoe's Politics: Parliament, Power, Kinship, and Robinson Crusoe* (Cambridge: Cambridge University Press, 1991).

6. DeLuna, "*Jure Divino:* Defoe's 'whole Volume in Folio, by Way of Answer to, and Confutation of *Clarendon's* History of the Rebellion,' " *Philological Quarterly* 75:1 (Winter 1996): 43–66.

7. Novak neatly disputes the traditional view of Defoe's "unconscious artistry" in *Realism, Myth, and History*, 98.

8. Watt, *Rise of the Novel*, 60–92.

9. Novak, *Realism, Myth, and History*, 21.

10. Watt here is referring to Moll Flanders; he goes on to suggest that that it is almost inadvertent that Defoe so effectively achieves the "characteristic utterance of such an uneducated person" since the prose of so many passages are in "Defoe's usual style" (*Rise of the Novel*, 101).

11. See note 31 to my introduction.

12. Flint, *Family Fictions*, 160.

13. See Paula Backscheider, *Daniel Defoe: His Life* (Baltimore: Johns Hopkins University Press, 1989) for details of Defoe's political principles, which she describes as "Lockean" (160–79). See Ashcraft and Goldsmith's "Locke, Revolution Principles, and the Formation of Whig Ideology" for their theory of Defoe's authorship of the three distillations of Locke.

14. There is simply no mention of these writings in P. N. Furbank and W. R. Owens's *A Critical Bibliography of Daniel Defoe* (London: Pickering & Chatto, 1998). Manual Schonhorn refers to the "anonymous Lockean author of *Political Aphorisms*" (*Defoe's Politics*, 81), but insists that this author agrees with Locke in precisely the way that Defoe disagrees with him—over the fact that for Locke, property (land) does not give one man authority over another, whereas for Defoe "Dominion is founded in property" (80). David Wootton argues that Ashcraft exaggerates Locke's radicalism in terms of class relations, which would make him closer to a more conservative Defoe. See *Political Writings of John Locke*, ed. David Wootton (New York: Penguin Books, 1993), 41–119.

15. Daniel Defoe, *The True-Born Englishman: A Satyr* in *The Shortest Way with the Dissenters and Other Pamphlets By Daniel Defoe.*

The Shakespeare Head Edition of the Novels & Selected Writings of Daniel Defoe, 14 vols. (Oxford: Basil Blackwell and New York and Boston: Houghton Mifflin, 1928), 13:57.

16. This ultimately resulted in the 1701 Act of Settlement guaranteeing a Hanoverian line of descent via Charles I's Protestant daughter Sophia. In her biography of Defoe, Paula Backscheider reminds us that there was plausible reason for Jacobite protest to the Act of Settlement, considering that "Thirteen people with better hereditary claims than the Hanoverian Sophia . . . had to be passed over to assure a Protestant successor" (78).

17. *The History of the Jacobite* Clubs, 4.

18. This image is used to refute Jacobite references to the "adultery" of those taking an oath to William and Mary (after previously swearing an oath to the house of Stuart). See *The Anatomy of a Jacobite, or, the Jacobites Heart Laid Open, with a Sure and Certain Method for their Cure* (Cambridge: [s.n.], 1692), 66–67.

19. Schonhorn, *Defoe's Politics*, 140.

20. *Jure Divino* (London: printed by P. Hills, 1706), Book 2:16. All subsequent page numbers are to this edition by book number and page number (although bound in a single folio, numbering recommences at the start of each "Book" in the epic).

21. Novak, *Realism, Myth, and History*, 15.

22. *Religious Courtship, Being Historical Discourses on the Necessity of Marrying Religious Husband and Wives Only* (London: E. Matthews, A. Bettesworth, J. Brotherton, and W. Meadows, 1722), 58.

23. *The Family Instructor* (London: Eman. Matthews; Newcastle upon Tyne: Jo. Button, 1715), 13.

24. Carol Houlihan Flynn has examined his conduct manuals in terms of how the ideology of individualism is placed under stress in a hierarchical household. She identifies "the strains that the fiction of justice exacts when domestic harmony and 'affective individualism' depend upon a subordination of the woman in the house." See "Defoe's Idea of Conduct: Ideological Fictions and Fictional Reality," in *The Ideology of Conduct: Essays on Literature and the History of Sexuality*, ed. Nancy Armstrong and Leonard Tennenhouse (New York and London: Methuen, 1987), 73.

25. Watt, *Rise of the Novel*, 61. Watt provides no footnote for his reference to Maitlin.

26. In *Rise of the Novel*, Ian Watt describes Defoe's novels as upholding economic individualism at the same time that they reveal the ways in which such individualism "tended to isolate man from his family and his country" (89). Maximillian Novak, in *Defoe and the Nature of Man* (Oxford: Oxford University Press, 1963), explains Defoe's fiction as resolving the contradiction between spirituality and economics through an understanding of natural morality. G. A. Starr, in *Defoe and Casuistry* (Princeton: Princeton University Press, 1971), adds

more historical detail to the prior attempts to understand Defoe's morality by explaining his novels as part of a casuistic tradition of religious and moral argument. In *Defoe's Characters* (Oxford: Oxford University Press, 1975), John Richetti adds a level of complexity to studies of "the individual's dilemma between the free self and the social and ideological realities which that self seems to require" (17) by considering how Defoe's characters perceive and so mediate their own unmediated experience. In *The Origins of the English Novel*, Michael McKeon adds nuance to this traditional account as he locates Defoe within a spiritual tradition that is being secularized: "In Defoe the balance between spiritualization and the claim to historicity has been reversed [since Bunyan]" (319).

27. Schonhorn, *Defoe's Politics*, 161; Speck is here cited from a private communication with Schonhorn.
28. On this topic see also Richard Braverman, *Plots and Counterplots: Sexual Politics and the Body Politic in English Literature, 1660–1730* (Cambridge: Cambridge University Press, 1993) and Gordon J. Schochet, *The Authoritarian Family and Political Attitudes in 17th Century England: Patriarchalism in Political Thought* (Oxford: Basil Blackwell, 1975; New Brunswick and London: Transaction Books, 1988).
29. Flint, *Family Fictions*, 154.
30. *The Fortunes and Misfortunes of the Famous Moll Flanders. The Shakespeare Head Edition of the Novels & Selected Writings of Daniel Defoe*, 1:viii.
31. Schonhorn, *Defoe's Politics*, 150.
32. *The Life and Strange Surprizing Adventures of Robinson Crusoe of York, Mariner. The Shakespeare Head Edition of the Novels & Selected Writings of Daniel Defoe*, 7:171.
33. As Watt points out, this is twice the sum Judas was given. *Rise of the Novel*, 69.
34. See note 27 above.
35. *The Farther Adventures of Robinson Crusoe. The Shakespeare Head Edition of the Novels & Selected Writings of Daniel Defoe*, 8:117.
36. Backscheider, *Daniel Defoe*, 429.
37. Woodes Rogers, *A Cruising Voyage Round the World* (London: printed for A. Bell and B. Lintot, 1712), 10.
38. See note 11 above.
39. Schonhorn, *Defoe's Politics*, 80.
40. See note 25 to my introduction.
41. C. B. Macpherson, *The Political Theory of Possessive Individualism: Hobbes to Locke* (Oxford: Oxford University Press, 1962), 248.
42. See Paul Kléber Monod, *Jacobitism and the English People*, 47 (see note 46 to chapter 1). Rather than representing truly popular sentiment, such songs were devised and distributed for broad publish consumption by artisans and laborers by "small number of extremely

productive Jacobite printers" (47). By 1716, the Mayor of London had proclaimed against the "epidemic of Jacobite ballad-hawking" (47). For a discussion of the "lost lover" motif, see *Jacobitism and the English People*, 62–69.

43. See note 49 below.

44. "The Dutchess of Monmouth's Lamentation For the Loss of her Duke" (n.p.: 1683), unpaginated broadsheet.

45. This wood cut showed "a knight and a lady holding a pierced heart— a symbol of love, of Christ, and of the Pretender" (Monod, *Jacobitism and the English People*, 64–65).

46. *The Fortunate Mistress or A History of the Life . . . of* Mademoiselle de Beleau . . . *Being the Person known by the Name of the Lady Roxana, in the Time of King* Charles II. *The Shakespeare Head Edition of the Novels & Selected Writings of Daniel Defoe*, 11:4.

47. Defoe, *Conjugal Lewdness: or, Matrimonial Whoredom* (London: T. Warner, 1727), 27.

48. See Novak, *Defoe and the Nature of Man* and Starr, *Defoe and Casuistry*.

49. David Blewett offers compelling evidence to support the claim that the time period described by *Roxana*, ostensibly taking place during the reign of George I, echoes the corruption and moral decay of the reign of Charles II, in "The Double Time-Scheme of Roxana: Further Evidence," *SECC* 13 (1984): 19–28.

50. *The Great Law of Subordination consider'd; or, the Insolence and Unsufferable Behaviour of Servants in England duly Enquir'd into . . . in ten Familiar Letters* (London: sold by S. Harding, W. Lewis, et al., 1724), 20.

51. In *The Politics of Motherhood*, Toni Bowers focuses on Defoe's depiction of "larger relations that create contradictions between ideals for motherhood and the behaviors required for maternal survival" (100). Bowers refreshingly dismantles two and a half centuries of criticism that has focused on the moral or psychological flaws of the heroine and underscores the fact that Roxana's struggle is not a moral one but a material one. For Bowers, Defoe faces the reality he glosses over in *Moll Flanders* in *Roxana* by "expos[ing] social formations that make a choice between autonomy and maternity seem inevitable" (123). Bowers thus praises Defoe for his realistic depiction of material reality at the same time that she shows its limitations in not providing descriptions of happy or effective single mothers (as Eliza Haywood does in several of her early novels). His critique of social conditions that impoverish single mothers speaks for itself, and is certainly one piece of the narrative's "realism." However, the narrative also achieves a different type of realism through, for example, its depiction of the necessary conditions under which marriage could convey the mutual liberty and responsibility embodied by the Whig social contract.

52. Although the genre of tragicomedy had certainly come to play a role in the early part of the eighteenth century, many contemporary critics

objected to it. Following the comprehensive list of plays typically staged in London in the mid 1730s in Eliza Haywood's *Dramatic Historiographer: or, the British Theatre Delineated* (1735), we may conclude that the majority are still either comedy or tragedy (even when a play such as *King Lear* had been modified from tragedy to comedy, it did not end up in the mixed form of tragicomedy).

4 PARTISAN DEBATE AND
MODERATION POLITICS IN SAMUEL
RICHARDSON'S FICTION

1. Ian Watt identified the social realism inherent in Richardson's depiction of class difference and in the economic plight of unmarried women in the eighteenth-century *Rise of the Novel*, 137–38. Michael McKeon links the "subversive strain" of "progressive ideology" in *Pamela* to parallel development in epistemology. See *The Origins of the English Novel*, 378. See note 14 below for an overview of the standard apolitical interpretations of Richardson.

2. For his reference to Monmouth, see his letter to Johannes Stinstra, June 2, 1753, *Selected Letters of Samuel Richardson*, ed. John Carroll (Oxford: Clarendon Press, 1964), 228. Eaves and Kimpel describe the 1724 issue of the *True Briton*, for which Richardson was probably the printer and which resulted in a trial of treason for the publisher: "Englishmen would do well to beware of a 'future' possible king who, being easy and inactive, might 'permit every Man in his Court to be a Tyrant but Himself.' " Richardson's biographers are here summarizing issues 5 and 7 (17 June and 24 June, 1724) of the *True Briton*. See Duncan Eaves and Ben Kimpel, *Samuel Richardson: A Biography* (Oxford: Clarendon Press, 1971), 26–29.

3. Margaret Anne Doody, "Richardson's Politics," *Eighteenth-Century Fiction* 2 (1990): 119, 123, 125.

4. Armstrong, *Desire and Domestic Fiction*, 132 (see note 5 to my introduction).

5. Ian Watt links Pamela to Moll Flanders and Robinson Crusoe when he concludes that "Puritan virtues" in an "individualist social order . . . offer women as large possibilities of achievement as men" (*Rise of the Novel*, 157). Michael McKeon similarly interprets Pamela's story within a rubric of bourgeois individualism.

6. Margaret Anne Doody suggests that while the novel offers a Whig critique of "the Church and the power of the secular establishment in the rural gentry," its apparent "Whiggism must be quite a thin veil." See "Richardson's Politics," 119. Toni Bowers also situates Richardson's work in a Tory context, and Christopher Flint observes that despite Pamela's radical rise from lady's maid to wife of Squire B., the novel never threatens "the precise demarcations of class." See Bowers, *The Politics of Motherhood*, 153–195 and Flint, *Family Fictions*, 163.

7. Samuel Richardson, *Pamela or, Virtue Rewarded*, Shakespeare Head edition, 4 vols. (Oxford: Basil Blackwell, 1929), 2:229.
8. Armstrong, *Desire and Domestic Fiction*, 113.
9. Esther 1:17–20 King James Version.
10. See note 7 to chapter 1.
11. [William Keith], *A Dissertation on the Liberty of the Subject in Great Britain*, 25–26.
12. This is part of Bowers's argument for his Toryism in *The Politics of Motherhood*, 156–78.
13. Samuel Richardson, *The History of Sir Charles Grandison*, 3 vols. (London: Oxford University Press, 1972), 3:470.
14. Cynthia Griffin Wolff's *Samuel Richardson and the Eighteenth-Century Puritan Character* (Hamden, CT: The Shoe String Press, 1972) focuses more on Richardson's universal descriptions of "character under stress" than on the historical context that might have caused the structural development of complex novelistic characters. Lawrence Stone uses the example of *Clarissa* as "literary evidence" of "a prolonged public argument during the late seventeenth and eighteenth centuries about a child's freedom of choice of a marriage partner." See *The Family, Sex and Marriage in England 1500–1800* (New York: Harper and Row, 1977), 280–81. Tony Tanner's *Adultery in the Novel: Contract and Transgression* (Baltimore: Johns Hopkins University Press, 1979) offers a Lacanian reading of the patriarchal Harlowe household. *Clarissa* criticism moves away from psychology to textual play when William Warner describes the ambiguity of the text. In *Reading Clarissa: The Struggles of Interpretation* (New Haven: Yale University Press, 1979), Warner concludes from such linguistic ambiguity that "rape is the most cogent response to Clarissa's fictional projection of herself as a whole unified body 'full of light' " (49). Terry Eagleton has a sharp response. Warner's book, says Eagleton, "is an ominous exposé of the truly reactionary nature of much deconstructionist 'radicalism', once divorced from the social and political contexts it so characteristically finds hard to handle." See *The Rape of Clarissa* (Minneapolis: University of Minnesota Press, 1982), 67–68. Terry Castle argues, in response to Warner's post-structural rhetorical analysis, that "the excruciating situation that Clarissa dramatizes is that a rhetorical system is *not* 'powerful' unless grounded in political power." See *Clarissa's Ciphers: Meaning and Disruption in Richardson's Clarissa* (Ithaca: Cornell University Press, 1982), 25. Toni Bowers describes how in *Clarissa* motherhood is represented in the language of public politics. See *The Politics of Motherhood*, 196–224.
15. Wolff, *Samuel Richardson and the Eighteenth-Century Puritan Character*, 131. Watt and Eagleton both make a similar observation.
16. See note 22 to chapter 1.
17. Morris Golden, "Public Context and Imagining Self in *Clarissa*," *SEL* 25 (1985): 575–98.

18. Eaves and Kimpel refer to Richardson's thorough knowledge of Locke's theories of education and his at least cursory knowledge of Shaftesbury, Mandeville, Bolingbroke, Hartley, Hume, and Berkeley. See *Samuel Richardson: A Biography*, 571.

19. Richardson, *Clarissa*, 95 (see note 14 to chapter 1).

20. This is consistent with Florian Stuber's observation that in a novel devoid of strong paternal figures, Clarissa becomes an example of prudent, mature masculine power: "In her Will, Clarissa uses power, but with restraint, and only for the purposes of love and nurture. She seems an ideal secular authority. The mind is father to the deed. Or, if I can break through the sexism inherent in the metaphor, Clarissa herself becomes a Father." See Florian Stuber, "On Fathers and Authority in Clarissa," *SEL* 25 (Summer 1985): 574.

21. Filmer, *Patriarcha*, 96 (see note 4 to chapter 1).

22. Letter to Johannes Stinstra, June 2, 1753, *Selected Letters*, 234.

23. See note 3 above.

24. *Oxford Dictionary of National Biography*, s.v. Wharton. Richardson may in fact have known Wharton, since he printed issues *The True Briton*, one of Wharton's forays into Jacobite propaganda.

25. Richardson, *Clarissa*, 573.

26. As Susan Fraiman explains, the narrator relates Darcy's first proposal to Elizabeth through Elizabeth's mental summary of it, and her full verbatim responses to it, rather than being represented in his own words. His subsequent letter to her signals the beginning of a narrative shift that presents him more directly in his own words and from his own perspective. See Susan Fraiman, *Unbecoming Women*, 77–78.

27. See note 22 above.

28. Richardson, *The History of Sir Charles Grandison*, 3:470.

29. Doody, "Richardson's Politics," 125.

30. Doody mistakenly conflates Maria Clementina Stuart (née Sobieska), exiled wife of James Edward, with Miss Walkinshaw, his mistress during his wife's exile, in her discussion of "Clementina Walkinshaw." See "Richardson's Politics," 125.

5   JACOBITE IDEOLOGY AND ELIZA HAYWOOD'S RESPONSE TO WHIG REALISM

1. See Dale Spender's comment that "Eliza Haywood was among the first with every experiment [of every genre of novel], and among the few who could claim success" (*Mothers of the Novel*, 81). Although Haywood is not yet universally recognized as an innovator, many of the works that Haywood is supposed to have imitated are in fact chronologically subsequent to her original versions, as Paula Backscheider has noted. The damage wrought by Haywood's continuing exclusion from literary history is considerable; Backscheider observes, "No wonder

the history of the novel is in disarray." See "The Shadow of an Author: Eliza Haywood," *Eighteenth-Century Fiction* 11:1 (October 1998): 102. Backscheider reminds us that *The Fortunate Foundlings* (1744) precedes both "Fielding's own foundling story" and "Richardson's greatest exploration of class and gender politics" (102).

2. See my conclusion for a discussion of the references to Haywood in Anna Barbauld's introduction to *The British Novelists* (1810).

3. George Whicher blurs the distinction between her life and her romances in his biography of her, thus making it difficult to take her seriously as a novelist. See *The Life and Romances of Mrs. Eliza Haywood* (New York: Columbia University Press, 1915).

4. See notes 31 and 32 to my introduction.

5. In *Popular Fiction before Richardson*, John Richetti suggests that Haywood is second-rate; he then leaves her out of his "line" of important novelists in "Ideas and Voices" (see notes 1, 11, and 14 to my introduction). More recently, he has discussed Haywood's use of romance formulae and her imitation of Richardson and Fielding, without acknowledging how they also imitated her technical developments in the novel. See his "Histories by Eliza Haywood and Henry Fielding: Imitation and Adaptation," in *The Passionate Fictions of Eliza Haywood*, ed. Saxton and Bocchicchio (Lexington: University Press of Kentucky, 2000), 240–58.

6. In elucidating amatory fiction's relationship to party politics, Ros Ballaster delineates the obvious satire of the South Sea Bubble in Haywood's *Memoirs of a Certain Island Adjacent to the Kingdom of Utopia* (1727) and Haywood's anti-Walpole stance in *The Adventures of Eovaai* (1736). See *Seductive Forms*, 153–62. More recently, Ballaster has expanded her analysis of Haywood's partisan politics in "A Gender of Opposition: Eliza Haywood's Scandal Fiction," in *Passionate Fictions*, ed. Saxton and Bocchicchio, 143–67. For all their focus on social history, Helene Koon, in "Eliza Haywood and the Female Spectator," *Huntington Library Quarterly* 42:1 (Winter 1978): 43–55, and Deborah Nestor, in "Representing Domestic Difficulties: Eliza Haywood and the Critique of Bourgeois Ideology," *Prose Studies* 16:2 (August 1993): 1–26, overlook the specific political allusions in Haywood's *The Female Spectator*. Catherine Ingrassia's observations in "Additional Information about Eliza Haywood's 1749 Arrest for Seditious Libel" establish the need for broader recognition of Haywood as "producer and distributor of surprisingly political texts in a heretofore unrecognized way." See *Notes and Queries* 242:2 (June 1997): 202. Ingrassia's *Authorship, Commerce, and Gender in Early Eighteenth-Century England: A Culture of Paper Credit* (Cambridge: Cambridge University Press, 1998) further elaborates the way that Haywood negotiates the "fundamental generic instabilities that characterize this literary period—was fiction 'political'? was political writing 'fictional'?" (125).

7. His wife retired to a convent over a dispute about the tutor whom James had chosen for his son, and divided loyalties for James and Clementina did "untold harm" to the Jacobite cause, according to Frank McLynn. See *Charles Edward Stuart: A Tragedy in Many Acts* (London and New York: Routledge, 1988), 17.

8. In "Histories by Eliza Haywood and Henry Fielding," Richetti acknowledges Haywood's political collaboration with Fielding at the New Theater in the 1730s, but then interprets her subsequent and "retrospective scorn for her old employer" in terms of personal affront at his contempt for the authors of "foolish Novels and monstrous Romances" (241). I suggest that we might interpret the 1740s rivalry between Haywood and Fielding not merely in formal terms, but in terms of her evolution from mere anti-Walpole politics to a stronger stance in favor of Charles Edward Stuart, a position that Fielding might well have mocked as itself a sort of "monstrous Romance."

9. See my "It's Not Easy Being Green" (see note 35 to my introduction).

10. See my "The Very Scandal of Her Tea-Table: Eliza Haywood's Response to the Whig Public Sphere," in Presenting Gender: Sex Change in Early-Modern Culture, ed. Chris Mounsey (Lewisburg, PA: Bucknell University Press, 2001), 255–73.

11. In contrast with my view here, Kathryn King has argued recently that Haywood's "achievements as a popular novelist" stem from "her creation of politically multivalent texts that oscillate between Tory and Whiggish tendencies" (265). See her "New Contexts for Early Novels by Women: The Case of Eliza Haywood, Aaron Hill, and the Hillarians, 1719–1725," in *A Companion to the Eighteenth-Century English Novel and Culture*, ed. Paula Backscheider and Catherine Ingrassia (Oxford: Blackwell Publishing, 2005), 261–75. I am grateful to the author for sharing this article with me in advance of its publication.

12. Austin, "Shooting Blanks: Potency, Parody, and Eliza Haywood's *The History of Miss Betsy Thoughtless*" in *The Passionate Fictions of Eliza Haywood*, ed. Saxton and Bocchicchio, 259–82.

13. A handwritten note on the British Library's copy suggests this identification, which is also given by the English Short Title Catalogue.

14. *A Letter From H----G----g, Esq.; One of the Gentlemen of the Bed Chamber to the Young Chevalier, and the only Person of his own Retinue that attended him from Avignon, in his late Journey through Germany, and elsewhere* (London: printed and sold at the Royal Exchange, Temple Bar, and Charing Cross, 1750), iii. Although dated 1750, the work appeared in late 1749.

15. Lynch, *The Economy of Character*, 86–94.

16. See my "It's Not Easy Being Green" for a full analysis of Haywood's treatment of the politics of friendship.

17. See note 43 to my introduction.

18. Although Haywood hints at an impending marriage between Charles Edward Stuart and a Polish princess, Frank McLynn describes him as

"brusquely" rejecting "a proposal to make him the next king of Poland" and instead pursuing an intrigue (possibly platonic) with the eccentric and already married Duchesse d'Aiguillon. See *Charles Edward Stuart*, 344.

19. Although all the booksellers implicated in selling copies of *A Letter* signed and swore to the accuracy of their testimony, Haywood and her maid apparently refused to do so. In the record of Streddon's testimony, at the bottom of the page, where in the other accounts Lord Stanhope wrote "Taken upon oath," the words "upon oath" are crossed out, and a note at the bottom indicates that the witness "refused to swear to her Examination," although Streddon's signature does appear at the bottom of the page. By contrast, a month later, after giving her own testimony, Haywood managed to avoid signing the paper altogether, without Stanhope making any written note calling attention to her refusal. See Public Record Office, State Papers Domestic 36/111 f. 204–14 and 36/112 f. 24.

20. Haywood adds, in order to further explain how she was unable to have written the pamphlet in November, "that she has lost her Eye sight about Six Months & kept her Bed above two Months" (PRO SP112 f. 24)—an excuse that Catherine Ingrassia has described as politically convenient "in a professional world where intentional 'blindness' to certain activities could be a great asset." See *Authorship, Commerce, and Gender*, 122.

21. Doody, *True Story of the Novel*, 286.

22. Bowers, "Collusive Resistance," 63.

23. Haywood, *Idalia: or, the Unfortunate Mistress* (London: printed for D. Brown, W. Chetwood, and S. Chapman, 1723), 2–3.

24. Haywood, *Lasselia: or the Self-Abandon'd* (London: printed for D. Browne and S. Chapman, 1723), 4.

25. Haywood, *The Rash Resolve: or, the Untimely Discovery*, 1724 (London: printed for D. Browne and S. Chapman, 1724), 49.

26. Haywood, *The British Recluse: or, The Secret History of Cleomira* (London: printed for D. Brown, W. Chetwood, J. Woodward, and S. Chapman, 1722), 51.

27. Both Earla Wilputte in her editorial comments to the Broadview edition of *Eovaai* and Paula Backscheider in "The Shadow of an Author" link *Eovaai's* anti-Walpole position to Haywood's support for Frederick. See Backscheider's "Shadow of an Author": 93–95 (see note 1 above); Eliza Haywood *Adventures of Eovaai, Princess of Ijaveao: A Pre-Adamitical History*, ed. Earla Wilputte (Peterborough, Ontario: Broadview Press, 1999). Acknowledging the iconographic links to Bolingbroke that Elizabeth Kubek traces in "The Key to Stowe: Towards a Patriot Whig reading of Eliza Haywood's *Eovaai*," in *Presenting Gender: Sex Change in Early-Modern Culture*, Chris Mounsey, ed., 225–54, Paula Backscheider traces interesting splits and fissures in the Bolingbroke camp as well as a fascination with

Frederick among some of its members. However, even should we assume a frustration with James Edward Stuart in the 1730s, this did not prevent Haywood taking up the Jacobite cause again more directly during the 1740s, when Charles Edward Stuart became a rallying figure for his father's long disaffected supporters. Correcting her earlier discounting of Haywood's partisan position, Ros Ballaster also seems to think that Adelhu is more likely to represent Frederick observing that "Haywood appears to have been attracted to the cause of Frederick in the 1730s and reverted to a Jacobite position in the subsequent decade." See "A Gender of Opposition: Eliza Haywood's Scandal Fiction," in *The Passionate Fictions of Eliza Haywood*, ed. Saxton and Bocchicchio, 154; 166 n. 19.

28. Haywood, *The Adventures of Eovaai, Princess of Ijaveo* (London: printed for S. Baker, 1736), 4.

29. Murray G. H. Pittock, *Inventing and Resisting Britain: Cultural Identities in Britain and Ireland, 1685–1789* (Basingstoke: Macmillan, 1997), 58.

30. Haywood, *The Fortunate Foundlings* (London: printed by and published for T. Gardner, 1744), 1.

31. Haywood makes condescending references in *The Wife* to a Jacobite husband who only toasts the cause but will not support it in any material way. See my "The Very Scandal of her Tea Table," 266–69.

32. In privileging Fielding over Haywood, John Richetti recognizes no irony in Haywood's narratives, a common oversight among those who read her novels as merely apolitical romances. Moreover, Richetti interprets as a personal vendetta Haywood's and Fielding's mutual and mocking references to each other's works, rather than as evidence of a possible difference of opinion over issues of political loyalty and Jacobitism. The passage from *The History of Miss Betsy Thoughtless* that Richetti cites, in which Haywood mocks "F——g's scandal shop" (quoted in "Histories by Eliza Haywood and Henry Fielding," 240–41), suggests less a personal anger against her former collaborator on stage, than a political disapproval of his desire to "wriggle himself into favour" with whomever was in power. Haywood herself advocated a consistent, long-term political loyalty by way of the cosmic Jacobitism evident in her later works. It may have seemed to her that the opportunism she ascribes to Fielding compared unfavorably to her own loyalty. I prefer Christine Blouch's interpretation of the supposed rivalry between Haywood and Fielding: "As exchanges conducted without real invective, at least relative to the period's norms, the mutual satires can also be seen as mutually beneficial." See "Eliza Haywood," Blouch's biographical essay in *Selected Works of Eliza Haywood*, ed. Alexander Pettit, 6 vols. (London: Pickering and Chatto, 2000), 1:lxii. Another explanation for their differences of opinion was that while they were joined in the 1730s by a mutual dislike of Walpole, after that minister's fall from power, their political sympathies evolved in different directions: Haywood moved toward the Jacobite cause while Fielding maintained a firmly anti-Jacobite position.

33. Szechi explains why Sweden looked to the Jacobites as a sympathetic force against the Hanoverian occupation of Verden and Bremen and why the Jacobites considered that "the gratitude of a warlord like Charles XII was a thing worth having." See *The Jacobites*, 106.

34. *The Monthly Review* 8 (1753): 77.

35. *Dalinda* marks the first of Haywood's works to be mentioned by *The Monthly Review*, as the periodical only came into existence in 1749, but it is only accorded only cursory and condescending acknowledgment. The brief mention is included after a heading that already acknowledges that while the editors will "*register all the new Things, in general, without exception to any, on account of their lowness of rank, or price*," although they anticipate that it would "*prove disagreeable to many of our readers*" to provide too much detail about the texts that they deem below their readers' notice (238). Accordingly, *Dalinda* is reduced simply to "the affair betwixt Mr. *Cresswell* and Miss *Scrope*, thrown into the form of a novel." Although the *Review* discounts Haywood's other plots for not being adequately true to life, it is clear that a fictional account of a "true to life" scandal chronicle does not satisfy its reviewers either. See *The Monthly Review* 1 (December 1749): 238.

36. Five English editions appears in the first two and a half decades, as well as editions in Dutch, French, German, and Swedish; the novel was then included in volume 13 of *The Novelist's Magazine* (1780–89). See Patrick Spedding *A Bibliography of Eliza Haywood* (London: Pickering & Chatto, 2004), 529–67.

37. Armstrong, *Desire and Domestic Fiction*, 3–27.

38. See Doody's introduction to the Oxford World Classics edition, xviii.

39. Haywood, *The History of Jemmy and Jenny Jessamy*, 3 vols. (London: printed for T. Gardner, 1753), 1:2.

40. Haywood, *The Female Spectator*, 4 vols. (London: printed and published by T. Gardner, 1744–46), 1:10.

41. Following Christine Blouch's biographical research, we may note that Haywood herself maintained a long-term romantic involvement (one that by 1753 had certainly moved beyond the sparks of first love) with the writer and bookseller, and Haywood's sometime collaborator, William Hatchett.

42. Booth, *Rhetoric of Fiction*, 64.

43. See note 42 to chapter 3.

44. See note 43 to my introduction.

CONCLUSION: PARTISAN REALISMS AND CANON FORMATION

1. "On the Origin and Progress of Novel-Writing," reprinted in *Anna Letitia Barbauld: Selected Poetry & Prose*, 400–01 (see note 36 to my introduction).

2. *The Monthly Review* 2 (January 1750): 167.

3. See note 2 to my introduction.

4. See William McCarthy and Elizabeth Kraft's correction the late twentieth-century assumption that Barbauld and Wollstonecraft represented
   opposite positions in matters of politics and attitudes toward gender
   roles in their introduction to *Anna Letitia Barbauld: Selected Poetry &*
   Prose, 28–30 (See note 36 to chapter 1).

5. Ballaster, *Seductive Forms*, 198.

6. See note 34 to chapter 5.

7. Irving Howe describes an encounter when he was asked whether
   A Tale of Two Cities should be considered "a political novel": "For a
   moment I was bewildered, since it had never occurred to me that this
   was a genuine problem: it was, I am now sure, the kind of problem
   one has to *look for*." See *Politics and the Novel* (Freeport, New York:
   Books for Libraries Press, 1957, 1970), 16.

8. *Clarissa, Sir Charles Grandison, Robinson Crusoe, Joseph Andrews*, and
   Tom Jones comprise the first twenty-one volumes. For a full listing of
   the contents of all fifty volumes, see Appendix D in McCarthy and
   Kraft's edition of Barbauld's works.

9. William Warner provides a superb overview and analysis of this type of
   canon-influencing essay from Clara Reeve's *Progress of Romance* (1785)
   to Watt's *Rise of the Novel* (1957) in *Licensing Entertainment*, 14–36.

10. Barbauld, preface to Henry Fielding, from *The British Novelists*
    (1810); reprinted in *Anna Letitia Barbauld: Selected Poetry & Prose*,
    420. In the last phrase, Barbauld is quoting Edward Young's *Love of*
    Fame, The Universal Passion (1728): *Satire VI*, "On Women," 1. 188,
    as the editors of *Anna Letitia Barbauld: Selected Poetry & Prose* point
    out (420 n. 4).

11. Robert Burns reworked many Jacobite songs for James Johnson's *The*
    Scots Musical Museum (1787–1803); such songs would therefore have
    become better known outside of Scotland in a de-politicized and
    romanticized context, a half-century after the last significant Jacobite
    attempt on the throne.

12. Barbauld, *An Address to the Opposers of the Repeal of the Corporation*
    and Test Acts (1790), reprinted in *Anna Letitia Barbauld: Selected*
    Poetry & Prose, 269–70.

13. See note 35 to my introduction.

14. McCarthy and Kraft explain that this passage comes from Fletcher's
    1704 *Conversation Concerning a Right Regulation of Government for*
    the Common Good of Mankind in *Anna Letitia Barbauld: Selected*
    Poetry & Prose, 416 n. 3.

BIBLIOGRAPHY

Allestree, Richard. *The Whole Duty of Man*. London: printed for Timothy Garthwait [1658].

Arbuthnot, Archibald. *Memoirs of the Remarkable Life and Surprizing Adventures of Miss Jenny Cameron, A Lady, who by her Attachment to the Person and Cause of the Young Pretender, Has Render'd Herself Famous by her Exploits in his Service*. London: printed and sold by R. Walker, 1746.

Armstrong, Nancy. *Desire and Domestic Fiction: A Political History of the Novel*. New York: Oxford University Press, 1987.

Ashcraft, Richard. *Revolutionary Politics and Locke's Two Treatises of Government*. Princeton, NJ: Princeton University Press, 1986.

Ashcraft, Richard, and M. M. Goldsmith. "Locke, Revolution Principles, and the Formation of Whig Ideology," *Historical Journal* 26:4 (1983): 773–800.

Astell, Mary. Preface to *Reflections on Marriage*, 3rd ed., London, 1706; reprinted in *The First English Feminist: Reflections upon Marriage and Other Writings*, ed. Bridget Hill, 70–87. New York: St. Martins Press, 1986.

The Anatomy of a Jacobite, or, the Jacobites Heart Laid Open, with a Sure and Certain Method for their Cure. Cambridge: [s.n.], 1692.

The Anatomy of a Jacobite-Tory: In a Dialogue between Whig and Tory, Occasioned by the Act for Recognizing King William and Queen Mary. London: Richard Baldwin, 1690.

An Attempt towards a Natural History of the Hanover Rat. London: printed for M. Cooper, 1744.

Atwood, William. *The Fundamental Constitution of the English Government*. London: printed by J. D. for the Author, 1690.

Austin, Andrea. "Shooting Blanks: Potency, Parody, and Eliza Haywood's *The History of Miss Betsy Thoughtless*," in *The Passionate Fictions of Eliza Haywood*, ed. Kirsten T. Saxton and Rebecca P. Bocchicchio, 259–82. Lexington: University Press of Kentucky, 2000.

Backscheider, Paula. *Daniel Defoe: His Life*. Baltimore: Johns Hopkins University Press, 1989.

———. "Introduction" to "The Intersections of the Public and Private Sphere in Early Modern England," ed. Paula R. Backscheider and Timothy Dykstal, *Prose Studies* 18:3 (December 1995): 1–21.

———. "The Novel's Gendered Space." In *Revising Women: Eighteenth-Century "Women's Fiction" and Social Engagement*, ed. Paula Backscheider, 1–30. Baltimore: Johns Hopkins University Press, 2000.

Backscheider, Paula. "The Shadow of an Author: Eliza Haywood." *Eighteenth-Century Fiction* 11:1 (October 1998): 79–102.

———. *Spectacular Politics: Theatrical Power and Mass Culture in Early Modern Europe*. Baltimore: Johns Hopkins University Press, 1993.

Backscheider, Paula and John Richetti, eds. *Popular Fiction by Women 1660–1730*. Oxford: Oxford University Press, 1996.

Bakhtin, Mikhail M. *The Dialogic Imagination: Four Essays by M. M. Bakhtin*, trans. Caryl Emerson and Michael Holquist, ed. Michael Holquist. Austin: University of Texas Press, 1981.

Ballaster, Ros. *Seductive Forms: Women's Amatory Fiction from 1684 to 1740*. Oxford: Clarendon Press, 1992.

———. " 'Pretences of State': Aphra Behn and the Female Plot." In *Rereading Aphra Behn: History, Theory, and Criticism*, ed. Heidi Hutner, 187–211. Charlottesville: University Press of Virginia, 1993.

———. "A Gender of Opposition: Eliza Haywood's Scandal Fiction." In *The Passionate Fictions of Eliza Haywood*, ed. Kirsten T. Saxton and Rebecca P. Bocchicchio, 143–67. Lexington: University Press of Kentucky, 2000.

Barbauld, Anna Letitia. *An Address to the Opposers of the Repeal of the Corporation and Test Acts*. London: printed for John Johnson, 1790; reprinted in *Anna Letitia Barbauld: Selected Poetry and Prose*, ed. William McCarthy and Elizabeth Kraft, 261–81. Peterborough, Ontario: Broadview Press, 2002.

———. "On the Origin and Progress of Novel Writing." Introduction to *The British Novelists*. London: F. C. and J. Rivington et al., 1810; reprinted in *Anna Letitia Barbauld: Selected Poetry and Prose*, 337–417. Peterborough, Ontario: Broadview Press, 2002.

———. Preface to Henry Fielding, from *The British Novelists*, excerpted in *Anna Letitia Barbauld: Selected Poetry and Prose*, 417–25.

[Barrington, John Shute]. *A Dissuasive from Jacobitism: Shewing in general What the Nation is to expect from a Popish King; and in particular, from the Pretender*. London: printed for John Baker, 1713.

Beasley, Jerry. *Novels of the 1740s*. Athens: University of Georgia Press, 1982.

Behn, Aphra. *The Works of Aphra Behn*, 7 vols., ed. Janet Todd. Athens: Ohio State University Press, 1992–96.

Bellegarde, Morvan de. *Lettres curieuses de Litterature et de morale*. la Haye [the Hague]: Adrian Moetjers, 1702.

Blewett, David. "The Double Time-Scheme of Roxana: Further Evidence." *Studies in Eighteenth-Century Culture* 13 (1984): 19–28.

Blouch, Christine. "Eliza Haywood: Biographical Introduction," *Selected Works of Eliza Haywood*, ed. Alexander Pettit, 6 vols. London: Pickering and Chatto, 2000.

Bolingbroke, Henry St. John, Viscount. *The Idea of a Patriot King* (London 1749), ed. Sydney W. Jackman. Indianapolis: Bobbs Merrill, 1965.

Booth, Wayne C. *The Rhetoric of Fiction*, 2nd ed. Chicago and London: University of Chicago Press, 1961.

Bowers, Toni. "Collusive Resistance: Sexual Agency and Partisan Politics in *Love in Excess.*" In *The Passionate Fictions of Eliza Haywood*, ed. Kirsten T. Saxton and Rebecca P. Bocchicchio, 48–68. Lexington: University Press of Kentucky, 2000.

———. "Sex, Lies, and Invisibility: Amatory Fiction from the Restoration to Mid-Century," in *The Columbia History of the British Novel*, ed. John Richetti et al., 50–72. New York: Columbia University Press, 1994.

———. *The Politics of Motherhood: British Writing and Culture 1680–1760.* Cambridge: Cambridge University Press, 1996.

Box, M. A. *The Suasive Art of David Hume.* Princeton: Princeton University Press, 1990.

Braverman, Richard. *Plots and Counterplots: Sexual Politics and the Body Politic in English Literature, 1660–1730.* Cambridge: Cambridge University Press, 1993.

A Brief Account of the Life and Family of Miss Jenny Cameron, the Reputed Mistress of the Pretender's Eldest Son. London: printed by T. Gardner, 1746.

A Brief Justification of the Prince of Orange's Descent into England and of the Kingdom's Late Recourse to Arms. London: printed for J. S. and sold by Richard Baldwin, 1689.

Brennan, Teresa and Carole Pateman. " 'Mere Auxiliaries to the Commonwealth': Women and the Origins of Liberalism," *Political Studies* 27 (1979): 183–200.

Brown, Homer Obed. "The Institution of the English Novel: Defoe's Contribution." *Novel: A Forum on Fiction* 29:3 (Spring 1996): 299–318.

———. *Institutions of the English Novel from Defoe to Scott.* Philadelphia: University of Pennsylvania Press, 1997.

Brown, Laura. *English Dramatic Form English Dramatic Form 1660–1760: An Essay in Generic History.* New Haven: Yale University Press, 1981.

———. "The Romance of Empire: *Oroonoko* and the Trade in Slaves." in *The New Eighteenth Century: Theory, Politics, English Literature*, ed. Felicity Nussbaum and Laura Brown, 59–60. New York: Methuen, 1987.

Brown, Marshall. "The Logic of Realism: A Hegelian Approach." *PMLA* 96:2 (March 1981): 224–41.

Bruyère, Jean de la. *Les Caractères de Théophraste traduits du grec avec les Caractères ou les Moeurs de ce siècle.* Paris: Éditions Garnier Frères [1964].

Burke, Edmund. *Reflections on the Revolution in France*, ed. Thomas H. D. Mahoney. New York: The Liberal Arts Press, 1955.

Butler, Marilyn. *Jane Austen and the War of Ideas.* Oxford: Clarendon Press, 1975.

Campbell, Jill. *Natural Masques: Gender and Identity in Fielding's Plays and Novels.* Stanford: Stanford University Press, 1995.

Canfield J. Douglas. "Royalism's Last Dramatic Stand: English Political Tragedy, 1679–89." *Studies in Philology* 82:2 (Spring 1985): 234–63.

———. "Tupping Your Rival's Women: Cit-Cuckolding as Class Warfare in Restoration Comedy." In *Broken Boundaries: Women and Feminism in*

Restoration Drama, ed. Katherine M. Quinsey, 113–28. Lexington: University of Kentucky Press, 1996.

Carnell, Rachel. "Clarissa's Treasonable Correspondence: Gender, Epistolary Politics, and the Public Sphere." *Eighteenth-Century Fiction* 10:3 (April 1998): 269–87.

———. "It's Not Easy Being Green: Gender and Friendship in Eliza Haywood's Political Periodicals." *Eighteenth-Century Studies* 32:2 (Winter 1998–99): 199–214.

———. "More Borrowing from Bellegarde in Manley's *Queen Zarah and the Zarazians*," *N&Q* 249: 4 (December 2004): 377–79.

———. "The Very Scandal of Her Tea-Table: Eliza Haywood's Response to the Whig Public Sphere." In *Presenting Gender: Sex Change in Early-Modern Culture*, ed. Chris Mounsey, 255–73. Lewisburg, PA: Bucknell University Press, 2001.

Carnell, Rachel and Ruth Herman. "General Introduction." *The Selected Works of Delarivier Manley*, ed. Rachel Carnell and Ruth Herman, 5 vols. London: Pickering & Chatto, 2005.

Castle, Terry. *Clarissa's Ciphers: Meaning and Disruption in Richardson's Clarissa*. Ithaca: Cornell University Press, 1982.

Clark, J. C. D. *English Society 1688–1832: Ideology, Social Structure, and Political Practice during the Ancien Régime*. Cambridge: Cambridge University Press, 1985.

Clarke, Bob. *From Grub Street to Fleet Street: An Illustrated History of English Newspapers to* 1899. Aldershot: Ashgate, 2004.

Colley, Linda. *In Defiance of Oligarchy: The Tory Party 1714–60*. Cambridge: Cambridge University Press, 1982.

"Come if You Dare." London: printed for P. Clifton, 1714.

A Comparison of the Spirit of the Whigs *and* Jacobites: *Being the Substance of a Discourse Delivered to An Audience of Gentlemen in Edinburgh, December 24, 1745*. Edinburgh: printed by R. Fleming, 1746.

Crompton, Virginia. " 'For when the act is done and finish't cleane, / what should the poet doe, but shift the scene?': Propaganda, Professionalism and Aphra Behn." In *Aphra Behn Studies*, ed. Janet Todd, 130–53. Cambridge: Cambridge University Press, 1996.

Corneille, Pierre. *Oeuvres Complètes*. Paris: Editions du Seuil, 1963.

The Counsel to the True English: or, A Word of Advice to the Jacobites. London: printed for S. Manship, 1691.

[Crouch, Nathaniel], *Female Excellency: or, the Ladies Glory. Illustrated in the Worthy Lives and Memorable Actions of Nine Famous Women* By R. B. London: Nath. Crouch, 1688.

Culler, Jonathon. *Structuralist Poetics: Structuralism, Linguistics and the Study of Literature*. Ithaca: Cornell University Press, 1975.

[Davenant, Charles]. *The True Picture of a Modern Whig, Set Forth in a Dialogue Between Mr. Whiglove & Mr. Double*. London: n.p., 1701.

[———]. *Tom DoubleReturn'd: or, the True Picture of a Modern Whig Set Forth in a Second Dialogue Between Mr. Whiglove & Mr. Double*. London: n.p., 1702.

Davis, Lennard J. *Factual Fictions: The Origins of the English Novel.* New York: Columbia University Press, 1983.

Defoe, Daniel. *Conjugal Lewdness: or, Matrimonial Whoredom.* London: T. Warner, 1727.

———. *The Family Instructor.* London: printed for Eman. Matthews; Newcastle upon Tyne: Jo. Button, 1715.

———. *The Great Law of Subordination consider'd; or, the Insolence and Unsufferable Behaviour of Servants in England duly enquir'd into . . . in ten Familiar Letters.* London: sold by S. Harding, W. Lewis, T. Worrall, A. Bettesworth, W. Meadows, and T. Edlin, 1724.

———. *Jure Divino: A Satyr.* London: printed by P. Hills, 1706.

———. *The Original Power of the Collective Body of the People of England, Examined and Asserted.* London, 1702.

———. *Religious Courtship, Being Historical Discourses on the Necessity of Marrying Religious Husband and Wives only.* London: printed for E. Matthews, A. Bettesworth, J. Brotherton, and W. Meadows, 1722.

———. *A Seasonal Warning and Caution against the Against the Insinuations Jacobites and Papists in Favour of the Pretender.* London: printed for J. Baker, 1712.

———. *The Shakespeare Head Edition of the Novels & Selected Writings of Daniel Defoe,* 14 vols. Oxford: Basil Blackwell and New York and Boston: Houghton Mifflin, 1928.

Deluna, D. N. "*Jure Divino*: Defoe's 'whole Volume in Folio, by Way of Answer to, and Confutation of *Clarendon's* History of the Rebellion.' " *Philological Quarterly* 75:1 (Winter 1996): 43–66.

Doody, Margaret Anne. Introduction to *The Female Quixote; or, The Adventures of Arabella,* by Charlotte Lennox, ed. Margaret Dalziel. Oxford: Oxford University Press, 1989.

———. "Richardson's Politics." *Eighteenth-Century Fiction* 2 (1990): 119–26.

———. *The True Story of the Novel.* New Brunswick: Rutgers University Press, 1996.

Downie, J. A. *Robert Harley and the Press: Propaganda and Public Opinion in the Age of Swift and Defoe.* Cambridge: Cambridge University Press, 1979.

———. "Mary Davys's 'Probable Feign'd Stories' and Critical Shibboleths about 'The Rise of the Novel.' " *Eighteenth-Century Fiction* 12 (January–April 2000): 309–26.

———. "The Making of the English Novel," *Eighteenth-Century Fiction* 9:3 (April 1997): 249–66.

———. "What if Delarivier Manley did *not* write *The Secret History of Queen Zarah*?" *The Library* 7th series 5:3 (September 2004): 247–64.

Dryden, John. *The Works of John Dryden,* 20 vols. Berkeley and Los Angeles: University of California Press, 1956–2000.

Duffy, Maureen. *The Passionate Shepherdess: Aphra Behn 1640–1689.* London: Methuen, 1989.

"The Dutchess of Monmouth's Lamentation For the Loss of her Duke," n. p.: 1683.

Eagleton, Terry. *Literary Theory: An Introduction.* Minneapolis: University of Minnesota Press, 1983.

———. *The Rape of Clarissa: Writing, Sexuality, and Class Struggle in Samuel* Richardson. Minneapolis: University of Minnesota Press, 1982.

Eaves, T. C. Duncan and Ben D. Kimpel. *Samuel Richardson: A Biography.* Oxford: Clarendon Press, 1971.

Ermarth, Elizabeth Deeds. *Realism and Consensus in the English Novel.* Princeton: Princeton University Press, 1983.

An Excellent New Song Call'd, The Female Duel; or, The Victorious Williamite Lady, Who was Challenged to Fight a Duel by a Jacobite Lady. [London]: printed and sold by P. Pelcomb, [1700].

The Female Monster: or, The Second Part of The World Turn'd Topsy Turvey. A Satyr. London: B. Bragg, 1705.

The Female Rebels: Being Some Remarkable Incidents of the Lives, Characters and Families of the Titular Duke and Dutchess of Perth, *the Lord and Lady* Ogilvie, *and of* Miss Florence M'Donald. Edinburgh; reprinted London: sold by L. Gilliver, Mrs. Dodd, and G. Woodfall, 1747.

Ferguson, Frances. "Rape and the Rise of the Novel," *Representations* 20 (Autumn 1987): 88–112.

Ferguson, Robert. *A Brief Justification of the Prince of Orange's Descent into England and of the Kingdom's Late Recourse to Arms.* London: R. Baldwin, 1689.

Fielding, Henry. *The Jacobite's Journal and Related Writings,* ed. W. B. Coley. Middletown, CT: Wesleyan University Press; Oxford: Oxford University Press, 1975.

Filmer, Robert. *Patriarcha and Other Political Works of Sir Robert Filmer,* ed. Peter Laslett. Oxford: Basil Blackwell, 1949.

Finke, Laurie. "Aphra Behn and the Ideological Construction of Restoration Literary Theory." In *Rereading Aphra Behn: History, Theory, and Criticism,* ed. Heidi Hutner, 255–73. Charlottesville: University Press of Virginia, 1993.

Flint, Christopher. *Family Fictions: Narrative and Domestic Relations in Britain, 1688–1798.* Stanford: Stanford University Press, 1998.

Flynn, Carol Houlihan. "Defoe's Idea of Conduct: Ideological Fictions and Fictional Reality." In *The Ideology of Conduct: Essays on Literature and the History of Sexuality,* ed. Nancy Armstrong and Leonard Tennenhouse, 73–95. New York and London: Methuen, 1987.

Forbes, Duncan. *Hume's Philosophical Politics.* Cambridge: Cambridge University Press, 1975.

Foucault, Michel. *The Archaeology of Knowledge,* trans. A. M. Sheridan Smith. Paris: Gallimard, 1969; New York: Pantheon Books, 1972.

Fraiman, Susan. *Unbecoming Women: British Women Writers and the Novel of Development.* New York: Columbia University Press, 1993.

Furbank, P. N. and W. R. Owens. *A Critical Bibliography of Daniel Defoe.* London: Pickering & Chatto, 1998.

———. *A Political Biography of Daniel Defoe.* London: Pickering & Chatto, 2006.

Gallagher, Catherine. "Embracing the Absolute: The Politics of the Female Subject in Seventeenth-Century England," *Genders* 1 (March 1988): 24–39.

———. *Nobody's Story: The Vanishing Acts of Women Writers in the Marketplace, 1670–1820*. Berkeley and Los Angeles: University of California Press, 1994.

Golden, Morris. "Public Context and Imagining Self," *SEL* 25 (1985): 575–98.

Gordon, Scott Paul. *The Power of the Passive Self in English Literature, 1640–1770*. Cambridge: Cambridge University Press, 2002.

Goreau, Angeline. *Reconstructing Aphra: A Social Biography of Aphra Behn*. New York: Dial Press, 1980.

Greenblatt, Stephen. *Will in the World: How Shakespeeare Became Shakespeare*. New York: W. W. Norton, 2004.

Greene, Jody. *The Trouble with Ownership: Literary Property and Authorial Liability in England, 1660–1730*. Philadelphia: University of Pennsylvania Press, 2005.

Guffy, George. "Aphra Behn's *Oroonoko*: Occasion and Accomplishment." Paper read at Clark Library Seminars, UCLA, May 11, 1974.

Habermas, Jürgen. *The Structural Transformation of the Public Sphere*, trans. Thomas Burger. Darmstadt: Hermann Luchterhand Verlag, 1962; Cambridge: MIT Press, 1989.

Hattigé: or the Amours of the King of Tamaran. A Novel. Amsterdam, 1680.

Haywood, Eliza. *The Adventures of Eovaai, Princess of Ijaveo*. London: printed for S. Baker, 1736.

———. *The British Recluse: or, The Secret History of Cleomira*. London: printed for D. Brown, W. Chetwood, J. Woodward, and S. Chapman, 1722.

———. *Cleomelia: or, The Generous Mistress Being the Secret History of a Lady lately arriv'd from Bengall*. London: printed for J. Millan and sold by J. Roberts, 1726.

———. *The Disguis'd Prince: or, The Beautiful Parisian. A True History*. London: printed for T. Corbett by J. Roberts, 1728.

———. *The Distress'd Orphan; or, Love in a Madhouse*. London: printed by T. Sabine, 1726.

———. *The Double Marriage: or, the Fatal Release. A True Secret History*. London: printed for J. Roberts, 1726.

———. *Dramatic Historiographer: or, the British Theatre Delineated*. London: printed for F. Cogan and J. Nourse, 1735.

———. *The Female Spectator*, 4 vols. London: printed and published by T. Gardner, 1744–46.

———. *The Fortunate Foundlings: being the Genuine History of Colonel M——rs, and his sister, Madame du P——y, the issue of the Hon. Ch——es M——rs, son of the late Duke of R——l—d*. London: printed and published by T. Gardner, 1744.

———. *The History of Jemmy and Jenny Jessamy*. London: printed for T. Gardner, 1753.

[———]. *The Husband. In Answer to the Wife*. London: printed by and for T. Gardner, 1756.

Haywood, Eliza . *Idalia: or, the Unfortunate Mistress.* London: printed for D. Brown, W. Chetwood, and S. Chapman, 1723.

———. *Lasselia: or, the Self-*Abandon'd. London: printed for D. Browne and S. Chapman, 1723.

———. *A Letter From H----G----g, Esq.; One of the Gentlemen of the Bed Chamber to the Young Chevalier, and the only Person of his own Retinue that attended him from Avignon, in his late Journey through Germany, and elsewhere.* London: printed and sold at the Royal Exchange, Temple Bar, and Charing Cross, 1749 [1750 on title page].

———. *The Life of Madame de Villesache. Written by a lady, who was an Eye-witness of the greatest part of her adventures, and faithfully translated from her French manuscript.* London: printed for W. Feales, 1727.

[———]. *The Mercenary Lover: or, the Unfortunate Heiresses. Being a True, Secret History of a City Amour, in a certain island adjacent to the Kingdom of Utopia. Written by the author of Memoirs of the said island translated into English.* London: printed for N. Dobb, 1726.

[———]. *The Parrot: With a Compendium of the Times. By the authors of the Female Spectator.* London: printed and published by T. Gardner, 1746.

———. *The Rash Resolve: or, the Untimely Discovery,* 1724. London: printed for D. Browne and S. Chapman, 1724.

[———]. *The Secret History of the Present Intrigues of the Court of Caramania.* London: printed and sold by the booksellers of London and Westminster, 1727.

———. *Selected Works of Eliza Haywood,* ed. Alexander Pettit, et al., 6 vols. London: Pickering and Chatto, 2000.

———. *The Wife. By Mira, one of the authors of The Female Spectator, and Epistles for Ladies.* London: printed for T. Garnder, 1756.

Hazlitt, William. *Lectures on the English Comic Writers.* London: Taylor and Hessey, 1819.

Heath, Stephen. "Realism, Modernism, and 'Language-consciousness.' " In *Realism in European Literature: Essays in Honor of J. P. Stern,* ed. Nicholas Boyle and Martin Swales, 103–22. Cambridge: Cambridge University Press, 1986.

Herman, Ruth. *The Business of a Woman: The Political Writings of Delarivier Manley.* Newark and London: University of Delaware Press, 2003.

The Highlanders Salivated, *or the Loyal Association OF M—ll K—g's Midnight Club: with The serious Address of the Ladies of Drury, to the Batter'd Strolling Nymphs of their Community.* London: printed for M. Cooper, 1746.

The History of the Jacobite Clubs. London: printed for J. Baker, 1712.

Holmes, Geoffrey. *British Politics in the Age of Anne.* New York: St. Martin's, 1967.

———. *The Trial of Doctor Sacheverell.* London: Eyre Methuen, 1973.

Holquist, Michael and Walter Reed. "Six Theses on the Novel—and Some Metaphors," *New Literary History* 11:3 (1980): 413–23.

Howe, Irving. *Politics and the Novel.* Freeport, New York: Horizon Press, 1957.

Hughes, Derek. *The Theatre of Aphra Behn*. New York: Palgrave, 2001.

Hume, David. *The Philosophical Works of David Hume*, ed. Thomas Hill Green and Thomas Hodge Grose. Darmstadt: Scientia Verlag Aalen, 1964.

———. *A Treatise of Human Nature*, ed. L. A. Selby-Bigge. Oxford: Clarendon Press, 1978.

Hunter, J. Paul. *Before Novels: The Cultural Contexts of Eighteenth-Century English Fiction*. New York: W. W. Norton, 1990.

Hutner, Heidi, ed. *Rereading Aphra Behn: History, Theory, and Criticism*. Charlottesville: University Press of Virginia, 1993.

Ingrassia, Catherine. "Additional Information about Eliza Haywood's 1749 Arrest for Seditious Libel." *Notes and Queries* 242:2 (June 1997): 202–04.

———. *Authorship, Commerce, and Gender in Early Eighteenth-Century England: A Culture of Paper Credit*. Cambridge: Cambridge University Press, 1998.

The Jacobite Curse, or Excommunication of King George and His Subjects. Glasgow: printed by Hugh Brown, 1714.

Johnson, James. *The Scots Musical Museum*. 1787–1803.

Jordan, Constance. "The Household and the State: Transformations in the Representation of an Analogy from Aristotle to James I," *Modern Language Quarterly*, 54:3 (September 1993): 308–26.

The Judgement of Whole Kingdoms and Nations. London, 1710; New York: Garland, 1979.

Kay, Carol. *Political Constructions: Defoe, Richardson, and Sterne in relation to Hobbes, Hume, and Burke*. Ithaca: Cornell University Press, 1988.

[Keith, William]. *A Dissertation On the Liberty of the Subject in Great Britain*. London: printed for J. Roberts, 1737.

King, Kathryn, "New Contexts for Early Novels by Women: The Case of Eliza Haywood, Aaron Hill, and the Hillarians, 1719–1725." In *A Companion to the Eighteenth-Century English Novel and Culture*, ed. Paula Backscheider and Catherine Ingrassia, 261–75. Oxford: Blackwell Publishing, 2005.

Koon, Helene. "Eliza Haywood and the Female Spectator." *Huntington Library Quarterly* 42:1 (Winter 1978): 43–55.

Kraft, Elizabeth. Character and Consciousness in Eighteenth-Century Comic Fiction. Athens: University of Georgia Press, 1992.

Kubek, Elizabeth. "The Key to Stowe: Towards a Patriot Whig reading of Eliza Haywood's *Eovaai*." In *Presenting Gender: Changing Sex in Early-Modern Culture*, ed. Chris Mounsey, 225–54. Lewisburg, PA: Bucknell University Press, 2001.

Laslett, Peter. Introduction to *Two Treatises of Government*, by John Locke, ed. Peter Laslett. Cambridge: Cambridge University Press, 1988.

———. Introduction to *Patriarcha and Other Political Works of Sir Robert Filmer*, ed. Peter Laslett. Oxford: Basil Blackwell, 1949.

Lennox, Charlotte. *The Female Quixote; or, The Adventures of Arabella*, ed. Margaret Dalziel. Oxford and New York: Oxford University Press, 1989.

Link, Frederick M. *Aphra Behn*. New York: Twayne, 1968.

Locke, John. *Two Treatises of Government*, ed. Peter Laslett. Cambridge: Cambridge University Press, 1988.

———. *Political Writings*, ed. David Wootton. New York: Penguin, 1993.

Logan, George. *A Treatise on Government; Shewing That the Right of the Kings of Scotland to the Crown was not Strictly and Absolutely Hereditary.* Edinburgh: printed and sold by the booksellers here and at Glasgow, 1746.

Lukács, Georg. *Studies in European Realism; a Sociological Survey of the Writings of Balzac, Stendhal, Zola, Tolstoy, Gorki, and* Others. Trans. Edith Bone. 1945; London: Hillway, 1950.

———. *The Theory of the Novel.* Trans. Anna Bostock. Berlin, 1920; Cambridge: MIT Press, 1971.

Lynch, Deidre Shauna. *The Economy of Character: Novels, Market Culture, and the Business of Inner Meaning.* Chicago: University of Chicago Press, 1998.

Macpherson, C. B. *The Political Theory of Possessive Individualism: Hobbes to Locke.* Oxford: Oxford University Press, 1962.

Manley, Delarivier. *The Selected Works of Delarivier Manley*, ed. Rachel Carnell and Ruth Herman, 5 vols. London: Pickering & Chatto, 2005.

Marilley, Suzanne M. *Womam Suffrage and the Origins of Liberal Feminism in the United States 1820–1920.* Cambridge: Harvard University Press, 1996.

Markley, Robert. " 'Be impudent, be saucy, forward, bold, touzing, and leud': The Politics of Masculine Sexuality and Feminine Desire in Behn's Tory Comedies." In *Cultural Readings of Restoration and Eighteenth-Century English Theater*, ed. J. Douglas Canfield and Deborah Payne, 114–40. Athens: University of Georgia Press, 1995.

McCarthy, William and Elizabeth Kraft. Introduction to *Anna Letitia Barbauld: Selected Poetry and Prose*, ed. William McCarthy and Elizabeth Kraft, 11–32. Peterborough Ontario: Broadview Press, 2002.

McDowell, Paula. *The Women of Grub Street: Press, Politics, and Gender in the London Literary Marketplace 1678–1730.* Oxford: Clarendon Press, 1998.

McKeon, Michael. *The Origins of the English Novel, 1600–1740.* Baltimore: Johns Hopkins University Press, 1987.

McLynn, Frank. *Charles Edward Stuart: A Tragedy in Many Acts.* London and New York: Routledge, 1988.

Monod, Paul Kléber. *Jacobitism and the English People 1688–1788.* Cambridge: Cambridge University Press, 1989.

[Montgomery, James]. *Great Britain's Just Complaint For Her Late Measures, Present Sufferings, And the Future Miseries She Is Exposed To.* [London], 1692.

Mowry, Melissa M. *The Bawdy Politic in Stuart England, 1660–1714.* Aldershot: Ashgate, 2004.

Nenner, Howard. *The Right to Be King: The Succession to the Crown of England 1603–1714.* Chapel Hill: The University of North Carolina Press, 1995.

Nestor, Deborah. "Representing Domestic Difficulties: Eliza Haywood and the Critique of Bourgeois Ideology." *Prose Studies* 16:2 (August 1993): 1–26.

Novak, Maximillian. *Daniel Defoe: Master of Fictions: His Life and Ideas.* Oxford and New York: Oxford University Press, 2001.

———. *Defoe and the Nature of Man.* Oxford: Oxford University Press, 1963.

———. *Realism, Myth, and History in Defoe's Fiction.* Lincoln: University of Nebraska Press, 1983.

The Novelist's Magazine; or a Gentleman and Lady's Entertaining Miscellany. London: printed for Harrison & Co., 1780–89.

Okin, Susan Moller. "Humanist Liberalism." In *Liberalism and the Moral Life*, ed. Nancy L. Rosenblum. Cambridge: Harvard University Press, 1989.

Owen, Susan J. *Restoration Theatre and Crisis.* Oxford: Clarendon Press, 1996.

———. "Sexual Politics and Party Politics in Behn's Drama, 1678–83." In *Aphra Behn Studies*, ed. Janet Todd, 15–29. Cambridge: Cambridge University Press,1996.

Pateman, Carole. *The Sexual Contract.* Stanford: Stanford University Press, 1988.

Patterson, Annabel. *Early Modern Liberalism.* Cambridge: Cambridge University Press, 1997.

Payne, Deborah C. " 'And Poets Shall by Patron-Princes Live': Aphra Behn and Patronage." In *Curtain Calls: British and American Women and the Theater 1660–1820*, ed. Mary Anne Schofield and Cecilia Macheski, 105–19. Athens: Ohio University Press, 1991.

Pearson, Jacqueline. "The History of *The History of the Nun*." In *Rereading Aphra Behn: History, Theory, and Criticism*, ed. Heidi Hutner, 234–52. Charlottesville: University Press of Virginia, 1993.

Perry, Ruth. "Mary Astell and the Feminist Critique of Possessive Individualism." *Eighteenth-Century Studies* 23:4 (1990): 444–57.

———. *Novel Relations: The Transformation of Kinship in English Literature and Culture 1748–1818.* Cambridge: Cambridge University Press, 2004.

Pittock, Murray G. H. *Inventing and Resisting Britain: Cultural Identities in Britain and Ireland, 1685–1789.* Basingstoke: Macmillan, 1997.

Potkay, Adam. *The Fate of Eloquence in the Age of Hume.* Ithaca: Cornell University Press, 1994.

Reeve, Clara. *The Progress of Romance through Times, Countries, and Manners.* Colchester: printed for the author by W. Keymer, 1785.

Richardson, Samuel. *Clarissa, or the History of a Young Lady*, ed. Angus Ross. London: Penguin Books, 1985.

———. *The History of Sir Charles Grandison.* 3 vols. London: Oxford University Press, 1972.

———. *Pamela or, Virtue Rewarded*, Shakespeare Head edition, 4 vols. Oxford: Basil Blackwell, 1929.

———. *Selected Letters of Samuel Richardson*, ed. John Carroll. Oxford: Clarendon Press, 1964.

Richetti, John. ed. *The Cambridge Companion to the Eighteenth-Century Novel.* Cambridge: Cambridge University Press, 1996.

———. *Defoe's Characters.* Oxford: Oxford University Press, 1975.

Richetti, John. *Defoe's Narratives: Situations and Structures.* Oxford: Clarendon Press, 1975.

———. *The English Novel in History 1700–1780.* London and New York: Routledge, 1999.

———. "Histories by Eliza Haywood and Henry Fielding: Imitation and Adaptation." In *The Passionate Fictions of Eliza Haywood,* ed. Kirsten T. Saxton and Rebecca P. Bocchicchio, 240–58. Lexington: University Press of Kentucky, 2000.

———. "Ideas and Voices: The New Novel in Eighteenth-Century England." *Eighteenth-Century Fiction* 12 (January–April 2000): 327–44.

———. *Popular Fiction Before Richardson: Narrative Patterns, 1700–1739.* Oxford: Clarendon Press, 1969.

Rogers, Woodes. *A Cruising Voyage Round the World: first to the South-Seas, thence to the East-Indies, and homeward by the Cape of Good Hope.* London: printed for A. Bell and B. Lintot, 1712.

Ross, Deborah. *The Excellence of Falsehood: Romance, Realism and Women's Contributions to the Novel.* Lexington: University Press of Kentucky, 1991.

Rothstein, Eric. *Restoration Tragedy: Form and the Process of Change.* Madison: University of Wisconsin Press, 1967; reprint, Westport Connecticut: Greenwood Press, 1978.

Rubin, Gayle. "The Traffic in Women: Notes on the 'Political Economy' of Sex." In *Toward an Anthropology of Women,* ed. Rayna Reiter, 157–210. New York: Monthly Review Press, 1975.

Saxton, Kirsten T. and Rebecca P. Bocchicchio, eds. *The Passionate Fictions of Eliza Haywood: Essays on her Life and Work.* Lexington: University Press of Kentucky, 2000.

Schochet, Gordon J. *The Authoritarian Family and Political Attitudes in 17th-Century England: Patriarchalism in Political Thought.* Oxford: Basil Blackwell, 1975; New Brunswick and London: Transaction Books, 1988.

Schonhorn, Manuel. *Defoe's Politics: Parliament, Power, Kinship, and Robinson Crusoe.* Cambridge: Cambridge University Press, 1991.

Scott, Joan Wallach. *Gender and the Politics of History.* New York: Columbia University Press, 1988.

Scott, Jonathan. *Algernon Sidney and the Restoration Crisis, 1677–1683.* Cambridge: Cambridge University Press, 1991.

Seidel, Michael. "The Man Who Came to Dinner: Ian Watt and the Theory of Formal Realism." *Eighteenth-Century Fiction* 12 (January–April 2000): 193–212.

Settle, Elkanah. *The Female Prelate: Being The History of the Life and Death of Pope Joan.* London: printed for W. Cademan, 1680.

Shaftesbury, Anthony Ashley Cooper, 3rd Earl of. *Sensus Communis, an Essay on the Freedom of Wit and Humour in a Letter to a Friend,* in *Characteristics of Men, Manners, Opinions, Times,* ed. Lawrence E. Klein, 29–69. Cambridge: Cambridge University Press, 1999.

Shaw, Harry E. *Narrating Reality: Austen, Scott, Eliot.* Ithaca and London: Cornell University Press, 1999.

Sidney, Algernon. *Discourses Concerning Government*, 2nd ed. London: printed by J. Darby, 1704.

Simeon and Levi: or, Jacobite Villany and French-Treachery, Hand in Hand. London: n.p., 1696.

Siskin, Clifford. *The Work of Writing: Literature and Social Change in Britain, 1700–1830*. Baltimore and London: Johns Hopkins University Press, 1998.

Southerne, Thomas. *The Works of Thomas Southerne*, 2 vols., ed. Robert Jordan and Harold Love. Oxford: Oxford University Press, 1988.

Speck, W. A. *Reluctant Revolutionaries: Englishmen and the Revolution of 1688*. Oxford: Oxford University Press, 1988.

Spedding, Patrick. *A Bibliography of Eliza Haywood*. London: Pickering & Chatto, 2004.

Spencer, Jane. *The Rise of the Woman Novelist: From Aphra Behn to Jane Austen*. Oxford: Basil Blackwell, 1986.

Spender, Dale. *Mothers of the Novel: 100 Good Women Writers before Jane Austen*. New York: Pandora, 1986.

Starr, G. A. *Defoe and Casuistry*. Princeton: Princeton University Press, 1971.

Staves, Susan. *Players' Scepters: Fictions of Authority in the Restoration*. Lincoln: University of Nebraska Press, 1979.

Sterne, J. P. *On Realism*. London: Routledge and Kegan Paul, 1973.

Stone, Lawrence. *The Family, Sex and Marriage in England 1500–1800*. New York: Harper and Row, 1977.

Stuber, Florian. "On Fathers and Authority in Clarissa." *SEL* 25 (Summer 1985): 557–74.

Sutton, John. "The Sources of Mrs. Manley's Preface to *Queen Zarah*." *Modern Philology* (November 1984): 167–72.

Szechi, Daniel. " 'Cam Ye O'er Frae France?' Exile and the Mind of Scottish Jacobitism, 1716–1727." *Journal of British Studies* 37:4 (October 1998): 357–90.

———. *The Jacobites, Britain, and Europe, 1688–1788*. Manchester: Manchester University Press, 1994.

Tanner, Tony. *Adultery in the Novel: Contract and Transgression*. Baltimore: Johns Hopkins University Press, 1979.

[Tate, Nahum]. *A Present for the Ladies: Being an Historical Vindication of the Female Sex*. London: printed for Francis Saunders,1692.

Thompson, Martyn P. "The Reception of Locke's *Two Treatises of Government* 1690–1705." *Political Studies* 24:2 (1976): 184–91.

Todd, Janet, ed. *Aphra Behn Studies*, Cambridge: Cambridge University Press, 1996.

———. *The Secret Life of Aphra Behn*. London: Pandora, 2000.

———. *The Sign of Angellica: Women, Writing, and Fiction, 1660–1800*. New York: Columbia University Press, 1989.

[Toland, John]. *The Jacobitism Perjury and Popery of High-Church-Priests*. London: printed for J. Baker, 1710.

The True Picture of a Modern Tory: In a Dialogue between Jack and Ned; Two Agents for the Jacobite Party. London: n.p., 1702.

[Tyrrell, James]. *Bibliotheca Politica or an Enquiry into the Ancient Constitution of the English Government, in Thirteen Dialogues.* London: printed for R. Baldwin, 1694.

————. *Patriarcha non Monarcha, The Patriarch Unmonarched; Being Observations on a late Treatise & Divers Other Miscellanies Published Under the Name of Sir Robert Filmer Baronet.* London: printed for Richard Janeway, 1681.

Villanueva, Darío. *Theories of Literary Realism.* Trans. Mihai I. Spariosu and Santiago García-Castañón. Albany: State University of New York Press, 1997.

Warner, William B. *Licensing Entertainment: The Elevation of Novel Reading in Britain, 1684–1750.* Berkeley and Los Angeles: University of California Press, 1998.

————. *Reading Clarissa: The Struggles of Interpretation.* New Haven: Yale University Press, 1979.

Watt, Ian. "Flat-Footed and Fly-Blown: The Realities of Realism." *Eighteenth-Century Fiction* 12 (January–April 2000): 147–66.

————. *The Rise of the Novel: Studies in Defoe, Richardson, and Fielding.* Berkeley and Los Angeles: University of California Press, 1957.

————. "Serious Reflections on *The Rise of the Novel.*" In *Towards a Poetics of Fiction,* ed. Mark Spilka, 90–103. Bloomington: Indiana University Press, 1977.

Whicher, George Frisbie. *The Life and Romances of Mrs. Eliza Haywood.* New York: Columbia University Press, 1915.

Williams, Raymond. *The Long Revolution.* New York: Columbia University Press, 1961.

Wilputte, Earla. Introduction to *The Adventures of Eovaii, Princess of Ijaveo: A Pre-Adamitical History,* by Eliza Haywood, ed. Earla Wilputte. Peterborough, Ontario: Broadview Press, 1999.

Wolff, Cynthia Griffin. *Samuel Richardson and the Eighteenth-Century Puritan Character.* Hamden, CT: Archon Books, 1972.

Wootton, David. Introduction to John Locke, *Political Writings,* ed. David Wootton, New York: Penguin, 1993, 7–130.

Zelinsky, Katherine. Introduction to *The Adventures of Rivella,* by Delarivier Manley, ed. Katherine Zelinsky. Peterborough, Ontario: Broadview Press, 1999.

Zimbardo, Rose. "Aphra Behn: A Dramatist in Search of the Novel." *Studies in Eighteenth-Century Culture* 19 (1989): 277–87.

Manuscript Sources

Public Record Office State Papers Domestic 36/111 f. 204–14 and 36/112 f. 24.

INDEX